Shlomo Kalo / LILI

Shlomo Kalo

Lili

English translation by Philip Simpson

© All Rights Reserved
Y   D.A.T. Publications
POBox 27019, Jaffa 61270, Israel
Phone: +972-3-5071239
Email: dat@y-dat.co.il
www.y-dat.com

Original Hebrew title: "*Lili*"
2nd Hebrew edition 2009
(based on Shlomo Kalo's novel "*Kehut Hashani*")
Cover photo: Old Jaffa
3rd English POD edition,
Printed by Amazon CreateSpace, 2015
ISBN: 978-965-7028-57-5

Table of Contents

FIVE THOUSAND – CASH

The twilight hour in Jaffa. Silver-winged gulls soaring high in the sky, in a widening arc. Stillness all around. The gulls fly on, receding until they are tiny black dots in the void, then wheeling and retracing their flight, approaching rapidly and growing back to their natural dimensions, diving in ceremonial mode, wings dipped in salute, and finally settling on the gentle swell of the dark and viscous sea.

Not the smallest of clouds on the broad blue expanse of a sky that is lost in thought. Not a sound, not a whisper. Fishing-boats which left the jetty of the ancient harbour just a moment ago have cut their engines; the gulls are still bobbing on the surface of the desolate waters, which rock them tenderly in token of affection. The horizons are faraway and people are walking shadows. A late-arriving spring tries to make amends, drawing out from its store a light, somewhat shamefaced breeze and sending it to rustle softly among the branches of the shrubs on the hillside, to stir the fronds of the palm-trees below. The branches of the dense shrubs and the fronds of the denuded palms move rhythmically in time to the tune sung by the shy breeze, and smile tolerantly.

I stood beside a clump of heather, its bloom already beginning to fade. I had just left the bank with five thousand new shekels in my pocket, a loan for a small apartment which I intended to buy and which was mortgaged to three different banks. The vendor of the apartment had insisted on "readies", and he had his reasons. And after a long process of persuasion, which was not conducted in the most amicable of spirits, the bank relented and handed over the "readies". My encounter with the vendor, still occupying the property, had been scheduled for eight o'clock. I had time on my hands.

I turned towards the alley beside the fenced section of the beach, a long and very tortuous, muddy alley, with crude steps cut into it, climbing the slope of the hill. Somewhere up there, I was supposed to be meeting the vendor of the apartment.

Evening descended, stars twinkling in a deep, purple and benevolent sky.

When I reached the top of the hill I saw to my right a broad, descending slope, on which abandoned, half-ruined buildings were strewn about in wild disorder, like the black vomit of a mythical monster. Elderly rats ambled across the fissured walls, by the faint light of distant stars. The sight resembled a derelict cemetery, with only the religious symbols absent from the memorial stones. Somewhere, to the South-West, at the furthest point, there emerged from darkness charged with the humidity of the sea, viscous as ink, a faint light – a torch perhaps, or the faraway flame of an oil-lamp. Maybe, the thought occurred to me, a solitary tenant remained here, or a destitute family awaiting rescue by the social services.

Impelled by a strange sense of fellowship, of sharing in adversity, and almost against my will, I focused my eyes on those distant glimmers of light... and then I sensed something dark and ugly, unbearably oppressive, emanating from that point and spreading all around.

I turned aside from my path, springing lightly over the crumbling blocks that were strewn in every direction, trying to avoid lumps of black filth, startled rats and rusting iron posts, and to find an expanse of soft ground to walk on, a surface to absorb the sound of my footsteps. I found the source of the dim light, approaching cautiously until I stood right beside it.

It was a hurricane-lamp, of the type used by campers, to be hung from the awning of a tent or placed on a table, and sure enough, this one stood on a long table – long, heavy and evidently rotten. The light juddered every time the table was struck and set quivering from end to end.

Beside the table were the silhouettes of three men, two at one end and the third at the other. At the feet of the lone man was a heavy bundle, reaching to the level of the table-top and stirring from time to time with a sleepy sort of movement; no suggestion of bitterness or resentment or alarm, just a blind quest for a more comfortable position.

I stood in the shadow, unobserved by anyone.

The man with the moving bundle at his feet held a cord attached to it in one hand and with the other he brandished, in a skilled and confident manner, an open razor, its blade catching a chance ray of light from time to time and gleaming with a chilly lustre.

"We agreed on three thousand!" he cried in a strange, shrill voice, like the blood-curdling shriek of an owl pouncing on its prey. "You're not going to cheat me!" he hissed, and raising the fist that held the razor he brought it crashing down on the rotten table.

"We agreed on nothing," one of the men at the other end of the table replied, in his voice a deep rasp of obscure pleasure, the malicious satisfaction of the professional hunter seeing his work accomplished and his intended victim falling into the trap.

"Take five hundred!" the other of the two suggested in a practical tone, trying to approach the man with the razor.

"Back off!" screeched the owl, letting the cord go and clutching another part of the bundle – which turned out to be a lock of long and luxuriant hair. The man suddenly yanked at the hair, exposing a gleaming neck to the murky light of the lamp and eliciting a muffled groan from its owner. "One more step – this throat gets cut!" he yelled, flourishing the razor and clearly intent on carrying out his threat. The man who had offered five hundred retreated reluctantly; the other, the one with the voice of cheerful malice, spoke again, calmly and with evident satisfaction:

"Go ahead and cut!" he taunted, his strange ebullience seeming to overflow. "You won't have her, neither shall we!"

"Take five hundred!" the rejected suitor repeated his offer, adding with finality: "You won't get more! So take it and go! Look at you," he said, pointing, "shaking like a leaf! You need it now!" he declared. "For five hundred you can get four fixes... five if you're lucky. Any minute now you'll be howling like a dog!"

"Three thousand!" shrieked the owl, but his screeches were sounding more tearful now, with hints of mental trauma and something beyond despair.

"Don't give him anything! We're not getting her, neither is he!" the other continued with a note of triumph which he made no effort to conceal. "Go ahead and do it!" he encouraged the razor-holder maliciously, with tense expectation and something like exaltation of spirit.

"Last chance!" the owl yelled his raucous, nerve-grinding cry. The razor was poised, decisively and with wondrous precision, the flamboyant style of a professional slaughterer about to dispatch a chicken – although in this case there was no angry squawking since the mouth of the victim had been gagged in advance with a thick wad of cloth. The razor began its descent...

The compressed air in the ruin did not whistle; instead a clear voice pierced the dim void:

"Five thousand!"

The death-blow was checked, but not soon enough to avoid making an incision on the exposed neck.

With a single abrupt movement, as one, the three men swung round to face me, and even the creature in the bundle tried to turn its head towards me, making unsuccessful efforts to struggle free from the owl who maintained his tight grip on its hair.

"Who are you?" hissed the predatory voice of the razor-man.

I ignored the question and repeated my offer in a calm and resolute tone:

"Five thousand I said!"

"Cash?" His eyes lit up.

"Cash!" I agreed.

The hand holding the luxuriant hair loosened its grip. But the owner of the hair made no motion of the head, or did not dare to. Is it still alive? – the thought occurred to me. But time was pressing and I couldn't afford to be delayed by any such speculations.

"Let's have it then!" snapped razor-man, releasing his hold at last. The bundle toppled over, rolled on its side and sank helplessly to the filthy floor. Whatever was trapped inside it seemed to have fainted... or died? There was no going back now.

I pulled out the banknotes, arranged so neatly by the pedantic teller, and laid them on the table. Still clutching the razor, he held out his other, trembling hand, grabbed at the pile of notes and riffed through them feverishly with a thumb curved like an eagle's talon. Abruptly he picked them up and stuffed them into the pocket of his trousers, then folded his razor, tossed a crumbling cube towards the men at the other end of the table, and without another word jumped over the ruined wall as if vaulting a fence and disappeared in the darkness. The other two men hurried after him.

The lamp remained. By its light I released the prisoner trapped in the bundle – freeing trussed legs and arms. The abject creature tried to stretch paralysed limbs, using its arms to crawl as far away from me as possible, then removing the mouth-gag and rising slowly.

It was a woman or perhaps – a girl. For a moment a ray of light fell on her eyes: they were hollow, like dark holes, eyes resigned to accepting everything, dead eyes.

"What kind of a jerk are you?" she hissed through lips tightly clenched to prevent them quivering, smoothing down her faded blue jeans and then yelling:

"Go to Hell! Leave me alone!" – in a valiant attempt to sound hard and defiant – "Stop staring at me like a bloody moron!"

She had a point. I was standing there as if I'd taken root, staring at her as I tried to marshal my thoughts. Her outburst roused me from my reverie as effectively as an alarm-clock. I turned and began slowly walking up the hillside, the way I had descended just a few minutes before.

Darkness all around. I glanced at my watch, and seeing that it was already time for my appointment I quickened my pace, arriving at the apartment I was supposed to be buying about a quarter of an hour late. All the way I had the feeling that something or someone was trailing along behind me, but sensing no hostility of any kind, no repressed resentment – I ignored it.

The vendor of the apartment and current occupier, a middle-aged man, stooping, gaunt and unshaven, his face a yellowish colour – fixed anxious eyes on me in an unsuccessful attempt to veil them or to preserve the last vestige of a smile. His wife stood beside him, tense and tight-lipped, wondering whether to greet me or wait for me to open my mouth, thus laying the responsibility on me. Quite rightly, she chose the latter course, and my greeting was polite and fulsome, apparently gaining their confidence; they melted a little, breathed more easily and returned my greeting. With a swift look I took in the apartment: two rooms, peeling walls, a closet with one of its doors hanging askew like the wing of an injured bird. A cheap joint indeed.

Three children huddled round their mother. They were barefoot and the cold of the cracked tiles on the floor forced them to shuffle and prance about. The youngest of them had her finger in her mouth and a stream of snot coursing down her abnormally broad upper lip.

Declining the offer of a seat, I informed them, calmly but clearly, that the deal was off.

The adults stared at me, astonished and clearly disappointed.

The children were unaware of all this and carried on prancing, without even a break in the rhythm. Their big, drowsy eyes showed only innocence.

"What, what does that mean?" The thin man with the yellowish skin and the cracked voice, the voice of a ghost, recovered something of his composure.

"I don't have the money," I explained and added hastily: "You can hang on to the deposit. Refund it when you find a buyer."

"We had such hopes!" the woman sighed – but recovered sufficiently to say: "Well, it can't be helped. Not your lucky day! Not ours either!" she concluded with a trace of her earlier resentment. "Just as well we didn't have time to put the mortgage in your name!"

I stepped forward and shook hands with all of them, starting with the father and finishing with the youngest child, the girl with the constant nasal drip and the finger in mouth. I retreated, bowed slightly and took my leave.

Outside, the Jaffa night was moist and violet.

I went to see Moshe Leon, owner of my rented apartment, and renew the rental contract. As I had hoped, I found him at home and after prolonged negotiation the matter was settled.

As I was leaving Moshe Leon's spacious house, a shadow detached itself from the high fence and stepped forward briskly to intercept me.

It was the same woman, or girl, whom fate had thrown into my path an hour before among the ruined buildings on the hillside.

"Well – what?" her voice hissed almost in my ear.

"Well – what?" I echoed, imitating her tone but unable to suppress a hint of amusement.

"I've been trailing along behind you a whole bloody hour!" she declared with indignation that was supposed to conceal weakness and exhaustion and frayed nerves, adding at once: "Are you taking me to a hotel or – what?"

"Not to a hotel, or what," was my reply.

"What kind of a weirdo are you?" she cried, attempting again, and with more success this time, to adopt a gruff and aggressive tone. "Throwing five thousand on the table and too mean for a hotel, or..." – with a change of tone as another thought occurred to her – "will you be fetching the clients?"

"No," I smiled at her, heartily amused.

I set off at a fairly rapid pace, along the street descending to the sea, turning from there towards the southern suburbs, climbing a broad-backed hill where narrow alleyways split and diversified like the branches of a family tree.

She wasn't far behind me. After a short silence, breathing heavily from the climb up the steep hillside, she tried to draw level with me:

"And just what do you reckon you're going to do with me?" – her sharp cry pierced the damp, compressed air.

"Nothing," I replied, in a tone intended to leave no room for doubt.

"Why did you buy me then?" she protested, sounding angry now.

"I didn't buy you."

"You put money on the table, didn't you?"

"It's my money."

"But you're so... stuck-up!" – a strange note of pain in her voice, which she tried in vain to swallow – "Such an egotist!" she continued, sounding ever more shaken and demoralised, "You got me for five thousand and now you're treating me like shit!" – she almost shouted, in an effort to disguise deep recesses of weakness and despair.

"You can go wherever you like."

"I've nowhere to go!"

"Have you no home?"

"No!"

"Where have you been sleeping up to now?"

"Where Shuki wanted..." – and when I didn't respond she added: "Usually there wasn't much time left for sleeping. He brought me clients in the night... in the daytime I slept at his mother's house."

By this time we were approaching my apartment. Night had long since fallen, enfolding us in that tender and benevolent darkness which is known only in Jaffa.

I pushed open the gate, recently painted but constructed from mismatched and ill-fitting planks.

"You can sleep here," I said.

"In the yard?" she asked, a strange note of resignation in her voice, which had softened a little.

"In the house," I replied.

I crossed the narrow strip of the yard, pushed lightly at the unlocked door, opened it and stepped inside. I pressed the switch. Yellowish light streamed over a jumble of property: overturned chair and armchair, cartons crammed with books, bundles of clothes, covers and kitchen utensils – graphic evidence of my intention to move house. I turned the chair and armchair upright and put them back in their place, shifted a table, pushed boxes aside, stuffed clothes into a closet in the inner room.

My guest stood on the threshold, gaunt but erect, looking on with an expression of mild disgust. For the first time I noticed what she was wearing: faded blue jeans, a grubby flannel blouse, bare feet in battered flip-flops.

The yellowish light in the outer, larger room was harsh and unwelcoming. I cleared the sofa, removing books, half a dozen assorted plates, a couple of pans and several cups.

"Sofa okay for you?" I asked.

"Okay for what?"

"Sleeping."

"It's narrow!" she replied.

I looked at her inquisitively.

"For two..." she explained

"You'll be sleeping there by yourself," I told her, with a bright smile but in a determined tone.

"By myself? It'll do!" she said, sounding relieved. She came inside, tested the upholstery with the air of an expert, and then looked up to scrutinise me, staring intently beneath brows that had never been trimmed, a few unruly bristles poking now through the clumsily applied mascara.

"Where are you sleeping?" she demanded to know.

"In there." I pointed to the inner room, which was still in darkness.

"Maybe I'll decide to sleep there!" she said, sounding indignant for no apparent reason.

"As you wish," I replied.

With measured tread, and sidelong glances watching every movement of mine, she entered the inner, smaller room, which contained an iron bedstead, sheets and blankets strewn over it in prodigious disarray. Unimpressed, she retraced her steps.

"I'll sleep on the sofa!" she announced, softening – and at once she regretted the softening and stiffened again: "Don't you dare creep up on me in the night!"

"I'm not like that," I assured her.

"What are you – a queer?" she asked, a strange note of hope in her voice.

"No."

"What then?" she persisted.

"Not what you think."

"Sure!" she cried, in a voice untainted by any expectation of anything at all. "You're a jerk, like all the rest of them!" she declared unequivocally and after a moment of reflection added in a more balanced tone: "I just don't understand why you bought me. I'd better warn you, you're not going to make much profit out of me... you should've left me there, with Shuki!"

"To get your throat cut?"

"Yes!" she cried with a finality that could not be other than sincere. "I'd have been free of him, and them, and do-gooding weirdoes like you!" And glaring at me viciously she added: "You're a hypocrite, did you know that?"

"How do you make that out?" I asked, without much interest. My indifference infuriated her:

"If you think you can impress me, forget it! It won't work!" she announced, kicking off her flip-flops and reclining on the sofa, pulling up the blanket that I had provided. Before covering herself she shot me a malicious look and pulled a black razor from her pocket, very like the one that had been brandished over her own exposed neck. Showing it to me, she intoned ceremoniously, pleasurably almost:

"You see, I'm armed too!" – adding, just in case the point had escaped me: "You have no idea who you've taken into your house! Now get out of here and let me sleep!" And in the same gruff tone, with the same affectation of aggression, she concluded – "Turn out the bloody light!"

I did as I was told, went into my room, stripped, put on pajamas and got into bed.

DREAMLESS SLEEP

This body of mine, this fleshly body, for all its processes and functions – dreamed no dreams that night. It fell asleep soon enough, breathed rhythmically and accumulated the particles of energy required for tomorrow's activities. But the mechanical process of accumulation was interrupted some time in the small hours of the new day while it was still night. The shoulder of this body was roughly shaken and its eyes were opened, taking in the shape of yesterday's house-guest.

"Can't sleep!" she announced in an unfamiliar tone of voice – plaintive, humble, almost helpless.

"Nothing I can do about that," I replied, still drowsy.

"There is!" she declared firmly, tense with anticipation.

"Really?" I asked in astonishment, fully awake now.

"Tell me something!" she demanded, then paused and added: "You know how it is... when you can't sleep... there's this thought I can't get out of my head..."

"What thought is that?" I asked, sitting up in bed.

"Why did you do this?" her abrupt cry ripped through the stillness of the night. Something in her recoiled from the sound of her own voice and she added in a tone that was more balanced and restrained – but no less tense and troubled:

"What do you expect from me in return? Where did the money come from? What kind of pervert are you?" Her last words were spoken almost in a whisper. She sighed.

I chuckled softly: "That isn't one thought," I pointed out, "it's a whole bundle!"

She ignored my comment and my mirth, perhaps didn't even notice them, absorbed as she was in her own preoccupations:

"All the time it's just going round and round, bugging me!" she went on, speaking with a kind of unnatural haste. "I've never felt like this, never met anyone like you before! And I still don't know how you get your kicks... I'm warning you, there are limits and I'm not putting up with any kind of filth just because of your five thousand!" And in an effort to restore the gruff and aggressive edge to her voice she added: "You saw the razor..." but her voice betrayed her, shaking, its former confidence utterly destroyed.

"If that's what's worrying you, perhaps I can help," I answered her very calmly. "Why did I do this? The answer is: it came to me."

"What kind of an answer is that?" she protested in the gloom.

"The only one I've got," I replied.

Cautiously she picked up my clothes which were strewn on the only chair in the room, laid them at the foot of the bed, sat down and taking a deep breath, resumed her unnaturally fluent style of speech:

"You look so nice, I mean" – she corrected herself hastily – "your face is nice. Your eyes... they're something else! The way you look at me is kind of scary, a bit embarrassing I'd say... no, very embarrassing!" she cried as if against her will, "But all the same, not too frightening... you see, all you're doing is confusing me!" she protested finally.

"As to the second question," I broke the silence, "what I expect from you in return, the answer is: nothing."

"I don't believe you!" she wailed as if in pain, as if trying to convince herself of something, and added: "You're a hypocrite! Sooner or later you'll want something!" She lapsed again into silence as if ashamed of her words, and hearing no response from me, despite her oppressive anticipation, she continued in a different tone – still hurt, but tinged with an inexplicable sense of guilt:

"Or maybe, you're the kind who does good works... maybe you're a sort of saint or a Christian, or one of those weird Indians... but they want something too!" she said, returning to her tone of bitter indignation. And after swallowing her saliva she continued, firmly but with a strange kind of tenderness, a surprising readiness for compromise and acceptance: "As for me – I don't take gifts! Five thousand – that's like a hundred times... some of us charge more, some less... We could start right now, if that's what you want... But I warn you, I don't smell very nice!" she declared in a practical tone.

"And my answer is the same as before, I don't want anything from you!" I insisted, with all the emphasis I could muster.

"I get it!" – she lowered her head with a kind of resentment or perhaps, unwilling submission to fate – "You're just too high and bloody mighty!" she declared in the same subdued tone, concluding with a feeble display of outward defiance as she raised her childlike head, with its arched brow: "I've done my part" – and after a long pause for thought, not content with leaving it at that, she added emphatically: "If you want it – take it! If you don't – that's fine by me!" and without transition she asked, while trying to catch my eye: "Now tell me – where's the money from?" There was nothing artificial about the gravity in her voice, the gravity of a mother about to catch her slippery son committing some misdemeanour. Her effort to catch my eye succeeded only too well; I turned my full attention to her and she faltered, looking away hastily and breathing heavily as she awaited my response.

"From the bank," I answered her calmly.

"You stole it?" she exclaimed as if involuntarily, adding hastily in an apologetic tone: "No, I don't think so! But you must have been up to something, forging a signature maybe... No, not that either!" she declared, as if debating with herself. "Anyway," she concluded finally, "it must be something like that..." and looking up again in the gloom she asked aggressively: "What did you do at the bank?"

"I took out a loan," I told her blithely.

"What for?"

"To buy an apartment."

She pondered this for a long moment and then responded with a strange note of triumph, almost of malice:

"So now you're not getting an apartment!"

"That is correct."

"Where are you going to live?"

"In the place where I live now."

"Where's that?

"Here."

She was silent, digesting my reply before asking with incredulity:

"This place – is yours?" – and she scanned the two rooms, a room within a room: the larger living room with its North-facing window, extending into the smaller bedroom with its South-facing window; off the bedroom on one side, a minuscule kitchen – on the other, toilet and shower; between the bed, set against the northern wall and the toilet – a narrow, ramshackle wardrobe and facing it, a tiny table serving as a writing-desk. There was the backless chair on which she was sitting, and a small shelf suspended precariously from the cracked and damp wall. Beside the long and low table in the living room – a simple chair and an armchair with battered and threadbare upholstery. On the other side of the table was the ancient sofa on which my guest was supposed to be sleeping.

"Rented," I replied, when her eyes had completed their tour of inspection and were once more staring into mine.

"So you'll have to carry on renting?" she asked in a conciliatory, or rather, apologetic tone.

I nodded.

Her head slumped as if of its own accord, her abundant hair falling in every possible direction – over her nape, her ears, forehead and face. Suddenly a tremor seemed to pass through her and she jerked upright, her long thin neck outstretched and tense, a tension supposed to convey resolve and determination.

"And now," she began bluntly, "the last question. What kind of pervert are you? Let's have it all! I'm bound to find out sooner or later! If you come clean now" – this with what was meant to be a coquettish leer – "we'll talk about it, maybe think of some way of repaying your five thousand…"

"I'm not a pervert," I assured her with a calm smile and in a tone which seemed to have the desired effect, dislodging her doubts and restoring her confidence.

"I…" she began hesitantly and with a tenderness that was quite unexpected and yet sincere and natural, "I don't understand!" After another pause she added, as if clarification were needed: I mean, if you're not a pervert – why didn't you… why didn't you even try… if only to keep warm?" she concluded, the distant bubble of bitterness returning to her voice.

"I don't need it," I replied.

"Then you are a pervert!" she declared, the bitterness in her voice mounting.

"There's something you ought to know," I told her. "I'm a monk."

For a long moment she stared at me, as if refusing to believe her ears. And then she burst into peals of laughter, rolling, ringing laughter, a pleasure to hear. I joined in. Something in the tone of my mirth, untouched by any kind of ulterior motive, got through to her and her laughter stopped. When I stopped too, she spoke to me in a voice that I hadn't heard before, a voice purged of the thick layers of revulsion and pretence:

"What a strange laugh you have!" she exclaimed, and after a prolonged silence and an apparently fruitless attempt to figure me out, accompanied by a sudden fusillade of inquisitive glance, she returned to her regular style of speech, supplemented now by a studied offhandedness:

"Call yourself a 'monk' do you? Well, they're all perverts!" and without waiting for a response she proceeded to offer irrefutable evidence of this: "A couple of monks are regulars of mine. One of them's old, Orthodox, the other's younger, a Catholic. All the others" – she concluded confidently, with a hint of good-natured ribaldry – "are poofs!"

"I'm not one of them," I sought to assure her, firmly and unequivocally, but my words seemed to have the effect of undermining her confidence. She hesitated and after a short silence, tried again:

"You're saying you're a monk... a real one?"

"Yes."

Slowly she raised her head and gave me a long look, faintly tinged with a bemusement which she did her best to conceal. And for the first time since we met she seemed to be removing veil after veil from her eyes, revealing quite unexpected courage and clarity, even something pure and childlike.

"I suppose there are some real ones," she admitted with a strange air of glad submission and added: "Why don't you dress like a monk... and what church do you belong to?"

"I don't belong to any church," I replied softly, adding: "I'm a Jew."

She turned to stare into my face again, utterly baffled:

"What kind of a real monk is that?" she demanded to know.

"The kind that by the grace and love of God enjoys the privilege of loving God."

"What kind of love do you love God with?" she persisted.

"There is only one kind."

"Which is?"

"God's love of man."

"You were talking about man's love of God!" she protested.

"Loving God is a privilege owed to the grace of His love," I answered her.

Again she lowered her head, weighing and pondering my words at length. Suddenly, with a sharp and unexpected movement she tossed her hair back, held her head up proudly, turned the piquant flash of her eyes to me and asked:

"Is God jealous?"

"He has no reason to be."

"How is that?"

"He who has earned the grace of God's love can love nothing else."

"Why?" she persisted.

"Compared with God," I replied, "nothing else has any worth, or meaning."

"Neither man – nor worm?"

"God is in everything," I explained – "in man and in worm."

Silence fell in the room, in the soft and steadily receding darkness. Was she considering my replies, or had she lost interest in the whole business. For a few minutes she looked utterly distracted.

"Some weird monk!" she concluded finally in a hushed voice, almost a whisper.

I looked around trying to locate the alarm-clock, usually placed on the chair, and found it among the articles dumped at the bottom of the bed. The luminous hands stood on 3 and 9 – two-forty-five in the morning. Two more hours and it would be time for this body, still sitting up in bed wrapped in a blanket, to be up and about its business.

"Are you okay?" I asked her.

"Uh-huh?" she responded, as if losing the thread of her thoughts. "Okay?" She seemed to be giving the question serious consideration, before finally answering with an unequivocal "No!" But then she added as if relenting: "I'm a bit more relaxed than I was..." She certainly sounded more serene.

"I'm going back to the sofa!" she announced, standing up with a sigh. "Maybe this time I'll get some sleep..."

"Goodnight then!" I said, sliding under the blanket, closing my eyes and falling asleep at once.

At five in the morning, as usual, I sat down for meditation. At six – I ran to the sea, bathed, returned and showered.

My guest was sleeping fitfully, tossing and twitching, emitting sighs, whistles and various odd sounds, lying still at times but not for long.

After shaving I made myself a cup of tea, as every morning. I drank it sitting at the little table which served as a writing-desk, eyes straying out through the window and settling on the wall jutting out from my neighbour's house, a thick concrete structure on which corrosive sea-breezes had carved some interesting patterns. Then I noticed the silence in the room behind me, as well as a stubborn and inquisitive force focused on my back. I turned and confronted the eyes of my guest, open wide in deep and undisguised amazement, bordering on wonder and underpinning it – that unexpected and unfathomable childlike innocence.

As if sensing she had been caught out, caught out in a manner not to her liking, she instantly veiled her eyes – mask after mask, shutter after shutter, knitting the smudged, black-smeared brows which gave her features a slightly comical, clownish appearance. Her expression became tense and hostile, with something closely resembling malice emerging from somewhere and forcing its way forward.

"What's so bloody interesting about my face?" she snapped, in a gruff voice which seemed to take on a tone of cold rigidity without undue effort on her part.

"Nothing," I replied, smiling at her and not shifting my gaze from her head, where the matted and dishevelled hair reminded me of a cossack-hat several sizes too large; most of her hair was light chestnut in colour although there were a few blond strands. I looked at her face, a little puffy, somewhat childish in appearance, its features at this moment strained and defiant. Under the 'cossack-hat' this face was rather long and virtually colourless, the colour of soil. But her neck was flawless, smooth and delicate, a delicacy at odds with her voice and the look in her eyes; her high forehead, visible through the tangles of hair, was likewise surprisingly limpid. Her nose was thin, sensitive and retrousse.

"You know what?" – she smiled suddenly, all the artificial stiffness fading from her face like a grey and diffident cloud dispelled by a bright beam of light – "You're just a snooper, a peeping Tom!" Her gruff voice did not accord at all with her face which had cleared completely. For a brief moment her face resembled that of a hurt and offended little girl – all her hopes shattered and yet still a child who may from time to time, at the times least expected, be enthralled by the innocent and radiant joys of childhood.

I smiled back at her, a warm and broad smile intended to encourage her, and converted it to a short, limpid laugh. And without pausing to consider the consequences I laid down my cup, went to the kitchenette and brewed another cup of tea, spread butter and honey on an ancient slice of bread and put them on the little table beside me.

She followed my movements, stared at the cup, looked up at me, at the cup again, then back to me. Her face darkened; the body under the blanket was tense, her brows knotted again.

"What's that supposed to be?" she asked at last with unexpected gravity.

"The tea and the bread?"

"Yes!"

"It's for you," I replied, "when you get up. I'll be going out soon."

"You may as well know I'm not coming back here!" was her immediate response.

I shrugged.

"Something else you should know!" – pronouncing each word separately, with special emphasis, demanding the full attention of the listener – "Shuki will get his fixes and if he doesn't go out of his mind – which he won't – he'll start taking an interest in you! You've got a week... maybe ten days at the most! After that he'll come looking for you. He likes soft touches!" she concluded in a tone of contempt.

"He doesn't know me," I pointed out calmly, in an effort to reassure her.

"He will!" was her succinct answer.

"How?" I queried.

"Someone will whisper in his ear!"

"Who will?"

"I will!" she muttered hoarsely, staring at my face.

"You're going back to him, then?" – it was a statement as much as it was a question.

"No."

I gave her a look which combined curiosity, incomprehension and a kindly smile. She took the hint and proceeded to explain:

"He'll find me. He can't do without me. It's true he put me up for sale and maybe... maybe he'd have cut my throat too... but now, knowing I'm alive... he'll turn the world upside down to find me! And he'll force me to tell him everything. Through me – he'll get to you. I suggest you get shot of this apartment, just disappear!" She paused and then added decisively: "He's not going to leave you alone!" After another moment of hesitation she continued in the same assured tone:

"My throat didn't get cut... but yours probably will be! I'd bet on it! Of course, if you came up with a few more thousand..." – she amended this, with a sneer of bitter contempt – "No, I can see how hard up you are... but if your life matters to you, you'll get the hell out before it's too late!" I didn't for a moment doubt the seriousness of this warning.

"And what about you?" I asked.

"My business is private!" she protested.

I smiled: "So is mine."

"Well – you've been warned!" she insisted with the utmost gravity.

I stood up from the table. Again I gave her a quizzical look. Suddenly she seemed like a creature from another world – unwanted, alien and outcast, to be kicked and spat on, abused and humiliated with impunity. My throat was constricted, my heart in the grip of an iron fist. I needed to say something encouraging, or do something, find some gesture that would exert a profound and illuminating influence, restore some spirit to this crushed and abject creature.

Without saying another word I turned, took the tray from the kitchen, put on it the tea which had cooled, the buttered bread dripping with honey, and offered it to my strange guest, still reclining on the sofa.

Her face contorted as if acid had been thrown in it, her body convulsed as if under the blows of a steel whip. She stretched out a lean hand to the tray, took the full cup and with an assured movement, a movement of cold, awakened anger, unrestrained and unanswerable – flung its contents in my face.

"Bastard!" she howled in a final, despairing wail, knocking over the tray with her free hand, grabbing her battered flip-flops and vanishing into the light of the new dawn.

AT WORK

I made my way to my work-place on foot. A long line of traffic blocked the street that skirted the hill, heading towards the bustling centre of the big city. Buses lumbered ponderously, brakes constantly uttering squeals of protest, rancour and impatience. Trucks emitted repressed, supercilious groans, while private vehicles honked in all possible registers. A pungent smell of scorched rubber, diesel and motor oil hung in the air, mingled with the light and invigorating breath of a good-natured sea breeze.

I quickened my pace and by ten minutes to eight I was already ensconced securely in my office: a narrow room crammed with professional literature, gilt-trimmed catalogues and tiny instruments, most of them defective. Two letters lay on my desk. Before I had time to open them, I was told that the manager wanted to see me immediately. The minion who passed on this message saw fit to warn me that he had sounded "stressed and anxious".

I made my way towards the executive offices where the manager was waiting for me, looking tense indeed. He was a middle-aged man, bespectacled with a bushy moustache masking his upper lip, of more than average height and smartly dressed – grey summer suit, matching shirt and tie.

Before I had even taken a seat on the other side of his big desk, he exclaimed impatiently:

"I asked you to promote Amelia!"

"It's not up to me to promote people" I replied calmly.

"Recommend then!" – he corrected himself, with undiminished insistence.

"There's no reason to do that," was the answer.

"What's that supposed to mean, 'no reason'?" he raged – and his high-pitched, grating voice took on a note of reproof. "You took her on in the first place!" he added in calmer tones – "You filled in the recommendation form, pointing out her qualities... Have you changed your mind?" He studied my face with an expression of veiled scorn and overt satisfaction.

"That's not what I meant!" – I smiled gently.

"Then what did you mean?" he demanded with renewed vigour,

his face darkening, as if determined not to let me evade the issue.

"There isn't a vacancy," I explained.

"Invent one!" he yelled.

"It isn't up to me to invent vacancies for posts that don't exist," I replied calmly.

"You're being insolent again!" – his voice shook with rage.

I said nothing.

He rose from his seat, did a broad circuit of his office, approached me from behind, leaned over me and said, in a remarkably calm, affable voice:

"You ran away from your wife and you're doing just as you please... as for me, I'm the one under pressure!" – his voice rising – "Someone like Amelia... Between friends, man to man! I promised she'd be promoted and I have to keep my word! Invent something!" He circled round me and sat down again behind his huge desk, looked at me keenly with a bizarre blend of entreaty, resentment, fear, pride and helplessness.

"I didn't 'run away' from my wife," I remarked coldly.

"You're living apart!" the manager grinned.

"An arrangement that suits us both."

"Do you really hate each other that much?" – a kind of sarcastic curiosity flashing in his eyes, their light green colour visible again behind the thick glasses.

"You wouldn't understand," I replied.

"What about all those glands and hormones, how do you cope with that, eh?" he cried, agog with curiosity, even shuffling his heavy body forward in anticipation of my reply.

I looked up at him and measured him with a steady glance.

"Okay, okay!" he said hurriedly, apologetically, before standing up again with renewed energy and performing a circuit of his office, one hand thrust in his trouser-pocket, the other describing weird geometric patterns in the air. Finally, he returned to his seat.

"I implore you most earnestly, I'm begging you please!" – his voice harsh and sibilant, bird-like – "Lend a hand, help me! Man to man! My wife I can't stand, but she's the mother of my children..." His voice softened for a moment and then he added bitterly:

"As for Amelia, what can I say – she wraps me round her little finger!" and looking back at me he almost yelled: "I promised! Invent something!"

I thought for a moment, then glanced back at him.

"As I said," I began equably, "I don't have the right or the authority, or the conscience, to invent things."

He grimaced, bitterly disappointed.

"I'd be prepared to invent..." he responded in a hollow voice. "But," he added – "I'm not familiar with your department..." And suddenly, as if coming to life: "Does Amelia understand the situation?"

"Almost certainly," I replied pragmatically.

"Many thanks!" he exclaimed, relieved, rising and standing behind his desk as a sign that the interview was over.

I had barely reached the door when he ran up behind me, laid a fleshy hand on my shoulder, a comradely gesture, and said:

"What should I do, do you think? I mean – how to get out of this mess?"

"Give it up," I answered him brightly.

He weighed my words, gave me a green-tinged sideways look in which surprise exceeded scepticism and muttered: "Subtle!" He removed his hand, took half a step towards me and opened the door with a theatrical flourish.

I turned to go. I had taken three paces when his strident-chirpy voice stopped me:

"Send Amelia here at once! Don't forget!" – and after a brief pause he added in the same tone: "I'm much obliged to you!"

I concentrated on my work and succeeded in clearing up a considerable number of items. And then I heard raised voices, from the direction of the lobby and the corridor where the washrooms were located. I listened. A gruff, guttural, masculine voice uttering a stream of crude expletives, answered by the shrieks of frightened women. A moment later I was phoned by one of the secretaries who told me, sounding very flustered, that some "low-life" had got into the building, was refusing to leave and saying he didn't care if they called the cops. In fact she had already called the police but they, as usual, were taking their time and until they arrived... She was turning to me, she added hastily, her voice shaking, as I was "the only man" still on the premises.

"What do you mean?" I asked.

"I'm begging you, pleading with you, please – do something!" she almost wailed into the receiver – "He's scary!" she protested and added feverishly: "We're trapped in the office! He's blocking the exit!"

I made my way to the corridor outside the washrooms. A big, in fact a very big man was sprawled there, his feet propped up on the wall on one side, and his head resting on the opposite wall. The corridor was approximately 1.80 metres in width, so the man had to be more than two metres tall.

He spat out a juicy curse – whether addressed to me or to the silent void above him, there was no way of telling.

I approached him, bent down and asked softly:

"What do you want?"

"To be got out of here!" he cried, his bulging eyes, laced with thick blood-vessels, shooting sparks of hatred at me.

"How did you get in here?" I asked, unperturbed.

"What does it matter, 'how'?" he challenged me. "Are you a cop?"

"No," I replied with a smile. "But before we can get you out, we need to know how you got in here…"

"That's none of your business!" he interrupted roughly. "You're a public institution – it's your duty to take care of me, do something… I'm not moving from here!" – his voice rising and spittle glistening at the corners of his thick lips.

"We'll do all we can to get you out," I assured him, and in the same calm and gentle voice I asked: "Why can't you walk out by yourself? Are you ill in some way?" I looked at him keenly. A quiver, which turned into a shudder, passed through his gangling body and brought a sour grimace to his bloated, unshaven face with its layers of compacted grime.

"All this talk!" the man sighed, seeming to melt a little. "Look!" he said, stretching out his swollen hands and waving them in front of my eyes. They were a mass of big, purple blisters.

"Burns?" I asked.

He nodded.

"Feet as well?"

Another nod.

"How did you get here?"

"Somebody threw me!" he exclaimed with a sudden surge of anger, but defensively, as if hiding something.

"I'll call an ambulance," I offered.

"I've no money!" he cried.

"That's not the point," I assured him, stepping over him and knocking on the locked door of the office, and when the girls trapped in there replied, I asked them to call an ambulance. And then I heard the man behind me shouting: "No! No!"

I retraced my steps and stood over him.

"Why not?" I asked.

He scrutinised me with his grey, red-rimmed eyes, eyes that were slightly scornful and yet seemed to hide some obscure fear in their depths, perhaps a lot more than simple fear, something resembling intense dread, uncompromising terror.

"You needn't be afraid of an ambulance!" I tried to reassure him, still standing over him, as if trying to work out what he wanted.

A distant flash passed through his eyes, which had changed their expression completely, exposing astonishing depth and startling sensitivity. He made an effort to sit upright, with some success. His clothes were tattered and encrusted with dirt: a shirt and sweater of indeterminate colour, trousers blackened by oil-stains. He wore army boots without socks. As he moved, abruptly, a pungent, mildewy aroma was diffused in the air.

"I've a confession to make," he whispered, breathing hard. "All this, the burns... the hands I mean," he stressed, grinning and trying to wink at me, in a display of superficial cunning, "there's nothing wrong with my feet!" – and returning to the train of thought which had been momentarily severed – "All this – it's just bullshit! It's not what I'm here for. I want to ask you a small favour!" He studied my face intently, a new gravity in his eyes along with a sort of pallid entreaty, arising from that indissoluble core of terror.

"Ask away!" I encouraged him.

"I'm a boozer," he announced in a clear voice, accompanied by a sigh. "Totally addicted to the demon drink!" he added, as if clarification was needed: "If you'll fetch me a bottle of something" – he gestured weakly with his hand – "I'll be up and on my way...You see, I've no money!" he wailed, "and if I don't have a drink – I'll go mad, get sick, don't know where I'll end up!" There was the ring of truth in his voice.

"The shops are closed at this hour," I pointed out.

"Maybe, you can still find... some kiosk or other," he suggested, barely able to control his impatience. Vodka or... just any liquor. You,

you're an understanding guy," – he tried a wheedling tone of voice and the first beads of sweat appeared on his purple brow. The expression on his face was that of a hunted refugee, with no prospect of escape. Suddenly he erupted:

"Run! Do something!" – the whole of his sturdy, bloated body shaking convulsively.

I left the Institute, and at the end of the street I found a kiosk that was open, and had a solitary bottle of arak in stock. The bottle had been there so long, the dust had congealed on it, entombing some variety of moth and an unfortunate fly. I paid the kiosk proprietor, roused briefly from his torpor by the unexpected transaction, took the liquor and retraced my steps. I handed the bottle just as it was, sealed and dusty, to our uninvited guest, still sprawled in the corridor outside the washrooms. Somehow he had shifted his bulk and was sitting upright. With a strangely solemn expression, as if participating in an arcane ceremony or performing some ancient religious rite, he took the bottle from me, his swollen hands shaking – from emotion or on account of the burns – and failing to open it manually, he tore off the cap with his yellow teeth and at once put the mouth to his lips.

He drank thirstily, spasmodically, continuously, silently tilting the bottle in accordance with the quantity of liquid remaining in it. Within a minute the arak had been drained, disappearing from the opaque glass vessel as if it had never existed. He turned sideways and with a flourish, hurled the empty bottle along the shady corridor. The bottle rolled noisily over the gleaming tiles, reached the end of the corridor and hit the wall, somehow surviving intact, without so much as a crack. The guest uttered a sound which might have been a sigh of relief, and with my help rose to his feet. He exuded a pungent, acrid stench.

"What's your name?" he asked impetuously. I told him.

"I won't forget!" he announced in a strange tone of pain blended with shame. And with confident tread, he left the building.

I told the secretaries trapped in the main office that the man had gone. Immediately the door was flung open and they swooped on me, eager to know how I had managed to get rid of him. When I mentioned his interest in me, the senior among them commented:

"You've made a mistake there!"

"Why?" queried her assistant, a young girl on the eve of national service.

"He's not going to leave you alone!" the senior declared authoritatively. "A shame!" she concluded with an emphatic air of gravity and sorrow.

I needed to go to the executive offices and I left the department temporarily. On my return, the office supervisor told me a man had been looking for me, and she gave a precise description of the drunkard. Not finding me there, she added, he asked her for my address and she gave it. I thanked her warmly and returned to my work. Within a relatively short time I had finished and I set out on my way.

RAHAMIM'S CAFÉ

On the shore, above the fish restaurant with the photographs of ministers and generals dining there, was a corner that I used to frequent, sitting on an upturned crate, well-hidden among the thick clumps of heather, and indulging in meditation to my heart's content.

The sun was veering westward; the horizon glowed in serene anticipation of something ornate and regal, hidden from human eyes. The sky above was blue, youthful, flawless. The raucous din of traffic was swallowed up entirely by the silvery void, giving added emphasis to the rhythm of the waves, the regular, insistent beat of perpetual rebellion.

I went down to Rahamim's café – with its massive and ancient domed roof reminiscent of a mosque or the tomb of a revered Muslim dignitary.

Unexpectedly, there were no customers present. The three small tables set up outside were untenanted. I sat in a corner on a bench with a seat of plaited reeds, a spot affording me an unimpeded view of sea and sky.

Rahamim was dozing in a corner of the café and it was some time before he became aware of my presence. When he finally awoke from his slumbers and noticed my silhouette he came outside, approaching me with steady gait, swaying slightly, either on account of his age or because of his habitual equanimity, and standing close by, he greeted me:

"Good evening!" – his voice still sleepy, but his small, mottled eyes alert and expressing interest and readiness to listen.

"Good evening!" I responded affably.

"Tea?" It was a statement, rather than a question.

I nodded assent.

He returned to the depths of the café and appeared a few minutes later in the broad frame of the door – a heavy door made up of panels of thick coloured glass, a later addition to an ancient structure – carrying a little brass tray. On the tray was a tall narrow glass cup and the liquid it contained was brown-amber, clear and sparkling as a precious stone. Rahamim's tea was unique in its flavour, its fragrance, its warmth and even its colour: sweetened but not so sweet as to impair the delicate flavour, a thin fragrance to purify and stimulate the mind, warmth to bring comfort, heart-warming colour.

Rahamim laid the tea down on the table, sat facing me and for a long while said not a word.

I took the cup and sipped placidly from the warm liquid. I gazed into the endless void of the sky, engulfing the sea beneath it, and filling up steadily with the young flickers of the stars, just now coming into being.

In a throaty voice, the voice of an elderly cat, Rahamim asked: "How's work?"

Unbidden, memories of the working day I had just experienced rose to the surface of my mind: those two letters laid on my desk which I had read cursorily – one from the management, warning me not to exceed my budget and the other – from someone who had been treated in the department, full of gratitude and compliments...

"Everything's fine," I replied.

He nodded his grey head, took a cigarette from an old-fashioned solid silver case, straightened it between his bony fingers, stuck it in his taut mouth, struck a match and lit it carefully. He took a deep drag of smoke, exhaled pleasurably through his nostrils and with a slightly awkward smile, a hint of self-justification, remarked:

"At least it's only tobacco..."

As there was no response from me, he saw fit to add:

"Not hashish, I mean... or – something else," and he shifted comfortably on the plaited seat of the bench. For some reason, Rahamim's comments reminded me of the events of last night.

I took another sip of the amber tea, still retaining its heat and delicate fragrance and its rich flavour – growing ever more rich, like the flavour of vintage wine. I put the cup back in its place, turning to my friend and asking him:

"A guy called Shuki – do you know him?" And to make it easier for him I added: "Some kind of pimp..."

"Shuki?" He pondered, racking his memory, took a long and deep pull at his cigarette, lowered his head behind a thick pall of smoke and when this faded and dispersed in the clear evening air, raised it again; an oval head, with wrinkled brow and cheeks – the colour of dull bronze.

"If you mean Shuki the pimp," he said in that steady, throaty voice, "he's well known..." – his eyes scanning the empty void behind my back – "known to the girls who need his services, and the police as well. He has a gang. A gang of extortionists. They'll kill for him too – at a price, of course!" And he continued:

"Rumour has it that he murdered a young girl with his own hands. A drug-addict and a drug-dealer, without conscience or restraints. For drugs," Rahamim added, listing the man's characteristics in his steady, modulated voice, weighing every word before it was said - "he'd sell the mother who bore him, or murder her... people like him – one plague that wasn't inflicted on Egypt!" Rahamim sighed and suddenly fixed his alert eyes on me – alert but benevolent as ever.

I took another sip of the tea.

"What have you to do with him?" the old man asked, with a faint trace of anxiety.

"Nothing at all," I replied.

Once more he focused his gaze on some point hidden behind me, took another drag from his cigarette, which was growing shorter, its glow intensifying in the darkness, and when he had shaken ash on the little tray and the butt-end almost disappeared between fingers reluctant to relinquish it – he asked again with no change to the guttural calm of his voice:

"Why do you ask?"

"I met one of his girls."

"He has three," Rahamim responded, and proceeded to list them: "Lili, Rosa and Sonya. The youngest and most profitable of them all is Lili."

"What kind of girl is she?" I asked.

"A born tart!" he declared, his voice changing, turning hoarse, deep and harsh – "Like all of them!" he added, attempting unsuccessfully to regain the gruff equanimity of before. His luminous face seemed to grow dark for a moment, as if a screen had descended, and he concluded his speech emphatically: "A disaster for the world!"

"How is that?" I asked.

"Their souls are corrupt and they corrupt the souls of all who have contact with them – even those who only see them or speak to them... they... they're like infectious diseases!" Rahamim insisted, leaning towards me.

"If that is so," was my conclusive comment, "the world is sick."

"It is sick indeed!" Rahamim agreed, with confidence but with unexpected restraint.

"Then it's been sick since mankind set foot on it," I suggested. "There have always been streetwalkers."

"No!" Rahamim objected. "Then they had a different view of it... Listen," he continued, turning to look at me keenly – "In those days it wasn't prostitution!"

"What was it then?" I persisted.

"In those days they didn't know what it was, they didn't have a definition. They thought things had to be that way – so they did it. Listen," – he turned his mottled eyes to me again, his broad smile exposing a gold tooth deep in his mouth – "as long as it isn't recognised that it's prostitution and it's forbidden – it isn't prostitution!

"So the reason why the world is sick – is that people recognise what's permitted and what's forbidden?" I asked with interest.

"It's the way to heal the world!" Rahamim declared with great firmness.

"How?" I still wasn't satisfied.

"When this business of not knowing the difference between permitted and forbidden began to sully the world and make it sick – it was decided to put an end to it. So they determined what was permitted and what forbidden. So laws and regulations came into being – without which – the world would have gone down the tubes!" Rahamim declared. "It's like a grown man continuing to behave like a child. The world grew up and it had to decide for itself what was permitted and what was forbidden... and then what?" – he smiled again, adding: "It, the world, did this – and fell into a trap! As so often happens, the world ensnared itself!" He took a deep, final pull at his cigarette, exhaled bluish smoke through his mouth and nostrils, stubbed out the smouldering butt on the tray before him, looked up, a kind of soft radiance rising from the depths of his eyes, and concluded:

"Now listen to me," – he demanded my full attention: "On the one hand, the world is instructed on what's forbidden and what's permitted, or to put it in archaic terms – 'Thou shalt' and 'Thou shalt not!' – but on the other hand, it's incapable of keeping these rules, upholding them! And the result," he added emphatically, stretching out his hand and waving it in an expansive gesture, "is a sick, degenerate, disintegrating world, crying out in its bitter pain, walking unblemished into the open arms of its only saviour..." He paused, looking grave, and sighed a deep sigh, apparently losing the thread of his thoughts.

"And that is?" I prompted him.

He replied in a distracted but clear voice:

"Annihilation!"

I took another sip of my tea.

Silence descended on us once more.

The waves went on beating out their ancient anger, restrained for the time being, on the dumb concrete down below, but with a different sound, softer and more submissive, as if straining to hear a secret divulged, tense with anticipation.

I had finished the tea some time before. Rahamim stood up from his place, silently picked up the tray and the empty cup and went into the café. He made coffee for himself, sat down at the counter, spread out an ancient newspaper and glanced at it while taking regular gulps of the hot and black liquid.

I came to the conclusion that it was time to leave. But I had barely risen to my feet when a dim figure emerged from the velvet enveloping darkness, heading towards the café.

It was Nessim, Rahamim's nephew – a man of middle age, short of build, a black cap perched on his balding skull – a junior clerk in the municipality. It was said he had been a yeshiva student in his youth.

He wished me a glutinous "Good evening", glanced at me briefly and went inside. His visits to the café were frequent and commonplace, but this time, for some reason, his appearance had the effect of undermining my decision, and finally changing it. Instead of getting up and leaving, I stayed where I was in the thickening darkness.

It wasn't long before the voices of the uncle and the nephew emerged from the café, sounding tense and with a strangely strident quality. A moment later Nessim came out hurriedly and took a seat at a table near mine, smiled a forced smile at me and waved a tiny hand uneasily, an improvised gesture of friendship, then stared at the table, waiting tensely for something. Rahamim followed him after a short interval, approaching his table and putting down two cups of steaming coffee on broad saucers. This was authentic Turkish coffee, Rahamim's speciality and reputedly the best in Jaffa, if not the entire country.

Rahamim sat down beside his nephew and asked how the family was faring. Nessim was blessed with a wife, five daughters and a son. He lived in one of the most rundown districts of the lower city; it was renowned as such and for this reason, rents for apartments there were among the lowest – little more than symbolic rents for dingy, neglected properties, sometimes not paid at all.

To his relative's question, Nessim replied that he had "fled" his home.

"Why?" Rahamim asked, and Nessim hastened to reply:

"Because of the frightful racket caused by the neighbour. You know, drums and cymbals and violins and clarinets and... what do you call them?" – he racked his brains and recalled – "Saxophones! And guitars and drunks, and tarts! I sent my wife and the children to her sister's and as for me, I came here – for a bit of peace and quiet!"

"Which neighbour are you talking about?" asked Rahamim in his normal, throaty voice, a question which had, apparently, been raised in their previous conversation.

"That ghastly pimp," replied Nessim with animation. "You know – the racketeer, deals in drugs and he's an addict himself."

"Shuki," Rahamim suggested with calm emphasis, gradually turning in my direction, giving me a silent, sidelong glance.

"That's him!" his nephew agreed, almost enthusiastically.

Rahamim drew from his deep trouser-pocket the solid silver cigarette-case, opened it solemnly, extracted a cigarette, closed it with a snap, tapped the end of the cigarette on the gleaming cover, stuck it between his lips, put the case back in its place, took out a box of matches and lit up. His movements were measured, leisurely and eloquent of deep thought and the pair of us, Nessim and I, followed them intently, as if compelled to watch. There was a silence that nobody attempted to break.

Rahamim exhaled the smoke in thick grey rings, darkening and dispersing into the void of the night. Then he leaned forward, raised the cup and took a clearly audible slurp from the hot and sticky liquid. His nephew hastened to follow his example, taking a swig from his own coffee – just as noisily as his uncle.

"So what has Shuki been up to?" asked Rahamim calmly.

"They say – he's had a stroke of luck," Nessim replied.

"At cards, roulette, dice?" Rahamim prompted.

"That's what you might think," Nessim rejoined and added: "But no one believes it!"

"What do they believe?" Rahamim persisted.

"There's another story going round," Nessim hushed his voice as if revealing a secret and then raised it to a dramatic pitch: "Some sucker threw five thousand at him... five thousand on the table!" Nessim cried in a tone of genuine bewilderment, blended with a certain degree of agitation and simple jealousy, and he concluded: "It seems to be the truth."

"Why do you think that?" Rahamim resumed his interrogation and his nephew replied willingly:

"I heard it with my own ears. From his mouth, I mean. I heard him boasting... I was standing by the door of his house and I could see right into the courtyard... and there was all that commotion – whores swigging wine and brandy, and champagne – would you believe! And a barbecue of course: kebabs and steaks and shishlik. And that wild music, and all kinds of dancing. I saw a man stripping naked!" His breath almost failed him as he relived the trauma of the spectacle he had witnessed. "As for the women," he added darkly with wrinkled brow, "the least said the better!"

"What did you hear?" In an uncharacteristically sharp tone, Rahamim brought him back to the main point at issue.

"I heard," Nessim began, a tense note to his voice, "I heard Shuki himself, in person" – emphatically – "saying:

'That sucker, I'm going to find him and milk him! By my life and the lives of all my loved ones I swear! I'll milk him and bleed him to the bare bones! He threw that five thousand at me as if I was a dog, without batting an eyelid! He'll live to regret that. He'll be sorry he was ever born!' At this point he was almost weeping with anger and pique," Nessim commented, going on to quote with mounting excitement, enthusiasm almost:

" 'He's going to find out who Shuki is! When Shuki lays hands on him – he'll have no bones left. No one insults Shuki that way!' And it seemed to me that here he broke into a strange kind of whimper, sort of dry, like a silent spasm," Nessim explained to us, adding an assessment of his own – "but maybe it was just the drink. The man was definitely drunk!"

"And angry," Rahamim tried to pin things down.

"And how!" exclaimed Nessim, and they both went back to drinking their coffee, taking deep and refreshing gulps. Rahamim puffed on his cigarette, exhaled smoke and commented off-handedly:

"So he took the money, threw a party and had a good time – and he's still angry..."

Carefully Nessim put the cup down on its broad saucer with the forget-me-nots painted on either side, and said equably, whether influenced just by the coffee or by the deep silence still prevailing all around:

"You know these types. They ask for a small favour and when they get it – they want your house as well!" And he grinned at me, in the hope of reading in my face a sign of appreciation of the astuteness of his perceptions. He wasn't disappointed.

"I'd be interested to know how this sucker came to be throwing his five thousand, good money, at a creep like Shuki!" mused Rahamim, before proposing what seemed to be a fairly plausible solution: "Or is there some new gang boss around here?"

"That's what I thought too, at first," Nessim replied, returning to his habitual, alert tone, from which the initial strains of anxiety and caution had dissipated, apparently under the calming influence of his uncle. "Especially seeing as one of his tarts, Lili, the one they call the 'gold-mine', disappeared the moment that five thousand was thrown at Shuki... but this wasn't a boss!"

"How do you know?" Rahamim showed lively interest.

"Deals between bosses don't end with parties! They're just...deals! And you won't find any self-respecting boss paying such a high price even for the classiest of hookers. In all of Jaffa you won't find a boss like that. Besides, all the bosses were at Shuki's place at that orgy and it seems they forced him to lay on the party for them. They're jealous of him. They're jealous of his luck and they're trying to get him worked up about this sucker, whoever he may be. I've heard them referring to him as a 'maniac', a 'mental defective' or 'totally off his head'. That seems to be the general consensus," Nessim concluded.

"Where did you hear this?" Rahamim showed no sign of tiring of his interrogation.

"There. At the orgy," Nessim answered him willingly and went on to sketch in some obligatory background. "As I told you, I sent Sarika with the children to her sister's. It started in the early afternoon. Actually," he corrected himself, "that was the time I came home from work, so it could well have started in the morning. After Sarika and the kids had gone I was left alone in the house and I went over to Shuki's place. I stood there in the gateway, or sat on the step. No one paid any attention to me. I waited. To see what would happen... you know what these parties are like – liable to end in destruction, vandalism, arson, looting... Neighbourliness, friendship, loyalty – they mean nothing to these guys! I sat there and watched and listened."

"You were eavesdropping!" Rahamim declared in uncharacteristically cold tone of voice.

"I was all ears!" Nessim agreed with undisguised triumphalism. "Get the cure in before the plague, that's my motto!"

"And that's when you heard them talking about the maniac?" Rahamim ignored the triumphalism and continued his rigorous questioning of his nephew: "The maniac or the mental defective or the guy who they say is totally off his head?"

Nessim measured his uncle with what was supposed to be an offended look, though not without a subtle trace of arrogance, and he continued his narrative:

"There were two who claimed they'd seen him with their own eyes. They were there when that guy threw the bundle of notes on the table. They were both ready to swear by everything precious to them that the guy is a weirdo, a psychotic nut!" Nessim cried with renewed heat and returned to his coffee, to steady his nerves a little and muster some energy.

Rahamim followed his example, accompanying his consumption of the black liquid with a dignified drag on the cigarette glowing between the fingers of his right hand, then lowering it slowly, delicately tapping ash into the broad saucer and leaving it there perched on the lip, still burning but with glow fading. In a thoughtful, muted voice, with head emphatically lowered, as if talking to himself, he half asked, half expressed his inner musing:

"I'd like to know who this madman is!"

A whole minute passed in deep silence, laden with tension and yet in spite of this, surprisingly – still bearable. And when another minute had been added to that dark river of increasingly self-conscious silence, my voice was heard, calm and miraculously clear:

"I am he."

They both looked up and turned to me at once. And their movement, though hardly exceptional, was so sudden and sharp, so unexpected, that their heads nearly butted together. And in the dumbfounded expressions on their faces, there was a strange kind of fear and the impulse to shy away from something frightful and flee from it, as far away as possible. And there was also a clear effort to convince themselves that the words that had just split the void had never been spoken.

"You?" Rahamim could not control his agitation; his lips contorted and when he picked up the cigarette again with the fingers of his right hand, his habitual gesture, it trembled and the glow at its tip seemed to be sending out a distress signal, a cry for help, a fateful warning.

And since I hesitated to answer the implied question, the invitation to confirm what I had said, the café proprietor hastened to make things easy for me, and maybe for himself, raising the logical objection:

"Where would you get five thousand from?" And he was all optimism now, expecting denial to follow, and admission of misunderstanding, in an acceptable and reasonable guise, or perhaps acknowledgement of a witty and successful experiment in winding them up – both of them at once – creating a kind of predatory tension that in the end would dissolve in peals of friendly laughter, the laughter of relief as well as amusement.

And because my continuing silence did not augur well, and the interest that I had earlier expressed in Shuki reinforced the darker side of the business, Rahamim continued with the same line of thought, though with hopes fading fast and an expression of unaccustomed severity:

"Why would you throw away five thousand to a mad dog like Shuki... you've heard what he means to do!"

I smiled in the darkness:

"What a lot of questions you're asking, and all at once!"

"Where would you get five thousand?" Rahamim eased a little, and his deep and sincere anxiety and the fear in his voice retreated, subdued.

"I got a loan to buy an apartment. I was supposed to be buying an apartment for twenty-one thousand, in the Ajami quarter. A mortgaged property. They agreed to let me have five thousand – a low interest loan over ten years. The money was in my hand, and I was on my way to see the landlord..."

"And now – no money and no apartment!" cried Nessim, the junior municipality clerk.

"No money," I agreed equably. "But I still have an apartment."

"He won't be homeless," the café proprietor saw fit to point out to his nephew: "Lives in rented accommodation, he'll carry on living in rented accommodation!" he concluded succinctly, then added thoughtfully, as if conversing with himself: "That isn't the question..."

"What is your question then?" demanded Nessim, annoyed for some reason by his uncle's words.

Rahamim turned to me again, and asked:

"What possessed you to throw that five thousand at Shuki?"

"There was a reason," I said, declining to elaborate.

The two slim, short-statured men, exchanged anxious glances.

"This thing is going to cost you dear" cried Nessim in a tone of warning and deep foreboding.

"Not only that," Rahamim interjected vigorously, "Why did you have to tell us that it's you?"

"Come on, Uncle," the younger man protested. "He has nothing to fear from me!"

"He most certainly has!" the uncle objected, shooting sparks at his nephew. "He should be afraid of me too. Still, what's done can't be undone," he concluded in an injured tone. "Anyway," he turned to me again, "now you know who you're dealing with and what to expect!"

"I know," I smiled with a serenity that nothing in the world could dislodge.

He observed my smile in spite of the darkness, which the neon light above the entrance to the café could not dispel, and cried out to me with unexpected fervour, in a yell which surprised him too:

"You're smiling!"

I didn't answer. He was incapable of tuning in to my wavelength.

Once more Rahamim concentrated his gaze on the unmatched, ancient flagstones, made a nervous movement with his foot as if stamping out a cigarette end, a movement serving as a lightning-conductor for fear and frustration, and murmured between clenched lips:

"And maybe they were right, those guys, what they were saying about some half-witted moron..."

And suddenly something in him seemed to melt and soften, withdrawing. He looked up and returned my smile with a surprising smile of his own – broad and amiable, and apologetic. His little eyes sparkled:

"All credit to you!" he cried – somewhat irrelevantly, I thought.

Nessim sat at an angle, his eyes staring ahead of him and the expression on his face tense and gloomy.

And then the fishermen started arriving – those coming up from the sea and those about to go down there. They came singly or in little groups of two or three, greeting one another with a raised hand, an awkward, almost embarrassed smile, speaking little and in hushed tones. Some of them had an anxious look, in the faces of others – a kind of blank unconcern, saying nothing. There were fishermen whose tranquil eyes held a spark of repressed happiness, a defence mechanism against the evil eye, and there were also some with cheerful faces. But the last were in the minority – two or three youngsters who were putting to sea for the first or second time, still thoroughly intoxicated by the open spaces and the humming breeze and the songs of the stars, and the silvery fish scales in the enchanted radiance of the moon. Given the opportunity, they would have started singing or dancing, or both simultaneously.

All the fishermen, young and old alike, those coming up from the sea and those on their way down there, the glad and the anxious, without exception – ordered Turkish coffee.

Rahamim hurriedly brought out extra tables and wicker-seated benches to the oval space by the entrance to the café. I helped him. He tried to thank me, but I succeeded in evading him. Finally, he put down the table he was carrying, approached and said emphatically:

"Thanks!"

"No need!" I replied.

"Oh yes there is!" he persisted.

"I should be thanking you," I said to him lightly, in the interval between putting down a bench and picking up a table.

"For calling you a half-witted moron?" he mumbled apologetically.

"For the opportunity to exercise my bones a little," I replied in the same bright tone.

"You can do that anywhere," he declared with distant sadness.

"I don't get the chance," I said with a smile, picking up another table.

A total of a dozen tables and some thirty benches were brought out into the open space resembling a small precinct at the feet of the impressive, ancient structure of the café – and all were immediately occupied.

Some of the fishermen stood by Rahamim's counter, inside the café, drinking their coffee with keen concentration and noisy slurping, absorbing the warm drink that both soothes and stimulates, and has the strange effect of dispelling hunger and any appetite for food.

Nessim, Rahamim's nephew, had slipped away in the commotion, so I also helped Rahamim serving the coffee and collecting the empty cups. Tucked away in the recesses of the café were some antiquated wooden chairs, with high backs. These too were brought outside, to be claimed by the fishermen who had abandoned their post by the counter inside. As the night was still young and there was a free seat available – I sat down too.

"Raphael!" – one of the fishermen turned to his older companion who had just drained his coffee, his empty cup still steaming on the table – "South of the Parsa Rock – did you find anything?"

"We haven't been there," the other replied and explained: "Tonight you won't find anything there – too much humidity and no moon. That means you have to go further to the West, and we found something there sure enough – touch wood!" he added hastily with a sincere, almost childish chuckle, winking at the questioner.

"Why do you need all these superstitions?" interjected a youth who didn't look like a fisherman at all – in his early twenties, lean and tousle-haired but clean-shaven, wearing a checked tricot shirt, in his eyes a flash of astuteness blended with innocence.

"You, learned Sir," Raphael turned fully towards him, speaking emphatically, "You should stick to writing poems in praise of the sea. You'll never make a fisherman!"

"Why is that?" the youth protested.

And Raphael the fisherman was happy to explain:

"What I said just now – is as far from superstition as East is from West. Many years of fishing experience are bound up in..."

"Anyone would think you were born a fisherman!" the youth interrupted him with a provocative air.

"Avinoam, my friend," Raphael continued: "I wasn't born a fisherman, but I learned the trade from one of the most famous fishermen in these parts... Peg leg Ibrahim... ever heard of him?"

"No," the youth admitted, honestly and with unexpected humility.

"He taught me!" Raphael went on, warming to his theme: "And taught me well! His father too, and his grandfather, and his great-grandfather – a whole dynasty of fathers and grandfathers made their living from fishing this coastline. A respectable living!" he stressed, "Fishing was in their blood. The experience they built up – you couldn't learn in any university in the world!"

"Where's this Ibrahim now?" the young man asked, with interest.

"He left the sea," – a note of regret was perceptible in Raphael's voice – "These days, everything's changing! And he, Ibrahim, smelt money and turned his back on poetry... and this... after hundreds of years... and deep roots. Like a kid offered an automatic toy... he doesn't play out in the fields any more. And he doesn't understand the terrible price he'll have to pay, the price of pure enjoyment..." Raphael sighed, slapped his thigh with his huge hand and concluded: "It's an age of upheavals... people don't feel it, but in ten, fifteen years from now – they'll stand and wonder!"

"What do you mean?" – a new voice joined the conversation, a fisherman sitting at a nearby table, wearing a woollen scarf around his head, like a tarbush.

"The changes!" cried Raphael, as if irked by the ignorance of the questioner.

"What are they?" Avinoam demanded to know.

"Look around you," Raphael invited him in a measured, didactic voice, pointing with a broad movement of the hand that evidently included all the customers in the café: "Will you find here a single veteran fisherman, a fisherman with roots... whose father made his living from fishing and his grandfather and his ancestors... or let's just stick to the father – will you find anyone like that?" Raphael waited for a moment for an answer, and when none came he answered his own question: "Not one! And that's what I mean when I talk about changes!" he concluded, with an air of triumph.

"Fishing is passing from Arab hands into Jewish hands!" was the incontrovertible statement of Raphael's middle-aged neighbour.

"It's just a matter of time," someone sitting in the corner commented with a grimace, in a diffident voice, before clearing his throat and adding in a clearer tone: "The Jews won't last the course!"

"Why?" Raphael demanded to know with emphatic, alert curiosity.

"Because it isn't a bank and it isn't a bourse, it isn't diamonds and it isn't politics!"

The speaker from the corner earned nods of agreement and approval, and someone even uttered a peculiar laugh, soft – and yet cynical and provocative.

"You're wrong, my friend," cried Raphael, "you're not reading the writing on the wall! The Jews are beginning to discover the sea. They're falling in love with it. The bourse and the banks – slowly but surely they're getting sick of them. Time is doing its job. As tension begins to ease and subside, there is a turning towards the profound and the beautiful, the true. There's no denying that the Jew is a pursuer of profit, but he has a head – and he has a heart as well! He realises that money isn't the answer to everything; in fact – it's the answer to very little... And all this anxiety and the pointless fraying of nerves, living in a whirlpool, short life spent in the pursuit of lucre – none of it is worthwhile. The Jews are beginning to wake up and absorb something of what is true in life!"

"You're naïve, Raphael!" young Avinoam shot at him, in a tone of overt scorn.

"It's not me that's naïve, it's you that's blinkered!" Raphael fumed. "You're a fool, a young idiot who puts marvellous poems together but has no conception of their higher meaning..." He softened his brusque words with a broad, friendly and apologetic smile, adding: "I'll ask you a question – Are you prepared to abandon the sea?"

"No!" Avinoam cried with surprising determination, sounding almost hysterical as if someone was trying to rob him of his most precious possession – "But I'm not the one you should be asking. To me," he explained, "money has never been that important. There's not many like me among you people, or in the whole nation of

Israel!" he grinned.

"Wrong!" replied Raphael, adding with firm emphasis: "Fatal mistake! Look!" – he rose to his feet, making another expansive gesture with his bony arm, a comprehensive gesture. "I turn to you!" – raising his voice – "Is there anyone here who's fed up with the sea and will leave his boat at the earliest opportunity, or maybe is already planning to vamoose?" And when no one replied, he egged his companions on:

"No need to be embarrassed, speak up!"

"No one's embarrassed!" came that voice again from the corner, or perhaps it was his neighbour at the table. "No one's thinking of giving it up, it's simply not an option!" he cried indignantly, before adding in a more subdued tone: "Not in my opinion..."

"Your turn, Avinoam!" Raphael announced, sitting down again at his bench.

Avinoam grinned awkwardly and made a further, final attempt to prove to his sparring partner that he didn't have all the answers:

"If you please, gentlemen," he turned to the assembled fishermen. "Anyone who has never, and I mean never – considered leaving the sea – raise your hand!"

"What's going on here, a bloody Knesset vote?" Rahamim was heard to grumble, clearly irritated. But it was too late – as one, all present raised their arms and held them aloft. Rahamim himself followed suit, unconsciously perhaps.

"Wonder of wonders!" said Avinoam, impressed, his own arm held high, "A nation of backhander merchants, turning into a nation of poets!"

One after another, almost reluctantly, the arms were lowered, as if their owners sought to demonstrate their unequivocal commitment to the business under discussion, their unshakable willingness to draw encouragement from one another.

"You're wrong about that too, pal!" Raphael rounded again on Avinoam.

"How?" asked the younger man, surprised but with an inexplicably cheerful gleam in his eyes.

"This people," Raphael replied with dignity, "has throughout its history" – and here he paused for added emphasis – "been a people of poets!"

"So who are its poets?" Avinoam scoffed.

"The Bible!" Raphael declared, and proceeded to explain: "You have the Prophets, and the Psalms of David, not to mention Solomon's incomparable Song of Songs! Even the kings of this nation – were poets."

"You're in a patriotic mood tonight!" Avinoam taunted him further.

"This isn't patriotism!" Raphael rebuffed him with dignity.

"What then?" Avinoam demanded keenly, thinking that finally the opportunity had arisen to deliver the knock-out blow and pin his opponent to the canvas. But the latter, it turned out, was not to be easily trapped and subdued.

"Prophecy!" he cried, adding – "I read what is written on the wall!"

"Who wrote this writing?" Avinoam persisted.

Raphael pointed upwards to the deep velvet sky, with the countless stars swimming in its infinite expanse, and said with perfect seriousness:

"And for this reason, flesh and blood cannot abrogate it!" And he added slowly, as if revealing a secret, but in a voice clearly audible to all those sitting in that open space: "This nation, in spite of its politicians, the bourse, the banks, the diamonds and the pernicious influence of Uncle Sam – is returning to what could be called 'the sources'."

"We're a seminar on the 'sources' now, are we?" Rahamim chortled with gruff good humour, emerging from his corner to collect Raphael's cold and empty cup.

This was greeted by a loud and prolonged shout of laughter in which all those present joined. The subject was dropped.

After a long moment of silence, Raphael turned again to young Avinoam, and in a tone of voice quite unlike anything heard so far that evening, appealed to him, almost humbly:

"Read the new poem you've just written!"

Without waiting for another invitation, the young man stood up by his table, drew his lean and lithe body erect, pulled a crumpled piece of paper from the back pocket of his trousers, and reading by the distant gleam of the neon light hanging in the doorway of the café, declaimed in a clear and metallic voice:

Heart's Desire

Evening falls, a ship ploughs on,
Pale the horizon, no sign of a star,
Black is the water, and leaden the sky,
The desire of the heart is to voyage afar!

Foaming the waves, the spars all a-shudder,
Soon we shall be at the heart of the squall:
Thunder and lightning, in dark brooding heavens,
Cold, angry rain is beginning to fall.

Up on the deck stands a young seafarer,
Taking his turn with the winch and the chain.
Loud is the wind that howls high above him,
He answers its rage with a cheerful refrain.

The laughter of freedom, a wave of the hand,
The sheen of the stars is the light in his eyes,
His heart's delight – the challenge of the storm,
The roar of the surf, its inexorable rise.

Smitten with fear, the bulkheads are weeping,
Timbers are quaking, the swell mounting higher,
Outside is the tempest's bold insurrection,
But deep in the heart, still bright glows the fire.

Time passes, the storm is abating,
Stars twinkle, we see the moon glow,

Defiant the prow, the ship undefeated,

The seafarer still has a long way to go!

The assembled company listened with rapt attention, and a kind of inner tension, keen appreciation which they tried for some reason to subdue and disguise, lit up their faces. When Avinoam reached the end, some applauded. One of the young men repeated the last lines: "Defiant the prow, the ship undefeated, the seafarer still has a long way to go...

Raphael appealed to the young poet once more:

"Is there a tune for those lyrics?"

"There is!" Avinoam replied, looking up at the starry sky, and singing. It was a lilting melody, expressing the spirit of the words in a style both fresh and combative; notes soaring and swelling, limpid and young, causing no disruption to the tranquillity of the night – enfolding them all and carrying them away with it to the silvery expanses of the open sea.

As soon as he had finished, the fishermen began trying their own choral talents, sometimes hitting on the original tune, but for the most part improvising for themselves, with loud guttural tones in all the lower registers. After a few minutes, they tired of it, and those who were on their way down to their boats began rising heavily to their feet and preparing to leave. Rahamim immediately began dragging tables inside, as well as the benches that had been vacated. I stood up, meaning to help him – and it was then that a heavy and insistent hand landed on my shoulder.

WHO IS YOUR BROTHER?

I stopped moving furniture and turned around at once. Directly before me was the broad, fleshy face of someone I had never seen before, a giant of a man. His eyes big and grey, slightly protuberant, his lips full and smiling confidently, his clothing simple but clean – T-shirt and shapeless woollen trousers. His massive feet were planted in scuffed and unsightly flip-flop sandals.

"Is your name – Adon?" he asked.

"Yes," I replied.

"That's a funny name," the man commented, hastily correcting himself with a hint of embarrassment: "Strange I meant," and with an abrupt change of subject, in a tone of forced gravity, he added: "You're the one who helped my brother, Shmuel, today."

"Who is your brother?" I asked, amused.

He stepped back, turned round heavily and pointed to a dim figure, as tall as he if not taller, but a little hunched, standing silently at the edge of the little square, which despite the pale light of the stars and a crescent moon was almost entirely dark.

The man approached, revealing his face to me and to the other customers in the café. It was the drunkard, the "burns victim" I had encountered that morning.

"So this is your brother?"

"You helped him!" the other exclaimed, his face, for some reason, turning grim.

"That was nothing!" I declared, and as a way of changing the subject, asked: "How did you find me?"

"We got your address from one of the staff at your office," Shmuel's brother explained, "We found the house and waited for you for some time... your wife arrived and tried to get rid of us. What a woman!" the man exclaimed with sincere bemusement and added: "A feather-weight, taking on a pair of big oafs like us and sending us packing!"

"My wife?" I interjected, surprised, in a calm and thoughtful tone of voice.

"She and no other!" Shmuel confirmed his brother's statement in a weary voice and added: "Or maybe she isn't your wife and you're not married…" Without waiting for a reply, he continued: "She refused to tell us where you were, said she had no idea and we'd better get out or she'd call the cops. What a creature – shooting sparks with her eyes and a voice to make you tremble…"

I wondered to myself: had my wife gone back on the agreement we had reached? On the other hand, the description didn't fit. There was a riddle here that needed solving, urgently.

"And then we approached your neighbour," Shmuel's brother took up the reins of the story again. "The guy with the limp," he pointed out by way of identification, adding with a distant hint of revulsion and artificial sympathy: "Crippled from birth, apparently… he was okay with us, once we'd assured him we weren't up to anything, and he told us where you often hang out… Rahamim's café, I mean," the speaker was momentarily confused and then recovered himself, "it's a well-known place. My shop isn't far from here, near the market… I come in here myself occasionally – usually in the morning, which is why we've never met until now." He sighed for some reason and added: "Rahamim knows me very well, the rest of the family too…"

"Yes, that's right!" Rahamim confirmed, approaching, a degree of tension in his voice that he tried to conceal.

"So – here we are," the giant concluded ceremoniously and added: "We've come to thank you, give you special thanks."

"That was nothing," I repeated, trying in vain to stem the effusive flow.

"It wasn't nothing!" the other insisted, studying me with a look suggestive of the distant relic of some strange, unshakable grievance. "We want to repay you!"

"There's nothing to repay," I replied.

"For your help, the money you spent."

"Nothing worth bothering about," I argued.

Rahamim approached us, touched Shmuel's shoulder and his brother's arm and interjected gruffly:

"So a guy does you a favour – no need to hassle him!"

"We want to express our gratitude!" the brother insisted, drawing a bulging wallet from his back-pocket, opening it, extracting a bundle of notes from one of many compartments, waving them in the air as if appealing for witnesses, then replaced the wallet with the same measured movements and in the same order, repeating:

"We owe you thanks!"

"I don't need your thanks or your money!" I declared.

"This money isn't going back in the wallet!" Shmuel's brother proclaimed in a full-throated roar, raising his hand again and waving the money menacingly.

"Give it to charity," I suggested.

At that moment Shmuel approached his brother and appealed to him in a shaking voice: "Give it to me! He doesn't want it," – he pointed to me – "and you said you're not putting it back in your wallet," he took care to remind him, as if in self-justification, before reverting to a wheedling tone:

"Go on, give it to me!"

"So you can spend it on arak?" his brother cried, inflamed with blind rage. "Pathetic creature that you are... I'd rather tear it up than give it to you!" And saying this he raised his other hand, gripping the notes at both ends and starting to rip them, powerfully and aggressively, into halves, then quarters, then tiny pieces... And having exhausted his indignation on the scraps of paper, he tossed the remaining fragments into the caressing breeze, just now rising from the sea, turned his broad back on the occupants of the café and left. His brother shambled after him like a beaten dog.

"A charming pair!" Raphael remarked, but without any hint of humour in his voice.

Rahamim stepped forward and said: "Lucky for Shmuel that he's got a brother... without him he'd be out on the street, dog-meat..."

"His hands are burnt," I commented.

"He's been that way for years," Rahamim replied, going on to explain: "When he has no choice and even his brother doesn't want him around, he goes and burns himself – so he gets rushed into some medical institution..."

"Why?" I inquired with interest.

"Either someone will take pity on him and give him a drink, or – and this has been known to happen – he'll steal raw alcohol from the sanitation-store..."

"Sad man!" declared Rahamim.

"His family are the ones to feel sorry for!" one of the fishermen commented from the shadows.

"He has a wife and kids?" asked another. The former speaker, evidently acquainted with Shmuel's family-tree, answered him:

"Elderly parents, the brother you've just seen, and seven unmarried sisters."

"What rotten luck," the second fisherman sighed.

It was time for me to go home. I stood up from my seat, smiled warmly at the fishermen, waved goodbye and left the café behind.

LILI

I climbed up the hill, and descended the slope on the other side, turning towards the winding alleyway and ascending again on the gentle incline that I knew so well, approaching that dark mass of wrecked buildings.

The memory of last night barely stirred in my mind. The cracked, bare walls, with their peeling plaster, resembled the predatory teeth of a mythical monster. The oppression, the neglect and the malice constituted a magnetic attraction for anyone whose mind echoed these things. By allowing sites such as this to fall into ruin, the authorities were uprooting with their own hands the last reserves of integrity and fairness remaining in their localities – a fact of which they were, no doubt, fully aware. Which raised the question: what value do these authorities place on the reserves of integrity and fairness in their localities? I didn't answer my question. Instead, I raised a cheerful anthem to my lips – a reminder of my schooldays – and was still humming it as I entered the yard of my rented apartment.

There was light showing in the apartment.

Had Shmuel's brother got it right after all, talking of my wife? It didn't seem likely. The agreement between us was still in force, to our full mutual satisfaction. Meaning – someone else had got there before me. Cautiously, I pushed the unlocked front door and it swung open without a sound.

On the low table, the first thing I saw, were two cups and between them a steaming pot of tea; in a little basket there were pittas that looked fresh and appetising; there was green salad in a big dish with a cracked rim, the only big dish in my kitchen; at opposite ends of the table were flat plastic plates, also familiar, and on them some kind of light-brown concoction garnished with red peppers and finely chopped green herbs – parsley, apparently; there were pickled cucumbers as a side dish, and in the middle of the light-brown concoction, a tiny, limpid-green pool of olive-oil.

"Tehina!" I heard the familiar, guttural-clear voice of last night's house-guest, who was apparently observing my own visual tour of inspection, silently and perhaps in a state of some tension.

"Come in, Adon!" she invited me, a trace of scorn in her voice: "What kind of a weird name is that, anyway?"

I smiled: "My parents' idea."

"I guess they must be on the other side by now!" – with a backward gesture of the thumb, evidently intended as a reference to the next world.

"My father – yes. My mother – still hanging on."

"Where is she?" she asked, surprised and curious.

"In the family home," I replied.

Suddenly, as if losing interest in the conversation or finding it distasteful, she changed the subject:

"Is this a custom of yours, leaving the door open?" she protested with dignity, before adding, in a softer tone but with equal gravity: "Anything might happen…"

"I don't think so," I replied. "Anyway, it can't be locked."

"So fix it!" she responded at once. "If you can't," she added in an utterly changed voice – from argumentative and aggressive to soft and plaintive – "Then call a professional."

I didn't reply. I approached the nearer side of the table, pulled out a chair, sat down before the tempting portion of tehina and asked:

"Why did you come back?" – not without a hint of levity in my voice.

"To check something out," she replied solemnly and saw fit to add: "For myself!"

"And that is?" I persisted.

"You'll find out," she replied, again with that strange air of dignity, comprising as it did a distant, unexpected brand of innocence. "And my name…" she tried to continue, but I held up an admonitory finger and said playfully, almost with a laugh:

"Let me guess!"

She gave me a sidelong look, surprised and a little suspicious, and responded in a whisper: "Go on then, guess!"

"Lili!" I threw it into the air, levity turning to quiet pleasure.

A short, thoughtful silence and then the restrained reaction:

"Pleased to meet you…" – and at once she added: "Some little bird been whispering in your ear?"

"One of the usual birds," I replied with a laugh.

"Of the two-legged variety?" she wanted to know.

"Yes," I assented, and added with a smile: "Though I've yet to see a bird with more than two legs!" I laughed and suddenly her laughter rang out too – clear, pure and surprising. She gave me a bemused look, then turned away.

"You know which birds I'm talking about..."

"I know," I assured her, in what I hoped was a soothing tone.

"That lot," she said grimly, with a shudder, "Birds of prey – all of them!"

She looked up abruptly, as if trying to shake off an unwelcome thought and went on: "Two men were here looking for you, like..." – she searched for the right word – "like a pair of bulldogs, great big beasts... Why did they want to see you?" she demanded to know.

"To thank me for something they thought was a favour," I replied and added: "You told them you were my wife..."

"When they asked me if I was your wife, I didn't answer. I let them guess..." And seeing my puzzled expression she hastened to explain: "When someone has a wife, he seems more respectable, don't you think?" Without waiting for an answer she demanded again: "Why were they really looking for you?"

"I've told you."

"Are you taking the piss?"

"Certainly not."

She chuckled: "I wish I knew!"

"You made an impression on them..."

"What did they say?" she asked, a note of childish curiosity in her voice.

"You scared them..."

"That was the idea... but they found you anyway!" she commented, sounding disappointed, then added: "They asked the neighbour... you've got a right chatterbox for a neighbour. You'll have to watch him!" she concluded solemnly.

"I know your nickname too," I declared, deviating from the subject as a means of lightening the atmosphere, which had become oppressive for some reason.

"And it is...?" – she cooperated, with a display of genuine curiosity.

"Gold-mine," I told her and added, "If Shuki stuck that name on you – then he's a poet!"

"Don't make light of him," she warned. "He's more dangerous

than a poet!"

"You mean there's something dangerous about poets?" – my bemusement was quite sincere.

"Stop bullshitting!" she snapped. And after a pensive moment, still standing where she was, she added with a smile that lit up her thin face with a kind of inner light, the light of uncommon faith: "That nickname – I got it from Shuki's mother, you see..." – the smile was erased entirely and her face took on a sealed, rigid expression – "It wasn't the job I did for Shuki!" she concluded with annoyance.

"Why did his mother call you that?"

"She's a pathetic case. Paralysed – arm, leg and face..." she recounted, continuing: "She gets around on crutches, or mostly in a wheelchair... I took care of her. I still do. I was at her place today... she can't cope by herself. Her husband's rotting in jail and so's her eldest son, Shuki's brother. She's only got Shuki left, and he's robbed her blind. She looks ghastly! If she goes one day without being looked after – she turns into a monster – and a stinking monster at that. The other girls can't stand her..."

"You mean – Sonya and Rosa?"

"You seem to know everything already!" She was impressed, but at the same time she raised her head and scrutinised my face with a heavy look. "Sonya and Rosa – they belong to Shuki too, but they won't touch his mother, not for any money!" She looked down and added: "She has to be washed, you see..." – she hesitated, thought for a moment and continued: "All that stuff. It's a smelly, messy job – but is that her fault?" She fixed me with a look that was defiant, indignant and in some strange way – accusing.

"I agree with you," I assured her.

"She tries!" she exclaimed, as if leaping to the defence of Shuki's mother. "Tries to wash dishes, wipe the table... sometimes, on her crutches... she runs a mop over the floor... but it's no good." She lowered her head as if beaten in some inner, personal struggle. "She's tough," she added, with a sidelong glance at me, "and not only on the outside... she has something else as well..."

"What is it?" I asked and she immediately replied:

"She's bitter, very bitter! Life has been cruel to her. She thinks she's a great sinner. But I don't think so..."

"What do you think?"

"That she's a saint!" she declared, with unshakable confidence.

"She's having to endure all the worst torments of Hell here, in this world!"

She looked up at me with moist eyes, as if appealing to me, with a strange kind of fear, to assent to her firmly-held conviction, if only with a look. I did so willingly, nodding my head for further emphasis.

She picked up the teapot and poured two cups. The light-brown liquid steamed. She approached me, offered me a cup and tried to touch my face. I flinched and backed away.

"What's the matter?" She was surprised, standing stock still for a moment and then she smiled an odd smile, tender and bitter and at the same time – childish.

"I don't eat people!" she explained. "I just wanted to check... if there were any scald-marks. You see, this morning I got a bit overwrought... I'm not used to things like that and" – raising her voice – "I don't like soft soaping!" And reverting to her normal voice: "People are such hypocrites, always hiding something, bringing you tea in bed on a tray, like in movies... and behind their back they're hiding a whip! Or softening you up, then moving in for the kill... I've had experience of life!" she insisted, turning a sidelong, inquisitive glance at me before concluding defiantly: "I know about monks too!"

"No scalds," I informed her calmly and explained: "The tea had cooled down by then..."

She studied my face intently, leaning slightly towards me:

"What about... the family jewels – not exactly..." She paused, waiting for my reply.

I laughed cheerfully: "I don't think so!"

"Fancy a test-drive?"

"No," I replied quietly but firmly, in a manner leaving no room for doubt or argument.

"Your will-power does you credit!" she sighed, straightening up. She poured herself tea, rounded the table and sat facing me, by the other plastic plate.

"If you'll excuse me," I said, "I usually say a prayer at this time," and without waiting for her response, I raised my joined hands and prayed. When the prayer was done I wished her good appetite, took a pitta, broke it, dipped it in tehina and put it to my mouth. After the first mouthful I turned to her, beaming. "This is great tehina!" I said. "I don't remember ever tasting anything like it." This was no more than the truth. The tehina was tasty, light and satisfying. I also felt it was time to say something encouraging to her, to thank her for the goodwill and the effort that she had invested in the meal, to make her happy. Indeed, I was all animated by that potent inner pleasure – radiant, overwhelming pleasure – the pleasure that you not only want to share in, but to share, to the full, with anyone who is prepared to accept it.

"Bullshit!" was her terse response to this. She drew a pitta from the basket, sliced it, dipped it and put it to her mouth, where the thick lower lip protruded slightly over the upper, as if to protect it. I let my gaze linger on her forehead, visible through the profusion of hair – not broad, rather high, domed and wonderfully smooth. If this were a reflection of her thought-processes – her thoughts too would be clean, even luminous. The luxuriant hair, gathered up this time behind the neck with the aid of a Spanish comb, was light-chestnut, tending towards the ruddy with a few golden strands. The cheek-bones were high and prominent, giving her a kind of lost, childish elegance. Her face was pallid, with the ugly hue of dust. This could be a symptom of disease, or it could simply be the reflection of an earthy, oppressed state of mind. The ears, matching the elegant cheek-bones, seemed to be seeking refuge in her hair, as if craving detachment from the world around. Her neck, appearing elongated at first sight, turned out to be thin and delicate, not particularly long, and clean – in stark contrast to the unhealthy colour of the face and the grubby collar of the cheap masculine shirt. The eyebrows had been worked on – another change from this morning – taking the form of short, black lines, not matching the colour of the hair. The lashes also looked black, and the eyes were astonishing in their dimensions – so big and yet seeming to hold back the depth of their penetration, hiding it behind multiple veils of rigidity, suspicion and illogical shrewdness. They were light-brown in colour, radiating a particular tenderness that undermined the display of toughness – or was it in itself a part of the display? Sometimes the colour of the eyes changed, with a sudden flash of green. So it was at this moment – she looked at me, a hint of remote disdain, shaded green, in her eyes, and said:

"Actually – you're right! I'm an expert in preparing tehina, a world-class expert." She dipped the pitta again, chewed pleasurably, pensively, then swallowed and added:

"I began making tehina at the age of ten... and not just for the family, for customers too. So you see, it was commercial tehina – not just any old thing!" She spoke without looking at me, her eyes seeming to stare straight ahead of her, utterly engrossed in what was suddenly emerging into her consciousness and agitating her heart: "My mother worked in a kiosk for a guy called Henri – a fat old bastard who never shaved. The kiosk was well-placed – between a school and a trading estate. School-kids used to come along, apprentices too, and shop and factory workers... usually they went for tehina in pitta... Henri's falafel wasn't that great... anyway, around midday, tehina's the best bet...

"So, my mother worked for him, making the tehina and falafel for him... but then she started drinking..." – she wavered, pausing to take a gulp of tea and shooting an inquisitive look at me, then as if guessing the question I was about to ask, she answered it: "I didn't have a father, you see... I never had the pleasure of making his acquaintance! To this day I don't know who he was... and I don't want to know either!" – trying to convince herself. She took another pitta, dipped it, chewed, swallowed and resumed her account, still staring moodily at the blank wall facing her:

"When she started drinking, she couldn't get up in the morning and go to work. Anri sent her a message – if she couldn't work she was to tell him and he'd hire someone else. And that's when I went along. It was a question of livelihood – well, no... it was just hunger really. She didn't send me, it was my decision," – for some reason, she thought this needed stressing, then continuing without a pause: "I realised this was the last resort... for me and for her... My mother had clients too and she used to go to their places, their houses or cheap hotels or parking lots... she didn't trade from home 'cos she didn't want to upset me... She loved me, my mum, in her own peculiar way. But the drinking changed her completely... she didn't do anything. Didn't go servicing her clients... or anything. There was hardly any money coming into the house, a few cents here and there from the social services – after you've filled in a thousand forms and questionnaires – and all of that went into a big hole full of bottles...

"So I went to Henri, and I learned the trade in no time, you know – preparing the tehina, spreading it on the pitta, serving with pickled cucumber... social services tried to put me back in school but I kept a step ahead of them, I was clever!" she declared with a bitter smile conveying neither triumph not indignation, just calm acceptance of the inevitable.

"Early in the morning I'd arrive at Henri's place and start preparing the merchandise – slicing pitta, opening jars of pickled cucumbers... and if there was food left over from yesterday in the big basin, and there usually was, tackling the swarms of cockroaches... Ugh!" – her eyes glinted – "They love tehina too! Some days there were so many of them I couldn't even see the basin – a thick layer of the busy little sods, jostling around, climbing over one another, sticking their antennae in the tehina, and sometimes – drowning in it. The ones that had fallen in I had to remove by hand, some of them still alive. The other ones I chased off with a big wooden spoon, the same one I used for stirring the tehina. They'd eaten so much they could hardly get air-born! At first I couldn't stand it when they landed on my face... but I got used to that too. Maybe I shouldn't be telling you all this," she said, in a tone of genuine concern: "Am I ruining your appetite?"

"It doesn't bother me at all," I assured her, and as proof I dipped a pitta into the savoury sauce and consumed it with gusto, smacking my lips for added emphasis.

"You're not the squeamish type, then?"

"No."

"Funny, you look like you are!"

"Appearances can be deceptive," I pointed out. This answer seemed to satisfy her.

"After the beetles and all that," – she continued her story – "I'd run to the school and make sure the caretaker and the teacher saw me, then disappear. If the social services were checking up, the teacher couldn't swear I hadn't been in school at all, and the caretaker would swear he'd seen me every day." She took a deep, refreshing gulp of tea, hot though it still was. I followed suit, picking up my full cup and sipping the golden, invigorating liquid.

"My mother never went back to the kiosk," she resumed – as if driven by some deep compulsion to reveal something not only to me, but perhaps for the first time in her life – to herself too. A compulsion that she was incapable of resisting and, so it seemed, unwilling to resist.

"Although sometimes she made an effort to get back to work, promising me and herself she would – nothing came of it. In the end, we both came to terms with the situation: she was the boozer and I was the breadwinner. She wasn't a bad woman, my mum, but life had been cruel to her, trampled her down!

"Henri used to pay me almost as much as he paid my mother," – she thought it was worth pointing out – "I used to do everything she did and more... and the money was enough. Social services used to chip in too, a little bit anyway... until... until... you want to hear the whole story?" she suddenly looked at me keenly, inquisitively, cold hostility in her eyes.

"Not really," I replied.

"Well, you're going to!" she declared, as if inflicting a well-deserved punishment.

"As you wish," I retorted with sincere equanimity. She ignored my response entirely, perhaps not even hearing it, and returned to her story with strange heat, with thirst almost:

"And then he started putting his hands where he shouldn't, that Henri, the fat, filthy, scruffy old man, always stinking of sweat, and shit... and he wanted... no, he didn't want, he demanded it. As if he deserved it!

" I told my mum. I was expecting to hear something from her, some big deal like 'I'll show that disgusting, filthy old creep!' or 'You're not going back to that job, you're jacking it in now!' or 'We can make do with the pittance from social services, you stay well away from that cess-pit!' That's what I expected to hear, you know?" – she was speaking as if to herself, distractedly, almost unconsciously, eyes staring far into the distance beyond my shoulder, striving against something for ever indefinable, something no one would dare to approach, let alone contend with.

"And she, my mother, right?" she continued without seeing me, without even being aware of my presence, her combative gaze not flinching from whatever it was she could see in the distance, behind me: "She says: 'Give it to him! You hear what I'm telling you. Give him whatever he wants. Just make sure he pays you, full wack! That's been my fate, and it's going to be yours too. You can't run away from your fate, you can't do it – however hard you try.'"

She was silent for a moment, as if frozen. And then, abruptly, she shifted her concentration from the point behind me, and fixed on me a glare of unutterable loathing:

"I fixed him, that Henri. Years later, I paid him back... with interest, the filthy bastard! That's when Shuki used to do what I asked him to… sent his hitmen after him… they castrated him. Since then he's swelled up like a balloon. If he gets any bigger, he'll explode!" And she let out a peal of artificial, distorted laughter, grating on the ear, and wiped her eyes and nose with a paper handkerchief. There was a pause.

"The truth is," she reverted suddenly to speaking in a colourless voice, her head lowered: "It wasn't because I asked for it. Henri tried to muscle in on Shuki's operation, get money out of his girls and not pass it on. So it was Shuki's idea, not mine. I even tried to warn the old swine, but he didn't believe me."

After a prolonged silence, I asked:

"And your mother?" To be honest, my interest in the fate of her mother was overridden by the need to get shot of the whole subject and return to the relaxed atmosphere that had prevailed at the beginning, on my homecoming, before the meal and before the mood had turned so ugly.

"Dead!" she announced. "I found her in her room. Collapsed on the floor, a bottle of arak in her hand, nearly empty… puddles of urine and excrement all around her…"

A long moment passed.

"The tea's getting cold," I said softly.

Mechanically she took the cup, raised it to her lips, sipped, and put it back on the table, with a grin:

"If the tea I threw in your face was this cold, no wonder you weren't scalded! All the same, I'm sorry." She tried to catch my eye.

"You're exaggerating!" I assured her.

"As for my mother," – she seemed compelled to return to the subject: "If only she'd said what I so much hoped she'd say! Things would've been so different, you know? Of course, my destiny's fixed and if it hadn't been old Henri, someone else would've come along. But if she…" Again she wiped her eyes with a clenched fist, leaving her sentence unfinished, then shook her head with a sudden, abrupt movement and looking up at me again – a smile on her face, she said:

"I'd like to do something for you!" Her voice suddenly cleared and with it – her gaze. And since there was no reply on my part she added: "Isn't there anything that you want?"

"Oh, there is!"

"What is it?" She withdrew behind the innumerable veils of her eyes.

"I want you to brew some fresh tea and finish off the tehina!"

A gruff laugh was the response, a laugh that shook her whole body, her head especially, until her hair rebelled against its confinement, springing loose from its clasp and shrouding her face again.

She carried out my request in every particular: poured away the tea that had cooled, brewed fresh and polished off the tehina in front of her, including the salad.

I poured myself tea and finished off my portion of tehina – and very tasty and satisfying it was. And then I began to wonder where all this had come from, since I don't keep the ingredients for tehina at home, nor pickled cucumbers. Leaving the table I opened the fridge – an antiquated machine, bought from the flea-market at a bargain price and working surprisingly well. What was even more surprising – the fridge was filled up with all kinds of grocery: numerous varieties of cheese, yellow as well as white, green vegetables, butter, margarine, eggs... I closed the door carefully and turned to face Lili, but before I could frame a question, she – putting into effect the principle that the best form of defence is attack – rounded on me in a combative and defiant style, in an attempt to forestall any protest on my part:

"I realised you're a vegetarian so I didn't buy meat or fish. Got a problem?" And the made-up brows were knitted.

"I'd just like to know where the money came from."

"Do you have to know?" Suddenly her voice rang out clear, and all the barricades folded and disappeared as if they had never been.

"Yes."

"I did one line-up!" she snapped, standing up from the table and, affecting a casual gait, walked across to the sink, as if intending to wash the few dishes piled up there.

"What do you mean by that – a 'line-up'?" I insisted.

"Professional parlance!" she said sweetly, with an ostentatious stab at eloquence. Her back was turned to me but I could sense her twisted, childish-bitter smile. "It means anything from fifteen to twenty or more clients," she added, "standing up..."

My silence demanded further explanation. She didn't flinch from it:

"It's a lower fee," – she explained – "but it's over that much sooner... there's no time and it's not the right place for sleazy stuff or nasty business... Anyway, it's a different class of customer coming to a line-up. You won't find old men there. Oldies – they really are the pits! What you get in a line-up is guys who want to get it over with quick, no fuss, and clear off. Professional types, you know... they get all these horny fantasies, stops them concentrating on their work. Apprentices, students, junior clerks on their tea-breaks, salesmen, greengrocers... those kinds of people... At night you can easily get a line-up together in bars and discos... but you'll never find married men in a line-up... married men are the ones who like it kinky – filthy-minded perverts... Ptu!" – she spat into the sink – "How do their wives put up with them? Give me a line-up any day. I admit, it's not exactly comfortable – standing in some dark corner that's normally used as a urinal, or a stinking stairwell, or some wreck of a building with shit all over the floor, but, like I said, it's soon over and though you earn less, I prefer it that way. There are some who don't. It's a matter of taste!"

"I'm having nothing to do with that money," I said calmly.

'S'where you're wrong!" she declared – whether the elision of letters was intended to give expression to a particular state of mind or perhaps underline it, I couldn't be sure. "You bought me!" she added in a triumphant tone, with just a hint of mockery blended into it. And suddenly, in a totally different voice, soft and conciliatory, she turned that statement into a question: "Didn't you?" She waited a long moment and when there was no response, continued: "Till now, I've worked for Shuki..." And after another fruitless wait, almost reluctantly, she said in her throaty-hoarse voice. "But 'f'you don't want me – I'm leaving you. And your five thousand's going down the pan!" She shrugged her narrow shoulders dismissively, and to give further emphasis to her indifference, turned the taps full on and began washing the dishes.

"To tell you the truth," she cried between plate and cup, a guttural cry, raised to make herself heard: "I reckon I could make out by myself. All the loss will be yours!" She turned down the volume of the tap, intent on hearing my response.

I capitulated, finally: "So what's Shuki going to do?"

Carefully she laid a plate on the rack, left the water streaming in a gentle, unexploited jet, turned to me and said with inimitable confidence:

"He won't give me up!" – her voice gloomy and heavy, and yet at the same time tinged with a kind of devilish amusement, demanding caution.

I cleared the table, sorted out my bedding and made up the sofa too.

"What makes you think I'm sleeping here?" I heard her call behind me, her voice wonderfully clear and suffused with an indescribable brand of purity. I turned to her, astonished.

She was holding herself erect, and for the first time I realised how statuesque her body was – statuesque, although not especially tall. Admittedly, a little taller than the body representing me in the sensual world.

Her big eyes focused their gaze on me and their limitless depths, unencumbered by any mask, radiated a unique light, the light of the first dawn of spring, dispelling many a heavy and gloom-laden winter, a light shedding rare grace and love unbounded, only now emerging.

"I never for a moment imagined you'd be staying here!" I answered her with a broad, clear smile, with a light very similar to the light radiating from her – and at the same time absolutely and utterly different.

"So why are you making up the sofa?" she wanted to know, her radiance undimmed.

"If you have no choice, if you're forced to stay here..." I began, my voice steady.

"I definitely have no choice and I'm definitely forced to stay here!" she erupted in high, throaty tones, purged of any trace of vulgarity or fraud – all of them, to the very last, suffused with tender benevolence, despite the hoarseness.

"Because I've nowhere to go," she explained, "and whether you like it or not, you're still my boss! At least," she back-pedalled hastily, "until tomorrow... I'm your 'girl'..." – her face darkened and the limpid radiance in her eyes began fading fast: "Because that's the will of fate!" she concluded, approaching the sofa, perching at the end of it and fixing her gaze on the floor, not the cleanest floor in the universe, although she didn't seem to notice this. It was astounding – the stark transition from exaltation of spirit to bitter despondency.

"You're just a crybaby!" I told her, simply.

"What's that supposed to mean?" – she raised her head abruptly and looked at me with the awe-struck eyes of a child bemused by a conjuring trick.

"You're weeping all the time," I explained.

"And why should I do that?" – she lowered her eyes, as if asking herself.

"Out of self-pity," I replied.

She weighed my words, weighed them again, finally conceding with a kind of gloomy pedantry – and there was no knowing what lay behind it: "You could be right."

After a brief moment of silence, she stood up and demanded:

"Go to your room and shut yourself in properly! I'm tired and I want to sleep. And tonight I've no intention of sleeping in my clothes! Have you got a night-shirt or something?"

I offered her pyjamas.

She inspected them with a critical eye, smiled sincerely and declared in her throaty-hoarse voice, apparently her natural one:

"These are okay... Goodnight!"

I went into my room, closed the door behind me, climbed into bed and closed my eyes. My body sank into deep sleep.

Shortly before midnight, or maybe at midnight, this body was awakened by hesitant but distinct knocking at the door. Not leaving my bed I asked:

"What's up?"

"Open it!" yelled my guest from the other side of the door, a tremor in her voice.

"Why?"

"Open it!" she repeated. There was nothing hesitant about her knocking now.

"What's up?" I insisted.

" Open it! Please!" – sounding positively distraught.

I jumped from my bed and opened the door, leaving it ajar. Seeing the door move she took a step backwards, with a sigh, whispering to herself: "At last, at last!" before adding in a louder voice:

"Open it properly, I'm not going to eat you..."

"What do you want?" I asked politely, in a steady voice, but with the distant hint of a cold edge.

"I'm scared!" she announced. "I'm asking you, please, leave the door open... I'm going back to the sofa... I won't do you any harm, I promise!"

I left the door and returned to my bed. A couple of minutes passed.

"Are you asleep?" she asked softly. At such close quarters, in the deep stillness of the night, there was no need to raise her voice.

"Not yet." In fact I was fully awake.

"D'you believe in fate?"

"Yes," I replied in the same calm and steady voice.

"What else d'you believe in?"

"Truth."

"And what's that?"

"Happiness."

"What kind of happiness?"

"Everlasting."

"Y'sound like a child!" – her voice emerged from the darkness, level, scornful and yet highly inquisitive: "What's in this happiness that makes it everlasting?" she went on to ask.

Without hesitation I declared: "Love."

Silence fell. But not for long.

"You don't mean..." – she tried to control her voice, with some success: "You don't mean the kind of love I trade in..."

"No."

"What kind then?" – she sounded alert, or possibly tense.

"The kind that depends on nothing," was the reply.

She took a deep breath, turning over once or twice in her improvised bed.

"There's no such thing!" she declared finally.

"There is no other!" I retorted confidently.

Silence again – deep and tense. She weighed my words, digested them slowly. Finally she responded:

"So whoever's capable..." – she began cautiously, but soon mustered more assurance – "of love like that... is happy forever?"

"That is the truth!" I assented. At that moment, anyone with ears in his head could have detected in my voice at least a distant echo of that very happiness I had spoken of.

She sank again into contemplation. Her tension seemed to fill the void, almost palpable.

"I want to ask you a few more things, that okay?" – there was a note of distant pleading in her voice, weak and pitiful, unnatural.

"It's okay," I answered readily.

"And tell you some things too, that okay?" – again she tried her hand at that style of cheap entreaty, so alien to her nature.

"It's okay," I repeated with no change of tone.

A silence pregnant with heavy thoughts. Perhaps she was making an attempt to impose some order on her problems, or her anecdotes, or both simultaneously. When she next spoke, it was to make a suggestion:

"Maybe I'll come over there and join you. I can whisper to you...you're that far away, it's a pain!"

"No!" I replied with all the clarity I could summon. I wanted no misunderstanding here.

She swallowed, digested, conceded.

"Why are you a monk?"

"I've already told you that."

"And you had a wife?"

"I have."

"What d'you mean, you have?" She expressed surprise by means of indignation, shifting restlessly in her bed. I visualised her sitting up and looking morosely in my direction. Before I could reply she added:

"Are you divorced?"

"No."

"So where's your wife?"

"At home."

"How's that come about?" – in growing bewilderment.

"When that true happiness comes along..."

"You mean," she interrupted, "that love you were talking about?"

"That's right," – I smiled into the darkness and continued: "When that happens, things change radically. Man is born again and his way of life is new as well. He is devoted entirely to that reality which he has woken up to know himself an inseparable part of."

"Does that mean you had to leave your wife?" There was still unease in her voice.

"Have you heard the expression, 'jealous God'?"

"I've heard it," – her voice fading – "but I never understood it! If God is jealous," she complained petulantly, "what's left for us humans?"

"This text, like other texts, can't be interpreted in fleshly terms."

"You can interpret it without using those terms?"

"I can try," I replied and added: "It isn't simple jealousy that the quotation refers to, but the determination not to think, look at, hear, taste, smell, anything other than Him. Him and Him alone... he who has the privilege of loving God can't love anything else..."

"But that's so cruel!" she interjected indignantly.

"Because nothing else exists," I concluded.

A long minute passed.

"What about her?" – she resumed: "How does she get by?"

"Half my salary goes to her?"

"And a house?"

"That's still hers."

"So you had a house?"

"Yes."

"Children?"

"Yes."

"Are they with her?"

"They're old enough to fend for themselves. The youngest" – I thought it wise to point out – "has just finished his army service."

"So officially – you're not separated?" – she asked, wanting the details spelt out.

"No."

"What if she wanted that?"

"She could have it."

"What about you?"

"It doesn't matter to me, not at all."

"So," – she sighed, "things like that don't bother you any more... aren't you the lucky one! All you're interested in is that God you've found in your heart! And I had to go and find someone like you!" There was bitterness in her voice, bitterness that she tried, unsuccessfully, to conceal. "You know," – she suddenly raised her voice – "I don't reckon you're as immune to those things as you make out! Maybe you've got more self-control than most, but I bet you could still snog someone... more maybe! It's just me, isn't it?" – a voice rising in pitch, heavy with accusation, painfully grating – "You can't stand the sight of me!"

"That's not true," I replied.

She sighed: "When my mother died," she began, "I was twelve years old… I decided to go to the mission, you know… hang out with the Christians – they give clothing and shelter there, food and even pocket-money… and they don't force you to convert… anyway, not straightaway…"

"The Jews have institutions like that too," I pointed out.

"There's a longer queue for those," – she declared emphatically – "and I couldn't wait to get away from Henri and his filth. He was going to start lending me to his friends… at a price, of course. I ran away. And then I met that monk… the young one, right? To start with he was teaching me science and geography and other stuff… I wanted to learn, tried very hard to make a good impression 'cos I liked the feel of the place – there were prayers and games, and the food was good and they taught us music, and the clothes were clean and everyone wore the same… and that's important, very important. Uniform – that's the thing. It's a pity all schools don't demand it… I mean – all the schools in the world. The same uniform all over the world… just think how different it could all be!" She was momentarily enthused by the idea, but her enthusiasm was fading fast: "They just don't understand, "she concluded sadly.

"And then," – returning to her story – "bit by bit this guy starts closing in on me… the young monk, the Catholic, y'know," – she sighed heavily, uneasily, with a kind of bitter indignation – "It was in the second year maybe, and he's behind me, bending down and looking over my shoulder, snorting like a pig with a hard-on!" She fell silent, swallowing spittle, or perhaps a tear, then cleared her throat, steadied her voice and continued: "I saw even here, in this place I liked so much, there was the same rottenness, the same dirt and sleaze. Even in the House of God… even among the Christians… so-called holy monks… right? It was about that time I stopped believing in God… it was worse than that – I started hating Him! Sometimes I imagined Him like old Henri – nice enough on the outside, but really, the filthiest-minded pervert ever! As for that monk…" – I heard her sit up in her bed and take a deep breath of air as if in danger of suffocation, before suddenly continuing in a clear, steady voice: "The time came when the choice I had was go to bed with him or get thrown out. Only it wasn't a bed exactly, it was the mosaic floor of that church, with all the icons and the statues around, and the images of Jesus, looking miserable, accusing you of something... Dying to save sinners is all very well, but why let the sinners carry on sinning?"

"That's not quite the way it works!" I interjected, taking advantage of a brief pause in her narration.

"So how do you see it?" she demanded, and I sensed that her throat was constricted by tears. I answered her with dignity:

"God is spirit, and any attempt to understand Him by way of the flesh is a serious mistake, and doomed to absolute failure from the start."

"But He gave us flesh!" she protested.

"And spirit too," I reminded her, "and spirit is the one that matters." Sensing that she was waiting for me to continue, I added: "If someone sets himself the objective of coming to understand God – which means, being awakened to know oneself an inseparable part of Him – he should examine his spirit, and only his spirit, and fight the flesh until he subdues it."

"That's something he'll never succeed at!" she cried, almost in despair.

"Flesh won't subdue flesh," I conceded, adding at once: "But the spirit is master of the flesh."

"That's not the way people see it!" she complained.

"That's because they're obsessed with the flesh," was my answer.

"So is it forbidden for humans to touch one another?" – it was a reasonable enough conclusion to draw.

"If it's liable to enslave them..."

"What does that mean?" she interrupted me.

"Make them dependent on the flesh," I answered willingly.

"Like a drug or something?" – she wanted to get it straight.

"Like a drug or something."

She fell silent, digesting my words.

"And what about that randy monk?" she cried out in a thick and hoarse voice. I imagined tears trickling down her throat, blending into the cocktail of saliva and nasal mucous.

"He was devoted to the flesh instead of to God."

"So he lied to himself and to God!" she declared with confidence and apparent relief.

"That is true," I assented.

"And his punishment will be – Hell!"

I didn't respond.

"What's your take on that?" she demanded.

"As long as there is spirit in the flesh, and the spirit is dominant," I began solemnly, "we are forbidden to judge."

"Aha!" she responded with alacrity almost, or at rate, with something fresh creeping into her voice: "Well... that's fine. But he'd agree with me... 'If God exists' he used to say – 'I'm going to roast forever in the fires of Hell! You too' he used to say, 'no less than me'. He threatened me, he enjoyed threatening me. Till I ran away, and fell into Shuki's hands... well, what could I do?" she asked herself and without waiting for an answer, continued: "He fixed everything... all the complicated, messy business that is..." she stressed, in a tone of scorn blended with bitterness. "He cut a deal with the monk too – he could have me once a month, at a price, for a limited period... he found me that other client too – the old orthodox creep... at least with him there weren't any sermons and lectures about sin... what is it about the orthodox?" – suddenly she was addressing me again: "Are they allowed to carry on that way?"

"No," I declared.

"So why all the hypocrisy?"

"What do you mean?"

"Monks!"

"They're not all like that," I replied. "The principle in itself is sublime. But," I admitted, "genuine monks are rare."

"Like you," she sighed.

I had no answer to this.

And suddenly, in the darkness, I sensed her kneeling beside me.

"What nonsense is this?" I protested, surprised and alarmed.

"I just wanted to kiss your hand!" she cried in a tone of repressed pain, adding in a confused flood of words, harsh and grating: "Believe me – I never kissed anyone before! Never, never, not ever! Nobody, nowhere, not even my mother! My mouth, my lips – they're clean... Just your hand..."

And before I had time to react, I felt moist pressure on the back of my hand. I didn't flinch, but let the coolness invade all its veins, nerves and sinews. A long moment passed.

"You're doing the same as I do," she rasped, releasing the inert hand.

"And what's that?"

"Fainting."

"I don't understand."

"When I'm working... I 'faint'... if you see what I mean..." She realised this wasn't an adequate explanation, and added: "I'm not there... I'm gone... faraway! My body's there, but I'm not. And I don't care what happens to it – the body I mean. You're doing the same thing, making your hand 'faint'. Do I really disgust you that much?" There was now no mistaking the pain in her voice. And without waiting for an answer she concluded with a despairing wail: "I'm cursed!"

"You're blessed," I retorted in a steady voice, a voice suffused by the light of true happiness. "And this blessing of love will stay with you always."

"Why are you running from me?"

"Not from you."

"Who from, then?" She had completely overcome the distress of a few moments before, and a few delicate snuffles were all that remained of her whimpering.

"From the flesh."

"I'm flesh!" she insisted.

"You were flesh – so much so they could have made steaks and rissoles out of you," I declared: "But you're something else that you don't know yet, you haven't woken up to it. And when you do wake up to it – flesh will no longer have dominion over you..."

"And if you've woken up to it," she interrupted me, "and flesh has no dominion over you, why are you afraid of it?"

"I'm not afraid."

"But?"

"I don't want to see it take control of someone else."

"That's bullshit!" she declared, hurt. "If I don't disgust you," she added, "let me hold your hand for a moment."

I held out my hand.

She took it between her two childish palms, held it a moment or two, released it, straightened up and left the room without any further delay, closing the door behind her.

I fell asleep at once.

I woke with the first dusk of dawn and, as usual, sat down to meditate.

Liberated from form and name, from time, from place and condition, I was, I myself, the perpetual delight of truth, the purity of boundless love, the joy of freedom, which no words or any other means of description could even begin to approach.

I went out to bathe in the sea. Passing through the outer room, I noticed that the sofa was empty. The bedclothes were folded. On the door-panel, crudely drawn with a make-up crayon, was a huge heart and in the middle of it – the letter "L".

GREY EYES

Arriving for work at my office, I met a young man pacing back and forth outside the main entrance of the institution, like the guardsman at a palace gate. His body was tense, his face pale and taut, like someone who has just committed a heinous crime or is about to do so.

Inside the building one of the secretaries was waiting for me, and in a hoarse, unnecessarily hushed voice, she hurriedly informed me that Amelia's husband was waiting to see the manager, and there was no knowing what might happen. Amelia hadn't come into work today, and it seemed she had been away from home all night.

The secretary looked up at me with eyes that were open wide and imploring, yet at the same time suffused with strange curiosity and just a flicker of malicious enjoyment. Raising her voice, she said:

"Do something, Adon!"

"Why not invite him to see me?" I suggested.

"I'll try!" – and she ran to the gate.

Through the window on the northern side I could see her, approaching the pale and tense man who was still patrolling the driveway in the style of a sentry, addressing him and leaning towards him with a look of emphatic concern stamped on her face. Her attempt to match her steps to his wasn't working, and her efforts to convince him of her good intentions with flailing hand movements weren't making much of an impression either. She looked like a midget beside him, or a puppy snapping at the heels of a disdainful and indifferent Doberman. Finally she gave up, hands hanging feebly at her sides, and turned to retrace her steps. I didn't wait for her to arrive. Instead I met her in the corridor, nodded mechanically at her garbled report and made my way to the gate.

"If you'd like to come inside," – I addressed Amelia's husband, "maybe you'll see things in a different light... entirely different."

"Who are you?" – shooting his words at me like pistol bullets.

"Amelia's immediate supervisor..."

"You're not the man I need!" – more withering fire.

"Maybe you should reconsider..."

"I'm not interested in what you have to say!" he snapped.

"If you change your mind, I'm inside," I concluded, undeterred, the bright, sincere smile not budging from my face.

I returned the way I had come and began attending to some routine work. I almost forgot Amelia's husband, but at intervals I glanced briefly through the window and saw him pacing to and fro with vigorous tread, as implacable as ever. Half an hour later the same secretary returned and reported that the manager had been alerted by telephone, and he'd decided he wouldn't be coming in today...

"What's to be done?" she asked.

"Tell him," I pointed to the gate.

Sure enough, a few minutes later I saw her talking again with the big "Doberman". He hesitated, stood stock still for a moment, released hands that had been clasped behind his back, waved them ineffectually, then wrinkled his brow, lowered his head and held the same pose for some time after the secretary had left him. According to her, he was still refusing to come in and hear what I had to say, and the next time I peered out of the window – he was no longer in sight.

Before I had time to return to my desk, there was a knock at the door.

"Enter!"

The door opened, and standing there was a red-haired giant, Shmuel's brother.

"Morning, Adon!" – he came into the office, on his face a jovial expression which seemed somewhat artificial – judging by his eyes which were having nothing to do with it, being tense with anxiety.

"Good morning!" I replied

"I..." he began hesitantly, wrinkling his fleshy brow, "...It's to do with Shmuel. May I sit down?" He pulled out a chair and sat on it before I had time to give my consent.

"It's possible... he might turn up here," – his voice was flat, practical. "Maybe you don't realise just what a sick mess you're poking that healthy head of yours into – if it is healthy, that is!" he added, looking up with an attempt at innocent levity which just didn't work. "Anyway, I came here to ask for your help..."

"I'll help you if I can," I replied.

"With a little goodwill – you can!" – he stressed the goodwill and invested unequivocal force in you can.

"What do you want me to do?" I asked after a prolonged silence.

"I want your cooperation…"

"In what way?"

He gave me a look that was both sullen and appraising, heavy somehow, and declared:

"I don't want you giving him a drink – or giving him money!" and before I could respond he added: "You see, Sir, we're used to it! We know all the tricks he gets up to! We know the devious ways his mind works… and nobody wants the best for him more than we do… the family I mean… that's me, my elderly parents and seven sisters… I have seven unmarried sisters… virgins, all of them!" he stressed, a faint note of pride creeping into his voice: "They have what you could call – a fine reputation. But in spite of that, not one of them is married yet… and that's mainly down to our brother Shmuel, the black sheep of the family. You have to understand, Adon…" he paused, pondering for a moment and adding with a grim smile: "Adon, what kind of a name is that anyway?" – and before I could respond he took up the thread again: "People aren't what they used to be – these days they're more choosy, they check the merchandise… and when they hear about Shmuel, all their ardour – goes down the tubes… and there's plenty of ardour, believe me – seeing as all my sisters, from the youngest to the oldest, are real angels, angels from Heaven, and eligible too… with a secure income… women who can fend for themselves, respectably, and not just for themselves either… whoever marries one of them will be set up – set up for life! Incidentally," he asked, that lady at your house – is that your wife?"

"No."

"Are you a bachelor?" he asked with a faint flicker of hope.

"Married."

"Just asking," he responded hastily. "You look like you're getting on a bit, but even older people these days are staying single. Some of them are scared, some are too stingy… do all kinds of calculations… about marriage, I mean. Who's going to support whom… It's a mistake, trying to calculate things like that…"

"What about you?" I asked, amused. "Are you a bachelor?"

"Yes," he replied and added hastily: "Not by choice! The whole family depends on me! I'm not talking about livelihood – though that's a part of it too...the main thing is... the honour of the family, its good name, and the worry of getting my sisters married off! How can I get myself married, before they do? It's a custom with us, a tradition! And even if you forget tradition – what kind of woman is going to want to join a household where there's a father-in-law, a mother-in-law, seven sisters-in-law and best of all – a dipso brother-in-law! And to get to the point," – he remembered the purpose of his visit and dismissed the querulous tone from his voice – "You must cooperate! We, the family I mean, are doing all we can to get him... rehabilitated... hoping... never giving up hope... two spells in the detox ward haven't done any good... maybe the third time it'll work. Our brother's still young! And he has a heart of gold, believe me! He was such a cute kid... but fate has been unkind to him. And through him, to us too. We're doing all we can to steer him away from booze... and not give him money to buy the stuff, of course. Clothing and food he'll get from us, but booze? – Forget it! For his own good, for our good and everyone's good!" – he declared emphatically, leaning forward and looking earnestly into my eyes to check that the message was getting through.

"There are some people," he continued, sitting up straight again, "good-natured and well-meaning people, who don't understand this! I mean... they see the guy's suffering and they do what he asks them to, just so they won't see him suffering. And that way they spoil everything!" he complained with more than a touch of bitterness.

"But," I responded, in an effort to stem the flow of verbiage and, rather to my surprise, succeeding, "otherwise, the police will be involved!"

"Who cares?" – the giant cleft the air with his heavy, fleshy hand – "I'd rather have the cops involved than lose the last shred of hope! Can you promise me," he continued after a brief pause, "you'll resist his pleading and those sob-stories he come up with? Don't worry," he added hastily, "he isn't violent... I mean, the things he says, the curses... there's no harm in them. If you need to – call the cops or whatever – but just no money, no bottles, please! Can you promise that?" he concluded, his voice tremulous.

"I promise!" I replied, with a cheerful smile.

He seemed rather taken aback by this prompt response. He rose to his feet, standing to his full height, and something of the brightness in my face must have transferred to his, as he smiled a broad smile – as if this was an expression he had never tried before – and his eyes sparkled as he said, irrelevantly I thought:

"A strange name for a strange man – and all for the best! Please make a note of our address... we live not far from here. If you see the need for it, call round and visit us. We'll always be glad to welcome you!" And when I had done as he asked and written down their address, he held out his huge fleshy hand and shook my hand vigorously, apparently reluctant to let go of it.

Shortly afterwards, Amelia's husband arrived.

"I changed my mind," he said, carefully closing the door. Turning to me, before sitting down, he demanded, making no effort to lower his voice:

"What do you know about Amelia?

"She's a good worker," I replied calmly.

"That's not what I meant!" he snapped, his eyes angry.

"What then?" I asked in a steady voice.

He was an energetic man in his thirties. The curls of his neatly combed hair were black as pitch, his eyes grey and sharp, radiating scorn and the same time – expressing clarity of vision. The ends of his upper lip were swollen, testifying to stormy temperament and strong libido.

"Her relations with the manager!" he insisted.

"Just rumours and nothing definite," I assured him in the same relaxed, entirely neutral tone.

He gave me an appraising look, and seeing his hesitation, I invited him to sit.

He nodded, and pulled out a chair with a vigorous, abrupt movement, as if meaning to throw it at someone or at something. The chair scraped the floor noisily, unexpectedly, as he shifted it, then deposited himself on it.

The door opened and a nervous secretary poked her head round it and peered inside. I sat there calmly, smiling, facing Amelia's husband – a reassuring tableau. The secretary closed the door carefully, almost silently.

"My name..." I began to introduce myself but he interrupted me in the same aggressive tone:

"I know! Amelia has talked about you! Several times..." and in a more restrained tone he proceeded to introduce himself: "My name is Valery. You wanted to talk to me..." he added, suddenly sounding quite conciliatory.

"That's right!" I assented.

"What about?" – his voice was sharper again.

"About Amelia..."

"You've spoken about her already!" he declared.

"... And the rumours about her," I added.

"Gossip!" – the man cried.

"That's one interpretation."

"What's that supposed to mean, 'one interpretation'?" He was suddenly tense.

"As long as there's no direct evidence – the allegation counts as unproven. Pure gossip."

"I wouldn't call it pure." – he surprised me with his carefully modulated tone: "Anyway, what are you talking about?"

"Adultery," I replied

"How can you say that?" – his instinct was to shout it out, and he had difficulty maintaining his cool composure. In fact, he looked close to tears.

"Who warned the manager?" he demanded, recovering himself.

"Not I," I replied. "Although," I added, "I wouldn't have hesitated to do so."

"Afraid I'd hit him?" he mocked.

"You'd regret it a great deal if you did," was my comment.

"Oh, sure! I'd teach him a lesson all right!" – he breathed heavily, and I could sense the warmth of the air expelled from his lungs.

"What the Hell!" – he slapped the top of the desk lightly with his open palm. "I'll find his address, in the phone book. At the end of the day – he'll get what's coming to him! So will she!"

"So will you," I interposed calmly.

He shot blazing eyes at me.

"The charge you're laying against them, could just as easily be laid against you," I explained patiently.

"Adultery?" he queried in a whisper, emphatically scornful.

"Adultery," I agreed.

"You'd better explain yourself, Sir, my patience is wearing thin!" he protested.

I treated him to a serene and perfectly friendly glance, far from any aversion or fear.

"In fact," I began to explain, my voice even and pellucid: "You are the guilty one – if indeed anything has happened between the two of them."

"You mean – I wasn't the right man for Amelia..."

"No," I replied. "I mean that you've been committing adultery since you married her, and even before you married her, and you're still at it today!"

"What kind of talk is this, what's going on?" he protested, glowering with menace. His jaws clenched, the corners of his lips swelled, I could hear his teeth grinding and at the same time – in the depths of his blazing eyes there was a quiet and distant pensiveness, bemusement and eagerness to hear more.

So I continued:

"Have you never coveted the wife of your neighbour, your employer, your colleague, your best friend, your brother – or any seductive woman who passes by you in the street, who has a husband and a family?"

"That's not quite the same thing," – he softened a little and the barest hint of a smile, a tolerant smile, flickered in the corners of his eyes.

"On the contrary," I insisted, "it's more serious."

"How is that?" he puzzled.

"It points to hypocrisy and self-righteousness," I explained with some vehemence. "Outwardly – you're chatting with your friend's wife and nothing's happening, but on the inside – you're someone else. You're not being honest!" – I declared and added: "And that is the vilest hypocrisy, the purest self-righteousness."

"If that is so," he responded with a strange sort of enforced awakening, "it seems that the entire human race is guilty of hypocrisy and self-righteousness!" He demanded an answer and it wasn't slow in coming:

"That is the truth, a truth which does not in any way extenuate your own self-righteousness and hypocrisy!" – my voice was steady, even, a tone intended to leave no room for doubt.

He pondered for a moment. Something that had been pent up in him seemed to be dissolving. His tensed arms were no longer flailing so aggressively. I added:

"Man should first do something for the cleansing of his thought and the purification of his heart and imagination, and then lay charges against others."

"But we're not talking about actions!" the man protested. "There's an essential difference between a theoretical murderer and a practical murderer!"

"Before a judge who is himself a theoretical murderer – that is so!" I declared. "But not before the true judge who dwells in the heart of every man!"

"What do you mean by a judge who is a theoretical murderer?" he wanted to know.

"Any judge of flesh and blood," – I answered him, adding by way of clarification: "One who has himself – not only once, not only twice – murdered in his thoughts. And on account of this he is flawed as a judge, flawed from the outset. Flesh and blood should not judge flesh and blood."

"The world appoints for itself judges of flesh and blood, and everything is done according to their pronouncements!" he commented with some alacrity.

"And that is why the world is mired in a dunghill of hypocrisy and self-righteousness and so far removed from the salvation to which it cries out!" And since Valery didn't respond but seemed attentive, weighing my words, I added: "So long as we don't hang the hypothetical murderer, and don't imprison the hypothetical criminal – courts of law are of no use, nor are prisons, nor the hangman's noose. External judgment is nothing more than shameful pretence, without any profit whatsoever. It's a disaster for humanity."

"You're going to have your work cut out hanging the inner murderer!" Valery commented thoughtfully.

"You can get there in stages," I replied.

"What's the first stage?" he asked – genuine curiosity dispelling the last remnants of tension from his face.

"Understanding the external killer and forgiving him!"

I watched the look in his eyes, and its gradual changes – from the mild and the bemused to the bitter and the mutinous, from the bitter and the mutinous back to the sullen and the aggressive.

"Impractical!" he declared and continued: "Anyway, external murderers and practising adulterers will take encouragement and have a ball – and their numbers will go through the roof!"

"There won't be more than exist already," I replied immediately.

"On the contrary, numbers will decrease at a certain point. And we're talking about the total number of killers and adulterers, actual and potential, which is the same thing. And thus mankind will take a significant step forward."

"I don't believe in atonement and forgiveness," he declared.

"Nor do I," I replied. He was clearly astonished by this, and I lost no time clarifying my meaning: "Not in 'technical' forgiveness, or what might be described as 'academic' forgiveness."

"So what kind of forgiveness do you believe in?"

"Inner forgiveness. In the heart. When man is capable of truly forgiving, that is, in the heart – then sin loses the solid ground beneath its feet..."

"What solid ground is that?" he interrupted.

"Hate," I answered him.

"And what is behind hate?" he persisted.

"Fear," I replied, "and the source of that is egotism."

He looked down, pondering my words for a long moment, and then asked, a twisted smile once more dilating the corners of his full lips:

"And what happens then?"

I replied without hesitation: "True love is what happens then. And redemption of the human species."

The smile was erased, the head lowered again:

"Forgiving..." he murmured, "forgiving..." He fell silent, contemplating, then looked up and asked:

"What does it mean, 'forgiving'?" – for some reason, he sounded scared.

"Loving," was the answer.

Once again he fixed a thoughtful look on the surface of the desk. His hands, which had been resting on it, slid off it, and down, as if of their own accord.

There was silence in the office, a blessed silence, which I did my utmost not to disturb, not even with heavy breathing. Finally, the man looked up, fixing me with a long and inquisitive stare. A kind of inner spark, a radiance – faint and yet real – caught fire in the depths of his eyes. For a long time the scrutiny continued, his sharp eyes focused firmly on mine. Suddenly, with an abrupt movement that couldn't have been foreseen, he withdrew his hand from under the table and held it out to me – a firm hand, suffused with warmth and apparent amity.

After vigorously shaking my hand, he stood up from his seat and left the office without another word.

The next day, Amelia turned up for work – as did the manager. Both were lavish with their compliments and expressions of acclaim. Amelia was the first to visit me in my office, and after sobbing for a while she assured me that I'd made a new man of her husband:

"I really don't recognise him! Really, really!" she repeated in the emotional tone so typical of her. "I'm so grateful to you! So grateful!" she kept on saying emphatically, wiping away the tears streaming down her face with a gentle, elegant motion of the hand. Elegance, in fact, was Amelia's hallmark, she was all elegance – but a type of elegance that has become outmoded, that few attempt to emulate today. She was statuesque, with clear, big eyes, lustrous straw-blond hair, like molten gold, high and smooth forehead, skin of gleaming whiteness, nose a little long, tending slightly towards one side. She was slimly built, and every one of her movements, so it seemed, calculated to the minutest detail, restrained with a firm hand. Her clothing always bore the stamp of something exceptional, yet there was nothing raucous about it – nor was it a hybrid of youthful rebelliousness and the chilly propriety of the establishment. Even her tears were under strict control, and the overall effect was to lend her an air of innocuous coquettishness.

"I'm sure he doesn't recognise you either!" I commented.

"What do you mean by that?" – she wiped away a tear and tried on an expression of pure and utterly innocent incomprehension.

"I'm assuming you've stopped stoking the furnace of his jealousy!" I explained.

"Oh! What a way with words!" Amelia replied with a chuckle. "Furnace of his jealousy – that's so apt!" – and after a pause for emphasis – "Did I ever stoke it?" She turned to me as if I was better placed to know this than anyone, herself included, qualified to appear as an eye-witness, as incontrovertible living testimony, before any interested party.

I shrugged.

"It's a kind of madness!" – she commented, evidently referring to "the furnace of his jealousy".

"No being of flesh and blood is exempt from madness," I declared, and before she could respond I added: "You have to prove to him that you're worthy of the changes he's made to himself for your sake!"

"I always was!" – she flashed me a look that was wondrously clear, calculated and not in the least bit plaintive, demanding vehemently that I acknowledge the truth of a conviction – valid in her eyes beyond any shadow of a doubt.

"All the same," I felt it worth stressing, "the time has come to prove this in practice!" I stood up from my seat as a sign that the interview was over.

Looking slightly abashed, Amelia also rose to her feet, but before leaving, turned back to me, her face suffused with cultivated grace and her habitual aristocratic style, and in a ceremonious kind of whisper said emphatically:

"I promise!" – and left the room.

Nor was the manager to be outdone, and in the course of a lengthy phone call he had nothing but praise for my sterling qualities which had suddenly become apparent to him. The man was an incomparable payer of compliments; his expertise in dispensing them at the right time, in the right place, right way and right quantities, to the right person – had no doubt contributed significantly to his rapid promotion and the attainment of all kinds of goals. His gratitude was warm and effusive:

"My sincere thanks, esteem and appreciation. I'll never forget this! Never, not ever!" The prodigious cascade of words swept on, leaving me no opportunity to respond. I moved the receiver away from my ear, and the cacophony continued, somewhere in the region of my nose: "Excellent work! Marvellous! Sensitivity! Consideration! You've acted... as a man to a man!" – stressed with questionable overtones – "One good turn deserves another, don't worry... it'll be my turn next!"

I raised the mouthpiece to my lips and in a light, albeit mechanical tone of voice, spoke into it:

"You're exaggerating!"

"Absolutely not!" the manager trumpeted on hearing my response. "You protected me from a... a very disturbed individual! He was harassing her as well..."

"If he's disturbed – then so am I and so are you and so is she – we're all disturbed!" I declared into the receiver.

The deluge of words was stemmed. A long moment of apparent self-assessment, and the soft and friendly voice, smooth as olive oil and jaunty as a mountain spring, turned authoritative, stern and emphatic.

"Now you're being hurtful!"

"So are you."

"Who have I hurt?"

"Him."

"Does he mean that much to you?"

"As much as you mean to me, and she means to me, and everyone else means to me..."

"That's you!" – the voice at the other end of the line mellowed a little – "You and your principles! But not to worry..." – a tolerant note creeping in – "I'm learning to appreciate them... appreciate you I should say... Forgive me if I've offended you and once again, thanks!"

The conversation was over. But the last sentences seemed to bear the precious seal of sincerity.

At the beginning of the following week, on arriving at my work-place, I sensed that something in the ambience was not as it should be. The employees who had already appeared, some of them before me which wasn't their normal practice, looked at me with frightened eyes, but averted their gaze when I tried to address them.

I went into my office, put on a gown, flicked through paperwork, organised a file. As I was about to begin analysing data that had accumulated during the previous week – there was a knock on the door and a secretary came in, stood close by the door, clasped her hands, fixed wide-open eyes on me and cried:

"Haven't you heard?"

"About what?" I asked.

"About Amelia!" – and being dissatisfied with my response she repeated her question: "Haven't you heard?"

"No." I let the printouts fall, in impotent disorder, on the desk.

"And Valery?"

"No."

"And the manager?"

Clearly, she was intent on coaxing some response from me.

"No," I repeated in an even voice, with a light, equable smile.

"It was on the radio!" – she was getting desperate now.

"I don't listen to the radio."

"We know that!" – the secretary restrained a bitter smile – "That's why I wanted to tell you… if you're interested, that is…" and without waiting for a response, she plunged straight in:

"He broke into his apartment!" Evidently, she didn't think it necessary to explain who "he" was, or to whom the "apartment" belonged. I was in no hurry to interrupt her.

"And he found them…" – she scrutinised my features, bemused by my unchanging expression – "in a compromising situation… to put it politely!" Again she scanned my face, now with unequivocal disapproval. "He got hold of some kind of stick, something to do with sport… I don't know what it's called… a 'bat' I think, or a 'club'… the manager played golf…"

"That's right," I chimed in.

She ignored my interruption and cried, almost maniacally:

"They've both got broken bones! Amelia – ribs and both hands, the manager – hand, legs and a minor skull fracture… at least, that's what they're saying. The pair of them are in hospital and he's in jail… the manager tried to get away – jumped from the second floor, from the kitchen window, the same way Valery got in…" she added to complete the picture: "Valery chased after him, caught him and whacked him over the head…"

The story was over. The secretary stole a last look at my face, noting the impression that her words had made and frankly, dissatisfied.

I returned to my normal work and was soon engrossed in the routine of data analysis. I solved as much as I could and put the rest back on the shelf, then went to the head office to look for something else that required my attention.

At the end of the working day I went down to Rahamim's café, ate humus on pitta, which he used to prepare sometimes for chance afternoon customers, drank tea and made my way to the hospital.

And sure enough, there they both were, the manager and Amelia, but I was unable to talk to them – those were the medical instructions and in any case, they were still in shock.

The manager's head was bandaged. Amelia's face, all suppurating bruises – was contorted with pain and elemental fear; the manager's eyes were suffused with sheer terror, as if seeking, in vain, some support, a source of consolation. I tried to convey a hint of encouragement to them and after a long spell of sitting quietly, watching those gaping eyes, it seemed that the hint had been absorbed and the fears had eased.

I rose from my seat, waved a goodbye and left the hospital.

I asked to be allowed to visit Valery in the jail in Tel Kabir. After prolonged negotiation between the deputy governor and the prisoner's attorney – I was granted permission for a twenty-minute visit.

THE DETENTION CELL

Slowly the heavy door swung open and I was admitted to the detention cell – dim, high-ceilinged, grey-walled – a dumb arrogance of cold, pitiable hostility. A pungent smell of urine hung in the air. Faint rays of light filtered through a high, netted window. When my eyes had grown accustomed to the gloom I saw the prisoner sitting facing me. His face was giving nothing away, the grey eyes scrutinising me closely. There was something special about the heavy set of the features, as if a distant calm had settled on them, a calm that was well guarded and fortified at all times.

To my astonishment, when I held out my hand to the prisoner he gripped it warmly and with friendship and the expression on his face changed completely: the rigour disappeared and a broad smile melted the tight lips, a smile that could not be described as other than amicable and yet showed no sign of excessive emotion, or an appeal for support and comfort.

"I'm sorry!" I began.

"Nothing to be sorry for!" he hastened to reply, adding, with an abrupt change of subject: "The justice that you demand, doesn't exist!"

I was silent.

"If you follow me," he proceeded to elucidate, the tone of his voice calm and even – "that isn't to say that it's not valid justice, in fact – it's the one and only justice. But it doesn't exist!" And after a moment's thought: "I've calmed down now. I did what seemed to me had to be done. Maybe I got it wrong – okay, I definitely got it wrong. But I'm not sorry. Anyway, how far are you supposed to pardon and forgive?" He looked up, and his eyes, a hint of something heavy beginning to cloud their vision, demanded an answer.

"As far as infinity," was my reply.

The old chair beneath him, with its damaged back and legs of blackened lead tubing, grated on the floor.

"There you are!" – he grinned a twisted, nervous sort of grin – "You have an answer! An answer for everything. A correct answer – and an impossible one!"

Again I was silent.

The silence lengthened. I assumed that he was engrossed in an intense, increasingly intense, process of self-appraisal, accompanied by the loud, persistent and penetrating sounds emitted by the chair, which he was simply unaware of.

At last he began, his head lowered, his eyes fixed on the floor, his legs set far apart:

"The outburst...I should say, my outburst," he explained – "a strange business! Quite unbelievable!" In a calmer tone he continued: "Yes, beyond the bounds of any logic!" Here he looked up and fixed on me a glance in which there was bemusement bordering on panic. My reply at this moment was very important to him.

"What's so strange, or illogical, in your opinion?" I asked, smiling. The tone of my voice had the effect of easing slightly the pressure and the tension perceptible in his entire demeanour.

Again he looked down at the filthy floor, took a lungful of the fetid air, full of the pungent aroma of human excrement, and spoke with a surprising change in the tempo of his words, from scared and fluid to slow and measured, almost torpid:

"I went quite innocently," he began and at once corrected himself – "well, there wasn't anything innocent about it really... I knew the manager's address, and phone number too. I called a few times. No reply... it seemed the apartment was empty. Later I found out the rest of the family had gone off somewhere. Some relatives in the North – he'd fixed that. Clever, or what?" he asked himself, then continued smoothly: "Amelia told some tale – working overtime or something. All very suspicious, the whole thing. Incidentally, I don't understand what she sees in him! But that's not the issue..." – he slowed the rhythm of his speech – "I left my house... there was nothing for me to do at home!" he explained and continued: "I made my way to that square, an exclusive square... in an exclusive square there's always something intriguing... the buildings...tall blocks, penthouses, bungalows, whatever.... they all look down their noses at you! From top to bottom, puffed-up and narrow-minded, just like the people who live in them!

"I soon located the manager's house. A two-storey building, elegant... a garden with flowers, lawn, parking-lot... I did a circuit, several circuits, surveys... making sure. I checked it out from every side... colour of walls – lurid yellow with creepers climbing up it – for camouflage! Balconies everywhere you look – sealed-off, private… the main entrance, a solid steel door… all this I took in at a glance. I checked, double-checked… and I found an open window. Stupid, or what?" For a moment he paused, staring up at me, and then looked away hastily, clearly intent on forestalling any attempt on my part to answer his question, or impede in any way the flow of his narrative.

"This open window," he continued, "got itself lodged somewhere – in a dark corner of the mind. A devilish business!" he complained bitterly – "I couldn't get it out of my head. It spurred me on to more and more reconnaissance, checking yet again that yes, the window was open, open in reality, not just my imagination…

"Suddenly I saw one of the neighbours, the neighbour from the house opposite, peering out of her window behind the curtains and giving me a suspicious, scared look, full of foreboding… and the moment our eyes met, she retreated out of sight, probably going to call someone, husband maybe or neighbour or – the police… This consideration, or intense premonition I should say – was the final straw, the jolt that I needed. From somewhere the thought flashed into my mind, I had to do something, and right now! Before it was too late…" he muttered to himself, falling silent for a long minute and then, without looking up, without any movement, sitting as still as a monolith – he resumed in a hushed but clear voice:

"Suddenly – I was inside. I could never describe how it happened. Not ever! I must have climbed up to the second floor and got in through the open window… but I don't remember it. That part's wiped from my memory. Absolutely. I didn't experience the climb and the break-in…" and he added, in an abrupt change of subject, in the same quiet and even tone of voice – "How stupid can you get! Cavorting with another man's wife – and leaving a window open!" His voice changed suddenly, revealing an odd but sincere bemusement, devoid of any trace of pathos or anger: "The strangest thing," he explained to me and to himself, "is that I was in control of myself at every moment," – a fresh, animated note now perceptible in his voice – "when I broke into the apartment, when I saw them, when I looked around for something to hit them with… this… this is incredible! When I was hitting them, it all happened as if it was some weird film, with me in the audience – and playing the leading role too… and the trendy director giving cool, precise instructions to his actors – that was me as well! Can you understand something like that?" As this wasn't addressed to me, I didn't respond, and he added, as if summing up:

"It's as if instinct disappears!" – and apparently consumed by wonderment and incredulity, he shifted his right leg and the chair beneath him emitted a strident, grating sound. Then he looked up abruptly and turned his grey eyes on me.

"All the same, what's done is done..." I remarked in a calm tone that might have sounded strange and misplaced to any other ears, but from the perspective of my one and only listener, seemed not only absolutely natural, but even required by the circumstances. Since at the end of the day, everything that we were discussing belonged to the past. This past, like the present and the future arising from it – belonged to nothing other than a unique world, a world of hallucinations that our imagination created for itself – something out of nothing. This pellucid calm aroused Valery to tell more of what was in his heart and thus to ease, if only by the tiniest fraction, the weight of depression that no doubt was lying in wait for him in the days ahead, between the blank prison walls.

"I didn't resist it... didn't resist the impulse!" he confessed suddenly, his words sounding like a preamble to something much more substantial, something pressing, needing to be said.

"It's understandable," I said, with the aim of nudging him towards it.

"Absolutely not!" he declared and gave me a strange, intense look, as if only now becoming aware of me, as if everything he had said so far was addressed to himself alone.

"Why not?" I asked, in the same equable tone, designed to convey to him and infuse in him the confidence that the prisoner needs – confidence that all is not over and in fact, nothing exceptional has happened, and starting over requires nothing more than moving from the point at which you stopped, and nothing has been lost, nothing can be lost for ever.

"Because even for a moment I didn't forget your words and didn't lose my faith in them! Even now I remember them and believe in them absolutely... but the strange thing, the thing beyond comprehension – it was actually because of your words and my steadfast belief in them – that I hit... and went on hitting!" He looked at me with eyes from which the gloomy clouds had cleared, to be replaced by a chilly, yet impetuous lustre, and his words flowed in a spirit of sincerity and profound self-awareness:

"It didn't happen until the moment I was standing there with that golf stick or club or whatever, some sporting implement I wasn't familiar with, the kind of thing snotty-nosed snobs play around with... anyway I had the stick and I crept up on them... Till that moment they weren't aware of me, too busy with their carnal frolics...and because of what you said, I could see it that way – pathetic carnal frolics, like a pair of naked worms writhing on a stinking dung-heap... it was ludicrous, fit to arouse pity and ridicule," – he was careful to point out – "certainly not a motive for murder... and something strange happens, as if it doesn't touch you at all, and you wonder how you got to this point, and ask yourself, what's it for?" He swallowed his saliva, apparently to moisten his dry throat and continued: "I took all this in... I saw it all for myself. As you know, at moments like these time is a very relative dimension. It seemed no more than a micro-second, and there were thousands of impressions, analyses, conceptions, conclusions and decisions flashing through my head... I saw everything; I experienced, analysed, weighed, decided. And my decision – was to throw away the heavy, primitive weapon and break into peals of laughter, derisive laughter – befitting the situation... or perhaps not derisive at all, but gentle, amicable, tolerant maybe... no malice intended... then bid a polite 'Goodbye' and leave.

"And instead of all this, suddenly, without any transition, as if I was detached from all self-control or innate logic – I saw myself beating frantically, landing blows on the revolting flesh of the worms, the two worms wriggling in passionate abandon on a stinking pile of dung, light brown dung..." – his lips curled in what could be described as a twisted grin, sarcastic and at the same time, bitter and cruel: "That's the colour of the sheets in his house – light brown..." He cleared his throat and continued:

"After a second or two, no more, I became aware of what was happening, and those words of refined truth returned to me and my belief in them – I was put on my guard. Everything worked quickly and the command was – to stop! Immediately, then and there – to stop!

"So – I stopped. For a fraction of a second... and then it happened. What I mean is – it was because I'd stopped and was seeing myself in the light of the refined truth that I heard from you and believed in with steadfast faith – and always will believe in!" – he thought it worth stressing – "…because of that I saw myself as I am – the ultimate weakling, the most despicable worm in the universe, a creature without backbone, worthy not even to be spat upon, incapable of accepting instruction or control…" Flecks of foam sparkled on his lips. He wiped them away angrily and went on:

"The effect of this was stunning… and in full consciousness and with absolutely clear vision I went on hitting, because of the truths I knew and my belief in them. I hit and hit. I even chased after him and whacked him on the head… It's a miracle I didn't kill anyone!" He breathed heavily, as if the whole incident had put on skin and sinew and he was experiencing it again. A thin thread of foam dangled from the corner of his mouth. His eyes met mine. A kind of green, chilly light appeared in them, but not cruel or lacking in vitality, not idolatrous fire but something filled with a strange intensity of pleasure.

"It's as if you were hitting yourself," I commented.

"Not just 'as if'!" he declared, covering his face with his hands, and knuckling his temples in an apparent attempt to restore his lucidity:

"I was hitting myself! In fact – I tried to murder myself…" A spasm crossed over his sallow features, his broad shoulders quivered. The expensive blue shirt he was wearing had become tattered overnight and was spattered with stains from an indeterminate source. His unshaved beard gave him a neglected look. The exposed parts of his face were filthy.

"Is there a way out?" – he looked up suddenly, his eyes clouded with deepening dejection.

"There is!" I declared.

He looked at me intently, wrinkled his brow and as if cherishing the distant spark of a lost hope asked: "What is it?"

"You'll find it for yourself," I replied and added: "It's not that difficult."

"What do I have to do to find it?"

"Search. Put idleness aside and search."

"How do I search?"

"Get rid of self-pity, avoid the temptation to chew over the past, and adhere to the truth!"

"How do you adhere to the truth?"

"Think the truth, tell the truth, act the truth!"

"Are you saying that I'm a liar?" he asked, suddenly tense.

"Yes," I said, unimpressed by his expression of surprise and chagrin – "because you don't know what the truth is!"

I stood up from my seat and held out my hand. Once more he surprised me with the warmth and cordiality of his handshake.

THE FARHI FAMILY

One warm bright day, as I was leaving my work-place, I heard someone running behind me, running heavily and clumsily. I didn't turn round and this proved unnecessary anyway – the man caught up with me, and wheezing like a steam locomotive, laid a huge hand on my shoulder. It was Shmuel. His face was flushed and sweating, unshaven, with a twisted sort of smile, and his eyeballs dilated, laced with red filaments.

"Adon! Please! Wait!" This request was superfluous, as I was already standing still. He put his free hand to his chest as if trying to calm the rapid beating of his heart, and the throbbing vein in his neck did indeed reflect some cardiac hyper-activity. For a long minute he stood thus, without uttering a word. The hand on my shoulder trembled and it was as if the whole weight of his body had been transferred to it.

His panting steadied, and without removing his hand from my shoulder, he began:

"Adon! I'm in a bad way, and it's getting worse! If someone doesn't help me – I'll fall down in the street and maybe – not get up again... I'd be better off that way! Please, help me!" – intense, incurable pain twisted his face – "One bottle!" he exclaimed and hastily added: "Or a little money... just enough for one bottle! What's a pittance like that to a toff like you? Just so I can stay on my feet... Adon, you're a gentleman, help me!" he cried, realising that the expression on my face wasn't as responsive as he had hoped it would be.

"Your brother came to see me," I replied, "some time ago. He begged me not to give in, nor to buy you bottles or provide you with money. He insisted this was the only way you'd get out of the mess you're in... the shame that you're bringing on yourself, your family and all those around you. I could tell he was really concerned for you, so I gave my word – I promised. I promised, and I'm not going back on it. The only thing I can do for you is make sure you get home."

"Bastard! Swine!" – Shmuel let out a full-throated roar. Passers-by stopped and stared at us for a moment, some hastily turning their backs and leaving the scene, others giving us baleful looks, others pausing to watch further developments with an air of frank curiosity. And there was one of them who offered help – a lean man in advanced middle age.

"Should I call the police?" he asked simply, without specifically addressing either of us, but on looking more closely at Shmuel he changed his tone: "Or an ambulance?"

In fact, it wasn't clear to whom Shmuel was addressing his curses – his brother or me – not that it made any difference, to him or to me. In any case, the locomotive was in motion but hadn't yet built up a full head of steam.

Shmuel approached the man who had offered his services, held out his hand, and still not relaxing his hold on my shoulder, cried:

"If you want to help – make a contribution!" – and in a tone of mild persuasion: "A tenner should be enough… give generously and save a lost soul from the fires of Hell!"

The man who'd been asked for charity looked in alarm at the gigantic, proffered hand, then turned to me as if seeking something in my face – encouragement perhaps, or sympathy, or advice to refuse the request. And as my eyes told him nothing – he backed away and hastily left the scene. I have no doubt that having rounded the corner – he broke into a run.

"Ho! Ho! Ho! Ho!.. Ho! Ho! Ho!" – Shmuel began yelling, leaping on the spot like someone treading on burning coals, unable to extricate himself from the blazing carpet beneath him. In the process he was shaking me back and forth. Spittle dribbled from his mouth and mingled with the stubble on his cheeks that hadn't been shaved for some days.

I remained where I was, immobile. His heavy hand was still on my shoulder, as if it were a last handhold in a disintegrating world.

The prancing and the yelling went on for some time. People behaved much as before – some passing by in a hurry, others eyeing us with frank disapproval, some lingering briefly, feeding their curiosity but hoping for more drama and ultimately dissatisfied, and again there were a few who, in one way or another, tried to offer assistance. Shmuel's outstretched hand and my blank expression repelled them and they turned and hurried away, bemused perhaps by what they had seen and relieved in the end to have got away from us.

In a bitter moment of despair, when we were left alone, Shmuel released his hold on me and sank to the ground, still kicking out with his feet and lashing the air with his hands, shaking his gigantic head like a man swimming in deep waters.

"Ho! Ho! Ho! Ho!" he shouted, rolling in the busy roadway, prostrating himself full length, arms and legs spreadeagled.

A sharp squeal of brakes, chilling the heart and curdling the bowels, tore through the air, seeming to lacerate the ear-drums of all who heard it. As the traffic backed up, scores of motor-horns suddenly joined in a demented chorus. All movement was at a standstill, and the wail of the klaxons continued to send vibrations through the airy void until a police patrol car arrived.

The cops slammed on their brakes, leapt down from their vehicle with great aplomb and pounced on Shmuel, grabbing the tattered fabric covering his heavy frame and with their combined efforts carried him, still waving and kicking, to their transport and bundled him inside. Moments later they were on their way.

The vehicles that had been halted emitted rancorous roars as their engines were restarted; the faces of the drivers, without exception, stared through the windscreens with expressions of icy anger as the traffic began moving again.

I set out in the direction of Shmuel's house, relying on the address given me by his brother.

It was no easy task finding the place. It turned out to be one of those dead-end alleyways, tucked away in some old and dilapidated suburb – invariably short, shapeless and reckoned unworthy of the distinction of a name. If it is called anything, then this is likely to be something weird and eccentric, like the place itself – "Crescent," for example, on account of its single bend, or "Investment Street", in memory of a financier who in former times bought up the entire neighbourhood and treated it as his personal fiefdom.

Late in the afternoon, sweating profusely, I discovered the substantial door, which could just about be described as a "gate", of the Farhi family, domiciled at "Menora Street", number 2. Nobody helped me in my quest. The name "Menora" evoked surprise, bemusement and suspicion when I consulted various local residents. There was one who thought I was pulling his leg, took offence and slammed his door in my face. Others whom I questioned assumed that I represented some authority and that my intentions were far from innocent. One way or another, no one had any information to give me regarding a street of this name, and as it turned out they had a point: no identifying sign was visible in the alleyway, which must have been all of thirty paces in length.

On the clumsy "gate", fashioned from heavy, unplaned wooden planks, the words "Fam. Farhi" were emblazoned in black paint – big letters, half a cubit in height. The script wasn't lacking in elegance and artistic flair: every letter was an entity in its own right, facing in its preferred direction, but in spite of this overt defiance of authority, combining submissively enough with the others for the sake of the family name.

I knocked on the gate. It wasn't long before it swung open before me, silently. The giant hinges were well oiled.

A girl of stocky build, in a frayed but clean housecoat, stood in the doorway with a friendly smile on her lips.

"Menora Street, number 2?" I asked, to be sure.

"Yes," she replied, her smile deepening, as the gate was opened further, revealing a swathe of backyard and a path paved with marble chippings of all types and colours, flanked on both sides by flower-beds.

"Shmuel's brother asked me to call if I thought it necessary."

In response to this, the gate was flung wide open and the invitation was forthright:

"Please come in!"

I entered. There was no lock on the door and it could be bolted only from the inside. The whole house, with its extensive grounds, was surrounded by a high wall. Beyond the flower-beds with their white and pink blooms, an old orchard had been converted into a vegetable garden, growing tomatoes, cucumbers, pumpkins and onions.

In the middle of the yard stood a tall building, its tiled roof crumbling with age, as were the antiquated sandstone walls. The front of the house was occupied by a broad balcony with a rail of blackened wood, scorched by the sun and nibbled by insects. On the balcony, at a broad and long table, sat six girls, very similar to the one who had greeted me, dressed like her and hard at work – handing one another glass lampshades and painting them carefully and diligently with wavy lines, flowers and geometric patterns. The completed shades were stacked up at the end of the table, where they were collected by an elderly man of stern appearance, with a bushy moustache, white as cotton-wool, who vanished with them into the house, soon to emerge empty-handed and repeat the process.

As I entered the yard the old man paused for a moment, checking me out with a keen look, as if making some calculation, wrinkled his broad brow, tanned by wind and sun, put down the shades he was carrying and came out to meet me. When we stood face to face he held out a small, callused hand and said:

"David Farhi!" – adding at once – "Whom do I have the honour of addressing?"

I introduced myself.

"Oh!.." – a cloud passed over his face, although I couldn't tell what it was and what it signified.

"Israel spoke about you..."

"Shmuel's brother?" I asked, wanting to get things straight.

"Shmuel's brother," he echoed, and added: "I'm their father and these," – he indicated with a raised eyebrow and a backward toss of the head – "are their sisters. Their mother, Leah, is in the house..." And suddenly, quite unexpectedly, a broad smile lit up his face, dispersing the stern and gloomy lines. The man resembled a retired army officer, with years of discipline and rigid routine behind him, suddenly reverting to the simple pleasures of childhood.

"Please, come inside!" he invited me with a broad, hospitable sweep of the hand.

I followed him. Climbing up to the balcony I greeted the industrious young ladies, and they looked up and returned my greeting in a tuneful chorus.

Inside the house the air was pleasantly cool, with the mottled shadow of the rays of the setting sun filtering through curtains. The lounge was spacious, paved with tiles of superior quality, covered by a carpet, and contained a sofa and armchairs arranged round a low table with ornately crafted legs, polished to a deep sheen, the colour of ripe dates. A light breeze rustled daintily, playing with the airy lace curtains. The windows were open. On the left side of the room four doors were visible: three of them apparently leading to bedrooms, and the fourth, standing ajar, revealing the polished porcelain of a bathroom.

"Sit down, please!" – my host invited me.

I sat in one of the armchairs. He disappeared into a dark and narrow passageway and returned a few minutes later carrying a tray, loaded with seasonal fruits and cups of tea.

"Would you prefer coffee?" he asked, laying the tray on the table.

"No thank you, this is fine."

"My wife isn't in the best of health," he saw fit to explain, taking his cup carefully and sitting down opposite me.

I sipped the warm liquid and the pungent smell of fresh mint rose in my nostrils.

"What brings you here?" David Farhi asked, taking a deep gulp and fidgeting absently with his moustache.

"A promise I made to Israel," I began, carefully putting the cup down.

"We're waiting for him now," Mr. Farhi announced. "He might come and join us at any moment," he added, still clutching the cup and absorbing its pleasant warmth into his body through the callused palm of his hand. He wasn't a tall man but even when sitting he held his body quite erect, unusually so in view of his age. Were it not for this exceptionally stiff posture, he would have disappeared from view in the deep recesses of the armchair. His fingers were thin but solid, bespeaking confidence and a firm grip. How old is he? – I speculated. As if reading my thoughts he continued calmly, from under the bushy moustache:

"I married young, at twenty-four years old. My wife, Leah, was seventeen then. Israel was born nine months after the wedding. And then came..." – he listed the names of his seven daughters. Shmuel was left to the last:

"The child of our old age!" – it sounded like a boast.

"How old is he?" I asked innocently.

"He turned twenty-eight last week, but he looks older than his age. Even older than Israel, the firstborn. That... unconventional way of life of his..." He grinned at me awkwardly, in embarrassment almost, as if the grin would suffice to cover up something, or distract my attention. "He's talented!" he added with dignity. "In his youth he wrote poems... I have a few of them here..." He glanced hesitantly, rather dryly, at an antique cabinet standing at one end of the spacious lounge, evidently the place where he kept his son's poems. His body shifted in the armchair, as if he meant to get up and fetch the poems, but in the end he changed his mind and stayed where he was.

Meanwhile, the girls on the balcony began to sing – a sad song in two voices, a song of a distant land with snow-capped mountains and limpid, fast-flowing streams and dark, perpetual forests and fabled heroes riding into battle on mighty chargers...

"Where does that song come from?" I asked, puzzled.

"They studied at the Mission," he replied, and added by way of explanation: "The education there is superior! The New Testament and the prayers and all that stuff – you can take it or leave it!" he stressed. "It will be a long time before our educational institutions can match theirs. They teach obedience there, and respect. Obedience to parents and respect for them. And in all the world there's no healthier foundation for the happiness of mankind than respect for the parents and obedience to them!" And without waiting for a response he continued: "I respected my father and I obeyed him, and to this very day I have happy memories of my father's house. Sometimes these memories are my only consolation!" he declared with a rueful smile.

"And Shmuel?" I asked "Where was he educated?"

"Like all of them," – his face darkening – "at elementary school. Then he did a spell with the religious mob, some kind of yeshiva. But he didn't stick at it..." – he took a deep gulp of the tea – "Israel studied at a technical school, he's a qualified electrician!" As if afraid I would ask more questions about Shmuel he added hastily: "He has his own shop, selling electrical equipment. The lampshades that the girls put together, they're for the wholesale trade. The girls are hard workers, and he is too. They're like me," – he grinned uncomfortably – "Israel and the girls..." – and reverting suddenly to his younger son: "Shmuel seems to take after his mother – big and strong, but sensitive... Israel's like his mother too, actually, in physical terms I mean... but in temperament, he's so different... has no time for poetry at all, doesn't understand it! He's good at his job, has golden hands!" An undisguised note of pride and satisfaction could be heard in his voice. "As for me," he added, "I studied at the 'Alliance'. Did my matriculation there... got a distinction in Hebrew..."

The singing outside was hushed. Some exchanges of words were audible, resembling the rapid chirping of birds, cheerful song-birds whose only concern is to celebrate the happiness that has fallen to their lot and the delights of music... and at that point the door of the lounge swung open and on the threshold stood Israel – erect and tense, his restless eyes scouring the room. He soon spotted us and approached with firm, purposeful tread:

"Hello Mr...sorry, Adon," he corrected himself hastily: "What brings you here?"

"My promise."

"Did he show up?" he asked anxiously, as if attempting to hide something from his father, by making his question as vague as possible. But the other, it seemed, had been keenly following every move he made, every word he spoke, brows knitted and eyes devouring every minute change in the expression of his face.

"He showed up..." I replied uneasily.

"Speak freely!" – came the persuasive, gentle and yet assured voice of David Farhi – "Nothing gets past me, at the end of the day!" He surprised us both with a soft and amiable laugh.

I studied Israel's tense face. He nodded in token of assent and agreement. I outlined the incident in a few sentences: Shmuel's appearance, his appeal for help – bottle or cash equivalent – my refusal in the spirit of that promise, his emotional outburst, his prostration in the street, the patrol-car that took him away... After a fraught silence lasting no more than a minute, Israel responded:

"I'll go fetch him!" – and without waiting for any rejoinder, let alone a word of agreement, stood up from his seat, turned to the door and with the same resolute tread as before, left the dim room and went outside. From the balcony, the sound of that tuneful bird-talk was heard again, followed by a new song, a simple song this time: rustic romance, and the broad river which is the only obstacle separating a pair of lovers.

The voices of the girls were wondrously clear, well-matched and harmonious, redolent of childhood purity as yet undefiled.

David Farhi, who didn't seem quite so old to me now – he might not be out of his seventies yet – raised dark eyes and gave me a long, deep and unhappy look:

"Why didn't you help him?" he asked in a downcast, hoarse and plaintive voice.

"Israel appealed to me, and made it clear this was what the whole family wanted," I replied, "It was the only way Shmuel could be helped – his last chance..."

"Israel, Israel!" he sighed, looking away – "What does he know?

Electrical gadgets are all he understands!" There was great sadness in the old man's voice. An oppressive moment passed.

"Let me explain it to you," he started suddenly, sounding more assured, "Shmuel is worried about the future of his sisters. It's an obsession with him. Seven sisters – and all of them virgins! He drowns his sorrows in drink, or tries to. That's how it started anyway. Then he used to bring all kinds of friends home, in the hope someone would take a shine to one of his sisters. And there were some with serious... intentions... except for the youngest, all of them went out at least once with one boy or another. Afterwards," he added, speaking with sharp, unnatural alertness – " it always turned out that the boy wasn't the right one: no proper income, no family to speak of... It had to be broken off, and that was no easy matter. And I'm not talking about the girls."

"Who then?" I asked.

"The boys, of course!" he declared with unassailable confidence. "They sniffed superior merchandise, and held on tight! Or, like the kids say today, they were 'all fired up'. They were burning, all right!" – with repressed notes of relish creeping into his voice – "One even threatened to drown himself..." He chuckled oddly and scrutinised the expression on my face with a look of mild scorn, blended with childish gaiety. Then suddenly, as if feeling the need to go into detail:

"The one who dated the eldest turned out to be a cobbler of all things! Worked in a shoe factory and at home, in his spare time, he repaired them. He walked with a limp... not a big deal but a handicap all the same! And she – I can't think why – was fond of him... or wanted to give that impression... maybe she still likes him. But he's not the one for her!" he declared resolutely. Again he studied my features, and finding no indication there that I was about to respond, added:

"And the next one in line – she found herself a plumber, one who specialised in cleaning out drains, as a matter of fact. She got involved, and it was a tough job getting her out of it. We had to call on some priest, one of the teachers from the Mission. He came round a few times, consecutive days even. He tried to talk her round, underlining the duty of obedience to your parents that begat you. And she gave in eventually. The third couldn't have cared less. Her suitor was the one who threatened to drown himself. No proper prospects at all. The fourth took up with an old man... almost as old as me…" – he broke off suddenly and stared down at the highly polished floor-tiles, waiting for my response. I responded:

"Who decides that the suitor isn't suitable?"

"The one authorised to do so by the very nature of things!" he replied, in a tone of absolute certainty, his whole body rigid with resolution. I noticed how his shaved head accentuated still further the thick, luxuriant moustache entirely covering his upper lip. "The head of the family," he explained and added, just in case this left any doubt – "David Farhi!"

"In cases like this, it's not easy to reach the right decision," I commented mildly.

Again he scrutinised my facial expression from under dense eyebrows that were turning grey, all suspicion and repressed rancour. But when he realised that I was sincere, meaning the words that I had said and nothing else, he softened and said:

"Exactly so. Not easy at all!"

Suddenly he put back on his weather-beaten face that pure and innocent smile that seemed so out of character, the smile of a child. And then, without any intermediate phase, he adopted a look of severity and dignity, the lines of his face hardened, and casting his eyes down to the floor, he complained:

"There are some who are sorry after the event, very sorry indeed. And the heart bleeds!" He sighed and with head still bowed, added: "But there's nothing that can be done – and no one to turn to!" he concluded, looking up and staring into my face.

"It isn't easy being a father and the head of a family," I said and added at once: "There's no point picking at old wounds. What's past is past. Listen to that," I continued – "the girls never stop singing and their song is as pure as a mountain stream, enchanting all who hear it!" – he listened intently – "It follows that they're not bemoaning their fate. If they were married, there's no knowing how things would look…" Seeing his rapt expression, demanding more, I continued:

"A family is a joy to a father, but it's only natural he should worry over the fate of his sons and daughters!" I smiled an affable smile, radiating confidence.

"That is indeed true," he hastened to agree with me, a vivid flash passing through his eyes – "the very best of the best is what a man wants for his children and especially – his daughters!" But his enthusiasm faded suddenly and he returned to that heavy, pensive tone of voice, once again looking down at the floor:

"After a while, doubt creeps in… Maybe I've done the wrong things and not acted in entirely good faith, without prejudice… maybe I've made a serious mistake, a fatal mistake, irreparable and unforgivable, something that can't be undone!" He looked up and gave me that heavy, inquisitive-insistent stare.

"As I said," I repeated with emphasis, "there's no point digging up the past. Better to give thought to the future. The future," I declared, "always brings hope." And seeing clearly that he wanted to hear more, I continued in the same light and assured tone of voice:

"It may yet prove that you've been absolutely right all along, and grooms will come who will ensure the happiness of your daughters!"

"What a way with words!" David Farhi exclaimed emotionally, adding in the same breath: "And what a shame you're not free, meaning it's a shame you're married, or at least, that what Israel told me. It's become a habit with me," he explained. "When I'm told about some male, my first question is, is he free or married… that's what things have come to…"

"I'm married and not young," I replied. "You'll find suitors yet who are right for your daughters. And I wish you luck!" I concluded cheerfully.

"The fact that you're not young doesn't bother me at all!" the old man insisted.

"We're going over and over things that are quite irrelevant," I pointed out.

"What kind of things are relevant then, in your opinion?" he demanded to know.

"Things that deal with the future," I replied.

He gave me a prolonged, probing look. Finally he said, as if admitting defeat:

"That's right!" – and having tried to put on a look of injured dignity and failed, he grinned in that sudden way of his, his face lit up, he leaned forward and seized his cup, raised it with a ceremonious gesture and cried: "To life!" – as if it were intoxicating liquor in there, and drank, with a toss of the head.

I picked up my own cup, echoed the toast and followed suit. The liquid still retained something of its invigorating warmth and pungent aroma.

Again the singing outside stopped, and the chattering, like the lively chirping of birds, again took its place – but this time more strident and alert, with a hint of remote fear and a touch of bewilderment blended into it.

The door of the shady lounge swung violently open and Shmuel – stumbling, dirty and bleeding from cuts on the face, was shoved unceremoniously into the room. Behind him stood Israel, simultaneously propelling him and supporting him.

Silence reigned in the room – heavy, oppressive silence, swallowing all the sounds from outside, including that fluid chirping of the birds of freedom, which seemed to have faded out altogether.

David Farhi froze in his seat, staring in disbelief at the two grown men, still standing motionless in the doorway. A long moment passed. Then the old man rose, and with surprising vigour, approached his two sons.

He stood close to Shmuel, scrutinising his bloated face intently. It was as if the latter was about to fall on his shoulder or at any rate, felt a powerful desire to do so.

The facial expression of the old man, standing with his back to me, I couldn't see, but I noticed the shudder that passed through his broad shoulders. And then, suddenly, he raised his small but firm hand and slapped his son hard across the face, slapped him again with the other hand and then began kicking Shmuel, kicked him again and again while uttering a strangled, blood-curdling yell, furious and yet strangely plaintive.

Shmuel fell at his feet, losing his balance as his brother let go of him, no longer supporting him. His expansive, heavy body sprawled on the floor, just as it had in the roadway at noon, gasping and panting and hissing, like a seal menaced by the hunters with their clubs – an impression reinforced by the old man's indiscriminate assault, kicking his son everywhere, from the head to the bloated stomach. He was completely out of control, sometimes leaping on the overweight body and stamping with his feet in a kind of weird and desperate frenzy. And the man beneath him, his flesh and blood was groaning, choking and sobbing and sometimes uttering a faint, strangled cry of "Dad... Dad..." in a tone that meant not so much an appeal for mercy as acknowledgment of the justice of the sentence and admission of guilt, unfathomable bitterness and unanswerable despair.

Suddenly, from outside the limpid voices of the girls were heard again, launching into a challenging, inspiring song, a song about God and His boundless love for mankind – in a solemn melody, redolent with faith.

I leapt up from my seat and gripped the old man's arm gently:

"Please! Have pity on yourself! You're the head of the family and these people are your responsibility. It's a heavy responsibility... don't let yourself down!"

He turned to me, raising a clenched fist with a thin strip of blood adorning it like a ribbon, as if intending to punch me in the face. But something stopped him and suddenly he collapsed on my shoulder and burst into bitter weeping, the weeping of a child abandoned in the darkness of perpetual forest surrounded by menacing sounds and wild beasts. And then, directly behind us, the door swung open with a crash and a big, heavy-fleshed woman, with dishevelled greying hair and a print dress, eyes flashing with all the sparks in the world, was yelling at the top of her voice:

"Bastard! Criminal!" – a shriek fit to tear the Heavens apart – "Shedding the blood of his sons! Choking his daughters! Digging a grave for his wife! I wish the earth would open and swallow you alive! I hope you roast forever in the fires of Hell!"

Israel ran to the woman with cries of "Mother! Mother!" – cries that combined alarm and tenderness with a strange variety of enjoyment – and succeeded in restraining her upraised arms and pushing her back to her room, shutting her in and gripping the outside handle of the door with all his strength, while she went on shouting and cursing and pounding with her big fists on the other side of the door.

The father sprang forward, swooped on Israel and dragged him away from the door and when this swung open wide again, to reveal the big, intimidating woman standing in the frame, he knelt at her feet, pleading:

"I blamed you! I wronged you! Forgive! Forgive me!"

The woman stepped back and slammed the door in his face.

David Farhi remained on his knees, frozen, motionless. Israel stood over him, not saying a word while young Shmuel was still sprawled on the floor muttering in a fading voice: "Dad, Dad!" And all this time – from the balcony outside the sublime sound of pure angelic voices was soaring – a chant without fear, without rejection, without care, without submission.

I turned to Shmuel, helped him to stand up and then sat him down in one of the armchairs. All the while he stared at me with frozen eyes, and before I took my leave of him he called softly:

"Adon..." – and held out a quivering, moist and fleshy hand. His red-speckled eyes smiled at me through the tears as I shook his hand warmly.

I left the room quietly and emerged into the open air, smiled at the girls still singing on the balcony, still hard at work, and bade farewell to Number 2, Menora Street.

NELLY

On entering my office the next morning, I found it already occupied; two men and a young woman were waiting for me. All of them were looking worried, the woman most of all. One of the men, in late middle age, was elegantly dressed and carried a gleaming briefcase. He smiled a greeting at me with well-practised cordiality. The other man was tense for some reason, all emphatic if somewhat artificial pedantry, with a gloomy set of features. A young man, wearing a fashionable suit, he favoured me with a rancorous look, at its fringes a cloud of hostility which he tried to dispel. He almost succeeded:

"Mr... Adon!" he addressed me with enforced solemnity.

"Good morning!" I greeted him brightly.

"Good morning!" the speaker replied, still seeming awkward. He told me his name was Havkin and went on to introduce his fellow-trespassers: Attorney-at-Law Mandelvich and Ms. Nelly.

I shook hands with them politely and with an affable expression, and was still standing when the gentlemen - the lawyer to be precise - deigned to explain:

"Ms. Nelly is the sister of Mr. Valery, who is currently detained on a serious assault charge. Mr. Havkin is her husband, thus Mr. Valery's brother-in-law, and I am his attorney. We have come here on a mission. A mission on behalf of Mr. Valery himself," he chose to explain. "If you are agreeable Sir, we'd like to sit down and discuss it. This can all be cleared up in few minutes. And our apologies for intruding like this, without prior notification. We are acting on the authority of your general secretary, who gave her consent when she was informed of the urgency... Anyway, it's not as if we were guilty of forced entry or unwarranted invasion of privacy, from a formal point of view at least." The lawyer chuckled one of his regulation chuckles, a transparent and dead sound, yet apparently masking some obscure trepidation.

I arranged chairs, dumped the tattered box-file on the law shelf beside me, invited them to sit and sat down myself.

For a long moment there was an awkward silence. The visitors simply didn't know how to begin - or perhaps the question was who should begin.

Ms. Nelly was sending me importunate glances, and when her husband saw this, he glowered; his face lost all its youthful freshness and for a moment he resembled an embittered old man. The lawyer regarded me with a honey-sweet look, the look of a contented cat.

And as so often happens in such situations, all three suddenly started at once, trying simultaneously to set out before me the issue that had brought them here at such an early hour. The result was a noisy outburst, an unintelligible cacophony of truncated sentences. And then the three of them laughed. I laughed too, thereby eliciting a renewed blast of mirth, to the point where even young Havkin's face lost some of its protective stiffness, to be replaced by a faint glow of bashful innocence - his natural expression apparently, but one which caused him such acute embarrassment that he tended whenever possible to obscure it behind a mask of anger.

"If you'll allow me," - the lawyer turned to his entourage, who gave their consent with simultaneous nods, and continued, in a mellifluous tone that was just about tolerable, while casting an eye over my cluttered desk:

"The situation is this: my client, who has been detained for some time..."

"A very long time!" Valery's sister interrupted him, sounding agitated.

"Just so!" the lawyer smiled at her, repeating her words with emphasis: "A very long time, indeed... My client," he resumed, "has applied to the court, through me of course, for his release on bail..."

"And this," the sister interrupted again, this time with a vehemence that left no room for objection, "in view of the discharge from hospital of Amelia and that... manager of hers, on the basis of valid medical reports... I'm sure you've heard about that, Sir..." Again there was a pleading look in her eyes.

"I've heard," I confirmed, seeing fit to add: "But neither of them is fully recovered yet..."

"That's true!" the young lady admitted, lowering her eyes, only to raise them again at once and continue undeterred: "It must not be forgotten that my brother has a son not yet five years old and he misses his father! Amelia can't handle him alone."

"And you're including that argument in your application for bail?" I asked without any special interest.

"Of course!" Mandelvich declared, hurriedly taking up the reins of the conversation again. "It's a routine matter. In fact, every application for bail is a routine matter. The reply to our appeal took some time, but it finally arrived!" He gave me a look which was a strange blend of cordiality, pedantry and confident stewardship - undeniably a professional amalgam.

"Much to our surprise..." Havkin tried to make his voice heard at this point in the proceedings, to remind everyone, including himself, that he was present at the meeting and an active participant.

The lawyer cleared his throat with eloquent affability, glancing alternately at Mr. and Mrs. Havkin, and choosing not to comment on the young man's intervention, he concluded solemnly:

"The reply was positive!"

"He was granted leave for release on bail!" the woman stressed in growing agitation.

"That is the truth!" the lawyer oozed through his practised smile.

"You understand what's being said, Sir!" young Havkin decided to try his luck again and added, before anyone could stop him: "Valery's application for bail has been granted. Are you clear on that?"

It was obvious to all that young Havkin was perturbed by the lack of response on my part. I assured him: "Quite clear."

At this he relaxed in his chair - not that this was a chair designed for uninhibited relaxation - and shot a furtive, sidelong look at his young wife to gauge the effect his words were having on her. She paid no attention to him but went on studying my face with that pained expression of entreaty and appeal.

"Anyway, the application was approved," Mandelvich concluded in a measured tone, "and we went to give him the news and bring him, as they say, from confinement into the open air, the freedom of the outside world!" He added an expansive and theatrical gesture for good measure and smiled ruefully, as if apologising for his poetic outburst. "This was yesterday..."

"Day before yesterday!" cried Havkin, in a further desperate attempt to draw attention to himself, any attention, however dismissive.

"The day before yesterday," the lawyer began in a mild, almost paternal voice, "late in the afternoon, the application was granted. And yesterday morning, we visited the detainee," he continued without looking at young Havkin. "The three of us went together, in high spirits," - focussing his learned gaze for a moment on his hands, placed on the desk-top - "and my client" - he added without emotion, "surprised us in the extreme!" - his thin, sallow, face reliving the experience of the "surprise" for the sake of atmosphere. "He refuses, so he says, to be freed! And this," he added, moving his hands this way and that in a gesture of utter bemusement and helplessness, "is nothing to do with the cost of the bail, which in fact has already been posted, or the fear that he might let himself down and not resist the temptation to do a bunk. Nor is it any kind of aversion to facing the outside world again!" He rubbed his hands together significantly, studied for a moment the expression on my face and continued:

"All these possibilities we put to him, but he rejected all of them one after the other" - his hands demonstrating "helpless" again - "In his own words, he just doesn't want to go free." His hands joined together as if in prayer, lightly touching his thin, pale lips.

"After negotiations that dragged on, intermittently, from yesterday morning to late in the evening, negotiations in which all logical paths were blocked by my client's obstinacy," - the advocate expressed sincere, surprising bemusement - "my client made a proposition and we're clinging to it, like the drowning man clutching the proverbial straw..." - at this point the lawyer chuckled affably, leaned a little towards me, fixed his big, gentle eyes on me and said emphatically:

"He mentioned your name, Sir. Immediately we inquired and pressed and cajoled, and as the stars were coming out he agreed that if you, Mr... Adon - that is your name isn't it?"

"It is."

"If you, Mr. Adon," he repeated for special emphasis, "will confirm and consent, viz - express your opinion that freedom from custody is permissible and even desirable, subject to certain restrictions of course," - Mandelvich didn't forget to mention - "in short, say that he should come out of there, on bail - then he, Valery, will obey you!" The lawyer's eyes scanned my face with a most unusual expression: there was disgust in it and perhaps jealousy as well, and above all else - awe that he himself was ashamed to admit.

"A very strange decision!" was young Havkin's inapposite comment, but this time he wasn't trying to attract attention or make an impression; it was a sincere expression of his thoughts.

"We're not concerned," Valery's sister responded decisively, "with how the decision looks or how it will be judged! For us it's a thread of hope, a way out of the morass! My brother's fate is now in your hands," - she turned to me - "for better or worse!" she stressed and concluded emotionally: "We're begging you, please!"

"We appeal to you most earnestly," the lawyer intervened, as if intent on forestalling any further inappropriate outbursts, "to understand our predicament and in particular the condition of the prisoner, whose response to events is already testimony to some disturbance..." - he laid excessive emphasis on the last word and even nodded his elongated head like one who is confident that his hint has been understood. But young Havkin couldn't resist the temptation to call a spade a spade:

"... of the mind!"

".... which undoubtedly, prison conditions could cause to people who are entirely sane," the lawyer continued, apparently ignoring Havkin's brusque and unhelpful interjection.

"All the more so," - Havkin tried to consolidate his position - "where the balance of the mind has always been in doubt..."

Nelly turned abruptly, and heaving with resentment or fury, or both at once, snapped:

"That's enough bad taste from you, Gil!"

And Gil duly recoiled, deflated, all his anger and animation diffused, and till the end of the conversation dared take no further part in it.

The lawyer meanwhile was warming to his theme, describing "prison conditions" in baleful terms and alluding to Valery's alarming appearance and to the distress he was inflicting, not only upon himself but also, and especially, upon his relatives and friends - and with a jerk of the thumb he made it plain that the reference was to Mrs. Havkin, his sister, who was raising her moist, beseeching eyes to me again.

"Just a little note with your signature - and the man will once more feast his eyes on his free fellowmen, the open spaces that inspire lofty emotions, such as liberty and love, and compassion, enjoy unfettered access to family and friends..." the lawyer insisted in that style of his own which somehow managed to be poetic and lifeless at the same time.

Silence reigned, heavy, oppressive.

I looked up at my guests. With tension that was rising, intensifying, becoming almost tangible - the three of them stared at me, unflinching.

"It's possible," I began calmly, "that it's actually because of those 'open spaces' and 'free fellowmen' and 'unfettered access to family and friends' that the prisoner prefers his cell to the world outside - and I'm not the one to decide for him what's good for him, and what isn't..."

"But he assured us he'd listen to you!" the lawyer cried impatiently, mounting an effective display of disappointment and profound mortification.

"Under duress!" I pointed out, adding: "And that's the last thing I want to be a part of!"

"But he asked..." Valery's sister interposed, in a dejected tone.

"You are the ones who asked," I declared, "pestering him until he had no other way out. It was the only way he could get rid of you, and that's what he had to do... when he realised just how far you are from understanding the depth of the pain that he's in... What's good for you isn't necessarily good for everyone else," I commented and added: "He shook you off. He knew I wouldn't impose anything on him, and that's why he appealed to me."

Again the room was plunged into silence. My visitors froze on their narrow chairs.

The first to recover was the lawyer, raising a wavering smile to his lips and stating, unwillingly almost:

"I've been acting in the explicit interests of my client..."

"There's no one better placed than the person himself to know what's good for him and what isn't," I answered him calmly, "and it behoves nobody to interfere in his business, trespass in the innermost recesses of his heart, and least of all, seek to influence his will and his aspirations."

"You disappoint us!" - the lawyer steadied his voice and wiped off the faint smile, and challenging me to reply, he added provocatively:

"This is inconsiderate behaviour bordering on cruelty!"

Although the demand for clarification and justification of my position could not have been more explicit, I chose not to respond. The others had no choice but to lapse into silence themselves. Young Gil seemed to recede even further into his seat while Nelly, her head between her hands, was pressing hard on her temples, as if her brain was liable to explode and shatter her skull. Finally, she broke her silence, saying in a surprisingly even tone:

"Would you be willing to see my brother and talk to him, Sir?"

"Gladly!" I replied

The three of them gaped at me in utter bewilderment. Young Havkin tried to catch the eyes of his colleagues, perhaps trying to gauge just how impressed they were so he could arrange his own features accordingly, but it didn't work.

I phoned the chief secretary and announced that I was taking the rest of the day off. I stood up and left my office with them.

Sitting facing me in the corner of the tall, dark cell with its bare concrete walls, a warder peering in occasionally through a peephole - Valery looked up and exclaimed gloomily, his voice like the sound of nails scraping a tin can:

"So, you've been pressganged too!"

"No," I replied. "I came willingly."

"What for?" - he stared at me with bitter, weary eyes, eyes in the process of submitting to some hidden enemy in a tussle that had lasted, it seemed, way beyond any reasonable time-span. His hair was close-cropped; the expression on his face preserved a kind of mask of fatigue, behind which something heavy and dark was seething.

"A visit."

"Is there any point?" he shot at me from under the leaden cloud of contorted brows.

"There is!" I responded brightly.

"So what is it?" he persisted.

"Sometimes," I began calmly, " - very often in fact, man forgets himself, meaning... his image."

"What image?" - he scanned the lines of my face grimly.

"The image of God in him," I insisted in a tone allowing for no further interruption and continued: "He imagines in his mind that he's a predatory beast or a vile insect. It's then his friend's job to come and remind him that it's not true."

"How's his friend going to do that?" - he demanded to know, without any softening of the lines on his face or the harsh timbre of his voice.

"It's not a question of doing," I replied.

"What then?" he asked at once, like a hunter in relentless pursuit of his quarry.

"Being there."

"And if the friend himself isn't immune to the predatory beast or vile insect syndrome?" he asked curiously, the seething behind the mask of fatigue approaching the point of climax.

"No one is immune," I replied confidently.

"You said that sometimes a man imagines to himself..." - a note of derision creeping into his hoarse voice.

"Imagines. Yes, that's what I said."

He remained seated, his body shaking, his gaze fixed on the dim, filthy floor - in silence. Suddenly he sprang to his feet, stooped, grabbed the simple chair he had been sitting on and with alarming ferocity, hurled it against the thick concrete wall, before charging like a wounded bull and butting his head on the same wall, falling flat on his back, then sitting up in the dirt, striking a strange posture, as if he was trying to figure something out. When he rose slowly to his feet, there was blood streaming down both his cheeks and dripping from his chin, falling to the floor in a steady cascade of heavy droplets

All this happened within seconds, before I had time to reach him and restrain him. The warder was too late to stop him too; he rushed into the cell and together we pinioned him in our arms. In the end, we succeeded in pacifying him. He breathed evenly and looked at us with a new expression in his eyes - sober and rational:

"I'm sorry!" he said, "I'm very sorry!" - his sorrow sounding profound and sincere - "I imagined myself a predatory beast or a vile insect and I couldn't bear myself! Now I see - I'm neither of those things! I'm ashamed of what I did. Tell my family I'm accepting the offer of bail and I'm coming out..."

About a week after the incident, I was told by one of our employees that Valery had been released from prison. Various rumours were going about, and opinions were divided: some alleged that he was adamantly refusing to see his wife, who was looking for reconciliation, while according to others, the opposite was the case - he wanted to see his wife and was sending a constant stream of intermediaries to see her, intermediaries renowned for their powers of persuasion, but the very mention of her husband's name was enough to traumatise her...

"It seems," commented another employee, a woman reckoned to be astute as well as eloquent, "he'll always remind her of the assault..."

A few days later, Mrs. Nelly Havkin, Valery's sister, showed up again. As in our previous encounter, she was waiting for me at an early hour of the morning, this time not in my office but outside the door.

I opened the door for her, offered her a seat, sat down facing her and waited for her to speak.

"First of all," she began, "I must thank you again, Sir. I'm very, very grateful to you!"

"Our time is precious," I responded somewhat dryly, determined to stem the flow of pointless platitudes. "Let's get to the point, shall we?" I spoke in a softer tone of voice, but she could be in no doubt I meant what I said.

"Yes, yes..." she replied hastily, rather flustered, anxious not to forfeit my sympathy and - more important still - my consent to the request she was about to make. "You're absolutely right, Sir!" She bowed her head submissively.

"There's no need to be quite so formal!" I smiled brightly, a smile not lacking in firmness. "We can leave that to the professionals!" Seeing her perplexed, inquiring gaze I explained: "Lawyers and the like..."

She relaxed, absorbing my smile. Her own features reflected the smile and it was a charming and endearing sight, its origins in truth and its intentions - pure.

"I'm sure you know, Mr... Adon..." - she made the usual mistake of combining the two*, but I didn't interrupt her and she went on to say: "Valery, my brother, has come home."

"I didn't know, as it happens, but I'm glad to hear it!"

"His first day out of prison - he went straight home!"

"More good news!" I replied, encouraging her to continue.

"He asked for Amelia's forgiveness... got quite emotional about it... stumbling over his words... obviously meaning what he said. And

---

* "Adon" is both "Master" and "Mister" in Hebrew

by way of reply - she fell into his arms... she was in tears too... begging him to forgive her. And the son, who was an eye-witness to all of it, was in an emotional state as well... Since then, they've been living in a sort of quiet happiness, like they've never known before, a rare sort of happiness. A wonderful relationship..." - she sighed and went on: "And then Amelia decided to go to the manager and ask him to drop the charges. She'd cancelled her own claims even before my brother got out of jail. Quietly, of course, without Valery knowing and after consulting me." She gave me a long look and then continued in a more sombre tone:

"I drove her there myself, to see the manager. I waited downstairs. She came back fuming. He refused, Mr. Adon!" she cried, a cry rising from the depths of the heart: "He refused point-blank! He's all rage and resentment... and it didn't do poor Amelia any good reminding him of the past and everything that he... how can I put it?" she wondered, looking at me with a display of helplessness that I responded to:

"Enjoyed with her?"

She blushed, lowered her gaze and went on earnestly:

"Nothing helped! Not even the child - whose father will be thrown into prison - even mentioning him got no response. And the praise and the compliments that she paid the manger - his noble qualities, his generous personality, his dignity - it was like battering against a brick wall! Amelia says he's never behaved in such an offensive manner before, she's never seen him like this..."

"What does she mean?" I asked.

"According to Amelia," Nelly carried on with her account, her voice both alert and anxious, "he's changed completely, as if he's taken off a mask. He's being mean and petty... you'd almost think he was retarded. Imagine him - stamping his foot, the undamaged one that is, and barking incessantly: 'Let him rot in jail, let him rot! That's what he deserves! I'm not interested in him, or you or the kid, or the past we shared!' And with that he turned his back on her..."

"She's very hurt!" my guest declared indignantly - "But her feelings aren't the issue here, and they're not what she's concerned about. She's worried about the fate of her husband... she loves him now more than ever before. She says her eyes have been opened, and she means it too!" Nelly stated emphatically, solemnly scrutinising the expression on my face, which hadn't changed at all.

"All she wants at the moment," she added, "is just to live at his side until her last day or until his, be a dutiful and exemplary wife... and suddenly - he's about to be taken away from her."

"Sent to prison, you mean?" - I decided it was time to call a spade a spade.

"Just that!" -she was pleased by my response, showing that I had paid attention to her rambling story, and hastened to add: "What I need to know, Adon, is - may I appeal to you on his behalf?"

I nodded in assent and she continued:

"If the manager drops his charges..."

"There will still be an official indictment against him," I reminded her and she hastened to reply:

"Mandelvich, our attorney, is sure he can get him off with a very short sentence, on top of what he's already served... if the manager will only drop his charges the way Amelia has done. Mandelvich says that in the circumstances as they stand - meaning the family unit that's been restored, and Valery's appeal for clemency, and the deep and sincere remorse he's expressed for his actions - it's inconceivable he'd be locked up again for any length of time... but if the manager sticks to his guns and doesn't give way..." - and again Nelly fixed those big, pleading eyes on me, holding my gaze with unflinching determination.

"You mean - you want me to try and sweet-talk the manager and get him to change his mind?" I suggested calmly, smiling.

Her eyes lit up with delight and a kind of relief spread across her tense features:

"I wouldn't put it quite like that!" she declared in a brisk tone of voice and added: " Just visit him! The way you visited my brother before... I thoroughly respect your view that our will shouldn't be imposed on others... but go to see him, that's all I ask..." There was entreaty in her eyes again, aggressive entreaty almost, as the young woman concluded: "You're my last hope!"

"You're learning how to play the game, Mrs. Havkin!" I chuckled.

She stiffened for a moment, taken aback, and then, recognising the humorous tone she melted, and laughed with me, her voice surprisingly guttural.

THE MANAGER

At an early hour of the afternoon, I went to visit the manager. He received me with a stiff, severe expression. On his crown, he still wore some kind of sticking-plaster, and he walked with the aid of one crutch. He invited me to sit and immediately launched into a loud tirade:

"I suppose you're another bloody go-between!" - his voice sibilant and chirpy, as in the past.

"No," I replied, "I'm one of the bell-ringers!"

He was surprised, opening his eyes wide, some of the severity withdrawing from them:

"That's a new one from you!" he exclaimed, almost with a smile. "What are you talking about? What 'bells' do you reckon you're ringing?"

"Alarm-bells!" I declared.

"What's the emergency that brings you round here, ringing your alarm-bells at me?"

"It has to do with the soul," I explained.

"The soul - that's a complicated business!" He hesitated, lowered his eyes behind the thick lenses of his glasses and, some of his stiffness dissolving, began pacing - with a slight limp and without recourse to the crutch - around the spacious room, where a bright but gentle light filtered in through massive windows. It was then that I noticed his right hand was encased in some kind of apparatus, covered by the sleeve of his expensive shirt. Suddenly he turned abruptly and with a sharpness of tone that distorted his face, a voice I hadn't heard before, cried:

"I've made my decision, I've stamped my seal... and there's no going back on it! I'm not a puppy, to be enticed by a juicy bone into jumping through burning hoops! I've had enough! They're pissing me off!" he hissed, his bushy moustache vibrating,

"Who's pissing you off?" I asked with interest, in a steady voice, not to be easily deflected. He sensed this, scanned me with a baleful look and replied, evidently with some reluctance:

"That woman... Amelia... the lunatic!" he cried, some distant spark of compassion flickering in his voice, "And that man's sister, the bimbo... quite attractive... what's her name?" He racked his brains, in mounting rage.

"Nelly," I reminded him.

"Nelly!" He reverted to that sharp tone of voice, repellent and unfamiliar, and suddenly abandoned it, stared at me from beneath quivering eyebrows and asked forcefully, brusquely almost: "She's come whining to you as well, has she?" And without waiting for the answer, which he already knew, he ranted on: "You as well! Anyway, she... however you want to put it... she's putting all her charms on the line, just to get her brother out of a scrape..." - he seemed to relax for a brief moment, but his eyes were still blazing: "The question is," he added in a solid, metallic sort of voice, not his own, "where does this willingness come from? Is it all genuine and pure, the justification of the end, over and above the means, or is there coquetry in it too, a kind of base, carnal instinct - to demonstrate power, convince, subdue! On the outside," he declaimed, "everything's fine, everything's innocent, and the signs can be read either way. But I," he was approaching me again, his limp heavier now and more pronounced: "I'm a guy with experience!" - he set off again towards the far side of the spacious room, lit from every angle with light that was sharp and dazzling, yet at the same time clear and captivating.

"I know what she's doing it for!" he declared, waving his hand, his back to me. "Her darling brother!" he scoffed and added, irrelevantly, in a lowered voice: "This I shall never understand! In fact - I do understand, but I'm shocked! Disgusted would be a better description...."

He reached the furthest corner, repeated his abrupt turn, almost like a sentry on parade, and with steadier and less halting gait came so close to me his heavy, laboured breathing was almost tangible. He leaned towards me, continuing with a sorrowful sigh:

"And... attracted! You get it? Attracted!" he declared with extravagant emphasis, unfathomable terror in his eyes and his whole body convulsed: "Attracted like metal to a strong magnet, like a slave in thrall to his master! What have you to say about that?" he asked, straightening up, in a tone that was tense but no longer strident, and waited for my answer. A light green flame danced behind his spectacles.

"Maybe you're wrong," was my calm response.

"What do you mean?" - he raised his eyebrows.

"Maybe you're imagining all this."

"Why should I do that?" he protested.

"Because of the attraction you mentioned."

He uttered a short and bitter laugh, held out his hand and reached for his crutch, and still standing facing me, leaning on the crutch, said with undiminished bitterness but with an air of confident authority:

"The opposite is the case! She or they," he explained, "whichever you prefer, she - that woman, or they - women in general - sense a diabolical attraction and they play with it, exploit it - all the way!" he insisted - "to bring me to my knees, to defeat me..." He fingered his moustache which was quivering again.

"That's a totally subjective view," I commented dispassionately.

He scanned me with a look of tolerant disdain, alert, cleansed of bitterness:

"You," he began with almost fatherly authority, "with all the respect due to age and daring exploits..." he strayed from the subject "...Separated from your wife... all credit to you for that... only a true man, a man of stature, is capable of that! I wouldn't be capable of that, I wouldn't dare! My wife deserted me once for... for two weeks... no, it was ten days and I... nearly went out of my mind!" Then he remembered and returned to the subject: "With all respect for your sterling qualities - when it comes to the absurd life that he and she are leading between them - you're no more than a child!"

Unimpressed by this speech I asked: "Which 'life' are you referring to?"

"The life of 'relationships' that for some reason they call 'love' and in fact are nothing more than dark servitude and the crude destruction of anything bearing the faintest resemblance to 'love'. Life of vice, I'd call it!" he mocked. "And anyway, what is love?" He looked up with a sudden movement, fixing me with sharp, inquisitive eyes, leaning on his crutch.

"Freedom," I declared without hesitation.

"Ha ha ha ha!" - he erupted into peals of spontaneous laughter which wracked the body still leaning on the crutch. The outburst was so strong and unrestrained that it seemed he was liable to collapse at any moment. His thick moustache vibrated to the rhythm of his mirth. He calmed down eventually, the palpitations mastered, and he steadied his weight on the crutch - half of it polished wood and the other half aluminium.

"You're a child and you'll always be a child!" he declared with a dismissive gesture of the hand, suddenly turning thoughtful, his eyes staring at the walls of his spacious room, and adding in a half-voice, a whisper almost:

"And maybe you're right... If love really exists, if this concept isn't just hypocrisy, devoid of any content - it has to be what you mentioned - freedom!" And then he turned his face back to me, with a look of bemusement.

"It turns out," he added in a voice that had thickened for some reason, "that love does indeed exist, but it's the property of children alone!" He grimaced sourly and became pensive again, pacing around the open space of the room. In fact, he made a broad circuit around the chair that I was sitting in - a big armchair upholstered in some expensive, iridescent fabric, silk perhaps, and contriving simultaneously to be both rigid and pliable, so comfortable you could think yourself disembodied. Eventually, he came to a stop beside me.

"And perhaps," he said, "the opposite is the case: it's the infantile ones who will never attain love... and they are the decisive majority of humanity... the herd!" he exclaimed emphatically and added: "And the one reckoned a child in the eyes of the herd - he is the one who is truly aware, entitled to love, which is - freedom..." And suddenly he broke out into a renewed eruption of rolling laughter, until he was forced to lean with his free hand on the back of the armchair.

When he'd recovered himself, he went and pulled some cord beside the big central window and the curtain withdrew to reveal glass doors, a broad, oval-shaped balcony and beyond it a panoramic view of the big city, with a lifeless strip of sea to the right.

"I forgot to offer you refreshment! You drink tea don't you? I thought so - tea!" He was gratified by this insight and he added as if to himself: "What kind of a host am I! Since you arrived..."

And sure enough, tea was brought to us, served by a liveried retainer.

"He's first class!" the manager chirped. "Better than a dozen women! I hire him from a local hotel to work half-days. The insurance contributes something," he saw fit to point out.

We sipped the hot, refreshing liquid in leisurely fashion.

"You're a strange creature!" the manager commented calmly, his thoughtful gaze focussed on the oval table, an impressive mosaic-topped table. "Wherever you go you sow unease, tension and confusion, and in the end, it all turns into something lukewarm…" he shot me a look combining disdain and uncertainty in equal measure, and hastened to add: "No, not lukewarm! I said that deliberately, to offend you… but there's no point, you're not offended… I can tell… you're not taking offence, it isn't in your nature!" he declared, sounding disappointed, and added: "There's a sort of serene light that radiates from you, something not of this world… and in the end - all that unease and confusion gets refined by some arcane process of remorse and is converted into contentment and satisfaction… if you like - a kind of ecstasy… Don't answer, don't protest!" - he held up an admonitory hand although I had not the slightest intention of answering or protesting. His words had no impact on me whatsoever. And after a short silence, broken only by noisy slurping and the arrival of another round of tea, courtesy once again of the liveried flunkey who brought in a full tea-service this time, the whole works - he spoke again:

"That guy - Amelia's husband I mean - Valery!" he remembered, "he came to see me. Some time ago, here. I wasn't sure whether to receive him or not, and before I could make up my mind he came bursting in, trespassing in fact… though it's fair to say I made no effort to eject him. He knelt down, here… yes," he stressed, while stealing a glance at the expression on my face, "knelt down in front of me and pleaded for mercy and forgiveness. More than that - he wanted me to hit him with the crutch, this one here," - he pointed to his crutch, half polished wood and half aluminium - "he bent his head submissively and waited for the blow to fall…" The manager stared at a distant point on the wall behind me, and added:

"I thought about it, weighed up the whole thing thoroughly… in the end, I decided not to hit him. You see," he turned to me, "I wanted to hurt him as much as I possibly could! Real, corrosive, lasting pain, that would give him no respite as long as he lived… and I decided that to attain my goal, hurt him to my satisfaction, I shouldn't hit him! Anyway, not with the crutch, not a simple physical blow, like the ones he inflicted!"

The manager leaned forward, took a gulp of his tea and replaced the cup on the table, then maintaining the same bowed posture, accentuated this time by a sigh, he wiped his lips with his hand and went on:

"And then I invited him to sit, and that's what he did. In the same place you're sitting," - he pointed to the big armchair - "and he pleaded with me, real pleading, that only a man worthy of the name is capable of! Not like his sister. Like a real man he pleaded with me, that on no account was I to drop the charges against him... because he said he deserved the punishment and he was prepared to go through with it..." The manager returned to his steaming cup and took deep, pensive gulps from it, his hand shaking.

"That was one request at least," I commented solemnly, "that you could comply with!"

"No!" the manager exclaimed, slamming the quivering cup down on the table and adding brusquely. "Yesterday I dropped the charge. Officially. To hurt him!" he snapped.

I stared down at the thick, fitted carpet and made no response at all. The silence continued. I pondered my next move and decided to get up and leave. When he saw me stirring, he stopped me with an outstretched hand, the one encased in some apparatus hidden by the sleeve of his expensive shirt.

"Just a moment!" There was fear in his voice, as well as entreaty.

I sat down again.

"And the result - do you know the result?"

"No," I replied.

"Instead of the relief and elation I expected - I'm tormented by a new pain such as I never knew before!" He scanned my face with a demented look. "I thought you'd sense it, you'd feel it," he complained, adding by way of clarification: "The moment you came in, you were talking about the soul! Well, my soul's in torment... it hasn't experienced its revenge! This isn't revenge..." he sighed, with a gloom-laden glance at me - "In fact, there's no such thing as revenge. Just lasting, endless self-torture... torture of the suffering flesh..."

"I thought of changing my mind... about dropping the charges I mean... it turned out I left it too late. Anyway, that's what my attorney told me, and I believe him." He sighed again, and without looking at me he exclaimed softly but forcefully, in a voice distorted by bitterness:

"I feel cheated! And hurting, hurting, hurting! How much I hurt!

It isn't the limp or the fractures, nor the crack in the skull - but the self, the soul... I'm tormented by a despicable desire to go to those two, Amelia and her husband, and apologise to them... It's such a strong impulse...there's no respite from it... for the moment, I can resist it. Can you do me a favour?" His tormented eyes fixed on mine.

"Willingly!" I replied.

"Tell them to stop coming!" - and in a more even tone - "I'm not sick. I want a break to think things over...consider... plan my future. Sometimes it seems to me I'm about to drop dead or go crazy!"

I promised to do as he asked.

"And you," - he scanned me with a prolonged look through his gleaming spectacles, as I stood at the door about to take my leave of him - "I don't want you coming round here either!" Here for some reason he saw fit to add: "Anyway, everything you wanted has been done. I've dropped the charges and there's no going back on it now!"

"I won't come," I assured him and added with a smile: "But remember, I'm your friend and if ever you want me - don't hesitate to turn to me!"

In the event, such an approach was not to come. About a week later, the manager returned to work and he took great care not to cross my path or address me directly. I received his instructions through his secretaries and sometimes - in typed memoranda bearing the official letterhead of the institution, rubber-stamped with his signature.

THE LAMP SHOP

At the end of the working day, as usual, I made my way towards the sea-shore. This time I deviated slightly from the normal route and entered the narrow alleyways of the market for ornamental bargains, known by the picturesque name of the "flea market".

There was a lot of commotion here, noise and bustle and overcrowding. Most of those visiting the market were tourists, with a minority of local bargain hunters who were likely to be disappointed; whenever a real "bargain" came their way, the crafty stall-holders charged a premium price for it.

I turned towards the broadest alleyway, skirting the market on the northern side, with a strip of sky visible high above it, and heading in the direction of the nearby hill, its lower slopes washed by the pellucid waters of the sea.

On both sides stood broad shop-fronts, displaying old and restored furniture, antiquated electrical equipment, domestic stoves, defective washing-machines and reconditioned freezers. There were also shops here selling carpets - old, new and renovated - and all kinds of lamps and lampshades, manufactured in-house. From one of these shops, through the thick display window, someone waved at me and seemed to be beckoning.

I approached and recognised Israel Farhi among the shadows of the interior, still waving in a gesture of friendly welcome, a broad smile lighting up his face. I entered. Two of his sisters were sitting there on big, antique chairs, at their feet - a pile of painted glass disks, the same shades that they had been making on the balcony of their house.

"Good afternoon!" - Israel rose to meet me, affably extending a huge hand, and then introduced his sisters:

"The two oldest!" he said emphatically, telling me their names which at the time I didn't take in. We shook hands.

"Gabi!" Israel shouted in a tone of unmistakable authority and from the depths of the shop, or more precisely - from the hidden interior, separated from the retail section by a thick curtain the colour of faded gold, a man appeared. He was thin and in his late thirties, with wisps of curly hair protruding from beneath a simple cloth cap, shaped like a tarbush, the type worn by convicts or factory workers. His face was smeared with black industrial oil, as were his overalls, of indeterminate original colour, his cap, his coarse shoes and his hands.

"A chair for the gentleman!" Israel commanded.

Gabi disappeared, returning a moment later with a gilt-trimmed chair which he placed beside me, one of those reconditioned chairs that the market was awash with.

"Fetch four cups of tea and some lokum!" Israel went on to order and Gabi, who seemed to be the general factotum, acknowledged these instructions with a slight nod of the head. Before leaving the shop he directed a strange, prolonged and mournful stare at the pure face of the older sister. The girl remained motionless and unresponsive, oblivious to this attention - or pretending to be so.

"What do you think of the shop?" Israel turned to me, suppressing a faint note of pride, his eyes sparkling.

"It's spacious," I replied laconically.

Evidently he was expecting something more fulsome than this, at the very least, a more enthusiastic tone of voice. But he realised he had to be satisfied with my statement, and he turned to another subject.

"My sisters" - he pointed to them - "bring in all the merchandise themselves!"

"Not too heavy for you?" I asked the two young women, eyeing the pile of glass at their feet.

"Not particularly," the older replied, somewhat taller and thinner than her sister.

"We're used to it!" added the latter, in a ringing voice.

"All that way?" I persisted.

"There's a bus!" Israel interposed.

"You take all that glass - on a bus?" I pointed to the impressive pile.

"We manage," the younger of the two smiled at me again, a smile that was friendly and at the same time, cautious and inquisitive. Her older sister, by way of contrast, had a smile that was open, broad and radiant; there was even something bold about it.

"We're happy to contribute to the family income!" she said and added: "In fact, we enjoy it!"

"What do you enjoy about it?" I asked with interest.

"Getting out, meeting people, fresh air, the clear, open sky..." She seemed to be speaking with some reluctance.

"As if!" - the brother chuckled, disguising his outburst behind a veil of humour.

"Oh," I responded, "fresh air, clear sky, meetings - look for these outside, and you'll never find them!" My words surprised the young ladies, and evidently made an impression on them. As one, they both turned to look at me, earnestly, without the slightest hint of jocularity, youthful mischief or feminine wiles; their gaze was deep, calculated, slightly chilly. Even Israel, their brother, was affected by the sudden change in the atmosphere, shifting in his chair uneasily, embarrassed perhaps, and asking in a thick, husky voice:

"What do you mean?"

"Those who search outside," I explained, "never find what they're looking for; what you discover inside - that stays with you forever... in fact," I stressed, "it is you!" - and seeing his look of blank incomprehension I added by way of clarification: "Happiness that has its roots outside isn't real happiness, and it ends in nausea, grief and disappointment; happiness that has its roots inside - that's real happiness and there's no grief in it, no nausea or disappointment."

He hadn't yet managed to digest my words, or maybe he hadn't taken them in at all. Unlike his sisters - who were following me with mounting awareness and giving me their undivided attention.

"Your sisters," I chose to point out, "understand what I'm on about."

"Yes," he retorted with a trace of bitterness, "my sisters would understand these things... because they studied at the Mission. To this day they're getting visits from one of the teachers there, a priest or a monk... Not that I've anything against that," he hastened to add, "but that guy... what's the word? - Detached from life, from everyday life I mean, detached from reality!" He was relieved, having found the word he was searching for.

"You couldn't be more wrong!" the older of his sisters responded with remarkable equanimity. "There is no life outside that man, no such thing as everyday life, or reality either."

Gabi came in, carrying a shining brass tray, with four cups of tea in decorative metal holders of silvery hue. There were sachets of sugar too, lemon-slices in a saucer and four lokums on frilly paper napkins. A low table was brought out and all those present, except

Gabi who had disappeared again into the gloom behind the curtain, helped themselves to tea.

"Of course," the younger sister returned to the subject, which was clearly still exercising her, "saying the words, hearing them and understanding them - aren't enough."

"What are you talking about?" - Israel tensed again, putting down the half-chewed lokum and the tea cup, and leaning towards me he remarked in a low voice, as if someone was eavesdropping and he didn't want to be overheard: "My sisters have some very weird ideas...you know, asceticism and monasteries and all that stuff... and it's all down to the influence of the Mission!" he concluded with petulance bordering on rage.

"What about the influence of the home?" I asked.

The two maidens smiled a secretive but perceptible smile.

"Influence of the home?" Israel was perplexed. "What are you trying to say?"

"That the basis of outside influence is the home," I replied and added: "It's very easy to blame the outside, and the real question is" - and I paused for emphasis - "does it help?"

No one answered.

The ensuing silence wasn't exactly tense - nor was it the pleasurable silence which is the precious reward of a shared state of mind. Israel seemed to be growing increasingly uncomfortable and his foot could be heard sporadically tapping the floor - something of which he was probably unaware. Eventually he pulled himself together and said, quite irrelevantly:

"That one," - he gestured with his chin towards the curtain that hid some kind of workshop from the view of casual customers - "that one," he repeated, clearly referring to Gabi, his factotum - "has got a beady eye!"

"What's he got a beady eye on?" the older girl responded immediately, with unexpected vehemence.

"You know perfectly well!" Israel grinned, gratified that he had put an end to the awkward silence, and confronted by the tense and quizzical look in his sister's eyes he hastened to explain: "The shop, of course!" Seeing that the effect of his words had been to dissolve the tension in her eyes and raise a tolerant smile to her lips, he added, as if intent on pumping up the stress-levels again:

"He fancies himself as the boss! Reckons the shop should be his!

As a matter of fact" - Israel pondered - "he deserves it! Hardworking, understands the business, and he's got a flair for commerce as well. Maybe one day there'll be big changes round here!" He grinned again and added mischievously: "When I get tired of it!" And having studied the impression his words had made he concluded triumphantly: "We'll just have to wait and see!"

We sipped slowly from the tea that was cooling. We finished off the lokum, wiping our hands on the paper napkins provided.

I rose to my feet, meaning to say farewell to my hosts.

"We've listened to you with great interest!" the older sister responded warmly, shaking my hand firmly, "And we're very glad to have seen you here today. If you should happen to be in our neighbourhood, please come and see us. Don't hesitate!"

I was on my way out of the shop when Israel, so bemused and distracted that he'd forgotten to return my benediction, suddenly gathered his wits together, just in time, and dashed forward, catching up with me in the doorway. He gripped my shoulder firmly, in a gesture of mutual amity and understanding and muttered confidentially:

"What happened at my house - forget it! Don't be too quick to jump to conclusions, please," he implored me and added: "My father is a wonderful man! But," - and here he fixed me with a look that demanded his words be understood and taken with absolute seriousness - "even a wonderful man makes mistakes sometimes and goes off the rails... It doesn't happen..." he began and corrected himself - "...very often. But you," he urged, "don't take too much notice. It isn't such a big deal. And as my sisters said - come and see us, any time. I can tell you've hit it off with them... So, come round! Things will look different! For the time being - Goodbye!" He parted from me and disappeared again into his shop.

OLD AHARON

I left the crowded, noisy alleyways of the market behind me and with light heart climbed the solid back of the hill overlooking the sea. I lingered there for a while, and by the time I returned to the hubbub of the world, the sun had set and I was greeted by the gentle gusts of an evening breeze, bearing with it the aroma of roasting meat and oriental spices.

I went down to Rahamim's café. I was surprised to find the place packed with fishermen, filling all the available space even though this wasn't their usual time.

"This evening we're going out early!" said one of them, correctly interpreting the puzzled look on my face, and he added: "The sea's calm, the wind's dropped and maybe fortune will smile on us!"

"This last two weeks the nets have been empty," complained another.

"Not quite empty!" Raphael interposed, taking a noisy gulp from his coffee cup, its dark contents apparently retaining their original heat. Not content with this comment he added: "It doesn't do to complain!"

"So as not to annoy the gods of fishing?" asked young Avinoam, partly curious, partly in jest.

"To stop young whippersnappers shooting their mouths off!" Raphael answered him, adamantly but without anger.

"Do you believe in superstitions?" Avinoam persisted.

Raphael didn't answer. His cup, clasped in his sinewy hand, looked smaller than before.

The big, pear-shaped electric light, hanging from the ceiling of the café and encased in a dark shade, like a barber's basin, swung gently in the breeze. Its lustre plucked gigantic shadows from the vaulted walls, set them dancing for a moment, then sent them back.

Another answered in Raphael's place:

"Any fisherman worthy of the name, one with experience, that is - always believes in superstitions!" And he went on to explain: "The sea isn't a solid body, and there's nothing solid about making a living from it either... There's no stability there and it seems it's all dependent on the whim of somebody..." and as no one interrupted him but on the contrary - all were listening attentively, he added: "Seafaring is detached from the certainties of dry land, you become a toy in the hands of unseen forces and it's they that decide your fate... for better or worse... You're helpless!" he declared in a faintly mournful tone, pausing for thought and surveying his still attentive audience, before continuing in a more upbeat vein: "Of course, the sea has a special charm... how shall I put it... the charm of risk, or perhaps that should be - the charm of gambling. The fisherman," he asserted with confidence, "is nothing but a compulsive gambler. He forgets everything - family, friends, the pleasures, great and small, that the dry land has to offer...he's chock-full of weird and wonderful superstitions, just like the compulsive gambler..."

"There are fishermen who won't board a boat without spitting three times to the left, for protection against the evil eye!" another spoke up in support of the previous speaker, an older seafarer, his thick moustache flecked with grey streaks and on his head a crumpled peaked cap.

This was greeted by a noisy but good-natured chorus of laughter. Everyone laughed, without exception. And the one who had previously compared fishing to gambling fever, turned to the moustachioed fisherman:

"You're talking about yourself!"

"I never said I was any different from the rest!" The speaker sounded offended, but at the same time he showed a smiling face and joined in the general laughter. Then he took a sip from his cup, set it down on the table and added in his thick, resonant voice:

"Gabriel, the one who's had no luck for two whole weeks and had to mortgage his boat - he's going out tonight with Crazy Nono..."

"Why's he doing that?" Avinoam wanted to know.

"They say that Nono brings luck," was the dignified reply. "If it comes to that, any lunatic brings luck!"

"You believe that?" a shrill voice was heard from the far corner of the saloon, the speaker hidden in the shadow of the wall.

"Yes!" declared the moustachioed man with surprising fervour and he explained: "The true lunatic is a pure soul; there's no malice in him, no greed, and he doesn't know what hatred is... He's always happy, the pure happiness of childhood! Give him a penny - he'll be glad. Take it back - he won't be angry or bear a grudge. Curse him -

he'll laugh. Bless him - he'll laugh. In the genuine lunatic, there's something holy!"

"That and more," the shrill voice from the shadows rang out again in the void: "The lunatic is a happy man. Always happy, that is! Whether he's in the kind of pain that drives rational people out of their minds, or having fun - it's the same happiness" he insisted and added: "Torments don't touch him! He's content with what there is. He's not out for flattery, property, ships. The whole world is his home and his life - a miraculous voyage on an ocean of bliss. Everything about him is simple, clean..."

"That's why they say he brings luck?" young Avinoam asked - or stated a fact.

"He brings luck!" the moustachioed man insisted stubbornly. "And anyway," he added with astonishing equanimity, "in this world it's better to be insane than normal..."

"What do you mean by that?" Raphael asked with interest.

"The whole of this world is one big pain, it's torment and depression," the other declared in a steady, almost metallic voice. "We don't know who created it, or why it was created this way. I'm told it serves as a refinery, it's designed for the purification of the soul... and I ask - couldn't some other method be devised for this purification? This way of doing things - through suffocation and the torments of Hell and chronic depression - does the Creator of the world think it's all right? The truth is - there's no end to the options open to him!"

Silence fell. No one stirred. The words spoken by the moustachioed man, infused with such sincere feeling and perhaps, personal experience of prolonged, debilitating pain, of despair even - affected everyone. Not a sound was heard, not so much as the tinkling of a coffee cup.

The evening thickened, and the light of the big lamp grew brighter and more intense. From behind his counter, Rahamim stared out into the void of the café, densely packed as it was, as if he had been transported to a strange place, to another planet, and he was frozen in limbo, waiting with anguish and dread for someone to decide his fate.

"Pain and suffering, disappointment, despair and death" - I suddenly heard my voice saying, loudly and clearly - "have their origin in mankind and not in the Creator of the world, who is love itself."

"What kind of love are you talking about?" - the shrill voice objected again from the shadows.

"Divine, true love that brings happiness, freedom and eternal life," I declared and added: "Love doesn't impose itself on anyone. Anyone who doesn't want it will be left without it."

Silence returned to the café for a long moment, as all those present slowly digested the words that they had heard.

"And I say," the moustachioed man broke the silence in a more stubborn, petulant tone, "the best thing in this world - is to be insane! Not to know depression, disappointment, despair!"

"Let's all go mad then!" suggested Raphael, partly in fun and partly in protest: "So we can endure the sorrows of this mad world that, according to this gentleman - we're responsible for creating!" He suddenly turned to face me with an emphatic movement, and then all those present were staring at me with inquisitive, assertive eyes. Rahamim came to life behind his counter, lighting a cigarette and steadily inhaling smoke. He looked at me with a hint of shame and yet at the same time, like all the others, his mottled eyes demanded a satisfactory answer.

"He's right," I indicated the moustachioed man with a movement of the head: "To go mad for God, as is written, is to be seen in the eyes of those in thrall to this world - as madmen. If only it was within your power to break through the barrier of worldly illusions, and be seen in the world's eyes as lunatics!"

Those sitting there had barely had time to digest my words when the moustachioed man was speaking again without addressing anyone in particular, his eyes on the wall and his voice strident:

"When my father died, he was screaming with the pain, he was in agony! And the doctors came and tried to console us, saying there were worse things than this... that's the mind-numbing consolation that the world has to offer!" he cried in anguish, and without waiting for any response he added: "So what's better than that, and where is it? - or are those just empty words?"

"Don't you go losing your mind, Aharon!" his neighbour at the table turned to him, his voice persuasive and impassioned.

"I wish I would go mad!" Aharon cried in bitterness bordering on dejection and added: "The doctors are telling me I'll go the same way as my father. And already the pains are attacking..." He shifted his gaze to the faces of his audience and continued: "All of you, going out in your boats - for the sea, the open spaces, the stars, deep sky, clear air... and for me all these things are one big darkness and unremitting pain... sometimes it's acute, sometimes it eases a little, as if it's doing me a favour! As if I invited it into my life, begged it to come and attach itself to me... And the consolers will come and console me, telling me there are worse things!" - the bitterness turned to incandescent rage.

"I'm telling you!" he erupted suddenly, again addressing his companions in the café: "Don't be happy about anything! Because it's bound to go sour and in the end you'll be left with bitter pangs, despair and pain!"

"Papa Aharon!" cried Avinoam, and when the other turned to him he changed the tone of his voice, sounding cautious and inquisitive, like someone treading on treacherous ground: "Have you forgotten? You were young once and you knew youthful pleasures, the joys of health and strength, the simple delights of love..."

"I haven't forgotten!" was Aharon's vehement response, "And that just makes the pain worse!"

"He's right!" - the shrill, rancorous voice rang out again from the corner. "His condition is - beyond despair! If I were him, I'd go and jump in the sea!"

"I'm not doing that!" moustachioed Aharon retorted with a kind of blatant, unnatural equanimity, cold and rootless: "I wouldn't give him the satisfaction!"

"Give whom the satisfaction?" his neighbour at the table inquired.

"The one who's urging me to do it!"

Silence descended on the café again, unexpectedly. A heavy, oppressive silence.

"Isn't it time we made a move?" Raphael suggested, with emphatic pragmatism.

"It's time!" Avinoam agreed.

The occupants of the café started getting up one after another, going to Rahamim, paying their bills and turning to the door. Soon there were just three of us left there - Aharon, Rahamim and myself.

Quietly Rahamim came out from behind his counter and approaching Aharon, he stooped to pick up the empty cup. Then, his brow wrinkled, he asked in a voice replete with compassion which he tried, unsuccessfully, to conceal behind a gruff and guttural façade: "Aren't you going down with the rest of them?"

"No!" retorted Aharon, panting. He grimaced and added: "It's already starting..."

"What's starting?" Rahamim wanted to know, all concern and willingness to help.

"The pain!" Aharon answered him, and continued: "Till now it's held off... I've taken some pills too... I should be thankful for any respite... it's only going to get worse from now on. I'll stay a little longer, if you don't mind," - he looked up hopefully at Rahamim - "I'll wait until my son goes out to visit his fiancée... then the house will be empty, at my disposal, and my son won't see me writhing and hear me howling like a beast under the slaughterer's knife..."

I stood up from my seat and approached him:

"Do you have a boat?" I asked.

"Moored in the harbour," he sighed.

"Why aren't you going out?"

"I don't see any point!" he declared in a tone which despite its bitter overlay, seemed to be showing the first signs of softening, faint stirrings of a willingness for concession and compromise.

"The boat can lead you towards that madness you talked about, divine madness!"

"How so?" - he sighed again but gave me an alert and inquisitive look, a dim spark of hope alight in his eyes.

"It can free you from your surroundings and even from yourself - if you know how to navigate properly... Go way out into the open spaces and if you feel like it - you can shout to your heart's content, as loud as you want! Address your tirade to wherever or whoever you please."

"And what good will that do me?" Doubt was creeping in, threatening to snuff out that dim spark of hope.

"It's the only way to get an answer," I assured him. "Try it!"

"I'm not sure I can make it down there..." he murmured, his resolve beginning to falter.

"I'll help you," I offered.

"I'll help you!" - that familiar, shrill voice rang out again, and a figure emerged from the shadows shrouding the far wall and walked towards us. "I'll go out in the boat with you!" he added confidently, with enthusiasm almost. I glanced at him: a tall man with wild, unkempt hair and a few days' growth of stubbly beard, eyes bright and intense.

"I don't have a boat," he declared and added, "not for tonight. I lent it to my brother-in-law," he explained. "I'll go out with you and together we'll shout at the heavens above and the earth beneath… maybe something will move, something happen, maybe you'll get an answer. It could be a turning-point for you… Let's go!"

With an effort that he tried to conceal from us old Aharon stood up from his seat, smiled a twisted smile at the man from the shadows and said with strange determination:

"I'm not going anywhere with you! Get off my case! I'm not done for yet! I'm still alive! So sod off!"

The other tensed like a highly tuned string, stood motionless for a long moment, making prodigious efforts to restrain something that was seething inside him and threatening to burst out, then took a step back, appraising us with a look of dull anger, a look seeing nothing. As nobody responded, he turned away, left the café at a brisk pace and was swallowed up by the gathering darkness.

I turned to the old fisherman, to repeat my offer of help, but he forestalled me, saying: "There's no need!" He lowered his eyes, loosened his knotted brows and trying hard to soften the tone of his voice, added: "I've thought the whole thing through… I'm not going out…"

"Why?" I asked.

"Too late!" he declared and concluded: "Leave me alone! Please!"

I left the café and followed the ugly, crumbling concrete fence leading down to the old port of Jaffa. One after another the boats were leaving the jetty.

The man with the shrill voice was standing there, watching in silence as the fishermen went out to sea. From one of the boats came a wild, rolling, strident laugh.

I approached the tall young man and spoke to him in the darkness:

"That laugh - must be Nono, eh?"

"That's him," he muttered, in a tone of indelible dejection.

"Why don't you go out with your brother-in-law?" I asked.

"I haven't got a brother-in-law," he replied and added: "I invented him." And as I didn't respond he continued: "I have relations - in Canada."

"What are you doing here?"

"I got into trouble over there..." - adopting a scornful tone for his own purposes - "I'm what they call... a hothead..." He grinned in the darkness, trying to obscure some sense of unease. "I got into a fight," - his lips tensed in a tolerant smile, and as if presenting an argument in self-mitigation he continued: "It's understandable... at my age, it's only natural!" He shuffled his feet, an involuntary movement, and when he spoke again, his tone was earnest:

"Here - I was passionate about the sea... I was drawn to it... it was like an obsession! Fishing's in my blood!" he declared with a strange kind of pride, and for a brief moment turned to me with a sharp look that penetrated the darkness in a valiant effort to figure me out.

"And the boat?" - I returned to the subject, ignoring his scrutiny.

"There was a boat..." He went back to scanning the thick darkness hanging over the heavy, viscous sea.

"What happened to it?"

"Creditors..." He turned to stare at the crumbling concrete of the balustrade.

"And the fishermen know?"

"They know..." He looked up and tried to resume his study of my face, then decided it was time to introduce himself. "My name's Danny, and there's no one in these docks who doesn't know me and my story..."

"Why didn't you ask to join one of the fishermen?"

"Too shy!" he explained, adding: "With the old man, Aharon, there was a reason... to help him. In his condition, he really needs help. Do you know about his condition?"

"No."

"He's seriously ill," he hurriedly filled me in. "A malignant disease, the same as his father had. If I was in his shoes - I wouldn't budge from the sea. In all weathers, and to the very end... I've always detested the smug petty-mindedness of the dry land - and those who live on the land, and their ways! Turns my stomach!"

"You're not the only one!" - a heavy panting, like that of a horse on the point of expiring, was heard behind us. "Come on," the voice continued, "let's go down to the boat. You're right - and so are you!"

And old Aharon nudged the young man's elbow.

Without waiting for another invitation, and without any expression of surprise or pleasure, Danny strode briskly towards the jetty.

"Joining us, Adon?" asked Aharon, his panting and wheezing growing ever more raucous and alarming, as if his airways were constricted by the pressure of the tumour.

"No."

"So you belong among 'those who live on the land' and you act according to 'their ways'?" Aharon quoted the young man, a thin smile visible beneath his moustache.

"It isn't like that," I replied. "I don't belong to anything or anyone. As for you - you must have been eavesdropping!" I smiled back at him.

"Didn't miss a single word!" he replied, adding: "I left the café just a moment after you did. As for the sea - Danny's right, and so are you. Anyway, what would I do at home? I guess my place is at sea... if the sea still wants me!" He turned and shuffled after the tall figure of Danny, and soon disappeared with him into the thickening darkness.

I left the harbour by the southern entrance and walked up the broad road, formerly a major artery serving the needs of importers and customs officers. Its surface was stained with patches of oil, reflecting the faint glow of the street-lamps and emitting a sickly yellow light that seemed to be fighting for its life. The whole length of the road I didn't encounter a living soul.

SHUKI

As I approached my house, the time was almost eleven o'clock. There was a light on in the house. Someone was waiting for me.

I had hardly stepped inside the yard when a shadow detached itself from the low, crumbling wall, built of clay and haphazard brickwork. Suddenly, as if springing from the ground, my neighbour was standing before me, standing so close I could feel his moist breath on my face. His finger, raised to his lips as a signal for caution, silenced my greeting. He whispered in my ear:

"You have a visitor. Not a very nice one! I tried to get rid... that is... I told him you weren't at home... you might not be coming back... he just laughed at me! Told me to go away... or words to that effect... Be careful! You'd be better off not going home tonight! Spend the night somewhere else, with a friend or a relative... till the dust settles!" He nodded his angular head to underline his warning and, duty done and conscience salved, turned to the low wall and only slightly hampered by his gammy leg, vaulted over it and disappeared in the direction of his own house.

I entered.

On the sofa, facing me, a man in his late thirties was reclining. His hands were clasped behind his head, which at first sight appeared finely crafted, manly and even handsome. A low and bulbous forehead rather spoiled this first impression. He wore a black shirt and tight jeans, and flip-flop sandals which he had taken off and dumped on the floor. He wasn't particularly tall, just tall enough for his feet, of less than perfect cleanliness, to dangle over the end of the sofa. His face, a dull grey colour in the subdued lamplight, showed a smile of deep and unnatural contentment - a variety of self-confidence, born of malicious and keen awareness of total control of the situation. This expression changed everything, turning his manly beauty into a twisted beauty, repellent and pitiable with a touch of diabolical menace about it too.

"Good evening!" - I greeted him in a tone of voice that couldn't possibly be mistaken for anything other than it was, a tone of friendly encouragement.

He heard the greeting but evidently chose to ignore it,

dismissing it contemptuously from his consciousness. For a long moment he was silent.

I went to the inner room, changed my clothes and was on my way to the little kitchen when I heard the voice of my uninvited guest:

"That heart with the 'L' on it, on the door - did Lili do that?"

"Cup of tea?" I offered, instead of a reply.

"Bring it here!" he responded, as if doing me a favour and giving an order at the same time.

I boiled water, poured out two cups, put them on a long tray along with sugar, spoons and slices of lemon. I returned to the outer room and set the tray down on the low and narrow oval table. I sat down in the armchair on the other side of the table, my face to the door.

"I asked you a question!" the visitor snapped without turning to me, without the slightest alteration in his posture.

"I gave you an answer," I responded, my voice still inflected with sincere affability, joviality even.

He turned his head to face me with a perceptible effort, stretching his neck muscles, obviously reluctant to change the rest of his posture.

"I didn't hear you!" he declared, scanning me with the amused air of a big predator, playing with a cornered mouse.

"I offered you a cup of tea!" I smiled back at him.

"That was an answer?"

"It was."

He rose slowly, accentuating every movement, swinging his bare feet to the floor, then added three spoonfuls of sugar to his cup, stirred it slowly and deliberately, took a slice of lemon, raised the cup to his lips, slurped the hot liquid noisily and said:

"You'd better learn to give answers - Shuki gets answers!"

Suddenly he burst into peals of raucous, malevolent laughter; the sharp lines of his face fragmented and for a moment he looked like a lunatic, escaping from his confinement and celebrating his freedom and his victory.

The laughter vanished just as it had erupted - suddenly, as if its vital cord had been severed, as if it never was.

He took a few rapid gulps of his tea, replaced the cup on the tray and said calmly:

"It's obvious she's the one who did that drawing. I can't see you doing anything like that! But" - he went on in a mellow, almost innocent tone - "she's no concern of yours! She's a pro when it comes to manipulating men, it's her profession after all. 'Gold-mine' - that's what they call her round here. It was my mother gave her that name. She can find the weak points in any man and exploit them - all the way, right down to the bone! Of course, money's what it all comes down too! And all the money" - he favoured me with a contemptuous frown - "she brings to Shuki! 'Cos he's her boss, and woe betide her if she gets her sums wrong!" He smiled pleasantly and added: "Not that she ever does!" He was looking directly ahead now, disdainfully, ostentatiously ignoring my presence. "Living with Shuki has been an education for her. She brings me every last cent that she earns! And waits like a scabby dog for a pat or a juicy bone, or both. And what she usually gets" - he studied the expression on my face, blithely, with an air of supreme, almost amiable satisfaction, and solemnly completed the sentence - "is a kick up the arse!" And once more he roared with coarse, guttural and provocative laughter, laughter that set his whole body shaking and his limbs waving in every conceivable direction.

"A kick up the arse!" he repeated after wiping the tears of mirth from his eyes with the back of his hand: "That's the best she can expect!" And suddenly he leaned towards me, and a pungent smell compounded of tobacco and sweat and something else - something like the stench of decay blended with acrid perfumes - assailed my nostrils.

"You following me?" he continued, with a rise in the pitch of his voice which could have been interpreted as evidence of sincerity, the flash of his tiny eyes - like glowing coals, a rodent's eyes - fixed on mine as if trying to pierce the mask of inscrutability and gauge the effect his words were having on me: "What she gets more often is... a kick in the face!" he hissed.

I picked up my cup, took a deep, pleasurable gulp of the tea, and without any change in the tone of my voice from before, I commented:

"A kick in the face sounds counter-productive. After a kick like that, she won't be much more use to you."

"Not a bit of it!" my guest exclaimed, waving his arms for emphasis: "She'll go running straight to the next client. Counter-productive? Hardly! After a kick like that, and it usually comes after a knock-out punch that's laid her on the floor in the first place - she'll crawl on her hands and knees to the door, take a second or two to recover, then stand up and get herself ready for the next in line! Yesterday, and the day before, I treated her to a kick in the face!" Again he tried to figure out what was in my eyes, with no more success than before. "You could say we understand one another!" He grinned suddenly under his thick brows and picked up his cup again.

He took a long gulp, put his cup back and without looking up, wiping his lips with his hand this way and that, asked quietly, gently almost:

"Do you feel sorry for her?"

For a long moment I pondered my reply, saying finally:

"I feel sorry for everyone. In the same measure."

"For me too?" He narrowed his brows and wrinkled his low, protuberant forehead.

"For you too," I answered him, without any change in the tone of my voice: "In the same measure," I thought it worth adding.

"And how do we earn your compassion?"

"Through suffering," was the answer.

For a brief moment it was as if something unfamiliar to him flashed through his consciousness, and he was on the point of mellowing, but the next moment - he was as drawn and tense as ever, his thick lips expanding into that dark, cold and malevolent smile - unfathomable, fortunately.

"What nobility of spirit! How very civil of you!" his voice rasped. "See yourself as the saviour of the human race, do you?"

"No," I answered him. "I'm a human being - like her and like you."

"In need of compassion?"

"No."

"What kind of human being are you?" he persisted.

"The kind that doesn't need compassion," was the answer.

He weighed my words, screwing up his face into an expression of emphatic disgust: "Listen, Mister!" - he leaned over the table again and the pungent smell of decay, comparable perhaps with the reek of nutmeg mingled with naphthalene, hit my nostrils again: "You're just, how can I put it..." He pondered for a long moment, the disdainful flash of his eyes focused on the table:

"You're just..." he repeated with emphasis and this time concluded: "Arrogant!"

He raised his clenched fist and brought it down on the table-top with great force, a blow supposedly demonstrating self-assurance. The tray, of lacquer-coated tin, protested, the spoons jingled, the almost empty cups resounded dully.

He remained in that pose - his fist on the table, trembling and tightly clenched, his eyes glued to it. I answered him calmly:

"That is possible."

"You're admitting you're arrogant!" he cried.

"I'm admitting it's possible."

"Yes or no?" he insisted.

"It's possible."

"Stubborn as well!" he shouted, hitting the table again, with more restraint this time, the crockery responding appropriately.

"That's possible too," I answered him, without changing my tone of voice or facial expression.

"And you're a queer!" he cried in wild exultation.

"No," I responded in a clear voice and a decisive tone: "I'm not a queer!"

"That's lucky for you!" he retorted, his voice as high and shrill as ever - " 'Cos I fancy a bit of that myself sometimes! That really bugs her! I'm telling you," - he moderated the tone of his voice but it remained abrasive, with a touch of hoarseness resonating in it - "when I met her, she was crazy about me, besotted... she's still that way now!" he insisted, seeing fit to add for some reason: "I'll prove that to you yet. I'll show you - and how!" He was shouting again, red flames of malice flashing in his eyes: "It used to make her mad, the way I was bedding queers... sometimes they pay good money for it, sometimes I do them a favour! When I want to wind her up..." He was silent for a moment, glanced at me and continued almost calmly:

"She used to plead with me, beg me to stop... you know what I used to do?" he asked rhetorically, "I used to..." he broke off abruptly, the word, whatever it was, freezing on his lips. For a moment he seemed utterly paralysed, then suddenly he exploded with renewed ferocity:

"I can't say it! I don't understand!" His eyes flared, dark flames seeming to set his whole face ablaze, his whole body, his soul. He struck the table again - a powerful, impetuous blow which finally upset the tray, showering sugar and spraying tea in all directions, as well as inflicting terminal injuries on the table itself.

"For God's sake!" he cried: "Are you a wizard, or a hypnotist - or what?" and without waiting for an answer he added: "Every foul word I try to say - sticks in my throat. It withers away there and dies... Words like..." he threw me a look that was wild and malevolent but at the same time pitiably helpless - "see what I mean! But I'm telling you this, and you pay attention to what Shuki says!" he continued with emphatic, unequivocal menace. "Don't get the idea that she's anything to do with you! Don't start indulging in fantasies like that. Bad for you, bad for both of you, very bad! And she knows this as well as anyone. You'll know too - when the time comes!" And with this he broke off the attack, opting for a dignified retreat, the muscles of his face slackening and something like a smile flickering there. He flexed his fist, wet with the tea that had spilled on it and spoke in a low, remarkably smooth voice:

"It won't come to that, don't worry. She came back to me of her own free will. Abandoned you and came back to me. She says you're a monk - 'just a pompous git' as she puts it. And she's right: you're the most pompous, arrogant git I've ever met! And when the money ran out, she sent me to you. Well, she didn't send me, exactly, but she gave me your address - and I didn't have to sweat it out of her either!" he declared, with some expansive hand gestures, presumably intended to underline the point:

"I didn't press her, didn't beat her or threaten her. I just asked her where the pompous git lived, and she came straight out with it. And here I am. Do you see the game she's playing?" He looked at me again, with that contemptuous lustre in his eyes.

"I don't see any game here," I commented and added: "You are, in a sense, her employer, and she's doing as you tell her."

"But she doesn't have to!" he cried, as if to himself: "She could get along by herself - she'd make a mountain of money!" he exclaimed in a shrill voice, leaning forward till his lips almost touched my ear: "What do I do for her?" he asked and gave the answer: "I torture her, kick her, abuse her, humiliate her, starve her, take all the money she earns with that skinny, sick and clapped-out body of hers... every last cent! And when her body finally breaks down - I'll throw her to the dogs! And she knows it! Some employer! Why does she listen to me?" He sounded genuinely puzzled.

"It seems," I responded equably, lucidly, "that her understanding of things isn't the same as yours. Neither you nor I can get into her mind and see things the way she sees them. Nor can anyone, no one in the world," I declared and added thoughtfully: "It's possible that she too isn't entirely clear about this."

"So who is?" he persisted, aggressive and menacing as ever.

"God is," I answered him.

"And He has no compassion for her?" he demanded to know.

"Not in any flesh and blood sense."

"Where is this God?"

"In everyone."

"So I'm God too?"

"You too."

He erupted again in a thunderous outburst of laughter, a sound reminiscent of the din of flood waters or a spur of the sea, buffeted violently in the dim recesses of subterranean caverns.

"You're off your head!" he cried and added: "Just like she said - a pompous git and a loony as well! And she gave me your address... and you know why?" - he leaned towards me again and the pungent smell of nutmeg blended with the reek of naphthalene renewed the assault on my nostrils. His words, spoken this time in a tone of malevolent triumph and accompanied by a fresh blast of venomous laughter, echoed in my ears: "So I could milk you! Milk you to the bone! Trust me - I'm speaking to you as one God to another!" - he grinned - "That's what I'm going to do and I'm not letting go... I'm going to milk you to the marrow of your bones and further... 'cos that's what you were created for and you're not worthy of anything else!"

"You won't find that quite so easy as you think," I commented mildly, with a broad, unflappable smile.

"And I'm telling you this!" - he withdrew to his neutral posture on the sofa and the tone of his voice was even, almost amiable, "I'm an expert in this! A top pro! I milk people to the marrow of their bones and further! I've got three of them, I'm sure you've heard about them, and they're my slaves, till death and even beyond. I'm everything to them - God and Devil, angel of death and angel of life, angel of destruction and angel of mercy. I give and I take, I bring to life and I kill! Without me they couldn't move, or think, or breathe!" - he shot me a look of overt, provocative scorn:

"You're in my sights now! You put on all these fine, gentlemanly airs and you tried to steal her from me - no one does that to Shuki and lives! You'll pay dearly for this, very dearly!" He scanned me with a look comprising scorn and disdain and a larger measure of malicious enjoyment, together with traces of tension and unease.

"You've only one chance left," he began in a new tone - soft, persuasive, almost silky, yet impenetrable, with nothing behind it. "If you want to come out of this a free man, not be squeezed to the marrow of your bones and not live in constant fear till your last day on the earth - you have to make sure Shuki stops breathing! Can you do that?" he asked curiously, sounding amused, "Have you got the nerve?" - and with an abrupt, unexpected movement he thrust a hand into his trouser-pocket and pulled out a long barber's razor, folded into its black handle, and offered it to me. As he did so, the razor opened halfway, its sharp blade glistening in the silvery lamplight.

Silence reigned. Total silence. Somewhere, not far away perhaps, a wall-clock ticked, or a tap dripped with steady, monotonous rhythm.

I turned to face my uninvited guest, held out my hand and took the razor. With a leisurely movement I opened it fully, and sensed the fraught, barely human tranquillity suffusing the body opposite mine.

My own tranquillity, devoid of any tension - steadfast, tangible, unassailable tranquillity - challenged the menacing current of fraught tranquillity emanating from the other side of the table, and collided with it. Shuki trembled.

I tested the blade of the razor, passing my thumb along its edge, and unimpressed by the mounting tension confronting me, folded the razor and offered it back, with a grin, to my sparring partner.

"A coward's weapon!" I declared, adding, "It's late."

"What's late?" he asked, looking up like someone returning from another world, and seeing the razor proffered to him, took it and with a nimble movement put it back in his pocket.

"The hour is late!"

"Usually asleep at this time, are you?" he asked, his little eyes regaining their scornful vitality.

"Yes."

"I'm going right away! I didn't mean to disturb you..." He spoke with emphatic, excessive courtesy - but the mockery and venom were only lightly disguised. He stood up and put on his sandals.

"There's just one small thing..." He turned to me with a gleeful sort of look in his eyes - repressed glee, which he himself was perhaps unaware of.

"And that is?" I asked.

"A small loan... I, as you know, need money. A lot of money! I'm on the hard stuff you see," he explained, managing to sound archly flippant and sanctimoniously humble at the same time - "Mainlining!" He waved an arm in the air, the other injecting it with an imaginary syringe. "And when I haven't got enough - and I can never get enough!" he grinned amiably, "I go crazy. I'm not responsible for my actions... They all know this. I'm grateful for the tea and the hospitality," he added in a softer tone. "We're almost mates now, aren't we!" He put on a jovial smile and continued: "What's a little thing like this between mates? Shall we say..." - he appraised me with a look of pure innocence - "... a thousand? Nice round figure, you see, and not too much to ask!"

"I don't have that much," I answered him with a broad smile.

"Five hundred will do for the moment, and we can leave the other five hundred for my next visit!" he suggested with an air of affable generosity.

"I don't have that much either," I informed him, still smiling.

"How much have you got?" he asked, prepared to compromise.

"A tenner."

"Ah!" he grimaced. "Not much respect for a friend, eh? A tenner? Okay, hand it over!" he demanded.

I handed it over.

"The rest - you can bring me tomorrow!" he declared, stuffing the crumpled note into his pocket and staring down at the floor.

"I won't have it then either," I replied, amused.

"Day after tomorrow," he suggested reasonably, looking up and scanning my face with that air of repressed glee, impossible to define.

"No."

"End of the week?"

"No."

"You're beginning to disappoint me!" he reproved me with an air of injured dignity. "A friend like me... shouldn't be disappointed!" He waved an admonitory finger at me, as a good-natured shopkeeper might, seeing a child pinching a sweet from the display on the counter. "Please do your best to find it by the weekend - a thousand... or nine hundred and ninety. You see," he twisted his features into a sort of smile, "I've taken the tenner into account. I'm a fair dealer! And if you're wishing you'd used that razor on me when you had the chance, forget it - I've got another one here!" He thrust both hands into his trouser-pockets, pulled out two razors, one in each hand, and waved them at me. "You see," he added cheerfully, geniality positively overflowing, "when it comes to pulling razors and slashing, I'm a faster mover than you!" He smiled again, then wiped off the smile as if it had never existed and added grimly:

"This one," - focusing his gaze on the razor in his left hand - "is hers. I take her to bed sometimes, when she's least expecting it... and when she wants it even less. After I've sodomised a queer. That disgusts her. It made her throw up once - and that's the biggest turn-on of the lot!" he declared with an air of delight, and more than a hint of challenge. "Shuki's not just a man. Shuki's the champ - you'll find no one else like him in the whole of Jaffa!" he concluded in a tone of malevolent enthusiasm, and a perverse affectation of authority.

"Do you know anything about these things?" he asked curiously, still brandishing his razors.

"I used to be married," I pointed out, then corrected myself: "I'm still married. I've fathered children."

"A razor in her pocket..." he reverted to the former topic, disregarding my reply, "that's dangerous! For me, I mean. You know," he turned to me with a changed expression, ingratiating, as if seeking complicity and understanding - "when a man's on the job he's completely defenceless. Even a little girl could slit his throat then... don't you think so?" - he asked for my opinion in a tone of surprising humility.

"Absolutely!" I expressed my whole-hearted agreement.

"That's why I took it off her," he explained, still clutching the razor in his left hand. "She kept it in the pocket of her jeans... I felt it, sorted it out. She tried to wriggle out of it, made up some excuses... I wasn't interested."

"Didn't she resist?" I asked, "Physical resistance, I mean."

"Oh, she resisted," he smiled contentedly, "but it didn't do her any good! As for you..." he reverted to the main issue, "I'm not going to slaughter a goose that's still laying golden eggs!" He put away his razors and then, in an abrupt change of tone, and topic, cried:

"You've hurt me and you'll pay dearly for that! I'll be getting the full price out of you! I turn to you as a friend - and you call me a coward!" His voice shook, his face contorted, even his shoulders went into spasm. "You'll regret this, I'll settle accounts with you yet! In the meantime," he softened a little, "I'll be seeing you! At the weekend, and you'd better have a grand with you! Yes, a full thousand," he stressed, going back on his former generosity, "that tenner doesn't count - that's the interest for a five day amnesty!" - and he left the house.

I cleared the table, put things back in their places, spread out blankets and went to bed, all joy and radiance, beyond the comprehension of flesh and blood.

A SHORT PATH

At an early hour of the afternoon I set out for Rahamim's café. But I didn't make it to the café, because on the way I met Rahamim himself, on the picturesque path that the municipality had paved with old stone tiles, excavated locally.

After the customary felicitations I asked him: "Something up at the café?"

"No," Rahamim replied, looking at me steadily.

I took his cue and asked: "What's happened?"

"You don't know?" he retorted with genuine astonishment and hastened to explain: "David Farhi's son, the boozer..." - he struggled to remember his name - "was knocked down yesterday. They've already done the autopsy, and today's the funeral."

"Blessed be the Judge of Truth!" I responded. "Is that where you're going, the funeral?"

"Yes," he replied. "If you want," he added, "come along too!"

On the way Rahamim lit himself a cigarette, calmly inhaling the smoke and then, for some reason, feeling the need to make excuses:

"I'm trying to kick this lousy habit!" - he flourished the glowing tip and added, as if explanation was needed - "Smoking, I mean. But," he continued, "there are moments when I couldn't do without it. Still, I've cut down... whole days go by without a cigarette!" he boasted. "My wife's pleased," he smiled and concluded, "so am I!"

After walking for about half an hour, we were both standing outside Number 2, Menora Street, at the big, ramshackle gate made of heavy, unmatched planks. The gate was already ajar, and we pushed it open. The big courtyard was thronged with people: neighbours, relatives and the simply curious. Members of the immediate family were sitting inside -David the father, Flora the mother, seven daughters and the surviving son, Israel.

In keeping with the customs of their sect, they wore black and sat on mats, keening softly. We approached, stooped, shook hands and silently took our seats on hard stools, set out for this purpose in all corners of the imposing lounge.

Rahamim followed tradition and convention, inquiring with great courtesy, in a tone of emphatic identification with the grief of the mourners, about the circumstances of the death. The question was addressed to David Farhi, but he pointed to his firstborn son and said balefully:

"He knows!"

Israel sighed, approached us and sat down at our feet, telling us in a hushed voice that yesterday, early in the morning, his brother left the house and made his way to the Petah Tikva expressway. Here, finding no one to take pity on him and give him a drink, or money, he pulled his usual stunt and "collapsed" in the fast lane... This time, his luck ran out...

The father, evidently listening with rapt attention to his son's account, interrupted him, exclaiming suddenly:

"He did it on purpose!" His voice was as I remembered it, sullen-aggressive, and his face was pale and grim. "After all, what more did he have to expect from this life?"

He looked up and fixed me with a look that was chilly and strange this time, eyes not so much frozen as blank and glassy: "What more did he have to expect of people? No one took pity on him... not his brother, not his sisters, not his mother, not even the father who begat him! They never learned to appreciate his warm heart, his excruciating pain, his talents!" He was silent for a moment, and seemed to be on the verge of tears, but managed, with some effort, to stem and restrain the impulse. And here, suddenly, it was Mrs. Farhi who intervened, this time dressed in black and her grey hair tied up in a broad black ribbon on her thick nape - her appearance utterly different from the appearance that I remembered.

"God gave!" she began with unexpected vehemence, "And God has taken!" She sighed and added: "The Name of the Lord be blessed..." Her voice lost something of its steadiness as she continued: "The boy went downhill, he drank... we did the best we could. There's no one to blame!" she declared, "It's fate! Bitter fate..." she concluded in a tone of resignation.

"There's no need for you to say anything," the son intervened. "You did all you could and more! It's down to me, I myself... Oh, I don't know... Anyway," - he abandoned this tack and seemed intent on answering his father - "I don't think he did this... what I mean is, he may have done what he did on purpose, but this wasn't the outcome he was banking on! You know him," he added hastily, "this was his way of drawing attention to himself, getting himself admitted to some clinic, or hospital, anywhere he could get what he wanted…"

"Drink!" the father interjected morosely.

The young women sat in silence, serene - it could be said - and solemn, with the same facial expressions that they wore every day of the year. The black modest dresses suited their fair complexions and accentuated their deep and lustrous pallor. One of them, the youngest, commented:

"If only he'd had a woman! A wife, I mean," she added hastily, "a loving and devoted wife! Perhaps he wouldn't have got into such a state. Perhaps his decline could have been halted before it was too late, even stopped altogether!"

David Farhi intervened again:

"No ordinary wife would have such powers of endurance! Not every woman can stand comparison with you or one of your sisters… I'm glad that you're all here with me, and I'm glad that Israel has been spared for us… he…he's the mainstay of the whole family!" And the old man patted his son's shoulder, but was careful to avoid eye-contact.

Someone came into the room and announced, in the whisper customary in these circumstances, that transport had arrived.

We began getting up and leaving the house of mourning. Outside, a shabby old motor coach was parked; it couldn't squeeze into the narrow alleyway and it waited for passengers a few metres from the gate.

People climbed the steps of the coach and pushed inside. Soon all the hard seats were taken and most of the mourners had to stand in the narrow gangway between the benches. Members of the immediate family were making their way towards an antiquated American Oldsmobile and a commercial van. Rahamim, standing with me alongside a crowded bench, pointed to the two private vehicles that were picking up the Farhi family and explained:

"Those are two of the daughters' suitors. One's a cobbler, and a very skilled one too, the other's a plumber… Both of them rejected by the father in the past… but as you see, they haven't given up hope! And David Farhi, because of the emergency, is having to make use of their transport, whether he likes it or not..." He paused for a moment, as if deep in thought and concluded: "Maybe those poor girls will get something out of their brother's death after all..."

The ceremony in the cemetery was short. Old David Farhi didn't weep, didn't stumble, said Kaddish in a remarkably clear voice and supported his wife, a whole head taller than him, who was suffering intermittent dizzy turns, her face contorted. The girls supported one another, sobbing quietly on one another's shoulders. When the coffin was lowered, only Israel was unable to restrain himself, yelling and waving his massive hands towards his brother as he descended into the pit, and for a moment it seemed he meant to jump in after him. The other mourners surrounded him in a tight circle and tried to calm him with hugs and kisses and commiserations. But he was inconsolable, and despite his own persistent efforts, his whimpering continued unabated. Otherwise, the funeral passed off in an exceptionally orderly fashion, in almost unnatural calm.

The coach picked up its passengers, as did the private vehicles, the antiquated Oldsmobile and the commercial van, and all made their way back to the house of mourning. Here the package unravelled as the mourners began quietly dispersing, taking their leave of the Farhi family and hurrying to go their separate ways.

"I have to go and open up the café," Rahamim told me.

"I'm staying," I replied.

In fact, besides three or four people including the midget cobbler and the lean plumber, the spurned suitors - none of the mourners was left. The family went back to sitting on mats, heads bowed and eyes staring at the floor. I sat beside the plumber facing the head of the family, David Farhi.

The silence lengthened and deepened, although it wasn't as oppressive as could be expected in such circumstances.

Suddenly old David Farhi stood up from his place on the floor, tensed and jerking spasmodically like a badly synchronised puppet, and rounding on the cobbler and the plumber, sitting there quietly and their faces showing nothing but the appropriate condolences, cried out at the top of his voice:

"Out! Get out! Out of here now! You didn't come here to pay your respects, but to sniff around my daughters! I don't want to see your faces ever again!" He accompanied his yells with menacing gestures.

His son Israel and wife Flora ran to him and folded him in their arms, stifling their own tears as they tried to soothe his grief. One of the daughters, one of those I had met at Israel's shop, turned to us and apologised on her father's behalf:

"He's not himself... it's understandable...it's a tragic time for him. Please, forgive him... and stay! Don't abandon us..." She glanced at the midget cobbler, owner of the Oldsmobile.

One way or another David Farhi managed to extricate himself from the embrace of his son and his wife, both of them whimpering softly, and he drew himself up to his full height, ready with a fresh tirade:

"What's left of this family?" he screeched. "Shit, that's what! The crown has been dashed from our heads, it has fallen, squashed flat on the road! The best and the finest has gone, and only the shit is left. Shmuel, Shmuel my dear," he cried, "how could you be so merciless to your poor old father, how could you leave him among these talentless, unfeeling, brain-dead nonentities? What's your brother compared with you? Zilch!" he exclaimed with a kind of vindictive, malicious delight, and without turning to face his son he added in a clear voice: "At the very best, he's a failure, he's ignorant and insensitive, and as for your sisters, what are they? - Streetwalkers, or they would be if I didn't keep an eye on them!"

Two of the girls turned to him with agonised cries of "Father! Father!" and a third fainted. The mother, trying desperately to silence her husband by any available means was forced to abandon the attempt and attend to her daughter, sprinkling water on her face to revive her.

"And your mother," the old man went on, as if hopelessly deranged - " a monster on two legs... who never understood you, and never will! What have you left behind? - An empty void! A cheerless, silent, empty void! A void of darkness and despair!" And suddenly, face contorted with rage, he rounded again on the cobbler and the plumber and yelled into their expressionless faces - a throat-splitting yell:

"Out! Get the Hell out of here! Move!"

The two of them stared at him, aghast, then cast sidelong glances at his daughters and picking up some hint from them, bowed submissively and walked quietly to the door. No one stopped them.

Moments later I stood up, intending to leave, but David Farhi detained me with a gesture that was anxious, and at the same time authoritative, saying:

"You! Please stay! I want to show you something," he explained. "Wait..." He mellowed suddenly and all those present in the high-ceilinged room - his son, his daughters, his wife and some distant aunt, an extremely elderly lady resembling a walking ruin, squiffy-eyed and in the habit of dropping off to sleep at regular intervals, just now roused by the noisy antics of the master of the house - stared at him in astonishment, astonishment which in some of them was blended with trepidation, in others with repressed anger and overt hatred.

David Farhi walked solemnly towards an antique cabinet, carefully opened one of the doors, which creaked loudly and stridently, and took out a little wooden box. It was intricately carved and polished, the kind of box normally used for storing small ornaments. He closed the door of the cabinet, which creaked again despite his obsessive caution, took from around his neck a thin gold chain with a tiny key hanging on it, and gingerly unlocked the carved box. Almost reverently he lifted the lid and drew out a folded sheet of paper, torn from a standard exercise-book.

"Listen!" He turned to me as if I was the only one present in the room and began reciting to me, with genuine feeling, in a deep and melodious voice, the following:

A Simple Man

A simple man
Sets out on his way
Tomorrow - he is lost
All is normal today.

There is plucking of roses,
And meeting a friend,
And burning of bridges,
*   To his questions - no end:*

What is the sky?
And where is the skyline?
What is the earth?
And the breeze on the brine...

And life, and the future?
And pleasure and pain?
Of the great and the chosen
What traces remain?

No answer is given,
No dream does he see,
The jewelled orb of the sun
His sole witness will be.

The path here is short,
Is all bramble and thorn,
This crop of wild flowers
Will be gone by the morn.

Tomorrow is barren,
A stranger draws near,
'Mankind' he will say,
Do they all eat dust here?'

A man passes on
While the day is still young,

His last friend has fallen,

The song has been sung.

The poem left a deep impression in the hearts of all who heard it; it had clearly been written at a time of severe emotional crisis - and by someone of outstanding poetic talent.

After allowing the simple words of the poem to elicit their mordant echo, and the silence that followed it to harrow the minds of all members of the family, fuelling deep feelings of guilt and irremediable regret, David Farhi re-folded the page with emphatic solemnity, replaced it in the carved and polished jewel-box, locked the box with the tiny key and hung the chain once more around his neck. He returned the box to the cabinet, then turned to me again saying simply: "That is Shmuel!"

His face, which had been radiant with childlike innocence and a rare and precious kind of purity, albeit accompanied by profound trauma - crumpled suddenly, and he broke into bitter and unrestrained weeping. He stood alone, set apart from all those around him, his short, lithe body shaking as if wracked by ague, and his tears trickling down, dripping on the crude mats with a soft pattering sound, heavy with guilt and grief.

"And now!" - he flared up suddenly, lunatic fire in his eyes: "Go!" - and he showed me to the door with an outstretched, tense, trembling hand.

I went to him, embraced him firmly and left the house.

About a month after Shmuel's death, at the end of the official mourning period, David Farhi's two eldest daughters rebelled against their father, defying him by marrying their suitors; the elder - the midget cobbler, and her sister - the plumber/van-driver. David Farhi, so it was said, shut himself away and refused to attend either wedding, unlike his wife Flora, her elder son Israel and her five remaining daughters. No other congregation was invited to the nuptials, which were very modest. Since then, it was said, David Farhi had become a recluse in his home, and had seen no one.

THE FORMER YESHIVA STUDENT

Rahamim's café was empty, but for the proprietor and his nephew, Nessim who, on seeing me, took a step backwards and retreated behind the counter; standing there beside his uncle he shot me an evasive glance and then looked away, taking care not to meet my eye.

Rahamim sighed and after returning my greeting, said:

"We've just been talking about you. My nephew asked after you, and he wasn't just asking - he was really interested! It seemed strange to me, suspicious even. I asked him why your well-being is so important to him - and that's when you came in..."

"After what I heard about you," Nessim interjected hastily, his face half-turned towards me - "some run-in you had with Shuki... I was worried! I was concerned about you!" he cried defensively, as if accusing somebody, me apparently, of sheer recklessness. And with lowered voice he continued: "Shuki's the kind of guy... you know, one of those special types who reckon they're free to think and act any way they please... everything's allowed. He's got all kinds of contacts..."

"He was at my house yesterday," I threw at Nessim, my voice entirely amicable.

"What did he want?" Rahamim asked, with some trepidation.

"A small loan," I replied.

"No!" Nessim exclaimed and added at once: "You'll never get out of that!"

"I have got out," I declared calmly. "You see me here, safe and sound!"

"And who told him your address?" Rahamim asked.

"Someone did," was my reply.

Slowly, Rahamim turned to look his nephew full in the face, and hissed between his teeth:

"So that's the reason for your concern and your sudden benevolence!"

Nessim regained something of his composure:

"You don't know anything, and you've no right to suspect anything either!" - he retorted, his voice resolute, even aggressive.

Nothing was left of his former awkwardness: "I'm entitled to manage my affairs just as I please, and no one has the right to preach at me or treat me like an informer!" he concluded.

"Your affairs are certainly yours to manage as you see fit and no one has the right to preach at you, not that I've been doing that either!" Rahamim replied. "But what I think of you - that's my private business, and it's not for anyone else to know or argue with!"

"Just a moment," I interposed. "I reckon Nessim's right! As far as I know, the information on my whereabouts didn't leak from him."

"Is that definite? Have you checked it out?" Rahamim asked hesitantly, his voice dropping.

"I haven't checked it out, but I've heard and it's more than just a rumour!" I asserted.

"You see!" Nessim turned to his uncle in the tone of voice of the slandered and unjustly accused, with an added tinge of triumphalism: "You were so quick to jump to conclusions, to preach and accuse - and you've got it all wrong."

"In that case, I shall apologise to you!" Rahamim conceded, even making a small bow of humility towards his nephew. "I didn't know anyone else who'd have an interest in revealing Adon's address to Shuki."

"And what makes you think I'd be interested in that?" asked Nessim, intrigued.

"You've got a wife and kids... and with a shark like Shuki breathing down your neck... I wouldn't actually blame you if you did let something slip... If your family was threatened, you'd give anything away... who wouldn't. I've been telling you for years to get out of that bloody neighbourhood, get as far away from it as you can. You've no future there, and more to the point - it's no place to be bringing up your daughters, either!"

"You're right there, a thousand per cent right!" Nessim agreed, his narrow forehead furrowing, "But you don't seem to realise that I can't! I can't get of there!" cried the former yeshiva student.

"Why is that?" I asked with interest.

"I'm used to the place, and it's not just me, there's my wife too, and my sons and daughters," he answered me brusquely. "And then there's all the hassle and upheaval of moving and settling in somewhere new!"

"That's no reason to stay!" Rahamim objected calmly: "With

someone like Shuki sitting on your tail, you should overcome all your objections and get the Hell out!"

"That's just the point," Nessim replied. "This Shuki who's sitting on my tail - he won't take it kindly if I leave... he'll sniff around... suspect that I'm running away! And woe betide me then, and woe betide my family! That's the main reason," he concluded tensely: "Shuki won't let me go!"

"And why won't he let you go?" Rahamim persisted, a sceptical look in his eyes.

"You don't understand, you're not involved!" Nessim retorted, adding a juicy Spanish expletive for good measure: "Just now, this Shuki is my best friend," he explained. "He supports me in everything. No one in the neighbourhood dares look at me with anything but respect, and my five daughters - they're the best protected girls in the world! Everyone respects them and defers to them. And all this because I've done Shuki, and still do Shuki" - he stressed - "a few small favours..."

"So you are an informer?" Rahamim pressed him, turning the full force of his limpid eyes on his nephew. His tone of voice was strange: gentle and tolerant, and at the same time clear and emphatic.

Nessim ignored him:

"It's curtains for me if I don't do him small favours," he cried and added by way of clarification. "That's what he calls it, 'small favours' - like when he means to stamp on someone's throat and squeeze him till his guts come out of his ears - he talks about a 'small loan'." He fell silent for a moment, staring at the floor. No one responded.

"Uncle!" Nessim cried suddenly in an impassioned and sincere voice: "You don't understand the pressure I'm under! There's no way out and I have to watch every step with great care - until there's some change and my daughters get married - every one of them - and my son goes off to do his army service and decides he wants a place of his own... and then, one night, my wife and I will slip away! Or maybe Shuki's luck will run out... I have to watch my tongue, I can't say any more!" And turning abruptly to me he said in a stolid tone of voice, quite out of character:

"I'm the one who gave Shuki your address. He didn't even have to demand it. For a long time I hadn't done him any 'small favours' and there was tension building up. When we met he'd be polite enough, but he was giving me these long, heavy, meaningful looks...

there were dark clouds looming. I'm a family man. I'm stuck, and there's no way out. Your address," he pointed out, " is my salvation, and it's up to you whether you forgive me or not!" He was silent again for a long moment, staring down at the floor, waiting for my response - and when no response came he added apologetically:

"I hope very much you'll understand the fix I'm in. You're a loner, with strange habits. Maybe you could find a way out... and anyway, the danger would only be hanging over your head, you wouldn't be putting your wife and sons and daughters in jeopardy..."

"It's a pity Adon was so talkative!" - Rahamim's regret sounded genuine.

"It's a blessing he was so talkative!" cried Nessim vehemently and turning to him he added: "You know what kind of guy Shuki is?" - and he went on to explain in the same ebullient tone, purged of any sense of guilt: "Boss of the neighbourhood, boss of half of Jaffa, the whole of Jaffa!" he declared with strange enthusiasm, "Everything depends on his say-so. He allows it - it's allowed, he forbids - it's forbidden! Can you imagine, Uncle, what kind of a life I'm living under his thumb?" And without waiting for a reply he hurried on, in a more stable, somewhat pensive tone of voice: "If you really had the faintest idea - you'd be congratulating... not me but Adon... doing me a favour and telling me his address. That information's going to keep me safe for six months at least... for six months I and my family can walk the streets without fear... and then when that time's up, maybe God will do me another 'small favour' or everything will change and Shuki won't be Shuki any more... Who knows what could happen? I'm already regretting my long tongue!" he said, suddenly alarmed - "But I know I've nothing to fear from you two. Real gents, the pair of you! You'd rather roast in Hell than betray a confidence... I'm not like that. I'm weak and I can't stand any kind of trouble, grief or suffering... And Shuki's the world expert in all that, the champion! So Adon did me a favour. Without knowing it, without meaning to, but he did it all the same and I'm grateful - with all my heart, for my sake and the sake of all my family! And I hope he'll come out of this whole and healthy, and have a long and happy life on the face of this blessed earth!"

"What kind of a stew have you cooked up?" Rahamim cut in, with a voice that was the next best thing to spitting.

Nessim didn't respond.

"But," I turned to Nessim - "it may be that at the end of the day you're not to blame. My impression is," I added, "that your revelation of my address came too late. Shuki already knew it."

"Not so!" Nessim grimaced with a certain bitterness, but at the same time, a strange air of superiority: "If I did him a favour he didn't need any more - he'd reckon I was up to something, or I'd lost my touch," he explained. "I'm very careful about the favours I do him, whether they're his idea or not..." He glanced briefly at the expression on my face and continued:

"I checked the ground carefully. It was clear. And it turned out later that my 'small favour' was highly satisfactory to him, very satisfactory indeed!" - he stressed with the smug, virtually unflappable smile of one to whom all the world's secrets are divulged: "My 'small favour'" he repeated, evidently liking the sound of it, "satisfied Shuki in two directions at once: there was the information itself, which he was very interested in, and secondly," - he smiled that smile again, tinged with a kind of self-indulgent cunning, good nature even, and yet not entirely exempt from anxiety - "it helped him check the honesty of one of his girls, the one who spent the night at Adon's house!"

"That sounds about right," I responded calmly. This was what I wanted to know: Shuki hadn't needed to extort my address from Lili, "his girl".

"That's what he told me," Nessim added and went on to quote: "'Now we'll see what my girl has to say!' he yelled at me with that brand of malicious joy that's so typical of him, when I gave him the address. I have to admit, I was curious. 'What do you mean?' I asked him innocently, all humble and obsequious, the way he likes it. And then he tells me in an undertone, as if we're mates sharing a secret: 'We'll see if she betrays that head-banger, or tries to cover for him. If that's what she does, we'll know how to deal with her. It'll be proof that she's got the hots for him!' And he laughed and slapped me on the shoulder in that spirit of pseudo-camaraderie of his..." At this, Nessim's face changed expression - turning dark and brooding, as if suddenly taken over by melancholia.

"Of course," he continued, raising his head as if trying to shake himself free of that black mood, "that's not to say that he feels the faintest shadow of anything resembling friendship for me... The fact is, he doesn't know what friendship is. Shuki's the boss of Jaffa - and the loneliest man in town! But," he added, "he knows how to evaluate people. He's got me figured for a wimp and so he isn't afraid of me. He can't imagine me ever doing anything he'd disapprove of, and he's right... except in this one particular case..."

"Did you feel sorry for Shuki's girl?" asked Rahamim in a heavy voice, but with a lot of interest, tension almost.

"No!" was Nessim's uncharacteristically vehement reply.

"Were you sorry for yourself?" Rahamim persisted in the same tone of voice.

"I wanted to prove something," his nephew replied.

"To whom?"

"To myself."

"And what exactly did you want to prove to yourself?" - Rahamim's interrogation wasn't over yet.

"That I exist!" - was the answer.

Rahamim sighed, passed his tongue over his dry, cracked lips, and turned once more to his nephew:

"And what was the outcome of this experiment?"

"Bad and bitter," said Nessim. He scanned the expression on my face, chuckled with capriciousness containing not a trace of gaiety and added slowly, solemnly almost, enjoying the taste of every individual syllable that he uttered: "Or it would have been, if I hadn't got the remedy in first, before the injury..."

I saw the look in his eyes which now, in contrast to everything it had displayed up to this point, was clear and alive with the faint flicker of a distant light.

"I managed to locate the girl and tell her in time that he - forgive me if I prefer not to keep mentioning his name - already knew it, the address he was interested in, he had the information... And she was absolutely livid, positively sobbing with rage... but, at the end of the day, I'm sure - she was truly grateful to me, from the bottom of her heart!"

Silence fell and diffused between the thick, concrete walls of the café. The sough of the waves of the sea was carried by the open air, a sough gathering strength and seeming to threaten something hidden, that in the end would be incapable of resisting it.

"That was a gallant thing to do," I declared succinctly, adding -

"and courageous. Shows strength of character!"

"It may be so!" Rahamim sighed again, "But I still think the best option would have been no 'small favours' for Shuki at all, and no divulging of addresses, certainly not Adon's!" He withdrew to his little kitchen and shortly returned carrying a little brass tray with ornamental engravings, and on it a cup of tea - the colour of clear amber gilded by the rays of the sun. For Nessim and himself, Rahamim served black coffee.

We sat around the low, oval table, on stools of plaited wicker and sipped at a leisurely pace. Rahamim lit a cigarette. No one spoke. A bright beam of light filtered inside, cleaving the ancient void of the café with its serene lustre.

HOT TEA

I arrived home at a late hour of a humid night.

Light showed from two of the low windows. Lili was inside.

She was sitting on the sofa - an erect, passably elegant posture, but there was also something stolid about her, as if she were competing for control of the open, empty, illuminated space before her, upon which I had just intruded. The bold lines of her pencilled eyebrows were incapable of hiding the gentle radiance of her eyes, always ready to forgive, without ever acknowledging the fact. And only the abundant hair, pinned up though it now was, foretold turbulence and rebellion. The tight lips, accentuating high cheekbones, testified to astonishing endurance of unfathomable limits.

On the low table there were two steaming tea-cups.

"How did you guess when I'd be arriving?" I smiled at her amicably.

" 'Cos the tea's still hot, you reckon I must have guessed?" she asked with strange, innocuous vehemence. Her posture was still tense, rigid almost, but at the same time something childlike and pure was encroaching upon her voice, somewhat that she no doubt construed as weakness and was therefore at pains to suppress.

"And what makes you think I haven't just arrived myself?" Her voice was deep and strange, spurning any attempt at coquetry or humour.

"That's possible too," I said with a laugh, "but I wouldn't bet on it!" I laughed again.

And suddenly, something in her artificial stolidity broke, something in the rigid tension of her body, in the taut lines of her face, in her eyes, trying so hard to survey her surroundings with ostentatious, cool disdain. My laughter was infectious and she laughed with me, uttering sounds that were wonderfully harmonious, smooth and radiant. The expression on her face changed completely; her eyes cleared and shone with bright innocence, the eyes of a child chasing a butterfly in a field.

And having finally subdued the melodious strains of her mirth, she spoke in tones that were lucid and clean:

"This is the fifth round of tea that I've brewed! The other four went cold... don't you have a thermos in this house? I've wasted gas... but that's a price you'll have to pay if you're going to stay out so late. A monk staying out late at night - now there's decadence for you!" Her eyes still held the last vestiges of laughter, like the rays of the setting sun, filtering through the branches of an ancient oak.

I sat down, prayed and took a sip. Lili also drank. For a while neither of us spoke.

"Shuki visited you," she said, finally breaking the silence. "I know, he told me himself," and in a resolute tone intended to inspire confidence, she added: "Don't take any notice of his threats. It's just his way of talking... at the end of the day - he's a man like any other man and his dignity means a lot to him..." - she looked into my face - "and it seems you wounded his dignity..."

"Not intentionally," I commented.

"That's what I thought. I tried to explain it to him too. Maybe I succeeded... in fact I'm sure I did!" she cried in a tone of emphatic, but probably phoney triumphalism, designed to convince and encourage herself as much as anyone else. "Don't be afraid of him!" she concluded, trying to sound authoritative.

"I'm not afraid," I replied solemnly, and added: "Fear is the result of identifying with the flesh, and the pain that it brings."

"So real monks don't identify with the flesh?"

"No."

She thought for a moment, with some slight wrinkling of her limpid, domed, childlike forehead.

"What I mean is, there's no need to be afraid of any physical harm happening to you or to anyone else."

"I'm not afraid," I repeated my assurance.

She looked up from under that smooth dome of her forehead:

"Not even afraid of what might happen - to me, for example?"

"No," I replied.

"That's good!" she declared, and it seemed she meant it. We returned to the tea that was cooling steadily.

When the empty cups had been replaced on the low table, she said on a playful note, but with an undertow of bitterness:

"If you decide to jump on me tonight - I won't have any means of defending myself," and giving me an evasive look under the straight lines of her pencilled eyebrows, she added: "He took the razor off me!" She shifted her gaze to the concrete wall facing her; it had been given a fresh coat of plaster not long before, but this wasn't enough to disguise its deep fissures.

"There was a moment when a dumb thought occurred to me... or maybe not so dumb after all..." - she tossed into the void as if conversing with herself: "I thought of using that razor when he was in bed with me... there was a moment like that... Don't get me wrong," - she turned to look at me - "I'm used to all kinds of kinks, and I know how to 'faint' and not be there... but he always succeeds somehow in bringing me back to reality, getting it on with me in the most revolting manner possible. That's what he enjoys," she asserted in a remarkably even tone of voice. "A perverted pleasure... but then everything about him is perverted! He does everything he can to make himself disgusting and hateful to me - all the way!"

"I didn't find him disgusting or hateful," I retorted firmly.

Something very sad flashed in her eyes, and she went back to staring across the table at the deep fault-lines on the opposite wall.

"That's when that dumb idea occurred to me - to use the razor... the razor was there, in the pocket of my jeans, beside me... close, so close... But it was like he was reading my thoughts, or picking something up... sixth sense or something, something unnatural, and he beat me to it.

"Shuki's one of a kind," she continued, staring at her empty cup, then picking it up and gripping the handle tightly, as she went on to say:

"The fact is, he didn't actually have to read my thoughts, and there was nothing very mysterious about his senses either, the way my hands were fumbling with the jeans... the pocket where the razor was. He had good reason to be afraid of me, you know..." She raised her head and without letting go of the cup-handle, turned to me - a bleak, unfamiliar look in her eyes. "I can put up with a lot... like..." She stopped as if unsure whether to continue.

"Kicks in the face?" I finished the sentence for her.

"He told you that too?" Something rebelled in her voice and she added hastily: "It's not that serious! Anyway, there hasn't been any kicking lately. He wouldn't dare! I'm not the greenhorn of years gone by... five years to be precise. Five years with him, that's like eternity!" she insisted - "And he's still trying to shock me with more and more outrageous behaviour... he's trying to get to the final frontier of filth, make himself as vile to me as he possibly can - to test me, find out just how tightly I'm tied to him, how dependent I am. He's pathetic!" She gave me another sidelong glance, put down the cup, and seemed to be sorting something out in her mind; when she spoke again her voice was briefly, crisp and clear: "He's like all men - he wants to be loved. And he has to have it proved to him, and it drives him wild and desperate - pathetic. And I'm prepared to put up with a lot, but every now and then, I reckon enough is enough..." A dull note of disappointment crept into her voice, disappointment with herself. And focusing on an invisible point on the table-top, she exclaimed: "These perversions!"

A tremor passed through her voice and through her lean body too. She needed a long moment to regain control of herself, and having succeeded, she leaned forward with her elbows on the table, looked up and glanced at me coolly:

"And then I remembered the razor. I didn't just remember, I reached out for the jeans beside me, touched the pocket... and I did all this so carefully he didn't even notice the movement! And before Shuki had time to suspect anything, before even I realised what was happening, the open razor was in my hand and the smooth, shiny blade intoxicated me... You should try putting yourself in my shoes!" she cried defensively and resumed her account:

"I was holding the razor somewhere above his head, very close to his hairy neck..." She scanned the expression on my face at length, and with meticulous care, and not finding there what she expected to find, whatever that might be, she turned away again. My lack of response, so it seemed, didn't disappoint her but on the contrary, brought her a kind of relief that she was ashamed to acknowledge and quick to suppress. Her eyes lowered. She was silent a moment longer, before continuing:

"Then he stopped me... the razor had been dangling over the back of his neck for some time, and my hand was starting to shake and I was all covered in sweat... and it was only then he came to his senses and grasped what was happening..." Lili grinned a bitter smile to herself, rueful, self-indulgent - "Moving quickly, just like a real snake, he turned over, grabbed the hand that was holding the razor with both of his, and got it off me - without too much effort, no effort at all maybe..." She gave me another appraising glance and went on: "He took it quite gently, folded it, reached out for his trousers and stuck the razor deep in the pocket. I was barely conscious at this moment!" The announcement was for herself as much as for me.

"So you weren't prepared to hurt him?" - it was a statement as well as a question.

The answer came immediately:

"No."

She stared down at the scarred, crumbling floor-tiles and after a prolonged silence spoke again, without looking up:

"I had one of those weird notions - the kind of thing you catch a glimpse of, and they scare you to death..." With an abrupt, candid movement she looked up at me and resumed: "All of a sudden I realised that you couldn't condone something like this, it would disgust you - and not so much the action as the one who did it - me! You wouldn't want me around, not ever! You'd find me repulsive!"

Her look softened, and with a sidelong glance at me she added:

"If I was sent to jail, you wouldn't visit me, ever... such a strange mixture of ideas!" She looked up at me again, with inquiring eyes.

"Very strange!" I agreed, not responding to her implied question.

"And that's what weakened my hand," she added hastily, as if this was an admission she feared she might regret. "I didn't want you to be disgusted with me!"

"I wouldn't have been disgusted," I answered her calmly.

"You wouldn't have minded if I'd killed him?"

"Yes!" I replied with unequivocal force. "I'd have minded it very much! I'd never condone such a thing! But," I added, "having said that - anything that you did wouldn't change in any way my relationship with you..."

"Oh!" A cry escaped her which she tried, in vain, to turn into a sigh of disappointment, and at once she resumed, her voice quite stable:

"Even without that, I wouldn't have done anything. I guess I just haven't got what it takes. But I wanted to give him a jolt, show him there are things I'm capable of... I'm not just a rag he can wipe his dirty boots on whenever he feels like it, wherever he feels like it..."

"How did he react?" I asked with interest.

"After he'd got what he wanted... if he ever gets what he wants, that is!" she commented sourly - "He stood up, waved those two razors at me like a maniac, laughed a strange kind of laugh, called his mother, called me a thousand filthy names and then started to cry, saying he hadn't a single friend in the world and he was lonely and even his mother saw him as a cheat and a villain who should never have been born, and if I'd carried out what I had in mind, she, his mother, would have been the first to rejoice..." She fell silent again.

"And then?" I encouraged her.

"He went away. Disappeared for two days. Yesterday he came back all hyped up, brought sweets and liquor and said he'd visited you and you'd impressed him and he could understand me falling for you... and then he started yelling 'But he's insulted me and he's going to pay for that'. And when he said this he was dead serious, and his face went all twisted and he kept on shouting 'He's going to pay the lot!' And I knew he meant every word he said... So then I called his mother and between us we managed to calm him down, pouring so much booze down his throat he didn't know his right hand from his left, and we tried to make him promise not to harm you in any way..."

"I'll bet you had your work cut out!" I smiled at her.

"Right!" she assented. "All our efforts were in vain. We couldn't get anything out of him, not his word of honour, that he boasts about so much, no promise, let alone an oath... although in the end you can't even rely on these... He just wasn't going to cooperate - even though he was pissed out of his head and in a weird mood! Still," - her eyes flashed - "he'll have me to answer to if he tries to have a go at you!"

She rose eventually from her seat and gave me a somewhat mournful look, combining the shadow of fear with helplessness, faint intercession - and a powerful desire to conceal all of this:

"You don't want me to stay?" It was part question and part statement

"No," - I put on a smile that was tender and bright, but at the same time, firm and resolute - "unless you really have nowhere to go..."

"I could always make up a story about having nowhere to go," she responded in a playful tone that didn't cover the residue of the steadily dissolving bitterness, "and the story wouldn't be that far from the truth!" she concluded quietly.

"You won't do that," I stated confidently.

She weighed my words, turning to me with the flash in her eyes, the childish innocence, that she was proving unable to control:

"If that's the way it is - I'm staying here!" and she added at once with dignity: "That's 'cos I really have no other place to go! At least, not tonight... So off you go into your room and I'll sort myself out here... and Goodnight! And don't close the door - I want to talk!"

I climbed into my bed and was already beginning to drift into a doze, the prelude to healthy sleep, when her voice roused me:

"Can you hear me?" she called from the outer room with a blend of anxiety and tenderness and something deep and inexorable, and a hint of gloom at the margins.

"I can hear you," I answered her.

"There's something I'm dreaming about," - she cleared her throat and restored the usual timbre to her voice, or at any rate tried to restore it - and seemed to be succeeding to some extent. What she was trying to hide behind this voice - perhaps she herself was not entirely sure.

"And now, in this situation that we find ourselves in - I mean, you in that dark and distant room and me here on your padded sofa - it seems to me it's okay to expose it... the dream I'm talking about!" she stressed and continued: "It's all the more okay to expose it, seeing there's no chance - or 'prospect' would be a fancier word - of it ever coming true, from any angle!" She chuckled melodiously, with a strange air of satisfaction, combined with unmistakable contrariness. And after a long pause, a pause of weighty consideration and deliberation, she spoke out with remarkable clarity:

"I'd like to be your wife... a real wife! Not a bed-mate... or anyway - not just that. Besides, if you wanted to keep your vow of chastity - bed wouldn't come into it at all! All I want... and I'm not sure how to put it - I'd like to serve you, cook things for you, guess what it is you want before you put it into words - and do it, do it in such a way you'll have no idea who's responsible for it, and I'll be thinking up all kinds of funny ideas to impress and amuse you," - she chuckled again - "and if was possible, if it was only possible - I'd work for you and make you a pile of money, loads of it. And you could do whatever you like with it. Build yourself a monastery if that's what you want. And I'd buy clothes for you too... things that I like - but they'd have to be to your taste as well. I want to see you happy, even happier than you are now, and that's a kind of happiness I can't even begin to understand! Give you some of my happiness, give you everything I have… and no pressure, absolutely not! You see - I'm not even asking to curl up with you on long dark nights… I'd go without that too - if that's what you want. I'd be happy just guessing what you want, getting it right, and doing it - all the way…"

I exploited a short interval to say in a soft but decisive voice:

"I'll tell you the truth. You and I don't exist as 'you' and 'I', but as a unity of light existing in Him - who is true happiness, joy and freedom and love everlasting."

"Those words don't tell me much," she commented, without changing the slow and dreamy tone of her voice, "but all the same, I'll take them on board and believe them - if that's what you want. I'm longing to be at your side always, close to you - not too close! To see you, at least once a day… and at night, hear your steady breathing, even like this, from your room… hear your breathing and be filled with this secret happiness, inside, in the heart - I couldn't ever ask for more than that!" And sensing that I was about to respond, she hastened to add:

"I hear your breathing and it gives me pleasure, pleasure like you wouldn't believe, 'cos it's a sign of your bodily health and good state of mind, and those are much more important to me than my own health and state of mind… Actually, I've never rated myself much. I know I'm the worst of sinners, a dissolute woman, without hope, without any remedy… but, you see, I have dreams: to be with you even the way we are now - you in that dark little room and me - here in this room that I miss so much so much whenever I'm away from it, miss it painfully, pain of body and soul!"

"Well, no one's going to stop you visiting," I responded with a degree of reserve.

"That's not quite the same, is it?" she objected.

"It's all there is!" I declared in a tone of voice allowing no interruption. "Supposing one day, the object on which all your happiness depends disappears or goes the way of all flesh - you'd be left in an empty void, hurt and helpless!"

"Something of all this would remain!" she asserted with strange confidence, "something worth more than all of this life, more than all worlds and dreams…"

She was silent for a long moment, and then in a more controlled, sobre tone of voice she asked:

"And those who've attained this happiness you've described - why should they carry on wandering around in this world?"

"To light the way for all those who desire their light."

Silence fell in the house. Shadows danced on the opposite wall. The gentle, silky shadows of the hours past midnight.

"That's not it," she said finally, in a troubled voice, a faint note of melancholy creeping in: "Although I can tell you'd rather be alone...with this happiness that you've talked about, this God that's in your heart... that you're so devoted to...they taught me" - she suddenly raised her voice - "taught me in the Mission I mean, that God is loved through His creatures!" There was a question in her words. I answered it.

"If love - is pure love, then - God is its source!"

"Yes - that is love!" she declared, as if stating the obvious.

I sensed the caress of her eyes. She was touching the happiness that no power on earth can spoil.

DAVID FARHI

This body inhaled a lungful of blue-tinted, invigorating evening air. There was silence all around, punctuated by the muffled, rhythmic rumble of the sea. And there was also a special silence, the evening silence of Jaffa, limpid and gentle and mysterious, on the one hand intoxicating and on the other - arousing the impulse to do something in utter defiance of convention; a yearning to hover above the turbulent, limitless sea, to melt and vanish into oblivion beyond the lustre of its far horizons.

When I turned my attention to this body, proceeding at a leisurely pace along familiar paths, I found that I was in the narrow defile between the two low hills of Jaffa, a long way from my own home but close to the all too familiar "Menora Street".

I had already turned to my left, heading in the direction of home, when I caught sight of a thin column of smoke rising to my right, turning black as it climbed higher and thickening rapidly.

Thoughtfully I retraced my steps and set out towards "Menora Street" which boasted all of two houses facing each other, Number 1 and Number 2.

Some ten minutes later I was approaching the two houses. The source of the towering smoke was Number 2. I saw the intermittent flash of yellowish-red flames at the base of the column.

I broke into a run.

Outside the gate of the house I found distraught neighbours and all the members of the Farhi family - daughters, son and wife - except the head of the family, David Farhi himself. They ran hither and thither, in a panic and utterly at a loss, like ants whose nest has been destroyed. The girls wailed, tearing at their dishevelled hair, the mother stared up at the sky. Israel was talking to himself.

"Has the fire-brigade been called?" I asked.

"Someone's got onto them," he replied and added: "He got all of us out, you see? All of us. Said he needed time to think... alone. Completely alone! He came with us as far as our neighbour's house and made sure we were all there, and made us promise - he was absolutely insistent - to leave him undisturbed for an hour... so we promised and we kept to it. We never imagined... He... he's still in there!"

"So why aren't you trying to help?" I shouted right in his ear, my voice already hoarse, throat seared by the acrid smoke billowing all around us.

"The gate's locked," Israel coughed in my face - "from inside! We tried to force it with that iron bar over there, but it didn't work...we've been looking for a ladder..." he added vaguely, "to climb over the wall, but we can't find one. Nothing we can do... nothing we can do..." He was almost whimpering now.

"If I climb on your shoulders, I can get across," I told him.

"No!" Israel objected brusquely. "You could get trapped in there with no way out! No!"

"Yes!" shouted Flora who had evidently overheard, her voice ringing out with astonishing clarity. "He can open the gate for us and let us all in. No one's going to get trapped!"

Reluctantly, muttering to himself, Israel obeyed his mother and knelt at my feet, letting me mount his broad shoulders.

A few seconds later I was over the wall, in the extensive garden with its neatly cultivated flower-beds and ornamental path - all of it shrouded now by a slow-moving, heavy, creeping pall of grey smoke, like an unearthly fog. There was a strong whiff of gasoline in the air.

It was no easy task opening the gate, which was not only bolted securely, but also barricaded with heavy old armchairs, a table, mattresses, upturned beds, odd breeze-blocks and planks. The main door to the house itself was locked too, and the windows barricaded.

When the gate was opened I turned at once to the backyard in the faint hope of finding an unlocked door or a window left open. Sure enough, the bathroom window wasn't barricaded or even locked. A light push, and it swung wide open.

I threaded myself through it and found myself standing between the toilet pedestal and the bath. The smoke here was thick, stinging the eyes. I found a towel, wetted it, wrapped it round my head, pushed the door open and cautiously entered the interior of the house. I realised I was standing in the spacious living-room where the few pieces of furniture, left over from the barricades, were in flames. Stifling smoke was everywhere. Through the smoke I caught sight of what looked like a big burning torch, flames gradually subsiding as the substance was consumed. I didn't approach it. After a long second of deliberation, and rational analysis of the situation,

I turned back. The incandescent torch was indeed nothing other than David Farhi who, as it emerged later, had doused his clothes in gasoline before setting himself alight. He sat erect in a smoke-blackened armchair, the polished wooden jewellery-box burning in his hands.

I staggered out into the yard and many hands were held out to me to pull me away from the danger-zone. A fire-truck was parked a few dozen metres from the burning house, the closest it could get. The hoses were in action, showering jets of water and foam on the flames which had now broken through the roof at all four corners. It took two more hours to extinguish the blaze.

Of the corporeal David Farhi, all that remained were chunks of charred flesh, blackened, brittle bones and a pile of thin ash.

After arguments and pleas and the payment of a suitable backhander, the burial company was prevailed upon to record the death as a tragic accident rather than suicide, and permission was given for the interment of David Farhi's incinerated remains within the perimeter of the cemetery. The funeral was modest and sparsely attended. No vehicles were hired this time for the transportation of the few mourners, who had to make do with their own resources.

DEPRESSION

I went down to Rahamim's café.

Grey clouds, low and heavy, veiled the surface of the sky, ambling slowly towards an unknown destination. The sun had set and a distant rosy pallor, glimpsed through a break in the cloud, was the final curtain-call of the daylight. A cool breeze rose in the west, skimming across the grey expanse of the sea and imposing its mastery on the narrow strip of shore-line, whispering between shrub and tree.

I drank my afternoon tea in silence. Having served it, Rahamim sat facing me, sipping strong black coffee from a tiny cup, as was his wont. Neither of us spoke. On finishing my tea I stood up and parted from him with a light wave of the hand, and his response was the same.

I left the café, walking along the deserted coastal strip where sycophantic breakers nuzzled the shore decorously, reflecting a soft and enchanted radiance of young stars. The wind was freshening and the darkness thickening. I turned my steps homeward.

As I climbed the steep hill, I was aware of a strange sense of depression, growing steadily   heavier and weighing on my heart, something amorphous and impenetrable, trying to paralyse my lungs and deny them air to breathe. From an objective viewpoint, such a depression could cause me no harm whatsoever, whereas from the viewpoint of the illusory existence of the body – it brought with it a kind of foreboding, a warning, not to be ignored, of forthcoming events, forthcoming, that is, in the immediate future.

I stood still, pondering to myself the meaning of this insistent demand. Mentally, I processed data, posited circumstances, dissected hints, as if trying to elude it, as if expecting it to dissipate and disappear of its own accord and no longer clog the limpid channels of consciousness. But all of this was to no avail. The depression didn't ease; on the contrary it grew ever stronger. Clearly, I needed to decide on some course of action.

After another moment of profound introspection, more

analysis of data and circumstances and this time, with the emphasis on the outcome to be anticipated, as ultimately arising from one or another pattern of behaviour – I decided to ignore the depression and its implied warning and continue on my way. After all, whatever is destined to befall the body cannot be substantially changed or influenced in any way and furthermore, as a point of principle, there is no purpose to be served in attempting to defer it.

Anyway, having located the depression I shrugged it off, as one shakes crumbs from a table cloth, and with light step and in buoyant spirits, humming to myself one of the "songs of freedom", I continued on my way.

When I reached the confluence of alleyways bordering on the Phantoms' Quarter, shrouded in heavy darkness, looming darkness evidently impervious to any whispers of the heart, the silhouette of a man emerged from the shadows, blocking my path and holding up his hand, a signal to stop. Before I had time to say a word, more figures appeared from the darkness, surrounding me.

"Would you be so kind as to accompany us?" asked the first with meticulous courtesy, his voice soft and quite pleasantly modulated. He stopped short of prostrating himself at my feet, but not by a wide margin.

"By all means!" I replied with a bright smile, my voice pellucid.

Before long my feet were treading the unspeakably filthy floor of the ruined building to which my physical destiny had invited me some time before, with five grand in my pocket, the bridging-loan for an apartment. As then, the empty space was dimly lit by the pale glow of a lantern mounted on the low wall.

The members of my escort, all dressed in leather waistcoats and with hands thrust deep in pockets, dispersed to the corners of the dark expanse and seemed to vanish from sight. Directly before me, eyes flashing with malice, the eyes of a hawk swooping on his prey, a mocking, cynical smile on his face – stood Shuki. The faint light of the lantern turned his face yellow, making it seem more grotesque than ever.

"Adon!" he began with emphatic solemnity, "With all the respect and esteem in which I hold you," – he bowed theatrically – "it is my duty to inform you that you are in breach of the law!"

"Which law is that?" I inquired.

"The law of men of honour!" he snapped, adding in a much more moderate tone, almost amiably, evidently enjoying himself: "Today, you were supposed to be bringing me a thousand…" He treated me to a gentle, caressing glance, as if trying to remind an old and dear friend of a favour owed: "That little loan I asked for! So, if you have it with you, hand it over and you can go on your way and forget the whole business. You'll come to no harm! You see, we too," – he indicated with a sweep of the hand the men leaning on the walls of the ruined building, half hidden by the darkness – "we are honourable people, and our word is our bond!"

He waited a long moment for a response and when none came, went on:

"If you haven't brought what I asked for as a friend, a friendly request for a modest loan – and we are talking about a loan, Adon!" he stressed, suddenly beginning to suspect that I was giving him less than my full attention: "Are you listening to me?" His face took on a stern expression, and his hand brushed lightly against the shabby old raincoat that I was wearing.

"Yes," I replied.

"So you're spurning my friendship, not interested in having a friend like me?" – it was both a question and an observation. He appraised me with an offended look, but without any loss of softness and warmth, and continued: "Underworld types like me – whoremonger, extortionist, mobster, drug-pusher…" he ran through the list with the same note of strange pleasure as before, both succinct and expansive.

Shuki's face turned grim, and again his flashing eyes scoured my face. And his appraisal, it seemed, failed to satisfy him. His twisted smile giving his face a grotesque expression, he tensed his lips and commanded:

"Give!" He held out his sinewy hand.

"Don't be ridiculous!" I retorted, maintaining a soft and genial voice. "Where would I get a thousand from?"

"You're pissing me off again!" he cried in a voice that would tolerate no interruption, his eyes shooting sparks: "I don't give a toss where you get the cash from!" – and with the ferocity of someone whose legitimate rights have been trampled underfoot in broad daylight, he insisted: "You owe it to me – since that evening when you threw five grand at me, right here, like you were throwing a bone to some scabby dog! What did you think? You bought God for five thousand? You hit me so hard I'd never get up again? That money was enough to buy my girl and save your peace of mind, not to mention your skin?" He paused, staring deep into my eyes, and added, a demented note of triumph in his voice: "Mistake, Adon, bad mistake!"

"What a funny name that is!" he said with a sudden change of tone, a hint of bogus petulance. "Adon? Adon indeed! What makes you a master?" – another change, to a full-throated growl – "I wouldn't put you in charge of a pig farm!" He chuckled briefly, before adding sternly:

"You snubbed Shuki – remember that! – why haven't you brought me the thousand I asked for?"

"I never had any intention of bringing it," I laughed, so serenely and confidently that for a moment he lost his composure, struck dumb with amazement. Finally he managed to say: "If you're not going to cooperate, you'll get what's coming to you!" He gestured into the darkness and I sensed someone approaching from behind me, with fist raised to strike.

I moved aside just in time and the blow cleft the void, setting up shock-waves that whistled in the air. The would-be assailant lost his balance and almost fell at Shuki's feet.

He stood up – a big man with heavy features and cold eyes, green, fishy eyes, slightly protruding and now, untypically, alight with destructive fury. He made to repeat his attempt, hitting me in the face this time, but Shuki intervened, grabbing his arm and hissing darkly in his ear:

"Are you a cretin or what! An elephant versus a flea – and you miss! Move!"

The other obeyed him with immediate, professional deference, lowered his clenched fist and returned to the shadows.

Shuki turned to me, on his face one of his gentlest, most amicable smiles, expressing solidarity in adversity and readiness to help. His voice changed too, accordingly, taking on a deep and velvety tone:

"What a hero!" – he pointed at the one who had retreated into the darkness behind me – "Big and brawny, and a tiny brain... But don't go judging the others by his standard," he warned solemnly, " 'cos you'll be in for a big disappointment!" And he continued, dispelling all the softer notes from his voice and speaking in total seriousness and with an air of unassailable confidence: "What you deserve, you're going to get! You'll get it all right... Maybe we'll send you back to Lili as a eunuch!" And here, quite unexpectedly he burst into strange, raucous laughter, metallic-sounding and tremulous, laughter fit to grate the nerves of anyone with nerves prone to grating.

For a long moment the sound shattered the silence of the night. In the leaden sky above my head the moon hid its face behind a big, low cloud. When the disturbance was over, Shuki turned to me again:

"Twice she's betrayed you!" he declared and went on to explain: "Then, when she told me your address, and today... you know how she's betraying you today?" He took a step forward, moving in closer and, in customary style, scanning the lines of my face. His look was suffused with seething hatred, with nothing but pain behind it – searing, deep, inexpressible pain:

"She knows that I'm here, and I'm going to do to you whatever I feel like... She knows it... down to the last detail. She probably reckons it's already been done and you're rolling about in the dirt – blood and pain and the greatest shame any man can suffer, any man at all, except maybe in your case... to this day I haven't got the faintest idea what you are!" He tensed, waiting for an answer and when none came, he melted a little, sighed and asked almost amicably:

"Where is she?" – and he stepped a full pace back from me. "Do you see her?" He waved his outstretched arms in a theatrical gesture that took in the whole of the dark void around us.

"I can cope without her!" I shot at him with relish, with a teasing note of challenge.

"Has your last brain cell flown away?" he cried in a tone of friendly reproof. "I thought you were smart! What you're going to 'cope' with is five men who'll do anything I tell them to do. Even if that's slicing up your flesh and eating it, to hide the evidence!" I saw he was expecting a response and decided not to give one.

"It seems your senses are all over the place! Or can't you see in the dark?" He raised his arms and moved his hands in a gesture of invitation, a gesture of command and authority, and from the darkness five men appeared, hands in waistcoat pockets, faces blank and eyes cold as death.

"A sign from me, and every one of these guys will turn his attention to one of your body parts! One apiece! They'll get to work on you... still alive of course, and squeeze out all the pride and insolence and arrogance built up in you since your first appearance on the face of the earth". He studied my face again, with that manic expression of triumph and satisfaction taking over his features and setting all this sinews throbbing.

A long moment passed.

"Maybe you'll claim," – he broke the silence that was lengthening and growing oppressive, "that six against one isn't fair! But I tell you, I reckon it's perfectly fair! Anyway, who decides what's fair and what's unfair? Six against one, that's my idea of fairness". And once more he broke into raucous, guttural laughter, the men, still standing at their posts, joining in with sounds of their own, sharing with him the undefinable delight of team-satisfaction, the joy experienced by a pack of predators closing on their prey.

And suddenly, in typical fashion, Shuki fell silent, lifted his arm and hushed his confederates. All repressed wrath and fury, he spat at me:

"I'll give you a chance. Last chance!" And he added: "I'll play by the rules accepted by you. Or the ones you represent! Here!" and with a contemptuous gesture he tossed down at my feet a razor, one of the two in his possession. He took the other out of his pocket, opened it adroitly and brandished it in his right hand.

"Defend yourself!" he shouted, signalled to one of his men, who came forward, stooped, picked up the razor from the cracked and grimy floor and handed it to me.

I took it in one hand and opened it with the other; it looked childish, ridiculous, tasteless.

"As I said once before," I responded in a clear and firm voice, "it's a coward's weapon." I threw the razor away behind me and called to Shuki: "Come on!" And my body tensed in anticipation of what was to come.

He responded to my call and leapt forward at once, with lightning speed.

At that very moment, the dark void of the roofless building was suddenly full of people. Shouts were heard, heavy blows, kicks, the dull thud of a heavy body falling to the ground. Someone grabbed hold of me and pulled me aside.

"Is your name Adon?" he panted heavily in my ear, a tall, unshaven, heavy-fleshed man.

"Yes," I managed to reply, gasping for breath.

"I'm supposed to be getting you out of here," he told me, and shielding me with his body, pushed me into a corner, beside a half-wrecked wall.

"How did you find me in this bear-garden?"

"The raincoat," he wheezed, still struggling for breath. " 'Thin, short, wears a light raincoat... the kind no one else wears these days' – that's how she described you. Said I was to rescue..."

"Who said?" I demanded to know.

"That girl... the one who gives it for free!" he declared and added with admiration and deep contentment: "What a girl!" And his face turning grim he concluded: "You'd better make yourself scarce. My job ends here, so scram!" And he was off, in one direction or another.

THE VOW

I found my way home.

This time too, someone had got there before me. I pushed the door open. I had barely stepped across the threshold when an incredibly light body – something more like a joyful surge of pure energy – hung itself around my neck, whimpering, in a manic spasm of pain, truncated phrases like: "God be praised... praise and thanks... forever and ever... what a miracle... it's a miracle! You're here... it's a miracle! Praise and thanks..." She wailed and whimpered, almost choking as the spasm tightened its grip.

All of this lasted no more than half a minute, before the body detached itself from my neck, took a step back and stood facing me.

Lili, awash with tears, her face crumpled, eyes red and swollen and their glassy stare crying out to Heaven that she had, really had, given up hope. And yet, already showing there were the first glimmers of a distant spark, of peace or perhaps – a spark of rejoicing. The frantic rejoicing of one who was, quite literally, struggling to believe her eyes. And suddenly Lili knelt on the floor, joined her hands, closed her eyes and spoke quickly, breathlessly:

"I'm thankful! I'm thankful! You are the one, You are the almighty, You are the merciful, You are the all-powerful. You worked this miracle! I'll do everything to make myself worthy! Protect him, protect him at all times, in all places... At least, as long as I'm here... No! – Even when I'm not here, protect him! I'll do everything to be worthy!" – and her body shook again spasmodically, in bitter, irrepressible weeping.

When she tried to stand up, she stumbled and almost fell. I leapt forward, clasped her outstretched hand and pulled her up, setting her on her feet in the middle of the room.

She looked at me through her tears, her eyes shining, clasped me again around the neck and at once recoiled, staring into my eyes from close range, mumbling:

"I still don't believe it! It's still hard to believe! Praise be to God! He will always love miserable sinners like me, always see their suffering, forgive them with grace and compassion, encourage them in their hardest moments, always perform miracles..." – and her face crumpled and dread returned to her eyes, dread of the living, recent memory. And tears filled those eyes and flowed in a thin, limpid, inexorable stream, dripping from her delicate chin and falling gently to the floor.

She turned her back on me, scurried to the kitchenette and soon returned with a tray of steaming tea and biscuits. Her hands still trembled, but she had dried her face with care, and her hair was tied up in a bun. She was careful not to look at me, for fear, I suppose, of repeating her tearful and emotional display. At the same time, she was sniffing back her snot like an urchin without a handkerchief.

"Sit down, Adon!" she commanded, her voice vibrant with joy – and the desire to conceal it. And before I had time to sit she continued:

"I'd just about given up hope of ever serving you tea and cookies again... Sit down, for God's sake! Don't stand there like a dummy... or like some prince out of a fairy tale, under a spell..."

"Listen to me for a moment," – I began gently, with a smile – "Nothing really happened! Nothing could have happened. When will you understand that the body is just a bundle of rags, and its only function is to serve as a bridge between spirit and the self!"

She sat facing me without looking at me, but the stream of tears on her cheeks, which seemed to have stopped, was flowing again.

"Why are you crying?" I asked in a changed tone of voice, still bright but also firm and sobering.

"From happiness!" – her voice quaked and took on a chirpy sound, the voice of a little girl. She wiped her cheeks, sniffed back more snot and continued in an even tone, as if in command of her senses: "It's because I'm hearing you and it doesn't matter that I don't understand what you're on about... although," she hastened to add in a tone that was suddenly stern and aggressive – "I know what you're after at the end of the day! It would have been so much better if I'd never met you!" she cried from the bottom of her heart, looking up and fixing me with the flash of her indignant eyes, surprisingly forceful and demanding a response.

My glance met hers, and transferred to her its luminous softness, its unflagging joy, its steadfast faith and undying love. Her face lit up. Her glare subsided, and indignation melted away as if it had never been. "No!" she cried out in a clear voice, purged of any trace of rancour, "God forbid! What dreadful things am I saying? I can't imagine my existence, the world, the air that I breathe and the light I'm beginning to see, the me that is myself – without you! This is the one thing that has any truth and meaning… God's wonderful gift!" And she continued in that clear and pellucid voice: "What matters is that I'm seeing you, and you're the way you are! I was sitting here, broken, deserted, beaten and helpless, worried sick and despair, more bitter than life and blacker than Hades, driving me out of my mind! I couldn't even figure out a plan of revenge… I just prayed. And hey, here you are – and I'm still shell-shocked and I can't believe what I'm seeing and what I'm hearing!"

"But Lili," I responded, reverting to that firm and cogent tone of voice, also tinged with light and designed solely to stabilise her spirit and finally restore her equilibrium – "from a certain point of view, it is thanks to you that I'm here. Someone broke in there, found me and got me out of that mess – at the last moment… which wasn't my last and wasn't even a moment!"

"You mean – in spite of everything they had time to do it?" she asked anxiously, strangely and unnaturally solicitous.

"I'm not sure I know what you're talking about," I answered her and added: "Shuki said he told you everything – even the place he was going to meet me, and the objective, and what I had coming to me. And true to type, he boasted that you were in on it too, encouraging him to go ahead."

"The man's a born liar!" she exclaimed brusquely, but then softened, letting the rapturous light flood once again her childlike face:

"Shuki," she began calmly, "told me he was going to wait for you – but here!" – she emphasised, pointing with an outstretched finger to the floor. "He changed the time too… he wanted to make sure that when I found out, it would be too late to do anything…

"So about the time, I just guessed and moved it forward, but the place…" – again her voice shook with unalloyed dread – "he had me fooled there all right!" She inhaled a deep draught of air and continued: "At the very last moment it occurred to me to send the boys to that place. It was just a blind guess, out of despair… I had to try something, even if it was suicidal…" She wrinkled her smooth, domed forehead, but it wasn't long before the wrinkles began to ease and her face shone with youthful light as before.

"And the boys," – she looked up at me, "they did a good job?"

"Yes," I answered her.

"I got them together in a hurry. From two discos and a bar. I had my work cut out, you know – one line-up, and the promise of second helpings if they did the job right..."

"Yes," I responded, "the man who asked my name and got me out of there,

mentioned that..."

"That was one little detail I'd rather have kept from you altogether!" She turned to me and studied the expression on my face with trepidation. The results of her scrutiny restored the light to her eyes and her face, and stilled the tremor of her shoulders – but only for a moment. Her expression turning serious again, she stared down at the floor and said: "This is something that has to stop too! One day, you'll see. I made a vow – when I was waiting for you here... and I was going out of my mind, in a real state... I vowed to be worthy of Him." She stared up at the ceiling with its flaking plaster, a gloomy look on her face. She sighed again and continued:

"It seems this is my curse... I'm a sinner, and the sin I go in for is one of the worst, seeing as it encourages others to sin... Maybe there's no atonement for me and no hope, and this is a vow I just can't keep. But I'll do anything – I'll try!"

"There's only one sin that exists in this world, and it has to be guarded against, in all places and at all times," I commented, my gaze again sinking deep into her eyes, which had turned grim and turbid, and restoring their life and vigour.

"And that is?" she asked, alert and expectant.

"Despair," was my answer.

For a long moment she pondered, then looked at me keenly and said: "That's one I've been guilty of myself, now and then. Still, if you say so, I'll try to resist it... but is it really the only sin? That's not the way I see it. Take Shuki, for example. He's got more sins in him than there are pips in a pomegranate..."

"If he doesn't despair," I retorted, "then he's innocent of any sin."

"He meant to murder you."

"Murdering's not that easy."

"It is for Shuki," she insisted. "He's used to it!"

"And maybe the idea was to scare you," I suggested – a flimsy suggestion, admittedly – and added: "To test your loyalty to him,"

"I don't think so," she responded, but a trace of doubt crept into her voice.

"Don't misunderstand me," – I tried to set the record straight – "If it's what you want, leave Shuki by all means, you must do as you see fit..." And in the same tone I added: "Maybe you're wrong about his intentions."

For a long moment she pondered my words to herself. Finally, she stated confidently "I'm not wrong!" – and went back to her tea.

We were still drinking tea when someone knocked on the door – or more accurately – someone clouted it three or four times. The door shook, and before I had time to respond it swung open and a big round head, with curly hair and stubbly beard, peered inside, inspected the interior with hungry eyes, focused on my guest and said:

"We're waiting. You promised, remember?"

"I'll be with you in a moment!" Lili replied with commendable professionalism, like a shop assistant dealing with an importunate customer.

The head disappeared, leaving behind it a pungent reek of tobacco and a trail of impatience.

"I have to!" She stood up, once again giving me a timorous look. "I promised! I have to keep my promise!" She skirted the table to pass by me, leaned towards me and asked, or perhaps stated a fact: "This doesn't bother you?"

"No," I answered her. "It's your private business."

"It doesn't change anything for you?" she pressed me.

"You would understand me better, and come closer to me in terms of that understanding – if you could give it up," I replied.

"I don't know if that's just a sermon," she commented, "but I'd rather it wasn't! I'd like it better if what you said really came from the heart!"

"It does come from the heart," I assured her.

"No, that's not it!" she protested. "What I really meant was – I hoped you'd mind just a bit..."

"I mind more than just a bit, and as for sermons," I smiled at her, "I only wanted you to reach out for the truth that's in you." And I saw fit to add: "For me, you'll always be the same Lili."

"Stupid and confused and up to her neck in shit!" she exclaimed bitterly, studying my face with big, inquisitive eyes.

"No," I retorted confidently, "you're not like that."

"So how do you see me?" she asked as if in desperation.

"You're simply, marvellous!" I declared with the composure of unshakable assurance, and concluded, "I've never known a heart as pure and as tender as yours!"

The knocking on the door was resumed – tentatively at first and then with greater force – heavy blows revealing the mood of those waiting outside.

"I'm coming, just a moment!" Lili called out in the gruff, throaty voice that she affected at such times – not always succeeding in expressing the firmness she was aiming for. Anyway, there was no emotion perceptible in her voice. She acted as if knowing very well what lay ahead of her, prepared for it from any angle.

She turned back to me and said: "I'm really very sorry. It's all gone wrong. If you tell me to – I'll stop it right now! I won't go out there, whatever the consequences. One word from you!"

"Are you trying to test me?" I smiled at her – a broad, placid smile. She was embarrassed. I added softly: "If it's really what you want – I'll go out there and get rid of the 'line-up'"

"Impossible!" she replied with a grimace. "I promised! And anyway," she added in a low voice, "it's too late now. But I'm grateful to you for the offer. I know it was sincere and genuine… wait for me – this won't take long… I've nowhere else to go tonight. And I'm not making that up."

THE FARHI SISTERS

At an early hour of a cool afternoon, ventilated by a light and yet mordant breeze, I dropped in at Rahamim's café.

He returned my gesture of greeting from behind his counter, then turned and disappeared into his little kitchen for a few minutes; on his return, he laid the cup of amber-coloured tea with its broad saucer on the table, and informed me in a hushed tone: "Israel Farhi, son of the late David Farhi... is looking for you. He'll be here in about a quarter of an hour..."

I didn't ask what exactly Israel Farhi wanted of me; I nodded my assent and calmly sipped the hot and clear liquid.

I watched Rahamim, standing behind his spotlessly clean counter, wiping cups and glasses that had just been washed with a freshly laundered towel, and putting them on a big tray beside him. The wind from outside did not penetrate the interior of the café, but the feel of the autumnal-wintry air was sensed, a good-natured Jaffa air, dreamy and intoxicating.

The drying-up done, Rahamim took one of the gleaming cups and poured himself a black coffee from a steaming pot on the stove beside him, then came out from behind his counter with the cup and its matching saucer and sat down beside me, to keep me company. His gleaming white apron matched the colour of the hair adorning his elliptical head and fringing his brow, furrowed with the creases of wisdom and experience of life.

"It seems to me he wants advice from you," he said between one calm sip and the next, in the same hushed tone as before.

"Why all the whispering?" I asked, surprised to hear my own voice dropping in volume.

"It's about not disrupting the harmony."

"What harmony are you talking about?"

"God's harmony," he replied, not looking at me, his voice still hushed but lucent and clearly audible – if restrained and strangely colourless.

"The harmony of God is always with us!" – I smiled at him pleasantly.

"But we're not always open to it!" he retorted, the furrows on his brow deepening and a faint note of reproof in his voice

I didn't answer him.

The silence lengthened and when he broke it, it was as if he did so to emphasise and consolidate it – if that makes any sense: "And when we are open to it, it's a sacred duty to take good care of it. The harmony of God purifies – it's the gateway to salvation!"

He took a last, leisurely gulp from his cup, and stayed where he was, sitting beside me quietly and barely moving a muscle, not even glancing at me, as if detached from himself and totally engrossed in that harmony of which he had spoken, unwilling to return to any other form of reality. And it was then that Israel Farhi arrived.

He pushed the heavy door open with a flourish, but on setting foot inside the café he stopped abruptly and gave us a sidelong look of surprise blended with confusion, in which a certain measure of chagrin was also perceptible. He didn't slam the door but closed it very carefully. Then he stood facing us, the fingers of one hand tapping the fingers of the other, nervously, and said:

"What secrets are you sharing, eh?" There was an unexpected note of serenity underpinning his voice, something which evidently disconcerted the speaker still further and added to his confusion.

"Ah-ha – Israel!" Rahamim turned to him calmly and rose to his feet, his face still holding an expression of solemn good nature and willingness to serve.

Israel pulled up Rahamim's vacated chair, ordered coffee, unfastened one of the buttons of his thick cardigan, stretched tightly over his broad chest, and began:

"You know about my sisters?"

"I heard they were married," I replied.

"Three of them..."

"I knew about two," I commented in a tone of agreeable surprise.

"Three!" – he stressed – "About four months ago. The two oldest... and the youngest."

"The two oldest," – I recalled – "the ones who were courted by the cobbler and the plumber? Your late father, bless him, wasn't particularly fond of the suitors..."

"The youngest married a teacher, a high school teacher, a geography teacher!" he chose to emphasise for some reason, ignoring my comment on the older two. Perhaps he considered this match the most auspicious and prestigious of the three.

"My congratulations!" I declared, my voice hushed as before and not expressing the degree of enthusiasm expected on such occasions.

"A bit late!" – Israel smiled awkwardly.

"Better late than never!" Rahamim interposed, appearing at the table with the coffee that had been ordered, black and hot as molten pitch.

"In this case," – Israel drew out the words into a kind of suppressed sigh, the awkward smile that still tightened his lips turning bitter and grim, "that statement too is out of place!" He took a noisy and emphatic gulp of his coffee, as if determined to savour the heat of the liquid and also to disguise his inner turmoil.

"What are you getting at?" Rahamim asked, standing beside us, and a particular kind of alacrity in his voice, the alacrity of one always prepared to take on board the suffering of another.

"The two older ones are already divorced, one after the other!" Israel replied promptly, adding in a more placid tone: "Only the youngest is still lasting the course..."

"Husbands a disappointment?" Rahamim wanted to know, his eyebrows knotted.

"From their point of view – yes..."

"And from yours?" Rahamim persisted.

"Well... what can you say?" Israel mumbled. "It's beyond me," he added as if still racking his brains – "We used to meet, chat... everything seemed okay, just fine... but who knows what was cooking there... I mean..." he sighed candidly, finally wiping the distorted smile from his face and choosing to conclude: "I really have no idea! I don't even have an opinion... But then what I think is irrelevant. I'm not the main issue here!"

"They're divorced already!" Rahamim muttered in quiet amazement.

"Already!" Israel confirmed, unfastening another button and returning to his noisy, emphatic slurping, still attempting to disguise the ferment of his feelings.

Without another word, Rahamim returned to the counter and set to with uncharacteristic energy on the task of washing the cups that had just been emptied, then turned to his little kitchen and disappeared into the storeroom.

"There's worse to come..." – Israel spoke without looking up at me, as if talking to himself – "A whole lot worse!" he stressed, turning his eyes to me and revealing the full weight of their turbid gloom: "They, the two oldest I mean, who were divorced not long ago, have got this very strange idea into their heads. In fact, it's not so much an idea, as a definite aspiration..." He waited for a response and as it was slow coming, continued:

"They want to go away and..." – he had difficulty expressing the essential point, as if he was recoiling from it, but eventually he managed to complete the sentence – "...and join a convent!" And once the seal of his heart was broken, he poured out all the bitterness and indignation that had accumulated in him thus far: "They're going to convert to Christianity, take monastic vows, both of them together, they want to be nuns!" And he broke off and fixed me with a mournful glance, an appeal for sympathy.

"And what can you do to stop them?" I responded equably. "After all," I added, "they're adults, and their destiny is for them to decide!"

"Apparently so," Israel sighed again, and continued: "But they're causing my mother a lot of grief... she was only just beginning to come to terms with things. I mean – after all the disasters that have befallen my family – Shmuel and my father dying, and the blow of the divorces – she supported them, had no choice I suppose.... Anyway, now there's this convent business..." He sent out a tentative, sidelong look, checking perhaps to see if anyone was listening to his conversation besides me, and went on to say:

"I've tried to talk them out of it, but I've got nowhere... absolutely nowhere! I tell them they're acting out of pure egotism, thinking only of themselves – and damn the consequences! They just carry on..."

"And what arguments do they put forward?" I asked.

"Love of God is higher than anything!" – he quoted, trying to convey to me the passion with which the words had been spoken, and at the same time to inflect them with a note of bitter scorn, reflecting his own state of mind at that moment. "I ask them what that means," Israel continued his account, "and they're happy to explain:

"Love of God is true love, embracing the whole world, and love of husbands is just submission to base desires, animal instinct, transparent sensual delights which never flourish unless there is hatred in the heart! Hatred – they say – blackens the heart! I ask them about their mother and they say with the same fervour, and not much in the way of remorse, that she should be proud of them!"

Slowly he turned his head and looked at me, ready to avert his bulging eyes at once if necessary. I met his gaze and held it. His expression now was a tormented, agonising appeal for support, or more than support – salvation, rescue from the valley of destruction. His whole being was dumb intercession, a cry for help.

"You want me to try and talk them of it, this intention of theirs that's so anathema to you?" I asked, my voice steady.

"If it's not too much trouble for you..." he sighed, with a kind of distant, hesitant relief. "For some reason," he continued, "you made a special impression on them, on my mother too... and on me! A positive impression, if I can put it like that. If you agree, I'll be only too glad to offer you hospitality! It wouldn't take too long. Now, if that's at all possible," he hastened to add, "because in the evenings there's some monk or priest or something who comes visiting... and he fills their heads with ideas! I'm not saying he's to blame. They invite him to call. They say he was their teacher at the Mission, in their high school. They studied at the Mission..." Israel leaned his heavy head forward, as if confessing a sin:

"They say he's the only one who really understands them... they're used to taking advice from him. Even my late father, bless him, wasn't averse to hearing his advice... and they warn us that if we throw him out, they'll up sticks and go off with him straightaway, to his monastery or church or whatever..."

He stared around him helplessly, then lowered his eyes and continued from the point where he left of:

"And that's the possibility that worries us most, much more so than the idea itself, in principle, that they're so hung up on at the moment. And they're neither of them prepared to give him up – the priest I mean, 'our only consolation' as they insist on calling him..."

I said nothing, keeping my eyes fixed on the low, oval table, with the droplets of spilled coffee on its clear formica surface.

"Complicated?" – Israel pressed me, trying to figure out what I was thinking.

"From a certain point of view – yes," I said, and proceeded to explain: "I'm not in the habit of getting involved in the affairs of others and controlling their thoughts and desires, nor am I prepared to influence their decisions. For better or worse, man is his own master. Interference from outside, not invited by the individual, does severe damage to his personal freedom. He has to decide for himself, by himself!"

"And if he asks for advice?" Israel asked me with a subdued look, hopes fading.

"Have they asked?" I demanded, fixing him with a stern, unflinching gaze. He recoiled, looked away and replied:

"They've agreed to listen... to you, I mean," – he stressed, in a voice showing not the slightest trace of optimism – "they're willing to listen, to you and no one else! If you agree," he pressed me, in desperation, "we'll be happy, my mother and I that is... and the others too, of course... to offer you hospitality... they respect you, at least come and hear what they have to say!" He was obviously having a hard struggle suppressing the impatience that was bubbling in his heart, and behind the mask of a forced smile he concluded: "And make any comments, as you see fit!"

I considered for a moment and said:

"I'll come," and at once I added, "but bear in mind that my visit could have the opposite result to the one you're hoping for!"

Israel sighed a heavy sigh, a sigh that seemed to be saying, I've no other option! – but immediately after it, his face was wreathed in a smile of sheer joy, as if the sigh had been merely for form's sake, a disagreeable obligation, and the smile that followed it was meant to show his relief at my answer; it had satisfied him, despite the caveat, and he was pinning his hopes on my visit. Indeed, he gave expression to this muddle of feelings when he said: "When all the exits are blocked – you've nothing left to lose!"

We paid our bills to Rahamim, who had reappeared behind his counter and was busily engaged in polishing some already gleaming spoons, waved our goodbyes to him and left the café.

After walking for about half an hour in the cool and refreshing evening air, we stood before the familiar gate of Number 2, Menora Street.

As before, the gate opened soundlessly, revealing the spacious garden with its flower-beds, vegetable patch and neat path. It seemed that the fire hadn't caused any real damage to the garden, or to the high wall, or to the heavy gate. The house, on the other hand, was substantially different. Parts of the walls had been rebuilt, and the new brickwork shone with youthful brio, combining serene self-confidence with the desire to find favour and show a welcoming face. The most obvious change was to the roof, thoroughly gutted and built again from scratch. Like its predecessor this was a tiled roof, but the colour of the tiles was emphatically vivacious and their flesh firm and young, a joyful sight to all observers and a poetic response to the solemn anthem of the setting sun. Even the gable-ends, whitening against the clear sky and fearlessly hoisting the tiles of the broad roof, seemed alive with song.

"We spent some money," said Israel, correctly interpreting the bright look in my eye, "we even borrowed, here and there..." And as I stood there a while, surveying the renovations with surprise and delight, he concluded confidently: "But the results speak for themselves!"

We went inside and were warmly welcomed by one of the girls who hurriedly spread an embroidered cloth over a new table – low, like its predecessor and polished to the same high sheen, but lacking the intricately carved legs. The armchairs, also new, differed from those I remembered, being more prosaic and less deep and plush, not so eloquent of the prestige of the family and the antiquity of its roots. These were decidedly from the popular – and cheap – end of the market. The walls of the renovated living-room had been painted a shade of light grey which bestowed a kind of controlled dignity on the entire house.

We sat at the table, in reasonable comfort but without the keen, indefinable anticipation that had permeated the living-room during its former manifestation. The absence of the head of the household, for better or worse, was clearly felt. The house had been purged, liberated from oppressive and destructive tension – but the magic and the beauty of the unexpected and the exceptional, these too were no more.

The younger of the two girls I had formerly met in Israel's shop came in carrying a gleaming brass tray laden with tea-cups, mulberry jam in little dishes and a steaming kettle. She greeted us amicably, laid the tray on the table, handed around the full cups and the dishes of jam – with whole mulberries designed to tempt the most jaded of palates – provided spoons and sat facing us.

"Not drinking?" – Israel turned to her with a question, trying to sound assured and succeeding only in increasing his own awkwardness.

"Oh, I'm drinking coffee," she chuckled with a kind of mischief, exposing rows of bright little teeth: "Mary's making it, for both of us!" she explained. And right on cue Mary appeared, the other girl I remembered from her brother's shop, with two big cups of coffee. Having added her own greeting, she put the cups on the table, sat down, took hers and sipped delicately. Her sister hastened to follow suit – as we all did.

For a while there was silence in the high-ceilinged room. An innocent, agreeable silence, a companionable atmosphere of fellowship, definable perhaps as "familial". Israel tried to exploit this, saying:

"Adon agreed to come – and here he is!" It was a clumsy introduction and Mary, the eldest sister, smiled tolerantly to herself.

"What's your opinion of the monastic life?" – her younger sister turned to me. I knew by now her name was Sylvia, and I was familiar too with her approach – direct and decisive, eschewing the roundabout routes of acquired courtesy.

"Positive," I replied with equal candour, and added: "But not everyone is destined to be a monk. Anyway," I continued, "it's not on account of a momentary disillusionment or a disappointment, however great and long-lasting it may be, even if it borders on despair – that people turn to monasticism."

"Why not?" Mary asked with interest.

"Because such an approach is bound to end in total failure!" I declared confidently. "The monastic life isn't a tranquillising drug or a fortifying drink, to soothe physical pain, or a psychological or emotional blow. It's a way of life and an ideal, capable of crushing without mercy anyone not fitted for it, that is, anyone who isn't drawn to it by true and powerful, inexorable zeal. The true monk," I continued, "is destined to be a monk. He's not someone drawn to the monastic life as a result of an acute turnabout in his life, or a traumatic change in his perceptions. Such a person is deceiving himself and others, and his soul is corrupted by lies; he will not pass the rigorous test of monasticism."

"Many monks are indeed people who have turned to monasticism in the wake of deep psychological trauma, after injury or disappointment or even – through attraction to the aura of the monastic community!" commented Sylvia, gazing down at the floor which was bare and, unlike the rest of the house, still showed vestiges of the fire – blackened and scorched tiles, serving as a warning of things liable to happen and beyond the control of flesh and blood.

"Those aren't monks," I asserted, "but residents in monasteries! Even if they don't transgress their vows – and such people are in the minority – to the end of their days they'll remain residents in monasteries and nothing more. True monks on the other hand," – I continued succinctly, cogently – "don't need monasteries, or monastic garb, to remind them day and night of the fact that they are monks. They don't need to make all kinds of vows either; they know that vows are no guarantee against failure to make the grade. Although," – I thought it only fair to concede – "there's nothing to stop them inhabiting monasteries, wearing the costume and making vows." And after a pause for emphasis, I declared:

"True monks are those to whom any other way of life is intolerable, and to whom any other aspiration is a burden on the soul."

"What is the way of life of true monks and what is their aspiration?" Israel asked with interest, as if aroused from his torpor.

"The way of life is freedom, and the aspiration is truth!" I replied, with a smile.

"What kind of freedom is this, and what kind of truth?" Mary asked.

"Total freedom from any kind of servitude, meaning non-dependence on any person or thing," I declared, adding: "Truth is the unshakeable knowledge that your nature is a divine nature, and you are nothing other than an inseparable part of the divine, meaning that your essence is love, pure true love, that conquers all."

"This way of life and aspiration of true monks – they exert a powerful attraction!" said Mary enthusiastically.

"Not where true monks are concerned," I retorted, and seeing the incomprehension in the eyes of my audience, I hastened to explain: "The monastic way of life and the aspiration of true monks – to them these are nothing other than the air they breathe, the essence of all things, the one and only essential reality, themselves!"

"So you're saying that a lot of monks are just residents in

monasteries!" was Sylvia's animated interjection.

"The decisive majority," I replied, adding: "Institutionalised monasticism is rotten to the core. But that is its hope."

"I don't follow you!" – Israel narrowed his eyes and knitted his fleshy brows in his sincere attempts to digest my words.

"The institution of institutionalised monasticism, which is necessarily corrupted and false from top to bottom," I began, "will expose the true monks in its midst, those whom it attempts to emulate. And they are the ones who will redeem it from falsehood. The bogus institution of monasticism will in the end be purified and refined by true monks, and disappear, thanks to them, from the painful memory of mankind! Anyway," I concluded, "there is no salvation for the institution without true monks."

"We want to go to a convent... become Christians and enter a convent!" said Mary, adding: "And what you've said has helped to reinforce that desire."

"If your desire needs reinforcing," I retorted, "it isn't genuine desire! Not the inexorable zeal that sweeps away like a storm wind every doubt and every question-mark and burns out with purifying fire every attachment to sensuality or emotionalism and every base instinct."

At that moment the door of the living-room opened and walking unsteadily, but with energy, in came Flora, matriarch of the Farhi family.

Her face was stern, her hands stretched out before her as if she were blind and needing to feel her way. She advanced, clutching for support at the back of the armchair closest to her, and then flopped into it, made an effort to sit up straight as if ashamed of her weakness and began:

"Everyone's a monk, a monk at heart. Everyone's an individual, isolated and alone!" – and as if to explain the manner of her arrival on the scene – "I heard your voices, too loud!" – and then returning to her theme: "Everyone wants to love, and more than wanting to love – longs to be loved... The man wants a woman to love him, and the woman yearns for a child to love her in return! And all of them, at the end of the day – are monks. Because there is no such thing as love and all are left by themselves, lonely and bereft. As they always were. It doesn't end at the door of the monastery. As for these girls," – she pointed to the young women, who were staring down at the floor – "it's the influence of their school. Their father, bless him, sent them to the Mission, and that teacher-monk – to this day he's filling their heads with ideas! It would be worth packing them all off to a nunnery – just to be shot of him!" she concluded with astonishing asperity, her voice tremulous. Clearly she was on the verge of tears.

I took a closer look at Mrs. Farhi, mother of the household. She had aged beyond recognition. Lean and wrinkled, shoulders hunched, she seemed to have shrunk to a fraction of her former self. Only her head stood out from her body, erect and proud, its abnormal proportions now accentuated still further, disdaining any association with the rest of her limbs. Her skin, the unhealthy colour of earth, was evidence of a physical or a psychological malady, or both. Reckoning a drink would do her good, I looked around for a spare cup, but couldn't see one. As if reading my thoughts, Sylvia stood up briskly from her seat, turned to one of the doors opening off the living-room, disappeared from view and returned with a cup. She poured tea and handed it to her mother.

"Thank you!" She sipped listlessly. The hand holding the cup trembled, the crinkled skin of her neck, like the skin of a lizard, quivered with every sip.

There was a long silence.

Flora laid her cup on the table, shifted in her seat to a more upright posture, as if regaining something of her composure and self-confidence, and turned to me:

"We all thought it would be good if you came and said something... David, bless him, held you in high regard. As they all do. Even Shmuel, bless him, admired you and had only good things to say about you. And I... I've heard some of the things you've been saying. I was in my room, listening. I didn't understand it all, but I got the general drift. And you're sincere. I can tell that by the tone of your voice. So in the end, I decided to come down. And maybe – to put a stop to all this!"

"Why?" demanded Israel, sounding hurt and indignant.

"Because I really don't know what's good any more!" she cried passionately. "Monasteries, convents... what difference does any of it make? Maybe a convent is the answer after all... so let them go and good luck to them, if it means they'll stop making their lives a misery – and mine too!"

"I don't understand!" Israel protested, adding: "So they're

divorced! Does that mean there are no eligible bachelors left in the world?"

"There's a lot you don't understand!" commented Mary, the eldest, giving him a dignified, rather sad look.

"Shortage of prospective husbands isn't the issue!" interjected Sylvia.

"What is it then?" asked the old woman, turning abruptly and unexpectedly to her eldest daughter.

For a long moment Mary pondered her mother's question, or more accurately perhaps, considered the wording of the reply she was going to give. She enfolded us all in a glance of profound sincerity, finally saying in a remarkably composed voice:

"The reason is – there's no love in me!" She paused for emphasis, and added: "I don't know what it is to love, or what love is! I'm ashamed of myself, and it hurts me, but that is the absolute truth! You" – she pointed to the members of her family – "didn't know this until now. Father, who was very sensitive but careful not to show his feelings – maybe he knew. That's why he was so opposed to my marriage."

"It was the cobbler he objected to!" Israel interjected, uncomprehending as ever.

"Only because it happened to be him!" she answered him coolly and added: "I'm sure he'd have objected to anyone. He knew, but he said nothing – that was his way. It's a handicap that I have, I think, and there's nothing I can do about it! I don't know how to love. I don't love anyone!" and with this she stood up from her seat, turned her back and strode briskly out of the room.

An awkward silence descended on those seated around the low table in the spacious room. It continued, turning turbid and oppressive.

Israel turned to Sylvia, the younger of the two would-be novices, and looked at her dryly:

"What about you? What's your reason?" he asked, his voice low, hoarse.

"I love her. I'll do as she does and go where she goes!" Sylvia replied with unexpected force, her face grim and pale. Suddenly this face crumpled and she burst into soft weeping that set her shoulders and her downcast head shaking. Tears streamed down her cheeks and over her contorted lips while she tried in vain to staunch them with a clenched fist. Israel handed her a crumpled handkerchief without looking at her. She swallowed a sigh, wiped her cheeks, folded the handkerchief and gave it back to her brother. And then one of the younger sisters came in and announced in a clear, rather solemn voice, "Father Michel has arrived!"

There was a tense silence in the room, and before another word was said, a tall, reasonably good-looking man in his early forties appeared in the doorway, his clothes old and not particularly clean. A rather foolish smile was pasted on his thin lips. He stepped forward, bade us a civil "Good evening", warmly shook the hands of all those present and sat down in the chair that Mary vacated for him.

Silence reigned once again. The old woman shifted uneasily in the chair, sighing deeply as if in pain. Finally, making an effort to sit upright, she turned to the priest or monk and said to him:

"No need for one of your chats tonight! My daughters have some important and urgent things to think about. If you wouldn't mind – come another time!"

Showing no sign of any resentment whatsoever, the man stood up, and after another round of affable handshakes, bade us a perfectly genial "Goodbye" and turned to the door.

"I'll be on my way too," I said, rising to my feet, and delivering my own valedictions. On leaving the house I met the priest who was standing in the yard, waiting for me.

"If you've no objection," he turned to me with a broad smile, "I'll walk with you…"

I had no objection.

"The night is young, the sky is clear and I have time on my hands!" he commented, looking up.

The sky was indeed clear and deep, with a few festive stars sparkling there, big and bright, like the songs of poets plucked in their prime.

FATHER MICHEL

We walked at a leisurely pace, careful not to disturb the contemplative depth of the silence, enwrapping all our surroundings – sky, sea and land – and absorbed in itself.

From the greying gloom of the alleyway where our journey began, a narrow and twisting path led down to the shore. Without speaking, as if by prior agreement, we turned, Father Michel and I, to this path and began descending, slowly and carefully.

The billows of the sea had evidently been tamed by an unseen hand, suppressing their energy and wiping from their heads the crests of angry foam, and now they cowered at the feet of the cliff and gently licked the narrow strip of shore. Their surging impetus halted, insubordination gave ground to brooding anticipation, age-old and hopeless, awaiting in vain the signal for the final assault on the still land-mass, and its towering mountains flushed with provocative pride.

We found a few sandstone boulders near the water's edge and sat there. The priest began proceedings with the comment:

"An unfortunate family, that has drunk the cup of life's bitterness to the dregs!"

"You can never know for sure," I replied.

"I've known them some twenty years," he continued. "All the girls studied with me. Talented girls. But their father, David, wasn't satisfied with them, for some reason. He was forever grumbling under his breath. In fact, it wasn't them he was dissatisfied with – it was himself!" the priest declared.

"Why?" I asked him.

He smiled into the blue clarity of the evening, picked up a pebble and without moving from his place, threw it with a flourish into the gently eddying sea – as yet still holding its wrath in check.

"He was disappointed in his sons – only two of them! He was depressed by the surfeit of daughters," he explained, "and he used to blame it on himself."

"Not his wife?"

"His wife, he admired!" the reverend gentleman declared, and continued: "She on the other hand, used to despise him. To her mind there was no doubt he was to blame."

"Their life wasn't easy," I said, tactfully offering a change of subject, but he declined it, or perhaps just didn't take the hint.

"The old man suffered, all churned up inside... a very sensitive person behind the stern front... he couldn't always stand it. I saw him crying when one of his daughters threw an insult in his face, or something that could be taken as an insult. He was interested in Christianity and he wasn't indifferent to that version of love that the New Testament preaches. Maybe his daughters' plans to join a convent would been some consolation to him!"

"Is that all his daughters?" I queried.

"All of them! Including the one who's still married."

"Is she getting divorced too?"

"She's started the process," he told me and added hastily: "Naturally, I'm trying to talk her out of it! As I'm sure you know, the sanctity of marriage is a central pillar of Catholicism! If she'd been married according to the rites of the Church, divorce would be out of the question. They shall be as one flesh, as the Good Book says," and he added a succinct quotation from the New Testament: "Whom God has joined, let no man put asunder..."

"Monasticism is a high calling..." I ventured.

"There is none higher!" – the priest's voice was suddenly infused with vigour and enthusiasm. "Monasticism is the lot of the elect of God's elect!" he exclaimed with undisguised pride and he continued: "Monks are those human beings who have finally fathomed out the meaning of the divine essence; they have absorbed its radiant happiness and they yearn for nothing else, see no purpose in the vanities of the world! They are the brothers of the Messiah and the true sons of God, the pure and the victorious. For whatsoever is born of God – overcometh the world!" the Catholic priest quoted with unabashed conviction, and he chose to underline the quotation by pointing out the precise reference: "First Epistle of John, chapter five, verse four!" He turned to me and scrutinised me with eyes radiating impassioned faith and the quiet light of unshakable confidence in the words he had spoken.

"There are few true monks," I said in an attempt to cool, if only slightly, the excess of his ardour.

"There are no others!" he declared, picking up another pebble and tossing it into the dark water, swirling calmly at our feet.

"They don't all pass the test," I persisted.

"Then they're not monks!" he answered me: "Because there's nothing to compare with the happiness of a monk who has earned the grace of God and knows what true love is, love of his God, pure and strong, that passes every test and fills him with light, to light the way of other mortals... and how can a monk such as this stumble and fall under the dominion of the flesh – flesh that is nothing other than dead matter, garbage that has no purpose but to feed worms and maggots – or however you choose to express it?"

"Not everyone is fit to be a monk," I said with a smile, in a measured, but clear and decisive tone.

"Too true!" he agreed, his enthusiasm showing no signs of abating. "And that is why the novice has to undergo numerous tests, and only after seven years of novitiate will he be accepted, if indeed he has passed these tests and his zeal to be a monk has not diminished but on the contrary, is stronger and firmer than ever... Those are the canonical rules of the Catholic Church," – my informant concluded – "and they guarantee the choice of suitable people!"

"Monks of the Catholic Church, like the monks of all other churches and sects the world over," I persisted, "are not all fit for true monasticism. In fact," I put it bluntly, "only a tiny minority are genuinely fit for it!"

"The unworthy – they're the ones who drop out!" he retorted. "That's why the rest of us are so few in number!" And he added, his eyes flashing sparks: "I'll give you an example. Take our monastery, by the sea shore – it's been standing on its mound for more than three hundred years, a fine, spacious building – and there are just five monks left there. Four old codgers, who hardly ever leave their cells, and I have the misfortune to be the youngster! It used to be a community of hundreds of monks... and now the upkeep of the entire place depends on us – and specifically on me! And I confess without shame, I can't always cope, even with hired help from outside!" he declared emphatically, with a faint note of complaint addressed to no one in particular. "If you like," he said in a sudden change of tack, "if you have time to spare, that is, why not come and see the monastery for yourself? 'Feast your eyes on it' – if you'll pardon the cliché. There's nothing round here to compare with it!" he concluded, making no attempt to conceal his youthful pride.

I had time to spare.

We left our seats on the sandstone boulders and turned towards the monastery.

We walked along the coastal strip at a leisurely pace. The sea was beginning to quicken the rate of its incursions on the shore, and quietly tightening its grip, at intervals uttering a dim and mournful groan, like the plaintive lament of a wild beast over a litter of still-born cubs.

"So, they got you involved in their agonising!" Father Michel shot at me.

"The Farhis, you mean?"

"The Farhis!"

"I suppose so," I replied off-handedly.

"The sisters told me about you... a lot of impressive stuff! A Jew and a monk as well – sounds like a unique blend!"

"Not quite unique," I corrected him. "You'll find people like that in various sects, in the deserts, even in your church, among all those far-flung communities of yours."

"They had nothing but praise for you," he continued. "In fact, it seems they see you as setting an example to be followed!"

"I'm not having that!" – I expressed my displeasure in genial tone but with some vehemence and went on to explain: "The only one who is fit to serve as an example – shines in every heart!"

"How?" my opposite number queried, stopping abruptly and giving me a sidelong, bemused look.

"The divine alone is capable of serving as an example," I answered him, "and the divine dwells in the hearts of all men!" I turned to him and smiled brightly. And for a brief moment everything faded and disappeared before my eyes – he and I and the landscape surrounding us, and all that was left was the unbounded light of that radiant smile.

"It seems," he mused, quickening his pace and catching up with me, "you're worthy to be a monk if ever anyone was! That's proved by your leanings towards the New Testament and the Catholic Church. And those exceptional Farhi girls have definitely been called to the monastic life, and it's the sacred duty of every true monk to support them in their vocation and encourage them to follow it!" he declared, like a superior authority on the subject issuing a final judgment.

"The Farhi girls are human beings with hearts that have been severely hurt," I retorted, "and in their distress they're searching for a refuge, or anything that could be described as a refuge, without first checking it out and seeing if it's really going to meet their expectations, without even analysing their own motives properly and working out what lies behind them. This isn't the way of true monasticism!" – I concluded.

"You mean," – he turned to me again – "that it's not through force of circumstances people become monks, but because they're chosen..."

"I mean, it's something that's perceived with clear and lucent knowledge, with the joy of vocation, with the energy of true love, and through powerful longings for the essence and for that alone!"

He was once more deep in thought, his head with its handsome, symmetrical lines lowered, and eyes fixed on the ground. While walking slowly, with measured step, he said, as if conversing with himself:

"That is certainly the way monasticism has always appeared to me! Since I was old enough to understand. I grew up in the region of Provence, a stronghold of Catholic piety. The seven years of novitiate I passed easily. And my heart was filled with joy and purity. And the potency of the vows that I made, in sanctity, and the love than which nothing could be more real, God's love of man!" He paused for emphasis, before continuing in a voice bright with awe and reverence: "There's no one on the face of the earth more happy than a monk! No one more worthy to preach the gospel of salvation to all flesh – than he who has conquered the flesh and suppressed all earthly desires!"

"Have you suppressed all earthly desires?" I asked casually.

In a low voice, with practised humility he answered me:

"By the grace of God, all such things are defeated and suppressed and never again will they divert me from my path!" His words were inflected with innocence and purity, and gave every impression of robust faith and adherence to the truth.

The rest of the route we covered in silence, quickening our pace without hurrying. We climbed the slope of a steep hill, and a few minutes later, Father Michel introduced me to the monastery.

We entered through a side door, into a spacious chapel, solemn and somewhat intimidating. The steady light of two neon lamps, set at opposite ends of the chapel, illuminated the faces of two big icons – the Holy Mother at one end and Jesus Christ, Judge of the Nations, at the other. The dome of the oval chapel soared high above us. Painted along the full length of the lofty walls were the images of the Messiah's twelve Jewish disciples, fixing stern glances on anyone entering the chapel, and following him with meticulous and merciless attention. Near the eastern wall, on a marble plinth, stood an altar.

Father Michel closed the side door behind us and turned at once to the altar. He knelt, crossed himself ceremoniously, put his hands together and said a silent prayer.

Suddenly his closed hands began to shake, then his shoulders quivered and the whole of his powerful, manly body seemed to go into spasm. Without any prior warning, Father Michel fell full length on the floor, lashing out with his feet like a drowning man, big fists pounding the ancient, miraculously preserved mosaics, crying out in his despair and wailing with loud, guttural sobs:

"I'm the swine of all swine, the sinner of sinners, the hypocrite of hypocrites, the sanctimonious, the criminal, the betrayer…"

I knelt beside him:

"What ails you, Father Michel?"

"No Father and no Michel!" he shouted. "I'm no monk and no priest but a detestable body chosen by Satan for his abode!" He shielded his face with both hands and his bitter sobbing continued unabated, shattering the stuffy atmosphere of the lofty chapel with its painted icons. The Apostles, three or four times life-size in their gilded frames, stared down at us; their censorious, inquisitorial air seemed to have softened a little.

"Won't you get up, Father Michel?" I suggested in a sharper tone.

"That won't help!" he wailed. "On this floor, in this very place, before the holy altar, I, the dedicated monk, the innocent boy from Provence who easily passed his seven year novitiate, seduced a woman, no, not a woman – a girl! And not just once, and not just twice! There's no atonement for me! I wish it was in my power to do something, something useful, positive…"

He regained control of himself for a moment and then his strange, guttural, high-pitched wailing resumed, sawing the air like cries from the death-bed – a dying man with his faculties still intact.

"Whatever has happened," I pressed him – "you have to weigh the situation as it stands and see what can be done! In other words – what can be salvaged and how…"

"No one knows better than me that there's nothing can be salvaged!" he cried, looking at me with tearful rancorous eyes, plunged into abysmal despair and yet – aglow with some strange light, soft and distant.

"If you think rolling around on the floor like this is going to help you somehow – I'm getting up and leaving right now!" I warned him sternly. I meant it too.

"No!" he howled maniacally, before adding in a more human tone: "I know it isn't going to help… this isn't the first time it's caught up with me… but what makes it different from the other times, this isn't following in the aftermath of the sin! Does that make any sense?" The very fact that in this instance, remorse was not the direct and immediate consequence of the sin repented, seemed to give him a precarious variety of hope. He stood up and sank into a wooden gilt-backed chair, set to the right of the altar.

"After I did it," he went on to say, eyes fixed on the opposite wall, face to face with the Apostle Peter, alias Simon the fisherman, "I was always assailed by regret and despair… after I paid her… yes – I was conscientious about paying! To start with it was free… my pupil… such a sad case. No known father, mother a certified alcoholic… I must have been out of my mind! I never imagined such a thing could happen to me! Till that moment… you see – I was a virgin! The Devil is so very powerful… if indeed he exists! He's the undisputed master of the flesh! I'm going down to Hell, I shall roast in Gehenna!" he concluded with an unearthly howl.

For a moment he seemed to be trying to impose some order on his frantic mind: he took a deep breath, stared fixedly at the wall facing him, wiped his wet face on a clenched fist and spoke again:

"She went downhill the way all her unfortunate sisters go downhill. By which I mean – I found her a pimp… He demanded money, and I paid willingly. That eased the pangs of conscience a little, the guilt… There's no doubt at all, I played a part in her decline… After all, whichever way you look at it she came here in search of a safe place, a refuge!" – with deranged emphasis on refuge – "I'm the one who destroyed her last hope, extinguished the light of her tender, fragile faith...

"Sometimes," he said in a more even tone, as if gaining a little confidence, "I think I did her a favour!" He glowered at me – a look which seemed utterly out of character – and added: "Instead of someone else doing this to her in some back alley, I was the one! A man with some education and values, if nothing else!" He smiled to himself sardonically, with a sidelong glance at me.

"I can't see her as anything than the envoy of Satan!" he continued. "The real test... not those seven years of celibacy... The fires of Hell enveloped me, the flames of Gehenna!" He was shouting again in wild desperation, a cry combining morbid self-pity with a challenge. Then, regaining some control over himself, he cocked his head and sighed:

"I paid every sum I was told to pay... they knew how to squeeze it out of me! That pimp... I used to steal the collection money brought in by those little innocents who looked up to me, a monk who had completed his seven year apprenticeship, a monk who could resist temptation – resist temptation!" – he derided himself in a surprisingly level tone of voice, looking up and focusing his gaze on the pointed apex of the splendidly soaring dome.

Once the mournful cacophony had subsided, the silence was heavy in the tall building, which seemed cramped in spite of its bulk, a silence apparently concealing within it some ineluctable threat. I stood facing him, motionless.

"I paid gladly," he resumed his litany, "I tried to atone... with money. And I got more and more deeply embroiled! And she seemed to understand everything, and you know," – his eyes trying to draw me into the darkness of their turbid gloom – " it was as if she pitied me! She – pitied – me!" he cried with stark and deliberate emphasis. "And it drove me out of my mind! It got to the stage where I dared to raise my hand to her. I couldn't control myself!" he concluded lamely, as if this constituted a mitigating argument.

He paused to collect himself, then turned away and spoke as if conversing with himself:

"Pride, you would say? – Yes, I think you could call it that! Real pride, arrogance springing up in the heart, the conceit of a boor and an illiterate peasant!" His voice flared up again to a furious pitch as he fulminated: "Brazen stupidity paving the way to Hell! No, I didn't know myself..." He hesitated a moment and then added, irrelevantly it seemed: "Suicide? That wasn't part of the equation! The Church forbids even thinking about it... but on the other hand – how much further could I sink? Is there any abyss deeper than this one of mine?" He fixed me with a wild and distracted look, a look of nameless despair, demanding my response.

"Certainly!" I responded confidently, taking a step towards him. "There is worse: the abyss of absolute despair! Hope," I declared with emphasis, "in spite of everything and no matter how far you have fallen – shows that God still has access to your heart!"

"Oh," he sighed, "she said something like that too... She... however much I knocked her about... no, she didn't enjoy it! She's not that kind of pervert! She just gritted her teeth and held on... like a prisoner standing up to brutal interrogation! And she pitied me. And when she realised her compassion was driving me crazy – she tried to hide it. She, what's her name..." – he made an effort to recall it, wagging a finger, clicking his tongue. "Her name, her name!" he demanded urgently, as if suddenly alarmed and assailed by a new form of despair: forgetting her name he interpreted as a sign presaging evil, more terrors for his damaged soul.

"Lili?" I suggested calmly.

"Lili, of course, Lili – that's it!" he cried, all at once radiant with joyful relief. And then just as suddenly he pulled himself up, lowered the arm that had been raised in exultation and slowly turned to face me, scanning me intently with a look that seemed clouded by smoky vapours of suspicion and dread:

"You know her? You knew? Knew all about it?" – he fired his questions at me in quick succession.

"I heard something," I replied. "The rest," I added, "wasn't too hard to guess."

"She told you?" He fixed me with a scared look, and there was no doubting that all his hopes and fears were pinned on my answer.

"Are you a monk or a cop?" I asked him with a grin, my voice steady.

"What do you mean?"

"All these questions!" I protested, adding in a more genial tone: "And why the subdued lighting?"

"Aha!" He took the hint, rose to his feet, went to the door by which we had entered, probed the wall and pressed the light switch.

The nave of the sumptuous chapel sprang all at once into radiant life, resplendent in its panoply of gold and silver, its purples and blues, like a royal bride presented before cheering crowds – and there was also the grey of serious thought and contemplation. The keen glances of the Apostles, from their lofty vantage-points, seemed to have softened further, their focus no longer so intense.

Father Michel invited me to sit in the gilded chair that he had vacated, pulling out another chair for himself from behind the altar – a backless chair this one, all flashing gold decorations and reliefs.

"You maintain all this by yourself?" I asked, pointing to the high walls and the soaring dome.

"Of course not!" he declared. "I hire in outside labour, and sometimes volunteers turn up, from all corners of the world. And as for the four old codgers who spend most of the time in their cells," – he added, lowering his voice – "they need looking after too..."

"Are you complaining?" I asked him.

"God forbid!" – he winced, and raised a hand as if to ward off a heinous accusation.

"A true monk," I began, "grows accustomed through will-power and through self-denial and true patience, and a temple such as this," I added, "opens up before you the opportunity to habituate yourself to things outside the realm of the habitual!" Again I pointed to the impressive nave of the chapel.

"Not for me!" – he contorted his face into an apologetic leer.

"Why is that?" I asked him evenly.

"Because, you see," he answered me uneasily – "I've just decided, I'm going to ask to be released from my vows... Perhaps I'll marry Lili... I've wronged her so much! I've behaved like an animal towards her! Then maybe I'll find the courage to look deep into myself, wrestle with my conscience... and somehow, put an end to this lousy life that I'm leading. Not an honourable end!" – he stressed – "My honour, whatever honour I ever had, has been pulverised into oblivion! Even in Hell they'll turn their noses up at me!" He tried to smile at me, but succeeded only in twisting his face into an even more grotesque expression. His lips quivered.

"I don't think that's what you really want," I commented in an off-hand style. "You're trying to flagellate yourself – and that's as far as you intend to go. It's your soul that's damaged," I warned him. "It has a serious defect."

"Lust of the flesh!" he cried with unseemly relish, as if answering a quiz question correctly.

"It's more than that," I asserted calmly, and added by way of clarification: "It's the defect that stops you resisting any impulse, and drags you down from one level of degradation to a level that's even lower."

"What defect is this?" he asked with a high degree of tension, managing somehow to still the tremor of his lips.

"Laziness!" I replied. "Your addiction to laziness is like addiction to a drug. You're sunk in it up to the neck, as if you'd blundered into a quicksand!"

"I've never been lazy!" the priest protested, his eyes fixed on the impressive mosaics of the floor of his chapel. For a while he seemed to be thinking, weighing something up internally, as if projecting scenes from his past life on the screen of his memory, analysing them quietly and carefully and coming to a conclusion:

"I was diligent, doing my work conscientiously! Always – I've never been lazy!" Midnight prayer for example," – he offered convincing proof – "to this very day I've always upheld it, to the letter... I've obeyed every ordinance – without complaint, without a murmur! I haven't valued bodily comfort above vigilance of the spirit... I think you've got it wrong!" – and he looked up at me, simultaneously assertive and inquisitive.

"I haven't got anything wrong," I responded with a smile, adding: "The man who contents himself with bitter weeping and pointless grief over past transgressions, instead of getting a grip on himself and mustering all his resources in order to stand up and start afresh – is the laziest man in the world, the laziest there has ever been!" And seeing his look of utter bemusement I continued:

"Laziness is a malignant disease, which prevents human beings from interpreting correctly the riddle of their lives and realising their potential."

"So, what you're suggesting...." – he studied me with a prolonged, hesitant look, expressive of disbelief and aversion, and underlying all this, something resembling hope which he was making a determined effort to suppress. "No!" he cried suddenly, "I'm not capable of that, not worthy... I should just give the whole thing up!"

"That's the victorious fanfare of laziness!" I declared

unequivocally.

"But... how?" Again he stared at me with puzzled eyes, and raised his hands in a gesture of powerlessness. The expression on his face exposed inner turmoil and deep, corrosive doubt.

"It's not a case of how? Just what?" I told him.

"What?" – he echoed the question mechanically without understanding it.

"What is to be done? That's all that matters," I explained, with a warm smile.

"What is to be done?" he pondered aloud and added: "What is to be done when I can't free myself from the summons of Hell... and I don't have the strength to resist that dark desire that I vowed would never defeat me! And Lili... inflaming my imagination and burning in my bones!"

"Get away from her!" I retorted.

"Well," he commented dryly, "she's not in my house, nor I in hers!"

"I mean really get away – to another country, another nation! To the North Pole – or the South if you prefer. And start all over again!"

His face turned grim. He seemed to be weighing my words, examining them from every angle, and finally he turned to me and said in a low voice:

"There's something about you... I don't know how to define it! In fact – I'm not familiar enough with it to define it properly, not that definitions are that important... From the depths I called Him – He answered me in a wide open place!" – he misquoted, consciously or unconsciously, and added:

"To my great shame, I find myself contemplating this crazy suggestion, the one and only idea that has resonance for me... the fact is," – he looked at me again and spoke with firm resolve – "I don't have the strength or the gumption required to cope with the ugliness of life outside. What I said about release from my vows may have been just empty words... but I meant it too! It seemed I had no choice. And you, you have put a new lamp into my hand and ignited in it a faint light of young hope... and you point the way and say to me 'Go!' And your advice is sound: this is the way and there is no other. If I prove worthy of it," he concluded. "Only time will tell!" He breathed a deep and heart-felt sigh. Standing up from his seat he held out a hand and clasped mine firmly, while announcing with some solemnity:

"Tomorrow I shall make confession to my superior, and the day after, I hope, I shall fly away from here, as far as possible – as you say, to the North Pole or the South. Wherever the Church needs me most!" he added with a touch of genial humour. "Peace be with you my friend, my dearest friend! It's safe to say we won't meet again on the dusty face of this earth!"

He stepped back and opened the door for me, and as I left he stood on the threshold and watched me go, alert and quizzical.

RAIN

The evening came down early. Skies lowered and clouds meshed together, with an expression of motherly concern – the winter skies of Jaffa. Big, heavy drops of grey rain were beginning to fall on the dusty streets with a soft pattering sound, as I made my way to Rahamim's café.

Rahamim replied to my greeting in a clear and slightly raised voice, as if apologising for not having time to approach me. A big pot of coffee had just started bubbling on the stove behind the counter. A few fishermen, who had correctly anticipated the change in the weather, were sitting on the benches by the oval tables and waiting patiently for the thick, stomach-warming and heart-reviving coffee. And Rahamim, predictably, didn't disappoint them: the black coffee that was served was, as usual, fragrant and invigorating, sweet and steaming. On his way back to the counter Rahamim switched the lights on, at once dispelling the shadows from the fringes of the spacious room. In the light dispersed by the high-powered hanging lamp, the lofty ceiling appeared loftier still, as if it had risen and subsided somewhere, in the violet-tinged gloom.

Anticipating my request, Rahamim brewed tea for me and served it on the usual ornate tray, along with a mug of coffee for himself. Without a word, he sat down facing me, looking solemn, and picked up his mug.

We sipped calmly – Rahamim from his mug, I from the crystal-clear glass cup, the liquid in it gleaming like polished amber.

One of the fishermen, evidently finding the silence disconcerting, made the comment:

"I've drunk coffee in many places – and nowhere is it the same. And no coffee that I've tasted till now could compare with Rahamim's!"

"Absolutely," Rahamim responded, reflecting the mood of the speaker. "You're right. You can't compare one coffee with another and besides – a lot of it depends on the drinker!"

"I don't quite see that," interposed a fisherman who looked older than his years – whether because of his hunched back and sloping shoulders, or because of the foolish smile sketched on his long, unshaven, leering face.

"It depends on the experience of the drinker," Rahamim explained patiently. "There are those whose experience is meagre and their judgment flawed, and to them coffee is just a black liquid, thick admittedly and scalding the tongue – sometimes more and sometimes less. And there are others who find in coffee a comforter and a friend, and they are alert to every slightest variation in consistency, sweetness, smell, warmth, colour and even, the cup it's served in, and who it's served by, and who you're drinking with, and at which table in which establishment..." The questioner was listening open-mouthed, bemused perhaps, the foolish smile not budging from his face.

Rahamim continued, warming to his theme:

"And there are those whose experience of drinking coffee is rich and varied, and they derive the utmost pleasure from it, and in fact – every drink of coffee is like a festival for them. They prepare themselves in advance and in accordance, and even at a distance they can tell between one coffee and another – judging by appearance, of course, and most of all, judging by aroma... It's only after this that taste comes into it, the personal taste of the drinker. And there are as many different tastes as there are coffee drinkers. And finally," – Rahamim sighed for some reason – "the taste of coffee depends on the state of mind of the drinker: if he's a grumpy mood, give him sewage to drink instead of coffee and he won't know the difference; if he's in a jolly mood, or success has smiled on him, he won't notice anything either, any more than the grumpy guy. But if the drinker's in a coffee-drinking mood, he'll know how to savour every single drop; every drop an entity in itself and put them all together – you're giving him the keys to the next world!"

"Is that the one above or the one below?" – the one with the silly smile chipped in again.

"Wherever you're not going to meet a twerp called Pini!" Rahamim retorted, smiling hastily as if apologising for the barb.

More fishermen were arriving now, driven from their boats by the weather. Rahamim had his hands full. I got up from my place and tried to help as best I could: I served coffee, collected empty cups, washed a few of them. I brushed aside Rahamim's expressions of gratitude, and eventually he got the message and let me get on with it.

Among the new arrivals in the café were Raphael, the veteran fisherman, and young Avinoam; beside them, grim-faced, sat the son of old Aharon, who was now being treated in the hospital. The son had no personal penchant for fishing, but his father was insistent that the boat should not be idle; whenever possible he leased it to another – otherwise, he had no option but to take it out himself. A number of middle-aged men were clustered in foursomes around the low, oval tables, rhythmically sipping the thick liquid, avoiding direct eye-contact with one another, most of them wrapped up in their own thoughts and in no mood for conversation. Danny, the one expelled from Canada by his family, was there too. A young man at the height of his powers, with unruly hair and a stubbly, spiky, long-neglected beard, he sat apart from the others, as he usually did, in a shady corner, his eyes glinting like the eyes of a bird of prey.

"It's no weather for fishing!" said old Aharon's son, as if staring at a blank and impenetrable wall of dejection.

"It wouldn't put me off!" put in Danny from his corner, his voice as sharp and confident as ever. Someone thought to ask old Aharon's son how his father was faring.

"He's in hospital," was the reply. "He's due to be discharged tomorrow," – and in the same heavy tone he concluded – "until the next time..." As there was no response to this he turned to Danny and asked him: "Interested in a boat?"

"Thank you, but no!" was the resolute answer. "I got my own out of hock." In Danny's voice for the first time there was a faint flicker of pleasure, allied with deep and provocative satisfaction.

"How did that happen?" Raphael asked.

"A little outside help – the family..." Danny explained. "Friends helped a bit too and – not forgetting some personal effort on my part. This week I've been working in Ashdod," he concluded.

"And you mean to go out tonight, in this rain?" asked Avinoam.

"It's the biggest thrill there is!" – Danny came as close to enthusiasm as he was ever likely to get, with no departure from the sharp and pugnacious tone of his voice.

"A wet thrill!" grinned Pini, from his table in the centre of the café. His close-set eyes, the glassy eyes of a fish, small and mottled, looked around for solidarity, but in vain. And then Gabriel came in – tall, broad-shouldered, lean-waisted, in his early thirties, hair black, dense and curly, low forehead, face and neck pock-marked with what looked like the residue of a bout of rubella. Immediately behind him came Nono, one of Jaffa's quieter imbeciles.

"Order coffee, Nono!" – Pini picked on him, without wiping the foolish smile from his face, his voice patronising and scornful.

"Gabriel ordering!" Nono cried, his shrill enthusiasm overflowing, in typical style, and he added: "Gabriel order coffee for Nono, Gabriel catch fish! Nono catch fish! Lots of fish, lots, lots!" Nono's excitement was mounting and his voice rang out clearly, a pure, childish voice.

"How many fish, Nono?" – Pini persisted, still seeking support among the assembled company with his grinning, glassy little eyes and trying to mimic Nono's voice.

"Lots, lots..." – Nono's excitement abated a little, and he knotted his thick-skinned brow in an effort to quantify and define the concept of lots. Not succeeding in this, despite the energy invested and the long minute consumed, he reverted to his former ebullience and bonhomie, repeating his cry of "Lots, lots!"

"A hundred thousand, Nono?" Pini went on to ask, despairing of any solidarity on the part of his colleagues, and the pleasure of the game steadily diminishing.

"Hundred thousand – ea-sy!" Nono drawled. "Hundred thousand – ea-sy!" he repeated in a more solemn tone, as if impressed by the scale of his own achievement, looking towards the centre of the café, the source of Pini's taunts.

"More than a hundred thousand, Nono?" – Pini persisted, evidently intent on flogging the dead horse.

"Why don't you leave him alone!" – Danny's warning-shot cut through the air.

"What's your problem?" Pini cried, with the bravado of one who has nothing to lose. "Nono and me – we're old friends! Right, Nono?"

"Nono friend! Nono friend!" came the spirited reply, and beaming all over his face, Nono concluded: "Gabriel friend, Nono friend!"

"Since you took him on your boat, you've had him as a permanent fixture!" was Raphael's comment, addressed to Gabriel.

"He's my good luck!" – Gabriel seemed to swallow a sigh.

"Does he really bring fish?" asked Avinoam, curious.

"He brings himself!"

"Does he really help at all?" one of the older fishermen interposed.

Gabriel turned, still standing by Rahamim's counter and apparently not intending to sit down. He looked at the one who had asked and snapped at him:

"You think a guy like that can help?"

"So why don't you get rid of him?" the fisherman persisted.

"How could anyone get rid of him – such a pitiable creature!" – Gabriel softened his stance and took a sidelong glance at Nono, who was staring at him fixedly; apparently as a result of what he had heard, and especially – what Gabriel's tone had told him, his unbelievably innocent eyes were full of dread.

"Are you sorry you took him on?" asked Rahamim, appearing on the other side of the counter.

For a while Gabriel considered Rahamim's question, his eyes fixed on the floor. At length he looked up and said:

"No. I guess not. In spite of everything he does bring luck! And maybe – more than luck!" he explained, continuing in the same reflective vein: "Fish – it's always the same thing... You're dependent on the season, the movement of shoals, species that are depleted and species in surplus... and on board, it's sheer bloody hard work. Nono brings something else – a kind of lightheartedness... and peace of mind... He's all willingness to help!" Gabriel cried. As almost all those present in the café listened intently he continued in a good-natured tone, with a hint of amusement: "You ask him to hold the end of a rope, he grabs the rudder; point to the rudder, he starts letting the nets out..." Gabriel suppressed a smile and went on to say: "But all this he does with such innocence and sincerity, and most of all – he has such a powerful and genuine motivation to help! Yell at him and he's upset, almost in tears – whimpering like a dog! Praise him and he dances around like a little kid who's got a nice birthday present. He brings along a special kind of mood... a bigger boost than a million fish could give you!" – he declared, and concluded, reverting to his former solemnity: "You've never experienced a mood like that till you've met Nono!"

Nono, seeming to sense the way things were going, cried out in beaming exultation:

"Nono help! Nono help! Gabriel help! Nono help! Nono friend! Gabriel friend!"

The fishermen laughed gently and tolerantly and invited Nono to sit.

"Gabriel sit, then Nono sit!" – he refused to take precedence over his employer.

"Gabriel wise, Nono crazy!" Pini interposed in a botched attempt to imitate the cries of the imbecile.

"Why don't you shut your mouth!" – Danny's mordant, provocative voice was heard again.

"It's no business of yours, boozy Canadian git!" shouted Pini, affecting a tone of malicious glee, an eager response to a challenge.

With lightning speed, before anyone could guess his intentions, Danny sprang from his dark corner, grabbed Pini by the shoulder, by the thick sweater he was wearing and dragged him out of the café into the pouring rain, as if dragging a half-empty sack of potatoes. And there he proceeded to hit him repeatedly, with a demented flurry of punches that laid his victim flat on the ground.

We ran after him.

"That's enough Danny, that's enough!" shouted Rahamim urgently. With an effort we succeeded in pulling the assailant away from Pini, who lay unconscious in the rain.

"What's up with you, Danny? What's the matter?" asked Raphael – questions not expecting an answer and intended only to express bemusement and mild revulsion.

I grabbed Danny's wrists and held him until Rahamim and Raphael had managed to drag Pini clear. They carried him into the café, where he was soon revived. Then Pini surprised everyone by staggering to the door and yelling at Danny:

"Crazy bastard! They kicked you out of Canada – where are they going to deport you from here? If you made it to the North Pole, you'd still be a savage beast! Where are you going to run to? Guatemala? Africa? There's no putting you right, not ever!" – and Pini's shrill voice fell silent.

Danny didn't want to go back into the café; perhaps he was ashamed, or perhaps he'd had enough of human company, for this evening at least.

"You can let go of me now!" he said in a low voice, adding: "That's a strong grip you've got... surprising! You must be tougher than you look!"

"I hope it's all over," I responded.

"I wish it was over!" he declared with bitterness bordering on depression and went on to say: "The truth is – Pini's right! I am an animal, a savage beast! I can't control myself, and I doubt there's anywhere in the world where I could settle and get along with people. I'll never understand why this happens to me and why I'm like this!"

"You," – I turned to him as the rain drenched my entire body, running in thin streams from my ears, my chin, and the corners of my lips, obscuring my words – "you're like most people. You pity yourself!"

He didn't seem to hear.

"It's depressing!" – he cried through the deluge of water that distorted visibility so completely that for a brief moment he looked like a flimsy shadow. "Well, good day to you!" he announced suddenly, his hands in the pockets of the baggy jeans he was wearing. They were soaked through, as were his sweater and scruffy Doc Martens. His voice was rough, with a barely repressed undercurrent of violence.

And before disappearing into the thickening darkness, beyond the angry screens of rain, he turned, drew a hand from his pocket, waved it at me and said:

"Thank you!" – in a voice utterly purged of the bitterness and dark dejection that just a moment before had dominated him inexorably.

THE AMAZON RAIN FOREST

About two weeks after I parted company from Father Michel, Lili came looking for me at Rahamim's café and when she found me, signalled to me to meet her outside.

"How did you find your way here?" I asked.

"I can find my way anywhere," she declared with a smile – "just as I please!" She walked on, found a bench in the garden nearby, sat down and made a space for me. And seeing I wasn't entirely convinced, she added:

"Half of Jaffa knows you spend your afternoons in Rahamim's café. That is," – she stressed – " the half of Jaffa that knows you. Like for example..." – with an expansive gesture – "Israel Farhi or Nessim, Rahamim's nephew, the fishermen, like Raphael and the rest of that bunch, and even – Shuki... He's been in a bit of a state recently, worried about the business..." she commented, with a hint of regret.

"Why is that?" I was interested to know.

"There's a season," – she proceeded to explain – "like for vegetables: cucumbers, onions and so on, or fruit: grapes, melons, oranges – well there's a season in his business too... our season that is... and it comes in the intervals between the seasons – in the heatwave that hits between spring and summer, or the dark evenings between autumn and winter, when the skies are low and people are wrapped up in themselves and don't socialise with one another – that's the boom time for our profession..." She paused for a moment, forced a grin and added:

"And that monk who used to be my teacher – he surprised me..."

"Has he left the country?" – I tried out my guessing skills.

"Why should he leave the country?" She was baffled, studying me with a strange look and adding: "There's no better place than this to hide his sinning! No one knows him here, no one takes any notice of him. He has hardly any congregation. There aren't many Christians in these parts, to sniff around him and check what he's getting up to, and Jews and Muslims aren't interested in him. They look down on him and as far as they're concerned, the deeper he sinks, the better! As for those four old companions of his – they're only interested in the angel of death and when he's going to come and release them from the torments of their interminable old age... Why should he leave?" she repeated her question emphatically.

I didn't answer.

"But something strange has happened!" This time her grin was bright and natural, as she reflected on the "strangeness" of the episode. "Ten days ago, or two weeks, I don't remember exactly – I went to his place, the church, the posh one. That's where he does all his fornicating. Maybe he doesn't want to defile his cell," – it seemed a reasonable enough hypothesis – "but that's where he always received me. Of course," she explained, "he used to lock the doors and the gates, and he always told me there was no danger of us being disturbed – as if that was likely to bother me!" – she protested, adding: "And as for his fellow-monks, those old men, he said they never bother to come down to the church except when they have to, you know – services or a feast-day or something. Anyway, be that as it may," – Lili returned to her story – "I came to him and would you believe it? – for the first time in his life, first time in my life – he refused it! Didn't want it. Shoved a few coins into my hand – slammed the door in my face! Yes exactly!" she concluded with a strange kind of relish that could have been interpreted as amazement at the eccentric behaviour of the monk, and a sincere sense of appreciation.

"What do you think?" she asked.

"What do you think?" was my answer to her question.

"To tell you the truth," she began with a bright smile, "I would have been proud of him! Only..." She gave me a sidelong glance and her voice fell, before fading into silence.

"Only what?" I prompted her.

"He didn't keep to his resolution. Yesterday, he was chasing after me like a maniac. Yesterday evening – he was back to his old ways..." Lili's voice spoke eloquently of disappointment and bitterness.

We were both silent for a while. Finally, I turned to her and asked:

"Did he hit you again?"

She scanned me with a frightened look, like someone forced to seek shelter in an exposed place where there isn't even an imaginary refuge.

"How did you know about that?" she asked in a quaking voice.

"He told me," I replied in a reassuring tone.

"Well, no," she replied. "Not this time. But something's happened to him. He didn't treat me to his usual routine of rolling around on the floor and bewailing his sins – after he's had his end away, of course... And though he got rid of me in a hurry, there was none of the groaning and bleating that I've been used to. It was like he was a human being again. In his own terms, perhaps..." she added hurriedly.

"And what was your impression of him when he hit you?"

She thought again, weighing up the words of her answer:

"Well," she began hesitantly, "I'm used to things like that, you know, getting hit... and he wasn't the worst by any means. And I think this is the kind of thing where a man gets shown up in his true light."

"And he?" I persisted.

"He seemed then the way he really is," – she smiled, not by any means a bitter smile, but on the contrary, warm and radiant – adding: "Like a kid! You know, an unhappy kid who wants to be a man and doesn't know how it's done. So he looks for a way to express his suffering. A kid who needs to be pitied and forgiven...." She looked up at me, her big eyes filled with a soft and kindly light, and concluded in a clear, melodic voice:

"As for me, it doesn't bother me either way! I'm well and I'm doing okay, no worse off than I ever was... but what I really came to tell you – I haven't forgotten – is to watch out for Shuki!"

"What's new?" I asked gently, in a tone of detachment from all the illusions of the ephemeral world.

"He's dangerous..." she replied, her eyes staring straight ahead of her. "You know, he's jealous and that makes him dangerous. Lock your door at night. Everything else – I'll take care of!" she assured me, giving me a prolonged and wistful look, as if yearning for something outside her reach and beyond her capabilities. And then she held out her hand and grasped mine firmly, blushing and stammering as she added:

"I wanted something else too... to... to see you and shake your hand... You're not angry?"

"No!" – I smiled with a pure pleasure that was conveyed to her, and she was all radiant light as if seeking to wrap herself in that moment forever. Her voice rang out again like a hymn of praise, like the song of a bird that has just heard freedom calling.

"I'm so happy!" she cried, and then fell silent. Something in her look grew darker, and it was if a heavy cloud had drifted across the source of her light, dispelling her joy.

"Father Michel," she murmured, "has booked a session with me next week..." She studied the expression on my face. "Shall I give him your regards?"

"Yes," I assented.

But the regards were not to be passed on. To Lili's utter amazement, Father Michel left the country and flew to some remote location in the Amazon rain forest, a place "where there are still gangs of cannibals and savage predatory animals" as it was described to her by one of the old monks, who took the trouble to come down and see who was hammering so insistently on the door of the chapel.

"A nice old man," Lili said – "All his hair white, and a pair of tiny, old-fashioned sun-glasses perched on his nose – and one of the lenses cracked!"

HOUSE MOVES

That bright winter day, with a quiet wind humming in the empty void and aspiring to rise and reign in the heights of the grey skies, skies hiding a bashful smile behind a rigid façade – I paid my customary visit to Rahamim's café.

There was more activity here than usual: two porters, supervised by Rahamim and his nephew Nessim, were at that moment unloading an antiquated fridge from a pick-up truck and manhandling it into the café, dragging and shoving it through the kitchen to the little store-room tucked away at the back. The fridge was closely followed by a closet with gaping doors, a heavy and shabby table, and a big padded armchair which could almost have doubled as a bed – all transported in the same manner and taken to the same destination.

I sat quietly in my usual spot, close to the glass window; from this point I could watch the sea-breakers with their mane of white surf and bathe in the fringes of the gentle sky and the blue and distant horizon.

Nessim paid the porters, adjusted his old tuxedo, washed his hands and sat down at the table next to mine. Rahamim disappeared for a while into his kitchen, before returning with the familiar gleaming brass tray – tea for me and coffee for his nephew and himself. He served the tea, sat down with Nessim, turned to me and said:

"House moves!"

And Nessim was quick to explain:

"Just for the time being – we're staying with my uncle!" he pointed to Rahamim. "We had to leave our old place in a hurry – just like our forebears in Egypt in their time!" he added exuberantly, obviously pleased with his ingenious analogy.

"A bit of an exaggeration!" – Rahamim smiled his gentle smile, steady and sweet as a children's song.

Nessim wrinkled his low forehead, touched the black cap on his scalp to check it hadn't fallen off during the furniture-moving process, and said:

"No exaggeration at all... Everything's changed in just a week – it isn't the same neighbourhood any more! And until we find a house," – he turned to me emphatically, to make sure he had my undivided attention – "we're moving in with Uncle Rahamim... My uncle has a heart of gold, all Jaffa knows that!" – and his voice rose to such a pitch it seemed he wanted all Jaffa to hear and absorb his eulogy.

"More exaggeration!" Rahamim objected, his voice betraying some faint traces of distaste. It seemed he was aware of this, and in an effort to make amends he added, having taken a slow and noisy slurp of his coffee: "We have a big, empty house... and by God's will, we have no children. It's true, my wife is complaining of creaking joints and pains and discomfort, and she day-dreams of bathing in the therapeutic waters of the Dead Sea... but is that any reason not to take the family in?" He raised his voice a little, perhaps with the intention of glossing over the non sequitur between his wife's dream and the issue of hospitality. "In fact," he added, his voice reverting to its normal timbre, "the way things are going, we'd even welcome strangers!" His mottled eyes alighted on my face, their expression heavy with implication. He took the solid silver cigarette case from his pocket and was about to open it, but thought better of it and returned the case to his pocket with a slow and deliberate movement. Taking the hint, I turned to Nessim and asked:

"So what's changed in the neighbourhood?"

"You don't know?" cried Nessim, with a somewhat excessive display of incredulity. He paused for a long moment, evidently expecting me to strain my memory in an effort to come up with what everyone else seemed to know, his tiny eyes following every slightest flicker of my features. Eventually he decided he's given me long enough.

"Shuki," – he cried – "has fallen off his perch! He's lost it all, gone way, way down! It's incredible! And with him, law and order have gone down the tubes as well... All kinds of weird types are muscling in on the action, shafting him too. His 'girls' have left him, and his 'boys' despise him!" Nessim sighed and looked down for a moment, but was quick to resume his narrative – eager to bring me up to speed on what he considered sensational news:

"Things have got to the point where he came to see me yesterday, in person, for the first time in five years!" – he cried in a tone of bitter resentment – "And he asked me for – a small loan... Then I knew how desperate he must be! And the lowlifes in the neighbourhood who used to be terrified of Shuki, who flattered him, worshipped him, and trembled at the sight of his shadow – they're strolling about with chests puffed up and heads held high, and doing whatever they feel like... So my daughters aren't safe any more, my wife feels threatened and in fact I reckon we're all at risk, including my son and me too! So, we had to leave the comfortable house we'd got so used to in a hurry. And we're very lucky to have Uncle Rahamim as a relative!"

Rahamim again made a dismissive gesture and his face turned grim, as if he meant to distance himself from what had been said. But Nessim was warming to his theme and he continued unperturbed.

"All praise be to God, and all blessings be His – for giving us a relative like our Uncle Rahamim – who without a moment's hesitation agreed to put us up, to take us in..."

"In the café?" I asked.

"Don't be ridiculous!" Nessim retorted, annoyed at losing his thread. "In his house! All of us, the whole family – wife, daughters, son and I."

"So why was that furniture being delivered here?"

"We didn't want to overload the house with all our stuff," Nessim explained. "It's a bit cramped there, whereas here," – with an expansive gesture of the thumb towards the kitchen – "there's a lot more space."

"This certainly is a fine building," Rahamim interjected in his soft, sibilant voice, like the purring of a cat by the fireside in winter. "It's definitely old, ancient I'd call it... they say it was built in the time of the Turks... but it's spacious and it stands firm on its foundations... walls are thick and that dome is a superb construction, an ingenious piece of design – it keeps the rain out in the winter and the strongest sea-breeze will be deflected off it, causing no damage, and the heat of the sun is tempered too... As for the floor, yes it's old and groaning under the weight of the many winters that have left their mark and the feet that have trodden and trampled it, but there's life in it yet!" Rahamim sighed and rounded off the eulogy of his café with the wistful remark: "They knew how to build in those days..." In a somewhat livelier tone he added:

"However narrow and cramped it may look from a distance – from close up, or from inside, the width and the depth are surprising, to say nothing of the height!" And turning to face me again, he explained: "We've moved some of the excess furniture in here, for the moment. We could of course have fitted the whole house inside the café and not known it was here!" Rahamim concluded with a note of restrained pride.

I turned to Nessim and asked: "Won't Shuki come after you?"

His face broadened into a bitter smile:

"Shuki's a spent force! He couldn't scare anyone any more – not even a dying cat!" He chuckled and added:

"There was a time – and it lasted five years or more – when there was some stability in the neighbourhood; it was a nice place to live. You could walk around in the alleyways... even the alleyways were, how can I put it..." he paused briefly, wrinkling his brow as he searched for the right expression – "reassuring, and clean... yes, clean! Even the local authorities respected Shuki, or more likely – they were afraid of him. Street cleansing workers did their job properly, and everything was different!" he declared, adding: "Granted, every one of the local residents was called on to do him a 'small favour' from time to time, but he was content with that. He never asked for more, never demanded gold or silver, or watches or diamonds... Women could walk the streets at midnight festooned with jewellery, and no one dared approach them! Now they're too scared to leave their homes!" Nessim sighed, staring down at the ancient, cracked tiles of the café floor.

"So how come Shuki's fallen from grace, all of a sudden?" Rahamim asked.

"It's not been all that sudden!" Nessim replied. "The final blow, in my humble opinion, came yesterday. But for weeks now, maybe months, Shuki's position has been eroded, nibbled away!" And after a pause for emphasis, boosting the tension in his uncle's mottled eyes, he continued as if gracefully fulfilling an obligation:

"They say it all started one evening... one of his girls rebelled and sent a gang of hoodlums to sort him out, him and his 'boys'. It was, by all accounts, a very efficient piece of sorting-out." And Nessim went into the details with a relish that he couldn't restrain: "The 'boys' were disarmed; flick-knives, knuckle-dusters and one of them, the hoodlums said, was carrying a loaded piece, a revolver, a Colt or something – anyway, a sophisticated weapon!"

"What happened to that gun?" – Rahamim interjected, apparently in a deliberate effort to cool, if only by a few degrees, his nephew's strange ebullience.

"It was confiscated!" Nessim replied and proceeded to explain: "That's the way things happen in such cases and at those levels of society... As for Shuki – they stripped him!" He looked keenly to see what effect the sensational account of Shuki's misadventures was having on us, and Rahamim and I adopted appropriate expressions of stupefaction. Apparently this wasn't enough to satisfy Nessim's expectations, and his voice dropped slightly. The intensity of his own enthusiasm was beginning to wane, but he still felt impelled to go further:

"They stripped him, but not entirely..." – his voice was quite steady now, even betraying a hint of resentment – "They left him in his underwear and that's how he turned up in the neighbourhood that night. He was on foot. The 'boys' didn't wait for him. Getting roughed up and robbed was enough for them, and they weren't hanging around to see what happened next. Anyway, they seized the opportunity to get clear of him, out of his clutches. In point of fact," – again the tension in his voice was rising and his little eyes scanning the expression on our faces – "he wasn't treated with much respect in the neighbourhood either... when he turned up like that, in his underwear!

"At first they couldn't believe their eyes – whether they were law-abiding residents, paying him off with 'little favours', or those who used to be hand in glove with him, partners in extortion, drugs, prostitution. And when they were sure what they were seeing, they started laughing. Laughing at him! Loud laughter, echoing round the backstreets! You could hear it all over!" He took another extended pause, controlling his impulses and wondering whether to tell what he knew or leave things as they stood – loose ends and all. In the end he opted to continue:

"I, personally, couldn't believe what I was hearing! For a moment I thought lunatics had escaped from the big asylum at the northern end of the neighbourhood. I didn't go out that night, I was too cautious... but in the morning – I heard all about it...

"Shuki shut himself away. Gave himself a fix, so they say... and when it wore off – took a double dose and then a quadruple. For about a week he wasn't seen in public. And after that week it was another week – and then another. His two most sensible girls, Rosa and Sonia, have left him, and his hitmen have vamoosed as well. And all those who used to shelter in his shadow and enjoy that protection, they've turned against him too and brushed him off. The only one who hasn't deserted him is his mother. Understandable I suppose. Mothers! If they give birth to vipers they don't deny them!" – and resisting the temptation to glance at our faces, he went on to say:

"She used to sit in the doorway of the house, in her special chair, with her crutches beside her and a fierce and suspicious look on her face, watching the passers-by. I'd bet on it – if anyone tried to get in, she'd clobber him with her crutches. One of them's got a lethal metal handle.

"Anyway, no one dares. There were some who hoped that once he'd got over it, he'd go back to being the way he was, restore the status quo. I was one of them. I couldn't wait for him to re-appear, but he was dragging his feet and then dragging them some more. In the end there he was. Hail the conquering hero – fat chance!" Nessim swallowed the spittle that had accumulated in his mouth, lowered his head, shifted uneasily on his chair and added with a hint of wistful regret:

"He doesn't have a trace of the old charisma, or the authority that he used to wield, that no one dared to resist. He's not even a shadow of what he was in days gone by, the glory days when he was imposing the kind of order and stability that were worth boasting about!" He scanned our faces again and said with apparent reluctance:
"He's turned into an abject creature, face all swollen, walking like a drunk, can hardly find his way round the backstreets, dead eyes... incredible, to think what he's become!" An odd, rather smug smile flickered over Nessim's face, a smile which he tried unsuccessfully to conceal: "Someone taunted him with a laugh, you see, just that – or maybe it was an experiment, testing the ground – and he, the mighty Shuki, didn't react at all! In the not so distant past – he'd have sliced his face up!" Nessim was taken aback by his own words, struck by their relevance to himself.

"No one dared abuse him in the past. Anyone approaching him without due respect, without head bowed in deference – he'd get his face slashed there and then, with the kind of cuts the most skilled surgeon couldn't sew up. He'd be a monster, disfigured for life. There's a couple like that still at large in the neighbourhood – twin brothers. And to tell the truth I was waiting, waiting with baited breath – to see how they were going to react to the new situation, how they were going to act towards Shuki..." Even at this moment there was a hint of curiosity in Nessim's voice – curiosity and tension:

"And they, the two of them, met Shuki, as he was lurching along like a cripple... and you know how they treated him, what they said to him?" These words were addressed to Rahamim, who shook his head.

"They met him in the wide alley, the main one, coming towards them, and they were walking straight at him, head-on. Getting closer... and when they were about two metres apart, face to face, those brothers – whom he had turned into monsters, disfigured for life, shunned by everyone in the neighbourhood, out of disgust and revulsion and the smell... yes, that special, hideous smell of suppurating wounds – they said 'Good morning' to him – no more and no less! They wished him a good morning at twelve noon. And there was no edge to this, no mockery, no hint of provocation, overt or covert... because for them, as for Shuki, twelve noon counts as morning. And I don't know why they acted this way," Nessim pondered, looking inquisitively at us in search of a solution and, failing to find it, deciding to attempt one of his own:
"Maybe they were still afraid of him, maybe they reckoned there was no point going after revenge for its own sake. Maybe they just hadn't noticed how much he'd changed, maybe they didn't know... I was curious, very curious," Nessim admitted, continuing in that cool, laid-back spirit that is a very close relative of schadenfreude:

"I followed them and caught up with them, the two brothers, and I asked if they knew about Shuki. They answered: 'We know.' I asked them what they intended to do and they said: 'Nothing at all.' 'You're full of compassion!' I said, and maybe there was just a hint of cynicism in my voice. 'For Shuki, yes!' one of the brothers replied, and the other said: 'Not for you!' They threatened me!" Nessim exclaimed in a tone of real fear, as if still confronting the pair and refusing to believe what he was hearing.

"Their appearance alone was enough to give me the creeps," he continued, sounding a little more relaxed – "two monsters with stitched-up faces! I was quaking with fear but I couldn't move – and though the hint was clear and they were waiting for me to turn tail and scarper, I stood there as if I'd taken root, sweating but immobile and apparently, quite unintentionally, blocking their path.

"They both pulled out their flick-knives, simultaneously, as if they'd rehearsed it, and at that very moment a shout was heard – not a yell or a frantic shriek or anything like that – but the calm and confident voice of command:

'Off with you, ugly bastards!' It was Shuki, coming up from behind, and surprisingly coherent considering his stoned appearance.

"They were taken aback, hesitating, but put their flick-knives away. One of them hissed through his teeth: 'We'll settle scores with you yet!' and the other put in: 'Lucky for you we still respect him!' – obviously referring to Shuki. Then they just walked away.

"Shuki ignored me after that, although I was still standing there like a statue, or as if I was bewitched. I wanted to thank him, show heart-felt gratitude for his timely intervention but he – collapsed, as simple as that... fell down in a heap and lay there, choking on the dust and dribbling saliva...

"I went to him and tried to help him up. I bent over him and took a firm hold with both hands. Suddenly, as if he was waking up, he pushed my hands away and growled in my ear – right in my ear, as I was stooping down – 'Sod off, worm!'

"He called me a worm!" Nessim exclaimed, still incredulous; I had never seen him so agitated. "I, who used to do him 'favours', large and small, who always praised him with all my heart, saw him in every instance as a figure capable of wielding authority, bending tigers and scorpions to his will and ruling them with a high hand, I who admired him and taught my family to admire and respect him – he calls me a worm! Me!" Nessim was almost in tears, still smarting from the insult.

"At that moment I was capable of murdering him!" he cried, his face contorted. "I was even looking round for a stick to bash him with... I'd have made do with a big stone. In the end I decided to kick him, kick him in the face! I had such a powerful urge to kick him, I was shaking all over, with rage and hatred, I was positively ecstatic...

"And just as I was poised to kick him – in the head that is," – Nessim thought it worth clarifying, although by now it seemed he was in the grip of debilitating depression, and giving no further attention to his audience; rather than addressing us, he was explaining something to himself: "What I actually wanted to do was kick him in the ear, that smug, diabolical ear of his... they say that's where you can cause some real damage!" He took a gulp of air, swallowed saliva and went on:

"And then he opened his eye... one eye opened, like the eye of a shark – cold, arrogant, full of contempt... and at the same time wild, pitiless, and utterly fearless...

"And the kick stopped short – by itself! I was shaking and sweating... and suddenly I turned and ran, ran all the way home, fleeing for my life, crying and blubbering like a little kid, and not knowing why..." Nessim fixed his tiny, mousy eyes on the surface of the oval table, as if it was capable of solving his puzzle.

"And the next day, Shuki came to me and had the nerve to ask me for a 'small loan'!"

"What was your answer?" asked Rahamim with interest.

"I said he could have it."

"And what did he say to that?" Rahamim prompted.

"He said he'd wait for me at his house," Nessim grinned awkwardly and added with an unconvincing display of composure: "He's going to have a long wait!"

As the first shadows of dusk descended, I left Rahamim's café. It was a long way home, since I was wrapped up in myself and my body carried on moving as if independent of me, slowly and hesitantly, getting lost in familiar alleyways as if I had never set foot in them before. An old man saw me and approached, frowning anxiously and asking:

"Would you like to sit down for a moment, Sir? Or should I call an ambulance?"

The body ignored him and carried on, feeling its way blindly. He watched from a distance, surprised and offended, probably nervous and pensive as well.

THE DEATH OF OLD AHARON

Old Aharon died. His son decided to sell his boat and abandon fishing and the sea altogether.

The rumour spread among the fishermen and some of them would have liked to buy the sophisticated and relatively new vessel, but couldn't afford it. And then, one violet-tinged, gentle and benevolent evening, Rahamim told me that Israel, son of the late David Farhi, only surviving son of the Farhi household, was buying the boat.

We were sitting in the café, quietly sipping our hot drinks – coffee for him and tea for me – when I happened to ask him casually what had become of that boat with its state-of-the-art technology, "Aharon's ship" as it was known among the fishermen, and he gave me the update, between rhythmic sips from his mug.

"What about Israel's shop?" I wanted to know.

"He got tired of it," he answered me in the same neutral, relaxed tone.

"And the family's livelihood?" I went on to ask. "Six or seven sisters and a mother to support?"

"It's only the mother who still needs support!" he asserted.

"So what's become of the sisters?"

"Some weird religious sect hijacked them... one of the bigger ones... headquarters abroad, in America," he explained. " It's run by this celebrity rabbi, does miracles and stuff... Well, when they heard about the sisters, their yen towards Christianity and monasticism, they got their bid in first. They rushed round there and succeeded in persuading all of them, including the mother and the brother too, and the youngest sister who's still married, that the free ones should emigrate to the USA... where prospective bridegrooms are already waiting for them, all of them carefully selected..."

"And they agreed – that soon?" I expressed my surprise.

"Actually, they were dithering for ages," Rahamim told me, "until the eldest daughter broke the ice, you know, the sensible one..." He chewed a finger, making an effort to remember her name.

"Mary," I reminded him.

"Mary!" Rahamim repeated with emphasis, taking a deep gulp from his coffee-mug and adding: "She's been told to change her name to Miriam. Anyway, she was the one who said: 'Come on, let's try our luck!' – that's the way Israel tells it – and the sisters followed her lead... five of them that is. One is still married and as soon as her divorce comes through, she'll go and join her sisters. When the eldest daughter speaks, it seems the others listen..."

"Israel and his mother are still here then," I concluded, adding: "And the youngest sister, the one who's still married."

"Since this business with his sisters started, Israel can't bear to be stuck in that shop any more – so he says... and when he heard about Aharon's ship – he swooped on it, reckoned it was a bargain. Maybe he imagines he can drown his sorrows in the sea, fishing, navigation..."

I didn't respond.

Outside the twilight was gathering, without detracting in any way from the pleasing softness of the airy void above the broad expanse of a quiet Jaffa sea. The first stars glittered in a deep and well-meaning sky.

CODE

I returned home earlier than usual and prepared supper – yogurt, pitta bread, tomato and cheese. I was about to sit down and meditate, when there was a thunderous knocking at the door, and before I had time to react in any way the door flew open and somebody tumbled into the room – quite literally: he lost his footing and if he hadn't clutched at the back of an armchair that happened to be handy, he'd have fallen full length on the cracked floor-tiles. It was Shuki.

He straightened up slowly, without relaxing his grip on the chair-back, his body quivering slightly, a quiver that he was trying unsuccessfully to suppress, and he shot me a keen, candid look, growing steadily clearer beneath his dark brows.

"You've brought ruin on me!" he began, his voice showing no hint of threat or reproof; it was a statement of fact.

"The wheel has turned!" he added with a sigh, focusing his gaze on the floor. He pulled the armchair towards him, sank into it, parked one foot, shod in a rubber shoe that had once been white, on the low, dark-stained table – and glanced at me again.

The look in his eyes was not as I remembered it: you could say it had become affable, open and conciliatory – yet at the same time it was shrewd and calculated. These disparate qualities neither competed nor blended with one another, but the overall effect was steady and uniform, lit by a dull lustre.

"You don't need to be afraid of me!" he hissed, turning away again. And in the silence that suddenly reigned in the long and narrow room, lit by a single yellowish lamp, my voice was heard, even and clear:

"I've never been afraid."

He scrutinised me again, trying to evaluate my expression. The mild scorn that had appeared in his eyes now faded, to be replaced by a kind of dread, bordering on dejection, which he tried to conceal by hastily averting his gaze.

"You've never been afraid..." he repeated my words as if weighing them up. "How very nice for you!" he cried in a voice that had thickened but sounded resigned and submissive. "I'm not afraid either, never have been, never will be!" he declared with rhetorical emphasis, adding: "Except of myself... I'm afraid of myself! And I suggest you should be a little afraid too... for your own good! Of me, I mean... 'Cos I'm always full of surprises!" he exclaimed in an unexpected spirit of arousal – "I surprise myself most of all!"

He passed a flat palm over his bulbous, simian forehead, slowly and firmly as if wiping away an imaginary film of sweat, and continued:

"It all began with that five grand... No! I should say it began with Lili! You tried to steal from me the most successful girl I have. 'Gold-mine' is what they call her... and that's what she is. And I'm not talking about the profits she brings in either, it has to do with..." – he hesitated, as if unsure whether to reveal his innermost thoughts or not – and finally whispered – "...her heart! 'Cos Lili" – he raised his voice again – "has a heart of gold! You won't find in this world, up above or down below, a heart like hers! Forget your cherubs, angels, saints and hermits... not one of them could hold a candle to her! And you tried to steal her from me, tried to take from me the only thing I had, the only thing I had left... It was down to you that she rebelled... mutinied against me!" he cried, thumping his chest emphatically and focusing his gaze on me again. And through that dim fudge of numbed senses and arrested thoughts, there was a flicker of sadness – distant, ephemeral, but real.

"Her boys abused me," he added as if in the confessional, looking for understanding and sympathy. "Her line-up!" he grimaced. "You see," he went on, suddenly turning to face me again, and in the process, planting his other foot on the table: "I'm the one who sorted out her line-ups!" He pointed to his chest with an emphatic finger. "I taught her how to get a line-up together, in factory canteens in the daytime, clubs and discos at night, how to makes sure of the money and how to get it over with, as quickly as possible. And I got her to see the good sides of the line-up – it's clean and it's commercial!" he declared with the verve of a salesman pushing a superior product, in love with himself and justifiably proud of his talents.

"There's no messing about in a line-up," he went on to explain, "no special demands, no drooling... it's all over, chop-chop – and a wad of cash in the kitty, my kitty that is!" – a wild, almost insane howl of self-derision distorted his voice, and when he spoke again he was choking:

"She learned fast... She's got an open mind and she learns everything fast." He took a deep breath and paused for a long moment. And then, as if suddenly roused from sleep, face grim and an admonitory finger wagging at some unseen figure in the void: "She... this Lili..." – his blazing eyes turned in my direction – "set her line-up on me! She got it together according to the principles I taught her – quick and efficient - got them all fired up, gave them what they wanted and promised second helpings – set them on me! I'm lucky they didn't finish me off!" he commented sourly, scratching his unshaven chin and adding:

"That wasn't what she wanted... I know. But sometimes it's hard to keep things under control. Especially when it's gang of men who've scored once already and they're expecting more..." He shook his head in a manner intended to express both sorrow and affronted dignity and resumed in a more equable tone:

"They kicked me, threw dust and sand over my head, and gravel... dragged me by the ears, stripped me naked. I was afraid then all right, shaking with fear like a little kid. I was afraid they were going to castrate me... I've done that to others, and I was afraid I was about to get the same. In the end, I suppose they remembered their instructions, threw me out into the street with nothing but my underwear..." For a moment he focused his heavy gaze on his hands that were clasped tightly together. When he eased the pressure slightly, both hands began to shake, an ague that could be neither controlled not concealed.

"I would never have believed," he went on, "that I could endure that level of humiliation! Never!" A wave of emotion flooded his voice, and he suppressed it at once, with perceptible effort, returning to his tone of affected composure:

"If anyone had ever described a scene like this to me and asked me: 'What would you do?' – I'd have answered him immediately, without hesitation, in full confidence: 'I'd run a bath and slit my veins!' Are you listening?" – he turned to me with a faint, distant smile and without waiting for a reply, continued:

"I was wriggling like a snake... hairy, sweaty arms and legs all over me – when they peeled off my clothes and I thought this was it, they were going to peel off my bollocks as well... I pissed myself, I was that scared!"

Shuki shifted in his seat, staring at the walls of the room with their flaking plaster, and ostentatiously ignoring me he went on: "I'm like you. I always believed, I was absolutely sure – I wasn't afraid of anything. Bullshit!" He suddenly removed his feet from the table and leaned forward as if nauseous and about to vomit. The moment passed and he leaned back again in the heavy armchair, replacing one of his feet on the table.

"Would you like a cup of tea?" I offered.

"No!" he snapped. "It wasn't for tea I came here, tea isn't what I need now! The situation is much more serious than you and I together could possibly imagine! And you're going to hear it! And I reckon this time you're going to tremble, quake with fear. Well, we shall see!" he declared, before going off at a tangent:

"With all the arrogance and insolence that you and your kind are capable of, you tried to steal my 'gold-mine'!" A note in his voice suggested a change taking place in him, something hidden and unidentifiable seething away beneath the thin veneer of artificial equanimity. And this "something" combined elements of the threatening, the malicious and the cruel, the pitiable too.

"I tell you!" he cried in his most metallic tone, looking at me in insistent demand for a response – "Never, never, ne-e-ver has she left me!"

"That is true!" I replied, adding: "So far as I can judge, she's tied to you by a very durable bond, strange – but durable!"

"Even now," his voice cracked, and in his tense neck the thick vein could be seen pulsating in rapid rhythm: "All the others have left me, kicked me in the teeth! But she came back, and she's the only one. The 'girls' scarpered, the 'boys' spat in my face... and she – who was absolutely free to act as she pleased, do whatever took her fancy – she came back to me, brought money in, went out to work... at her initiative, you see... and caring for my mother..." He sighed deeply, wheezing as if the air had been drained from his lungs, and continued: "I kicked her, and she didn't react. Really! I thought of killing her..." His face contorted, and his eyes flashed with malice, but his voice turned plaintive and edgy:

"I haven't the guts for that! I'm sorry I didn't cut her throat then! I reckon she regrets that too and you," – he turned to me abruptly, unexpectedly – "aren't you sorry too?" For a brief moment the tension in his voice eased, as if he was succeeding in controlling that inner eruption, which was swelling and threatening to shatter the fragile supports of his crumbling personality.

"I'm not sorry," I replied calmly.

Shuki grinned, tried to laugh but instead coughed a deep, cracking, lung-curdling cough. And so doing he put his other foot back on the table, in an effort to display composure and control of the situation.

"She returned to me!" he cried that climactic declamatory cry that has nothing behind it but empty void. "She's the only one of the whole bunch... the bunch that I nourished and supported. I made them big and I made them respected! She's the only one who's prepared to accept me the way I am, bruised, beaten and pissing myself out of fear – and still terrorising her the way I always have... You see," – he looked at me thoughtfully – "she came back to me but," – something flashed in his eyes, cold as the blade of a dagger, utterly hostile – "she belongs to you! And don't you try telling me anything different!" – forestalling with an outstretched hand what looked to him like readiness on my part to respond – "We all know that's how it is! You know it, I know it – and she knows it!" He withdrew his hand, trying to control the tremors that were wracking his body with increasing regularity, and succeeding to a degree.

"And you know," he said suddenly, his voice quite even, "I understand her. Or what would be closer to the truth..." he was silent for a brief moment and continued: "I don't mind... I only pretend to mind, but deep down – I know it's good for her. In fact, I'm almost grateful! This is incredible! I hear what I'm saying and I can't believe my ears. But that's the way it is," he asserted with renewed vigour. "I'm ashamed of the whole business and I wish I could change it all, run away from myself, run away from the truth, but you can't run away from the truth... 'cos it's the truth!" His lips, almost blue, contorted, his chin quivered, moisture glistened in his eyes – and was dried by sheer will-power.

"However," he went on, making some progress towards controlling the quaking of his voice, "at that meeting with you, at the abandoned lot – I wanted to murder you! That's what I wanted to do, wanted it with heart and soul, with every fibre! Throwing you that razor – was just a tactic. I knew you wouldn't use it. Even if you did surprise me and use it, you wouldn't get the better of me! Even if all the luck was on your side, and I slipped on a banana-skin – that's been known to happen – the boys would have finished you off. Those were my specific instructions... I had you in my pocket!" The last words came out as a barely human wail, after which he sighed deeply, drawing air into his chest and releasing it slowly, in an attempt to calm and subdue himself. Big drops of sweat began sparkling on his bony forehead. He glanced around the narrow room, took both feet off the table, perched them on the edge of the armchair and went on to say:

"When we met there, I didn't intend to murder you – not at first. To start with, I was just going to slash your face. The kind of deep cuts that can never be properly sewn up. Ugly cuts – and a face that will smell foul for ever. I was going to turn you into a monster, so no one would come near you. So you'd know what it is to be reviled, defeated, an outcast...and the idea was to make you repulsive to her, a failure in her eyes, spurned by her. And then I realised this wasn't going to work, it wouldn't happen! She'd stand by you despite the foul disfigurement. In fact, the more you were spurned, the more you were rejected – that would have drawn her even closer to you... if she could be any closer to you than she is already!

"She'd be yours not only in spirit, as she is now, but in body too... the body she despises so much she throws it at me, like a cracked bone to a mad dog, a mad dog like me!" He took a gulp of air, one of those deep gulps intended to mask emotion and restore self-control. And it seemed to work; his voice settled in a lower register:

"She'd have moved in with you, and not left you... she'd have come to serve you, 'cos then you'd really be needing service – and this brought me to a decision..." His voice faltered. He was silent for a long moment, coughed a rasping cough, swallowed phlegm and changed the subject:

"Maybe, after all..." he raised his cold, narrowed eyes to me – "How about that tea you offered?"

I went to the kitchen, boiled water, brewed tea and returned with two steaming cups, one apiece.

There was a great weight of weariness etched on his face, which seemed to have aged and grown wrinkled all at once. He seemed to be in the grip of a malignant fever, liable to collapse at any moment and lose consciousness.

With a sinewy, almost blue hand, he wiped his lips which were also bluish-violet in colour, and ploughed on regardless:

"My mind was made up – to finish you off, bury you then and there, get you out of the world or more to the point – out of her world! I suppose she'd have kept your memory alive for a while...maybe, even remembered you for the rest of your life. She goes for sentimental stuff like that. And as a reaction, she'd run away from time to time, but she'd always come back in the end, having nowhere else to go! And nothing else to dream of. And she'd be mine, all mine!" – his voice rose to a shriek – "the way she was before you turned up that evening!"

He leaned forward, picked up the cup and took long and deep gulps of the liquid, still unable to control the tremor that was now setting his whole body shaking. Then he wiped his lips, and tried to adopt a more relaxed pose – putting his feet back on the table, and then replacing them on the edge of the chair, which quaked beneath him and creaked ominously.

"The strangest thing that happened that evening, you know what it was?" – he asked, or stated, or was talking to himself – "It wasn't when those boys from the line-up jumped us, in spite of the clever way I'd deceived her about the place and time of the meeting. In fact," – his eyes glowed with a heavy, sickly lustre – "the deception was no deception really. I was sure in the end she'd figure it out. I dropped enough hints, broad hints... I was hoping she'd guess what was happening, that was the idea. But I didn't expect her to act on it! The thought might occur to her but in the end, trusting me, she'd do nothing..." He chuckled, a dry, nervous sound.

"What a fool I was! The strangest thing that evening wasn't those bastards spitting in my face and kicking me and sending me home in wet underwear and scared out of my wits, but..." – and at this point the heavy weariness dispersed from his features, which briefly regained their brash vitality – "when I drew the razor, and looked into your face – with scorn and contempt – I realised at once, it was clear to me beyond any doubt, like a lightning-flash in my mind – that I wasn't going to kill you! You weren't going to die that evening!" The weariness returned to his face, crumpling it and putting a dry and ugly look into his eyes. His arms were shaking again, and his voice dropped further, becoming barely coherent:

"It wasn't that my intentions changed, or my nerves betrayed me or my conscience was aroused," he explained in a tone that was hollow, but surprisingly equable given the circumstances. "Far from it! I was all fired up with determination to finish you off, put an end to this charade... my conscience was clear from every angle, pure and clear as the snow in the hills. I was going crazy, I couldn't wait to put the razor to your throat – just enough pressure, it doesn't take that much – and slash from left to right, and feel the spurt of warm blood...

"All this was driving me out of my mind, my imagination was in overdrive – I wanted it more than anything else in the world. And yet," – his voice sinking a fraction – "when I looked in your face, the face I hate more than any face in the world – I knew for a fact I wasn't going to kill you, I wasn't capable of killing you. I wouldn't have the guts to kill you, however much I wanted to do it.

"But it didn't stop me trying. You'll remember – I pounced on you although you were unarmed, and in some quarters that might be considered unsporting... so you may as well know – I threw that razor to you quite deliberately, so that when the story got out, people would say you were given a chance, meaning that I, Shuki, gave you a chance! This would be common knowledge, she'd know it too...

"And then I read in your face that it wasn't going to happen... not that your face scared me or appealed to my compassion or anything like that... Not at all! It was something else, something strong that doesn't have a name. Somewhere between my sharp razor and your bare throat, I was stopped in my tracks. I was helpless, couldn't move a muscle. Do you understand me?" He looked at me keenly, his eyes narrowed.

I nodded in assent.

"Some other power was involved here!" he exclaimed, his voice rising in pitch again, hoarse and strident. "For the first time since I came into this world, and met you – I acknowledge the fact that something else exists – real, even if it's untouchable." He was short of breath, and making renewed efforts to steady his breathing by inhaling deep and controlled gulps of air. He was silent for a moment, then smiled a pale and twisted smile, and declared solemnly:

"So I wouldn't have got to kill you even without the line-up that she sent to save your skin – and hers! That's what I've been trying to explain to her – and she has no idea what I'm talking about! It was out of despair that I attacked you... And now," – he looked up at me, brows knitted – "to the point!" For a moment he let the emphatic silence fall between us like a partition, before mustering his strength and saying loudly:

"I need money, now, right now! I'm trembling, I'm sweating..." he wailed – "I haven't got the gear! I've got the syringe, I've got the needles, I haven't got the stuff that matters... What she brings in – not even enough for half a fix! And I need more than that, lots more! Double, quadruple! And you'll have to supply this, 'cos if you don't," – and feverishly he thrust a shaking hand into the pocket of his grubby shirt and put down on the table beside him a standard barber's razor – "I'll slit my wrists right here, in front of you, open my veins. You couldn't stand that, could you! You're such a softy!" – he grimaced angrily.

"You're wrong," I answered him calmly. "Not only could I stand it, I'd be sure to call an ambulance and get your veins sewn up in time!" – and in a clear voice, almost pleasurably I added: "That's not what I call a threat!"

He listened to my words in astonishment, was silent a long moment. His mouth was gaping, his eyes twitched in their sockets as if the man was demented, and all his limbs were shaking with a tremor that could be neither hidden nor controlled. The armchair he sat on, the table under his feet, responded to the rhythm of his spasms and palpitations with loud and strident creaks.

Suddenly, his face contorted, he sprang from his seat, knelt at my feet and pleaded:

"I'm on fire, I'm burning up! The world's collapsed around me! Help me, please, and quickly! Hurry! I'll kill someone! I'll kill myself! Go out and mug someone! Please – a small loan..."

I drew out a wallet from my back pocket, opened it carefully, extracted a blue cash-card and handed it to him.

For a moment he froze. He looked stunned. And despite the fever that dominated him, he took the card, muttered his thanks, stood up unsteadily and turned to the door – a manoeuvre requiring all his effort and concentration.

"Just a moment!" I stopped him.

He rounded on me, twisted face ablaze with anger.

"You haven't got the PIN number," I explained.

"Oh, yes!" – he slapped his forehead with the flat of his hand –

"What an idiot I am!"

Impatiently, swaying on his feet like a man in urgent need of the bathroom, he waited while I wrote the number on a scrap of paper and handed it to him, and then he nearly collided with the door, trying to open it on the wrong side – and when it was finally wide open, he stepped out into the darkness with a flourish,   and disappeared as if he never was.

OVERDRAFT

The time was four in the morning. Outside, and in the house, thick and humid darkness still reigned. Through the north-facing window opposite my bed, from a vantage-point deep in the blue yonder, a big, elderly star peered into the room with an air of total indifference, a resigned humility.

I was just about to sit down and meditate when the entrance door was flung open with a thunderous crash, and someone landed with a thud on the floor of the outer room.

I got up cautiously, put on slippers, switched on the light in my room, then standing on the threshold I pressed the switch in the outer room, flooding it with yellowish light. On the cracked tiles of the floor, Shuki was sprawled.

He lay on his back, his hands under his head and a strange expression on his pinched face.

"Good evening!" he cried to the empty space above him, as a string of bubbles of spit or foam trickled from the corner of his mouth. His clothes – shirt and jeans – were crumpled and rucked in every conceivable direction, as if he'd been attacked by a pack of rabid dogs.

"Good morning!" he corrected himself, addressing me this time, and his eyes, gradually returning to their customary opacity, tried to catch sight of me.

I approached him, bending down with the intention of helping him stand up, or sit up at least. He resisted vehemently, with unexpected, almost frenzied vigour:

"No!" he cried, "Don't touch me! Don't! I'm unclean... no, it isn't me... you're the one who's unclean! The most unclean in all the world! You defile everything you touch! And you do it in a special way, your own way, reckon you're a saint or a hermit or a yogi or something... doing good works and putting things right! So why did you give me the cash-card?" he cried, as tears welled in his eyes.

"You asked for money," I reminded him, my voice even.

"And if I'd asked for a gun to blow my brains out – you'd have given me that too?"

"No."

"What's the difference between a cash-card and a gun?" he spluttered through the tidal wave of saliva that had flooded his mouth, still supine on the floor, his position unchanged in the slightest degree.

"There is no difference," I answered him.

For a moment he was silent, staring at me with wide open, astonished eyes, and then he seemed to sober up, briefly regaining some composure.

"Why did you give it?" he asked quietly, frankly curious.

"You weren't going to kill yourself with it."

"Do you believe everything you're told?" he cried with a blend of pain and bemused delight, yellow-green flames flashing in his eyes.

"Yes, I do."

He tried to chuckle or find some other way of expressing his scorn. And another string of bubbles appeared on his unshaven chin.

"Wouldn't you be more comfortable if you got up from the floor?" – was my practical suggestion.

"No!" he exclaimed, recoiling as if stung by a scorpion. I was halted in my tracks, standing frozen to the spot, still wearing only pajamas and bedroom slippers.

"Not yet!" – and he went on to say: "The cash-card worked a treat! I can't remember how many cash-machines I activated... in spite of all those warning messages I was getting about only paying out once a day... I filled my pockets with dosh... one fix and then another and maybe another after that – I lost count!" He broke off, sounding aggrieved, as if I was demanding a precise record of his drug intake, and this was an unreasonable imposition on my part.

"And then I had a brilliant idea!" he continued. "Only someone like me could have come up with a wheeze like that... Shuki the downtrodden, the has-been, the pathetic, Shuki the... boss man!" He succeeded, with an effort, in stifling what could have turned into an emotional outburst, adding in a hushed, slurred voice: "Of times gone by...

"You," he said, turning his head and giving me a weary look, "you have a kind heart. You're not afraid of anything, you throw money around, your own money – and it all turns out the wrong way! It's about time you realised that, once and for all!" He looked away from me and transferred his gaze to the scruffy ceiling with its cracked and flaking plaster.

"When I came here, to you – you should have thrown me out! Like a dog, like a sick dog! You should have waved a big stick at me, given me a proper kicking, punched my face in!" And without looking at me, without any change in his position, staring at the ceiling, he continued:

"It's open season now, I'm fair game for anyone. They're already spitting in my face, and I'm getting used to that!" He grimaced and added: "If I'm fair game for anyone, I'm fair game for you most of all. More than that, it's your duty! You should have kicked me, driven me out, thrown me in the gutter... The cops would have come and picked me up and who knows... some miracle might have happened. You believe in miracles, right!" He tried to look down at me, a project for which – lying flat on his back on the floor – he was not ideally placed. He abandoned the attempt with a petulant air which he tried unsuccessfully to hide, and in an effort to conserve his energy and resist whatever it was that was clouding his consciousness, he closed his eyes.

"You believe in miracles!" – he droned on, sounding like a shaman with sinusitis – "And so do I! Even those who scoff at miracles and pretend they don't believe in them – miracles are still what they're looking for all the time. Any miracle that will rescue them from squalor – and from hypocrisy, especially! From hypocrisy – remember that! It takes a miracle, 'cos will-power alone just isn't enough... no one can do it...

"The cops – maybe they're my miracle, and maybe – you are... But I don't believe in you!" he exclaimed suddenly, opening his eyes wide. Their expression was absolutely empty and yet – still ablaze with that yellow-green fire. "You are my curse!" he moaned, and continued: "As long as you're alive, as long as you're in this world – I'm cursed! And when you make your last exit – it's going to be too late! I'll be used to you, dependent on you, addicted to you, like a drug! If you hadn't given me the cash-card, I'd be in a bad way! Without the gear – I'd have gone out of my mind... on the other hand – maybe I'd have kicked it! You hear about people doing that – locking themselves up in sealed rooms, telling their families not to take any notice of their pleading, ignore all their curses and pathetic appeals... so they're shut up in there and going cold turkey and banging their heads on the walls... and if their relations really love them – they won't give in! And after however long it takes, a month or two, they come out of there different people, changed, new! No more dependence, no more addiction, no more drugs... that's the only way and it shows you what real love is!

"As for you," he added scornfully, "they only have to ask – and you hand it over! What are you going to say about that?" he asked, still staring fixedly at some point on the damaged ceiling.

"You're right," I declared.

"You shouldn't have given me the cash-card?"

"When someone asks to be locked in a sealed room until he's weaned off drugs – his wish is granted," I thought it worth pointing out. Before I could continue he interrupted:

"If he asks for a cash-card..."

"He gets given it." – I completed the sentence

"And a gun?"

"No – absolutely not!"

"You've got it all worked out, haven't you?" he sneered. "You've really got your head together! Just as well I didn't ask you to lock me up for detox! Mind you, this wouldn't be the ideal place for it... people coming and going all the time... Your door's always open, to anyone. Why is it always open?" he asked, sounding genuinely interested.

"I've nothing to hide."

"What about robbery?"

"There's no such thing."

"And what if someone gets in here and steals when you're not at home?" – he persisted.

"That isn't theft," I replied. "Anyone who comes in here, with me or without me, is my guest and the whole of the house is at his disposal."

"And I thought it was because of the broken lock..."

"That is another reason..." I admitted with a smile.

"Some other time," he said, "I'll ask you to lock me up somewhere... if I can think of somewhere suitable. And maybe, in the meantime you'll get the lock mended!

"When I got the cash-card," he added, "the cash-card and the PIN number too – I was delirious with joy... But it wasn't one of your best ideas, giving me the card. Cash would have been healthier, for you and for me... I'd have made do with less...one fix, or two, but no more than that! As it is, for all I know I've overdosed already! I could drop dead on you!" he declared, his voice thickening.

"And it'll be on your conscience!" – a sly, somewhat clumsy smile flickered over his face – "But you're not afraid are you, not even of Hell!" His smile broadened and turned into a blend of oily disdain and cold contempt: "Guys like you don't go to Hell, it's only guys like me... You'd send me down there, given half the chance!"

"Hell doesn't exist," was my response to this.

"So how sinners going to be punished?"

"By the sin itself."

"I'd rather go to Hell!" he muttered thoughtfully, and after a long moment reverted to his theme, his voice calm but blank:

"I didn't come here to weep and winge... you see – I could have gone home, to my house I mean, and that would have been better. Give my mother a fright and maybe – she'd have had another stroke... snuffed it. They say she's got money stashed... in her underwear. Somewhere I'd never get my hands on it! But the undertakers might do me a favour and give it to me. It's going to be found... when those nice charitable ladies come along to clean her up. At the moment I'm the sole heir. My father and brother – both of them banged up, and they're not getting anything... don't deserve it!

"And maybe – it's all bluff! Anyway, I didn't go home and I came here... and there's a reason for that. More than one reason – but one of them's important. First off, I wanted to tell you what I think of you... and I've done that! I'm glad you're here and you're the way you are but if you weren't – maybe the world would be a better place! We could have carried on the way we were... everything in its place... sorted..." He spoke in a dreamy, steadily diminishing voice, of variable tempo, but his words were still coherent.

"I didn't come here to tell you what I think of you. Forget I said that. I wasn't going to get bogged down in philosophy either. I came here to tell you about your cash-card. Fact is – I sold it!" He hooted with a blast of hollow, inane laughter that set the whole of his wiry body shaking, still lying flat on the floor.

When the laughter abated, he added hastily, as if afraid that at any moment death or something similar might overtake him:

"Five hundred I got for it! Clean and kosher money! You'd better get moving quick, cancel the card! You're losing money by the minute!" he warned me. "They're using it all over town, and then they'll try it in other towns too. I just couldn't resist it! I needed a double dose, a double-double! But you see... there's something in my nature – flawed maybe... or maybe it isn't flawed at all – something whole, natural, straight, true to itself, not resisting temptation, always under pressure, no thinking through, no conscience, no questions, no analysing – primitive, I'd call it – or should that be primeval? Something recognising no authority, no routine. That's what the true and the divine is all about!" he cried in a tone of sardonic fervour, before remembering the point at issue and adding more soberly: "You'd better get moving. Run, I tell you, run! Every minute's costing you money!"

I said nothing in reply to this. Instead I approached him, put my shoulder under his and disregarding the pungent smell of decay he exuded, lifted him onto his feet. This time he didn't resist, even cooperated a little.

I put him on the sofa, took the sweaty rubber shoes from his feet, went into my room and pulled a blanket from the closet, returned and spread it over him.

A smile flickered across his face and his simian forehead seemed to clear briefly. The sounds emerging from between his misshapen teeth were part words, part sigh of relief: "A quilt as well..." And with that he sank into a deep sleep, like a stone falling into a bottomless well.

I sat to meditate. There was nothing I could do about the cash-card until the banks opened, at eight-thirty. So I followed my standard daily routine: after meditation, a swim in the sea, shower, shave, tea with honey and departure for work.

When the banks opened I went to the branch handling my account, and after a long wait in the queue, it was my turn at the window. I reported to the clerk on duty that a cash-card was no longer in my possession. Without looking up he asked me:

"Stolen?"

"No."

"Lost?"

"No."

At this point the clerk finally looked up from his papers, wrinkled the smooth brow under a thinning thatch of hair, and studied me with a display of utter bemusement, backed up by a vague awareness of superiority, and resentment at the irritating and tasteless breach with convention that he was having to cope with.

"So what has happened, Sir?" – the words were spaced out emphatically. He tried to give his voice a metallic edge and succeeded only in producing a raucous, grating sound like the faulty mechanism of an antiquated wall-clock.

"It's no longer in my possession."

With commendable composure the clerk repeated the questions he'd already asked, to which he received the same answers. Finally, his patience fraying, he took some initiative and wrote "Disappeared" in his file.

It seemed the anonymous purchasers of my card hadn't managed to exploit it to quite the extent they had hoped for. It got stuck in one machine, which proceeded to swallow it. Still, the money withdrawn prior to this mishap amounted to more than twice my monthly salary. I rang my wife and arranged a meeting, to explain to her my changed financial circumstances.

THE WIFE

With my wife, from whom I had separated in the wake of the liberating change that I experienced, and in accordance with the changed perceptions emanating from it – I had come to an agreement whereby the house was registered in her name and my income was shared with her. The agreement had stood up to all kinds of tests and vicissitudes, and proved its worth. And now the issue of the cash-card had arisen.

We met in a small café, near the Tel Aviv sea-front, a businessmen's café where the vista of the sea served as a kind of painted backdrop, a minor accessory when compared with the important stuff contained in the briefcases clutched by patrons and clients, or whirring around among the well lubricated flywheels of their finely tuned computer-brains. There were some who were dissatisfied with this antiquated apparatus, supplementing it with the mechanical versions – neat pocket-calculators and even laptop models with their tiny monitor-screens and integral keyboards.

The atmosphere was solemn and businesslike, ruling out the possibility of any infringement of routine.

As expected, my wife showed up on time. The look in her eyes was heavy and even now tinged with blame, or perhaps it was the opposite – blame was the overwhelming factor and the rest was an unsuccessful effort to alleviate it. Avoiding my eye seemed to be her only option.

After the customary felicitations and the smiles that accompanied them, a kind of neutral, undemanding silence descended, a blessed silence that lasted until the tea was served.

"Coping?" I asked.

"Coping!" she replied, a dull echo. She was studying me now with a keen look, somehow contriving to combine accusation, sorrow and disdain.

"Do you want me back?" I asked evenly.

"No!" she cried as if seized by a spasm. "After everything that's happened – no chance!" And in a flat tone she went on: "Let's carry on the way we are... the children are used to it too... not that they're children any more but adults, with minds of their own – and homes of their own. As for me, I'm used to it... Any, what kind of a question is that – Do you want me back? It's one of those word-games you're such a dab hand at!" she protested, adding:

"If I say 'yes', it'll come out in the end as if I said 'no', and vice versa. I know you so well!" she continued, her tone turning grimmer. "If people want to come back they just do it – without asking questions. But don't even think about it!" she added hastily, suddenly alarmed. "I wouldn't take you back for all the money in the world! After everything that's happened..." her voice was shaky, starting to crack, and although she refused to shed tears, her eyes were moist.

"You're right," I responded as calmly as I could. "I'm the one who's to blame, I admit that, and yet – it's my way! You know that, you know me," I pointed out in a whisper, a whisper with some vigour behind it. If I chose a different way I wouldn't be true to myself... we'd both be untrue to ourselves!"

"I've never been untrue to myself!" she asserted stolidly.

"Absolutely!" I concurred.

"You can keep your absolutely's!" she snapped.

"Sorry."

In a thoroughly changed tone of voice, calculated and practical, she declared:

"There never was any love between us!"

"Now," I replied, "there's more of it than at any other time."

"You've got some strange ideas about love. What kind are you talking about now?"

"Love without carnal passion, which is the source of venomous, sterile hatred. Love that doesn't depend on time or place – and there's nothing physical about it."

She considered my words, finally conceding:

"There's something in that. As far as I'm concerned, you might just as well be dead!

"From a certain point of view," I responded, "I have died."

"The grandchildren are asking about you!" she told me in a sudden change of tack, adding: "Aren't you interested in seeing them?"

"I certainly am," I assured her.

"But you never show up!" she objected.

"I'm not hiding!"

"So they're supposed to come looking for you?" she sneered.

"They're always with me and I'm always with them."

She retreated into herself. Perhaps she was considering my words, perhaps she was engaged in thoughts of her own. Perhaps she just wanted a break from sterile verbiage, which was doing little for her, and clarifying nothing.

I sipped the tea which had cooled.

All around, the routine of the place and its clients ran on smoothly and efficiently, all with the absolute minimum of wasted time and effort. People with dossiers came, people with dossiers left, people with dossiers sat at plastic tables and sipped black coffee, or cappuccino, or espresso, while spreading out the paperwork, leafing through it, adding swift and adroit handwritten corrections and confident, no-frills signatures, putting the papers away and glancing around them briefly, hollow looks hemmed in by spectacle-lenses of varying thickness.

Somebody waiting for someone shifted anxiously on his narrow-seated chair and when the other arrived, greeted him with a nod that went unacknowledged. The newcomer produced a sheaf of documents which he spread out on the minimalist table, pointing with a long thin finger that seemed to have no flesh on it – just bone and transparent, waxy skin – to the places where signing was required, and the other, his face almost as emaciated as the pointing finger, began signing. He signed and signed and went on signing, without saying a word, without so much as a murmur, with confidence and alacrity.

"When I remember…" my wife began suddenly – "the whole thing… and see myself… how I reacted… how I stood up to all the tests…" she sighed, a tone of bitter wonderment creeping into her voice, "I can't help asking myself: How did you manage to hold on?!"

"That's true," I concurred without hesitation.

"I don't need your agreement!" she protested, trying the tea and not finding it to her taste, grimacing and replacing the semi-spherical cup with its oval saucer on the violet formica-topped table. And after a prolonged pause she spoke again:

"The truth is, I'm happy! Now more than at any other time." Her voice was sincere, with a ring of clear and resolute truth: "With a little fortitude, we've arrived at the situation most natural for me and apparently – for you too! After everything that's happened with you, after your 'change' as you call it, or 'rebirth' or whatever – there was no point carrying on together, except for the sake of the children – and they're all grown up now, thank God, and going their own ways, and the house is empty... it's not easy adjusting to that, but you can adjust to anything in the end, and it's the highest achievement in life, getting used to living alone! I should be grateful for that!" There was a perceptible quiver in her voice, advance warning of an overall outburst which she was so far managing to restrain.

"Sometimes I'm angry..." she added in a calmer voice, as if taking part in a banal conversation between neighbours – "or sad... but it soon passes. I visit one of my sons or daughters – it's all forgotten and I hurry back home. Forgetting... when there's nothing to forget! That's painful sometimes too...having nothing to forget! Everything's as smooth as I once dreamed it would be, and now that I've got there – it's boring and sad as well..." She lapsed into thought, lightly fingering the rim of the semi-spherical cup, its glass almost opaque after too many automatic washes.

"A sweet sort of sadness," she went on to explain, "a kind of melancholia... that's somehow addictive!" And after a brief silence she suddenly declared in a loud voice – quite unexpectedly and with scant regard for time and place:

"I haven't even got anyone to argue with!"

No one, not even the waiter, took the slightest notice of the raised voice. All were applying themselves to their own affairs with the same energy, the same concentration, the same diligence. Those sitting at or rising from tables went on riffling through papers, opening and closing briefcases, tapping on laptop keys and between times, as an afterthought, sipping the drinks served to them. The waiter, apparently also the proprietor, was engaged in vigorous wiping of his cups, fresh from the automatic dishwasher, which stood there with all the patience of a stuffed donkey. There were no flies; the background buzzing was the sound of distant traffic.

"Who'd have thought I'd miss arguments!" – she spoke with head lowered, addressing herself, "And that's what it's come to!" She looked up, without looking at me and added: "As I said, there's nothing better than this! It really is the apex of human achievement – to miss arguments! Nobody to argue with, nothing to argue about!"

I took another sip of tea, which was now lukewarm and utterly insipid.

"You let me down badly!" she cried suddenly, and this time a number of heads were lifted from laptops and turned momentarily in her direction.

"All the way!" she insisted, but with a little more restraint: "How I longed for warmth, security, love... and what did you give me?" – and she answered her own question succinctly: "Eccentricity, a life with no point and no respite, and a God who's not like any God I've ever known! How I wish I could turn the clock back, not be married to you, not even to have met you, ever!" – her voice rising to another crescendo.

"Not asking for much, are you!" I commented with a smile.

"I've been learning from you!" – she declared, adding: "Everything about you is weird, surprising in the wrong kind of way. I've never known any peace, always on edge, always under pressure, trying to figure out what the day was going to bring... I never got any satisfaction out of you, and as for you, I reckon you got even less out of me!"

"That's a bit of an exaggeration," I put in, in an attempt to focus on the main point at issue and move away from the incidentals. It was an attempt that failed utterly; there was no diverting her from her theme:

"Your behaviour was strange to me, and I didn't understand the way your mind worked... I never really figured you out, your demands or lack of demands... It was all strange to me, over my head, maybe, and maybe – not... Maybe it was all true, or maybe – it was all a lie, a pack of lies! There never was a middle way, a golden mean or a silver mean.... Not even a Milky Way!" she asserted with a sour smile, taking her hand away from the greasy table and continuing:

"There was a time when I felt as if I was frozen solid, I'd stopped existing...maybe – one of the happier times. The children..." and again she smiled a cryptic smile, entirely for her own benefit – "they really were a source of consolation. For them, I suppose I should be grateful to you – not for anything else!" she stressed, not looking at me but over my shoulder, at the opposite wall with its posters of

Alpine landscapes, advertising some airline or another.

"When I look back," she said in a softer tone, "it hurts me. I feel misused, disappointed, abandoned... and all this, I don't know how to say it – makes me happy!" she exclaimed vehemently, as if surprising herself. "It's an interesting life that I've lived, to this day it still interests me! A life of leisure I didn't want, and a life of servitude was a hateful idea! No still waters. And how I longed for them, the still waters! But it seems they only exist in the world of dreams, and so it will be for ever, to the end of time... and perhaps that's why we're so enthralled by them..."

She looked at me now, a heavy look with nothing behind it. After a long silence, she jumped abruptly to a different subject entirely:

"What's it really about, this meeting?" she asked, coldly practical.

"This month," I began, "I'm overdrawn at the bank; there's not a cent left over from my salary..."

"Is that my fault?" she interrupted sharply. "I haven't been withdrawing funds!"

"I know that," I replied. "I'm hoping that next month it'll all be sorted out. I'm appealing to you to try and cope this month. Somehow."

"What kind of an appeal is that?" she protested. "I'm supposed to 'cope' – 'somehow'? You're living it up, and I'm picking up the tab?"

"At the moment," I added, "I don't see any way of getting any cash together. Maybe by the end of the month, things will be sorted, but I can't guarantee that!"

"Has someone cheated you?" – she fired from the hip, trying to decipher the look on my face.

"That's not the point!" I objected sharply, and in the same resolute tone I added: "If I can find some way to do this, you won't get hurt!"

"I've been hurt already!" she responded firmly.

"How?"

"By this strange request of yours," she explained – "You won't tell me what's happened – but you expect me to sympathise!"

"It may be you're right," I said, weighing things up – "but that's all I'm asking for."

"And this is why you called me?" – her astonishment was genuine, and acute. Not waiting for an answer, she added hastily:

"You could have told me over the phone!"

"I didn't think it was appropriate."

"And I was thinking to myself," she raised her voice again – "God knows what I was thinking!"

I didn't answer.

She didn't touch any more of the tea. After a long minute of silence, she spoke, as if explaining things to herself.

"Maybe – it's better this way... that's there's nothing else. Business as usual! Everyone in his own little cubicle, with his own little view of the world..." – and in a totally different tone of voice, sober perhaps, practical:

"I don't know how I'm going to manage this month. We'll have to see" – in a distant, scornful tone, without looking at me – "if there's no choice..." And then she scanned me with a bitter look, a look of reproach clearly showing the direction of her thoughts, something like: How on earth does he imagine I'm going to cope? – and the self-evident conclusion: He hasn't changed at all. Just swans around in his own sweet way – and sod the rest of the world!

This train of thought, so familiar to me, led me to the natural and inevitable decision – to spare no effort, neither to rest nor relax until a sum equivalent to half of my salary could be paid into her account on the first of the month, this coming month.

She stood up from her seat.

"I'm going," she announced.

I stood up too.

"Sorry!" I said, meaning it.

"Don't bother seeing me to the door!"

"Goodbye," I said – "Be well!" She nodded grudgingly and left the café.

I walked round the table and approached the proprietor, who all this time had been busy polishing his cups. After paying the bill I went out into the clean, sunny street. There was no one else in sight.

NOTHING "DIFFICULT"

The sun had just kissed the narrow brow of a fading horizon. The world shone with the glitter of innocence, in youthful, ever hopeful expectation.

I found Rahamim sitting by himself, at ease, quietly sipping his habitual coffee. He responded to my greeting, stood up without another word, walked across to his counter and disappeared behind it, returning with a cup of tea which he put down on the table beside his own half-empty mug. The tea was the colour of ripe dates, with a pungent taste capable of awakening and healing every faltering cell encountered on its way, delicate fragrance, and soothing warmth to broaden the mind and boost the spirit – solid foundations for brotherhood and true friendship.

We drank companionably, without sullying the silence that permeated the open spaces of the café and purified them, so that the thick, concrete walls, painted in light pastels, began to glow, putting on their habitually blank faces a bright, if bashful smile.

We finished our drinks, and sat on, still silent. Outside the sea was foaming its waves and sending up straight and limpid shafts of light to the endless blue sky, like the pure prayer of an infant. Little by little, hesitantly, the sky began responding to the sea and the land, dimming its radiance and drawing closer to them. And something calm and solemn, like twilight, spread across the void, turning it a shade of pale violet.

Rahamim picked up his empty mug and my teacup, rinsed them in the sink, boiled water, brewed tea and coffee and returned with refills which he placed on the table, sitting facing me as before and sipping the dark, viscous liquid. He put his cup down, leaned back slightly and said:

"You've come late today."

"I had something to sort out."

"Something difficult?" he asked.

"There's nothing 'difficult'," I replied. " 'Difficulties' are things man makes for himself." He considered my words gravely and said:

"But that's human nature."

"Man is master of his nature," I retorted.

Rahamim fell silent, then took a noisy gulp and commented:

"But he doesn't know that."

"He knows."

"So why does nature rule him, and not vice versa?"

"Because that is his explicit will!" – I smiled.

He took another sip of his coffee and after replacing his cup on the table with deliberate caution, asked:

"And this business of yours... it's been sorted out?"

"Not yet," I replied. "It has to do with my wife," I thought I should explain.

"The one you're separated from?" – he wanted to be sure he had understood.

"In the geographical sense."

A little awkwardly he cleared his throat, perhaps about to say something and anxious to get it right:

"This business of separation... even if it's only in terms of place," he said in a rather creaky voice – "after so many years of living together, it just doesn't make sense to me."

This comment of his was really a question, and as the answer was slow in coming, he tried to raise another:

"How many years were you together?"

"About thirty-six..."

"Children?"

"Two sons and two daughters."

"Long life and good health to them! Grandchildren too?"

"Grandchildren too."

We returned to our silent drinking.

When Rahamim's cup was half empty, he looked up and asked again:

"And that business you mentioned – what's it about?"

I smiled back at him and replied: "That's why I came here. Maybe you can help."

"Gladly!" he responded sincerely.

"I need work in the afternoons, for two or three weeks. Enough to earn –" I named a sum equivalent to half my monthly salary.

He didn't reply immediately. He thought it over, then thought it over some more. I was beginning to think his mind was off on another tack, when he spoke again, in a deep voice:

"In fact, this is a happy coincidence, a real godsend!"

"What is?" I asked, surprised.

"You... needing work! And asking for such a small sum in return!" And he went on to explain: "My wife and I have wanted for ages to go on a trip to the Dead Sea – for her rheumatism and my heart condition. Doctors have been recommending it, prescribing it in fact, for years... and we've been putting it off from year to year. The café, you see... no one to look after it. The customers, I mean. And then you come and ask for something that I should be asking you for! In fact, I've often thought about this, but somehow I didn't have the nerve to approach you. I thought it would be degrading for someone like you, working in a café. For some reason, that's what I was thinking. Even now, I'm feeling a bit awkward about it. Still – you're the one who asked!" He smiled at me, and added at once:

"Here's my suggestion. Work here for two or three weeks, a month! Afternoons only, so the regular customers can stick to their routine. And you'll get the salary you asked for, plus heartfelt thanks from me and from my wife... from her especially!" Rahamim cried with almost childish enthusiasm. "She'll be beside herself with joy!

"And if this doesn't appeal to you, if for whatever reason you find my offer unacceptable," he added in a more sober tone of voice – "I'll lend you the money, and you pay me back when you can."

"I'd rather work!" I declared, adding: "But I'm not much of an expert when it comes to making tea or coffee..."

"It isn't expertise that's needed here, but something else altogether..." He looked at me keenly.

"And that is?" I prompted him.

"Love," he replied simply.

"There's a nice thought!" I commented, my face lighting up.

And Rahamim went on to reveal the secret of his astonishing expertise:

"Love of God which is love of mankind, which is love of the work that's assigned to you. It means working not for your pocket or your stomach, but for the greater glory of God, for the love of the Almighty and in His name."

"Thank you." It seemed the only possible response.

"Thank-you!" he insisted, adding: "You can start a week or two weeks from now, if that suits you. And the money, if you like, you can have now."

I glanced at my watch: another half-hour and the banks would be closing.

"I'd be very grateful if you could pay in advance."

He drew a battered, ancient-looking wallet from his trouser-pocket, peeled off a few high-denomination notes and handed them to me:

"There's an extra two hundred there," he explained. "Hang on to it, in case we're held up. That could happen – if the Dead Sea lives up to its reputation!" He chuckled amiably, his face radiant with the delight of a little boy receiving an unexpected present, and concluded: "We can settle up then!"

I thanked him, took the money and left the café almost at a run.

I arrived at the bank with only moments to spare. The security man at the door, brandishing his bundle of shining keys, gave me a meaningful look. I deposited the cash in my wife's account, and briskly retraced my steps, to Rahamim's café. Some of his regular clients were already arriving and taking their seats at the tables.

Rahamim had an announcement to make: "A week or two from now," he began portentously, " Adon will be taking my place for a few weeks, or maybe – a month! I'm taking my wife down to the Dead Sea, on doctor's orders!"

There was a chorus of good wishes and felicitations, and then somebody remembered to ask:

"And Adon, does he know the secret recipe of your special coffee?"

"He'll learn!" Rahamim assured him, and added: "The secret of my coffee is very simple. Anyone could figure it out in no time at all."

"So what is the secret of your coffee?" the sceptic insisted.

And with dignity Rahamim repeated the enchanting word that underlies the great secret of every undertaking:

"Love!" – and saying this he signalled to me to join him behind the counter and proceeded to show me where everything was, and how the gas stove worked, and the quantities of ingredients required to produce fine coffee and tea worthy of the name. He also pointed out the cleaning materials, dish-cloths and three clean aprons hanging on hooks in the little back-kitchen.

The way Rahamim explained what needed explaining – with a hint or an apposite word – it all seemed simple and infused with the pleasure of activity and true willingness to serve.

I decided it was time to test the efficiency of the bodily systems and their capacity for the absorption of instructions – as well as my willingness to serve: I brewed tea and made coffee, as the orders came in. Nessim, Rahamim's nephew, said something about excessive sweetness, and I thanked him for the comment and made some minor adjustments to the sugar-content. Raphael, on the other hand, strongly approved of the coffee served to him, as did young Avinoam. One of the fishermen asked Nessim:

"Are you still living with Rahamim?"

"Still," he replied without any special inflection.

"Not found a suitable apartment yet?" the same fisherman went on to ask.

"No," Nessim answered him and added: "I keep on looking – and sometimes I find it. But it isn't the right one."

Gabriel, coming into the café with Nono and sitting him down on the wicker bench, heard Nessim's reply and reacted at once:

"If you want it – you'll find it!" – and he ordered coffee for Nono and himself. Nono sat by the low, oval table, eyes wide open, submissive as an obedient dog, long arms hanging limply at his sides.

"You think I don't want it?" – suddenly there was a note of asperity in Nessim's voice – "We're putting pressure on my uncle, I'm well aware of that! But it's all in the hands of Providence!" he went on to say. "We haven't found anything suitable yet, though we've spared no effort and we're still sparing no effort. And I hope," – he turned to his uncle, with a simpering tone – "we're not being too much of a nuisance!"

"Not at all!" Rahamim answered him, and after a moment of reflection he added, sounding utterly sincere: "On the contrary, it's a pleasure... Anyway, in a week or two, God willing, I'll be going away with my wife for a vacation... since we came to this country we've only been away once – after the Six Day War. Everyone was celebrating then; there was jubilation and everyone was out on the street and the café didn't seem all that important... we closed up and vamoosed. For three days. We couldn't afford more than that. We didn't want to let our customers down, and there was more demand when the mood started to turn sour..."

"You mean to say people come into your café when they're

miserable?" asked the anonymous fisherman who had started the conversation.

"When people are happy," Rahamim explained, "anywhere will suit them just fine! It doesn't matter where you are, so long as you're in a good mood. It's a different story when things are going wrong. If you're depressed and you need some space, somewhere to think and make some sense of whatever it is that's bothering you – there's nowhere better than a café. A real café that is," Rahamim stressed, adding: "Not one of those places on Dizengoff, with the pastries and the milk-shakes and all kinds of juices, where bored women go with their poodles. And they piddle all over the fancy table legs – the poodles that is – and sometimes over the legs of their mistresses too..."

This sally provoked noisy laughter among some of the fishermen. Nono, who all this time had been sitting wrapped up in himself, staring blankly at Gabriel's face, also burst into unfettered laughter, high-pitched and discordant, and it was up to Gabriel to try to calm him down with weird and wonderful proverbs and parables, such as: The fish will flee from Gabriel's net because they're not laughing, but Nono, on the other hand, is laughing. At this Nono curbed his laughter and gave Gabriel a scared look. Gabriel was quick to reassure him, saying that at the end of the day fish do laugh, but they do it quietly, and so it's perfectly okay for Nono to laugh, only quietly. Nono grinned at this, much relieved.

"The best café," Rahamim returned to his theme, in an effort to draw the attention of the assembled company away from Nono and ease the pressure on Gabriel – "is a place that heals the heart!" He declared this with all the authority of a specialist and an expert, whose verdict brooks no argument.

"And I say," Raphael interjected, "that all this is a matter of habit!"

"That's true as well," Rahamim concurred. "When you're used to a certain place, it's not easy to give it up. That's why I'm so keen to keep this place open. Starting in a week or two, Adon will be standing in for me here, six days a week, every afternoon. And I wish him every success!"

"And so say all of us!" the fishermen chorused. "Best of luck to both of you!"

For a while there was silence in the café. And then the

anonymous fisherman turned to Rahamim again:

"Isn't it cramped at your house – with Nessim and all his family? As far as I know, you have one bedroom and a lounge," he added as if needing to account for his question –"and that's all."

"It's a big lounge, and we have a small spare bedroom as well as the main one," Rahamim replied, keen to stress that there was no shortage of space.

"And who's staying in the spare bedroom?" the questioner persisted.

"My wife and I," was Rahamim's answer.

At this point Raphael turned to Nessim.

"You've taken the master bedroom for yourselves and exiled the hosts to the annexe?" The tone of the question was friendly enough, but the same couldn't be said of the content.

"We never asked for the master bedroom!" cried Nessim as if refuting a slanderous accusation. "Anyway, these are family matters and they're no business of yours!" – and sounding flustered, he hastened to add: "We even offered to pay my uncle rent... but he was offended." He glanced at Rahamim.

"Nessim's right," the uncle confirmed. "He offered and I was offended, and I was glad when he changed his mind. The spare room's more convenient for a mature couple, and things are working out fine. As for family matters – this café, and everyone who comes to it – it's all family!" Rahamim declared, getting a sudden and enthusiastic round of applause from young Avinoam, in which he was joined by Raphael and the anonymous fisherman who had opened the conversation, and who now turned to Nessim again:

"You're saving a packet on rent and all the other expenses, so I hope you're keeping a record of it for the future!"

"I've told you that for my part – I was prepared to pay rent!" Nessim protested. "But he refused it," – pointing to his uncle – "so what could I do? I'm looking for a suitable place, searching everywhere, but the truth is I know I'll never find anything to compare with Uncle's. I'm not talking about comfort and amenities, but about something else, something completely different!" Nessim spoke with heavy emphasis, possibly directed at himself.

"What is that?" the fisherman demanded to know from his corner. His face was in shadow and only his eyebrows – thick eyebrows knotted in a frown speaking eloquently of obstinacy and dogged persistence – were visible.

"The atmosphere!" Nessim replied, in a calmer, clearer tone. "You wouldn't find an atmosphere like that if you lived in the palace of King Solomon himself! And for that I'd be prepared to pay whatever price could be agreed... because my sons, and my daughters and my wife – are precious to me. And I can see how their mood has changed, not like it was in the old place... and it's going to change again, and not for the better, if we have to move, uproot ourselves yet again.

"We're bound to move eventually, as that's the way things have to be in the real world. But we'll be sorry, we'll miss the arrangement we have now! And the modest sum I offered to pay Uncle – that's not going into my pocket, but to charity. The synagogue I go to is raising money to buy a Torah scroll..."

"And you'll make sure your name's on the list of contributors?" – a barbed shot from Gabriel.

"I wanted to put it in Rahamim's name but he refused it," Nessim explained. "Refused point-blank. He's such an obstinate guy, he just won't be persuaded!" He turned his head this way and that, as if seeking the support and the solidarity of the assembled company.

"Put it in his wife's name!" – thick eyebrows interposed in a quiet voice, evidently not anticipating a response. Sure enough, there was no response from Nessim, and as a new batch of fishermen arrived in the café, the subject was dropped.

I went on brewing tea and coffee and serving the new arrivals, while Rahamim made sure they were all aware of his forthcoming trip and his temporary understudy.

Satisfied with my rapid progress in the preparation and serving of drinks, he suggested I should return to my usual seat and celebrate the occasion with a cup of tea of my own making. I accepted the suggestion gladly.

The noise levels in the café had risen for some reason. The fishermen were engaged in a fervent debate, talking loudly with one another or across one another, or muttering to themselves. There was a lot of stress in the air, tension that was virtually tangible – but tension blended with repressed excitement, and anticipation of good and propitious developments.

From what was being said aloud, it could be deduced that fish of a rare species, of exceptional size and weight, were swarming in big shoals around the shores of Jaffa, promising a fish bonanza of a scale that for years they hadn't dared to dream of. The more far-sighted among them were already contemplating the long-term dangers inherent in flooding the market with cheap merchandise. Ingenious ideas were being exchanged, ways of duping the wholesalers, eluding their professional vigilance and keeping news of the glut – not only expected but as good as guaranteed – a closely guarded secret, thus preventing a collapse in prices and a slump in the market.

Nessim took advantage of the commotion, picked up his chair in one hand and his coffee cup in the other, came to my table and sat down facing me.

For some time he sat in silence, his head a little bowed.

"How can I put it," he began without preamble and without shifting his gaze from the empty cup clasped between his fingers – "The people here... they don't understand... they interfere in things that don't concern them, and they're liable to do damage, real damage!" He lifted his black eyes and gave me a look that somehow managed to combine anticipation, suspicion and fear of rejection – with a desperate appeal for solidarity, understanding and encouragement thrown in for good measure.

"Meaning what?" – I tried to respond to this strange amalgam of demands.

"People!" It was a non-committal opening, but a brusque and a tense one as well; Nessim seemed quite oblivious to whatever else was happening in the vicinity. "Look at Rahamim," he went on. "He's happy... so happy he doesn't know himself how happy he is! Since we came to live with him..." He eased the tension in his fingers, but seemed reluctant to let go of his cup, still holding it limply in one hand.

"For the first time he can remember, he's in the bosom of a family! In the bosom of a warm family, where all the sons and daughters love and respect him... him and his wife too! They listen to what they have to say, do as they ask gladly, keep their places for them at the head of the table, on either side – and all this isn't just automatic, it's done willingly, with true happiness, with love!" At this point he recoiled slightly, stiffening his hunched back:

"They enjoy it," he went on, "they both enjoy it, Rahamim and his wife... they don't show this to anyone, not even themselves, but they enjoy it and when we leave – it's not going to be easy for them. They're going to miss us... it could be devastating for them! And that's what I'm trying to avert. Not that I don't intend to leave!" He gave me a meaningful look, as if promising that he meant what he was saying – a promise that he hadn't been asked for.

"We'll be going! But not like that, not all at once... it'll be step by step, gradual! First we'll find a house, then there'll be alterations to do, decorating, furnishing... we'll be going to and fro, staying there a night or two, back to Rahamim's so he won't feel rejected. And that is the way he's going to feel – mark my words!" he declared, stabbing himself in the chest with the thumb of his free hand. "I know people!" He withdrew his hand, laid it flat on the small oval table.

"I love the man," he continued, his voice light now and steady, "he's my only surviving relative... My father had six brothers, and Rahamim was the youngest. Two of them were killed in the war – the big, European one I mean – another had a stroke, was paralysed and died after years of suffering. My dear and esteemed father," he spoke with strange reverence, "was a victim of stomach cancer. Another uncle was knocked down by a truck, here, in this country, and the last one to go died on the operating-table..." Nessim scanned me with narrowed eyes and continued:

"He's the only one left, Uncle Rahamim. He has no children. And he loves us and feels tied to us, it's a very special bond. And his wife too – she has a heart of gold!" – and he raised his free hand, pointing up to the shadowy dome of the café, as if calling on Heaven to vouch for the truth of his words.

"I am looking for accommodation," he resumed suddenly, his voice unwavering – "Rahamim's apartment, when all's said and done, is small – and there are ten of us altogether! And the fact he cleared the main bedroom for us and moved into the spare – gives him a great sense of pride and satisfaction. And who am I," he demanded, his voice rising, "to deny my last surviving relative pride and satisfaction?" There was a strange ardour in his voice, a kind of impatience to let his feelings overflow, and to enjoy the relief that is guaranteed to follow such an outburst. "As for us, me and my wife, we wouldn't mind moving into the spare room. Being younger, the smaller space would suit us better than it suits them. In fact," – this with lowered voice and the faintest hint of a wink – "we could even make do with one bed! Like most people of their age, they're used to separate beds, separate rooms even. But they insisted, and we gave in.

"And as for the charitable fund, and putting his name on the list of synagogue benefactors, they don't know it..." he leaned forward, very close to me and whispered in my ear conspiratorially – "but both their names are going to be there! I'm preparing a surprise for them! They don't know, and I don't want them to know!" – he stressed the final words, recoiled slightly, scrutinised the expression on my face with an air of suspicion, put his empty cup on the table and sat back in his chair.

It seemed he wasn't expecting an answer, being all wrapped up in himself, knitting his brows and loosening them, and tapping with his foot – shod in a narrow, uncomfortable shoe, on the ancient floor of the café. At intervals, he made an indeterminate gesture with one hand, or shifted awkwardly on his seat. Finally, he turned to me and said:

"If you hear of an apartment anywhere, let me know!"

"It could be that my landlord's got a spare apartment," I told him.

"He's in that business?" he asked and before I could answer he added: "An agent?"

"No, not exactly. The apartments belong to him. He bought up several properties in the past and now he rents them out."

"I bet he's expensive!" he said suspiciously.

"Depends on the apartment. I got mine fairly cheap."

"Could you give me the details?" he asked in an unexpectedly brusque manner, a certain reluctance, that he was trying in vain to conceal, detectable in his voice. He took a little notebook, with pencil attached, from his shirt pocket, and carefully jotted down the information I gave him. He inspected what he had written and thought for a while, before replacing notebook and pencil in his pocket. Without pleasantries or valedictions he rose, gave his empty cup to Rahamim, stationed behind his counter, waved to me and left the café.

Some time later, when the exuberance of the fishermen had abated, and they were starting to leave, Rahamim gave me an ornate key to the glass-panelled door of the café, which he had installed in place of the heavy oak door of former, pre-café times.

HEART'S DESIRE

I went out into the night and headed for home. The light of the stars above me flickered uneasily, not their usual style at this time of year. The moon made an effort to hide behind occasional wisps of cloud. A cool breeze blew steadily, persistently.

I made my way all wrapped up in the delight of the truth in me, which is the one delight of all creatures in the infinite spaces of the universe. I was myself – the freedom of light, immortal reality, whole and everlasting happiness.

I found Shuki sprawled on the sofa. Half of his blanket had fallen to the floor, half of it still covered his stomach. His unsteady breathing was urgent, hurried, rasping. On the table, around an empty cheese-packet, coarse breadcrumbs were strewn. There was also a half-empty bottle of water and a cup which looked as if it hadn't been used. I picked up the bottle, rinsed the cup, binned the packet and wiped the table down with a damp cloth.

As a result of my movements, or my very presence, or maybe because he had slept long enough – Shuki woke up. He spent a long time staring at the solid door-frame without moving at all, as if detached from the world and all his surroundings, or choosing to ignore them.

"This idea of an unlocked door – sheer genius!" he said suddenly, his voice rising from the depths, slightly hoarse and crackling, the drone of a shaman. "If everyone took up this idea – maybe the world would be a better place! You know why?" He turned his head to look at me, nape still resting on his linked hands.

"You tell me."

"Everyone would feel at home wherever he was, in any house, making full use of its contents. And legally too – and no questions asked. There'd be no need for break-ins, burglaries, pilfering. Cops, courts, prisons – they'd be redundant too..." He lapsed into silence.

"Cup of tea?" I asked him.

"All right, go on then. Seeing as you've nothing else to offer me. Some host you are!" – the familiar, guttural tones rang out again.

"There's water, if you'd prefer it," I suggested amiably.

"Is this the way you treat all your guests?" he retorted. "Welcome them with open arms and a big smile – just so long as they'll make do with whatever's in that pathetic fridge of yours... That your idea of hospitality? The door's unlocked... You can't say the same for the heart!" he sneered.

"The drinks cabinet may be locked, but the human heart never is," I replied with a playful smile.

I served tea and sandwiches on a flat plastic plate. I took my seat at the table, prayed and picked up a sandwich.

Shuki stood up heavily from the sofa, dragging the blanket with him and sitting down on it for some obscure reason, joined his hands and seemed to be trying to pray. Then he hawked coarsely, noisily, looked around in vain for somewhere to spit, then changed his mind and swallowed his phlegm instead. He picked up a sandwich and bit into it, chewing noisily and swallowing with difficulty, as if his throat was dry or inflamed or somehow constricted.

I looked up at him: he seemed emaciated, as if being consumed by some malignant disease. At intervals a light shudder set his shoulders quivering.

"The tea's good!" he declared, and added – "Not that I owe you any gratitude. Seeing as you're the one who brought me down to where I am now... And that cash-card, have you stopped it?" he asked, inconsequentially.

"Yes."

"Much damage done?"

"No."

"Pity!" He put a cunning smile on his lips, which for some reason seemed to have slackened, now resembling withered and drooping flesh. When the mouth wasn't chewing, the upper lip hid the lower – and the effect was like the toothless mouth of a very old man.

"I was looking forward to seeing you cop a huge debt!" he said sounding quite sincere – "You lot, geezers on decent salaries, you haven't got the faintest idea how to cope with real life, or anything outside your narrow frame of reference! You think it's the end of the world if you get the teeniest bit overdrawn. You fight over every cent... and that's about what you're worth!" he declared with ostentatious scorn and suddenly chuckled, a sour and menacing sound: "I don't mean that," he added, his voice steady and his mouth full – "just a joke! You," he turned to me – "you're something else! A sterling example of the salaried class!" he sneered, threatening me with an outstretched finger that was turning black, all skin and bone.

"At the end of the day," he declared, "you're really making me very happy – and that's the absolute truth. If it wasn't for you, I'd never have known how much Lili loves me, and how devoted she is... ha, ha, ha!" – he laughed dryly. "And I'd never have known just how vulnerable I am to the kind of disaster she's brought down on me, that lousy bloody bitch!" These words only inflamed his own rage. His teeth grated, and his mouth stopped chewing.

"Small people," I commented, in a calm but unequivocal tone – "always lay on others the blame for their own failures."

Shuki studied me with a protracted look and turned away, with a restrained air.

"It really doesn't bother me any more!" he said, trying to infuse some indifference into his voice. Then turning to me and leaning slightly forward, an affable gesture, he explained:

"You see, I used to have competitors who always needed neutralising – that meant being alert and keyed-up all the time, finding out everything about them down to the last detail: the state of their 'working capital' as the banks call it, and their sources, and the new guys joining them and the guys leaving them – and why. Finger always on the trigger, knowing the market and its shifting moods, predicting developments way ahead... The market in drugs and whores, that's the one I mean," he pointed out, as if clarification was needed.

"Then there's warming up the market when it's necessary, cooling it down when that's what time demands. Knowing how to improvise, evade, attack, steal, threaten, murder!" he cried. And after staring straight ahead for a moment, he took a deep breath and resumed in a much more even tone:

"There was a charm in that life... a bogus charm... shit!" – he spat on the plate, ignoring the sandwiches that were still there – "All that crap they show in the movies, fooling people into thinking there's something glamorous about the lifestyle of drug-dealers, pimps, gangsters, dodgy cops and killers, in a word – the underworld – there's not an atom of truth in it! It's a lousy, stupid lifestyle! Kids get taken in by the myth, corrupted, seduced, want to try their hands at it, get a piece of the action, and soon they're up to their necks in shit. What can you do with someone like that – except stamp on his head and push him under, all the way till there's nothing left, till he snuffs it in some stinking back-alley knee-deep in sewage." He grinned a bitter and sardonic grin, and added:

"It's an exhausting business. All that pressure – it's like the devil's chasing you, trying to snatch your soul. And you're always on the move, always running away... one marathon after another! And the cops – whether they're smart or dumb – that's all bluff as well! It's all a game – and they're a part of it!

"In fact, it's like Hell... No... not 'like' – it really is Hell!" he stressed with some force, "And anyone who gets through it has earned himself full rights of admission to the Garden of Eden – after his death or even before it!" – he cried with provocative certainty, inviting a response. He grinned broadly, turning inquisitive eyes on me.

"The only way a man can hope to earn anything in this life," I replied, "is through detachment from the world, or at least – sincere and continuous effort to be detached – and this can't fail to bear fruit, if it really is true effort!"

"There's no one in that world, the underworld as it's rightly called," Shuki cut in – "who isn't doing everything he possibly can and investing supreme efforts – every day, every hour, every minute and every second, in every situation – to be detached from it. But it isn't in his hands! It's a kind of curse! Now and again, by some happy fluke, someone manages to get away... but it's a drop in the ocean. Where's that God of yours?" – he demanded to know, accusation in his blazing eyes.

"In the heart of every man," I replied, picking up a sandwich.

"And the residents of that 'underworld' – don't they qualify as human beings?" he insisted, his eyes narrowing uneasily.

"They're human beings like all other members of their species," I replied with finality. "And God – is in their hearts!"

Again he thought for a moment, taking a sip of tea before speaking again:

"That deprives them of any excuse! Clever! There's no one to complain to! No one to blame! Superb!" he cried, his face lightening momentarily – "Wonderful. Your fate's in your own hands. Whatever you build, you're the one who built it, and whatever you destroy, you're the one who destroyed it. If you're a monster, you're in for a monster's fate – if you're a saint, a saint's fate!" He bit violently into his sandwich and tossed it away.

"That's the way it looks, but I guess it's not quite so clear-cut!" he declared, adding: "There's no knowing who chose whom – whether God chose man or vice versa – but man is an instrument..." he searched for an apposite expression – "that can't be relied on. What does man amount to, what's his sum total? Untrustworthy, feeble, vacillating, thinking one thing and saying another, saying one thing and doing another. A bundle of contradictions – that's mankind!

"And it isn't that he doesn't mean to be true to himself – it's just his way! A frivolous way of drifting in all kinds of weird directions, that he really doesn't want. He's opposed to them with every fibre, he's declared solemnly, before witnesses, and even vowed to himself – that he won't be tempted to touch them with the tip of a little finger... and as soon as he's said what he's said, declared what he's declared and vowed what he's vowed – it's not just a finger but the whole of him that gets shoved into it, up to the neck and over, against his explicit, declared and solemn will! He scanned my face and added:

"Whoever created such a spineless, irresponsible creature, a ragbag of grief and delusion – made a fatal mistake!"

"Perhaps it was His intention to experience for Himself the life of this kind of creature," I suggested and added: "Seeing Himself as strong enough to withstand the test."

He was silent. Perhaps he was pondering my words, perhaps he was ignoring them altogether, or trying to.

"In spite of everything," he turned to me suddenly, with a fairly relaxed tone of voice – "without some stimulus from the outside – there'd be no future for the underworld... or perhaps I should say, the underworld man. And I mean something genuine and sincere that could serve as a model, like for example – doors left open, unlocked... or a cash-card willingly given away, along with the PIN number... that could be a start. Maybe... that is the start..." he said, momentarily earnest, his eyes downcast – "Maybe luck will smile on me in the place I least expect it. My meeting with you – an event to be blessed from every possible angle – maybe! And Lili..." he paused for a long moment, a shadow of distant gloom flitting across his consumptive face, droplets of sweat appearing unexpectedly on his bulbous forehead:

"I'll never understand," he continued, "how an angel like that got shoved into filthy hands like these!" – and he held up both his hands before his eyes, fingers splayed, and moved them this way and that as if inspecting them meticulously, then gave me a probing look, dropped his hands and asked:

"Do you have an answer?"

"No."

"God has showered his mercies on me, his love... and I'm not worthy of it... not at all, no way!" he went on, paying no attention to me – "This God who's inside me, in my heart, who's judgment can't be evaded, who's the one truth... full of mercy... and cruelty as well! Have I got it right?" He demanded an answer, turning fervid eyes on me.

"God is love," was my answer.

"How is that love expressed?" he queried.

"In the saving of mankind from his torment."

Gradually he lowered his head and fixed his gaze on the cracked tiles of the floor. He seemed to be figuring something out, and then figuring it out all over again, wearing an expression of earnest concentration.

I waited, finishing off my sandwich and calmly gulping down the last mouthful of tea remaining in my cup. Eventually he said:

"God – that's an aspiration, a yearning, hard to attain... and maybe – impossible."

"Some people look for fire when they're sitting right beside a massive blaze, claiming that it's 'an aspiration, a yearning, hard to attain... and maybe – impossible'" I quoted him.

He was taken aback, scanning me with a long look, his frayed, loose mouth gaping. Finally he said in a hushed voice, either furtive or nervous:

"Is He that close?"

"To the one who truly desires Him, yes."

He sighed and lapsed again into silence.

Suddenly he remembered what was left of his sandwich, bolted it down hastily and brushed the crumbs from his trousers, drank thirstily from the lukewarm tea and slammed the empty cup down on the table. He rubbed his hands together, gave me a strange, composed look and said:

"You know, I've got an aspiration too. A realistic aspiration – one that can be attained and implemented. It isn't God, though God might have a finger in it! My one true aspiration," – he scanned me acutely, tensely – "the strongest desire I ever remember feeling, the dream of my life..." He smiled a calm, but malicious and provocative smile, still submitting my face to a meticulous scrutiny: "This one and only aspiration of mine," he continued, "sanctified and sanctifying, giving taste to my life and justification for my continued existence here, which took shape in my mind not so long ago, my aspiration..." – he moved his eyes slowly, held them on mine with a gaze of extraordinary, controlled, chilly serenity – serenity from another world, belonging to another creature, and after a long pause, without a flicker of movement or change of expression he concluded – "is to murder you!"

He didn't check the impression his announcement had made on me; at that moment at least, it seemed this was the least important thing to him. Instead he shifted his look from my face, gathered his saliva into his mouth with a strangely pleasurable air, hawked, swallowed, sat back easily and without looking at me, chose to continue in a surprisingly even, off-hand tone:

"As long as I'm alive," – his lips widened into a warm smile – "there's danger hanging over your head. Mortal danger!" he stressed, Hawking again before going into detail:

"You'll never know what dark corner I'll be jumping out of! Your habit of leaving the door unlocked makes things easier for me, no doubt about it! But even without that I can sort you out. I'm an expert at this, a world-class specialist!

"You won't know when and how I'm going to act!" he added, clearly relishing the prospect, and continuing in a coarser tone: "When you least think something's going to happen, when you least expect it – that's when the hit's going down! And this time," he concluded with solemn conviction: "No power on earth is going to stop me! Trust me!"

He raised his hand in a theatrical gesture, with an obscure, unfathomable air of excitement and added in a more restrained voice but with the same cold, venomous conviction, his head tilted in a reflective pose:

"The slash of a razor – there's nothing more noble, smooth, purifying! Takes real artistic flair! I've experienced it often enough.

You see," – he turned to me with unexpected enthusiasm and a voice that had veered from one extreme to another, as if he were telling an interesting anecdote, or unravelling the intriguing plot of a film, his eyes showing nothing but simple, almost childish eagerness to share his experience with a friend: "At first, the throat is intact. Still. For a long moment it stays that way, very long... or that's how it seems. A moment of tense expectation. Till you start wondering and worrying and it seems the whole thing's a dream and you've done nothing and achieved nothing and you can't breathe and the blood's pounding in your head. And then... and then..." He paused as if trying to relive the experience in every facet and every detail, with no omissions, no deviations:

"And then – something like a sigh of relief. A faint tickling in your throat, and a kind of voice whispering to you that you should've changed your mind – as if you had the choice! But deep down in your heart you reject this foolish notion, 'cos you know, somehow, the job's been done and there's no going back, it's impossible! And that's when you feel a sudden surge of disappointment: what a feeble coward you are! Hands of a woman... put a sharpened razor in them – what the Hell do you expect?" At this stage it seemed his words were directed solely at himself.

"And then... just then..." – it was as if a fire was ignited within him, emitting waves of choking, malevolent heat, sinister enthusiasm bursting from every pore and flowing like molten lava, burning and consuming everything in its path:

"Then a thin red line appears on that lovely, pure white throat – like a gleaming jewel. And all your senses are paralysed. It's like the moment before orgasm... or the orgasm itself! No!" – he wasn't satisfied with this image and hurriedly amended it: "It's beyond orgasm... it's – power!

"And immediately after that, in fact – it's virtually simultaneous, a diabolical chain-reaction that there's no stopping – you feel blood spattering your face and your hands, the one that's holding the razor and the one holding the head back... a warm, sticky, therapeutic cascade... like the caress of a loving hand. You'll never know feelings such as this!" he told me, his voice rising to an impassioned crescendo: "It's a serious gap in your experience! It's stronger than a drug, stronger than love, anything you care to mention. The world... no, not just the world, the whole universe is quaking under your feet, beneath your sway, and you are its master, glorious and terrible, and murderous, you're the highest of the high, the king of kings, even superior to the Devil, who urged you to do it, seeing as he can't do anything with his own hands! In comparison with you, he's impotent – his power amounts to zilch! It's true you're a tool in his hand, but a willing tool – well up in Hell's hierarchy!" Again he turned on me that triumphant look of his, provocative, cold and fierce at the same time – but now with a kind of exhaustion beginning to nibble at its fringes.

"What do you have to say to all that?" he asked.

"You're a sad man!" I replied, and began clearing away the cups and the plastic plate.

A long moment passed in silence. I brushed the crumbs from the table, went to the other room, put the cups in the sink, and tipped the crumbs into the bin.

"Will you pray for me?" Shuki asked when I returned.

"Day and night!" I replied with a bright smile, picking up a paper napkin that had fallen to the floor and returning to the kitchenette.

"I wish you all the best!" his voice reached me from a distance, from outside the door in fact, and somewhere out there he added in a remarkably clear voice, untypical of him:

"Watch out for me!"

THE SEA

In the afternoon, on leaving work, I went down to Rahamim's café and spent some time sweeping the ancient floor, setting out clean cups and glasses and a cavernous china jug, also coffee, tea, sugar and various condiments. I'd agreed with Rahamim that serving food – pittas and sandwiches – would be deferred until his return from the Dead Sea.

About an hour after opening up, I was ready to welcome customers, and sure enough, they began arriving. These weren't the fishermen whom I was familiar with, but locals – artisans, petty tradesmen, day-workers, clerks and passers-by. At first they came in ones and two, then in a thin but steady stream, and as the day was turning, in groups, occupying all the available space. I had my work cut out – trying to fill all the orders promptly, prepare, serve, take money, collect the cups and wash them – and repeat the process over and over again. Patrons of the café smiled in response to my smile and were tolerant of delays and the inevitable, slight variations in the taste of the drinks presented – the kind of glitches encountered by any novice.

By evening, the little cash register was stuffed with notes and coins. The first shift of café regulars began dispersing, to be replaced immediately by the fishermen, arriving singly at first like their predecessors, and later, en masse. The café was filled again, packed to the very limit, as the fishermen prepared for their night's work, gulping down the hot drink that both soothes and stimulates.

For the first time, Israel was intending to put to sea in the boat he had obtained from the late Aharon. He looked a little shy and ill at ease, masking his lack of confidence with a broad and childish smile.

"Till now," he explained, "I've been going out with Raphael and Avinoam. Till I got my licence. I've been watching, gaining experience... Their boat," he added, a note of concern creeping into his voice, "had a prang the other day. Not a serious one – but you never know. They're assessing the damage today. As for fishing," – he returned to the point at issue, poppy eyes looking up at me – " it's a great life and a fascinating job, what can you say... Fresh air, open spaces, wind... sea!" he exclaimed with restrained enthusiasm, as if describing, confidentially, something exceptional and marvellous, without equal and beyond compare. "The sea puts an end to all griefs and depressions", he declared, adding – "I say to myself: Israel, what kind of a fool have you been, wasting the best years of your life, trapped like a mouse in a cage, selling lampshades to ignorant oafs!" And leaning towards me he concluded:

"The sea – it's a rebirth!" The exuberance in his voice was tinged with a hint of reverence, respect for the new deity that had taken over his heart.

"And what about Gaby, your assistant in the shop?" I asked Israel.

"He's the owner now," he replied with a strange blend of envy and complacency. "He wanted it so much, he pleaded and whined and in the end – he got it dirt cheap. He persuaded his family and friends to help, mortgaged everything he could mortgage, and paid cash. The lot! Now, he's making a bomb!" His face contorted and there was a resentful rasp in his voice, but he quickly regained his composure and concluded in a tone of mellow resignation:

"Now he's a slave to the shop, having to lick the boots of his customers... I'm glad I'm out of it!"

At that moment Raphael and Avinoam arrived, looking gloomy.

"What's up with you?" someone asked from the corner.

"Nothing much," Raphael replied, evasively, but Avinoam had no such qualms.

"The boat's out of commission!" he declared. "The hull's sprung a leak. It's going to need sealing and caulking, the works, and that could take anything up to a week!"

"And this has to happen to you now of all times!" the questioner commented with genuine sympathy.

"Now of all times!" Raphael echoed, frowning as I handed him the cup of coffee he had ordered on his arrival. Avinoam was drinking tea.

There was silence for a moment, and then Israel rose heavily from his seat, crossed to the table where Raphael and Avinoam were sitting and suggested, rather awkwardly:

"You can come out with me if you like! Join me! It's a big boat, the biggest of the lot, I reckon, and it's sturdy and it's got all the top-class gear. The gadget for lowering the nets isn't working... so I could use your help! Join me on my maiden voyage! We'll split it all fifty-fifty," he assured them, with a genial smile. Then, still smiling but with a hint of his former diffidence he added:

"I'm not dependent on fishing yet, as I still have money saved from the shop. I know it's... different for you. What do you say?" He studied their faces with some tension, afraid of their refusal.

Both Raphael and Avinoam looked up at him, in unison, inspecting his impressive stature with an air of warm solidarity, and Raphael cried:

"We say yes! Absolutely! And we're very grateful. This is a real godsend!"

"We can carry on like this, as a team, all week!" Israel went on to say, his voice steadier now and his face radiant – "Until your boat's been fixed – and my lowering gear!" Avinoam held out a hand to him and shook his hand firmly, and Raphael followed suit. After the handshakes, Raphael pulled up a bench and invited Israel to join them at their table.

One by one, the fishermen began leaving the café and heading for the boats in the harbour.

The takings were respectable. I rolled up notes, counted coins and stuffed it all away in an old leather bag, as per Rahamim's instructions, to be deposited in his bank account the day after.

Last to leave was Israel, accompanied by Raphael and Avinoam, his partners for the night's work. On the threshold, he turned to me and asked:

"Fancy joining us? There's room on the boat," he hastened to add, "and we could use another pair of hands. You'll get a fair share!" For a moment I considered the offer. I reckoned I could help out on the boat, and the remuneration sounded reasonable.

"What do Raphael and Avinoam think?" I asked.

Israel grinned: "It was their idea!" he said, adding, "They reckon you'll bring us luck!"

I joined them.

Outside it was cool. As if reading my thoughts, Israel announced: "There are some old sweaters and coats on the boat!"

After clambering aboard we found various items of clothing: thick sheepskin jackets and collarless long-sleeved capes, everything smeared with engine-oil, but guaranteeing protection against cold and wind. The boat was broad and spacious, fitted with a high-powered motor – a real seagoing craft...

"You could get to Cyprus in this, in no time at all!" Raphael observed, testing the bow-panels with a tiny hammer. Avinoam added:

"You could tour the whole of the eastern Mediterranean... even further!"

"An excellent craft!" was Raphael's verdict, on completion of his inspection. He tossed the hammer on the canvas-covered heap at the foot of the tall mast, with the big lamp suspended from the top.

The sky was light, with stars twinkling and a new moon climbing majestically, taking up its position above the heads of the mariners. The air was clear and the spaces wide open, the breeze cool but not too strong, a friendly, invigorating breeze – the stuff of old sea-shanties.

"Weigh anchor!" Raphael shouted from one end of the boat.

Avinoam answered his call and operated the capstan-motor. The links of the rusty chain clanged, shattering the silence of the night.

"Anchor weighed!" Avinoam reported, and sure enough the racket ceased, fading into a hoarse sigh, the sigh of relief of a proud vessel, yearning for the open spaces and braced for cast-off.

"Come here, Israel!" Raphael cried and the other approached him, walking clumsily and groping his way in the darkness. Raphael stood him at the wheel, its brasswork gleaming in the cold light of the moon. "You steer!" he commanded. "Avinoam and I will see to the motor." And he joined Avinoam at the stern.

The motor roared, before settling into a steady throb, light and graceful, with the soothing rhythm of a lullaby. Gradually the big boat moved away from the narrow jetty and began skimming sedately across the dark, oily waters enclosed between the beach, the jetty and the sea-wall.

The anchorage was left far behind, and suddenly we found ourselves confronting the awesome, intimidating spectacle of the open sea, the stillness of its repressed energy enveloping the entire field of vision.

The constant whine of the motor, turned up now to operate at full power, shook the void all around. The prow of the boat rose up proudly and forged ahead, cleaving like a knife through the dark body of the viscous waters. The stern left behind a long, double track of white surf, dispersing somewhere far away in the cold clarity of the night.

When the din of the motor was curbed, resuming its controlled, harmonious throbbing, and the boat slowed to idling speed, Raphael and Avinoam signalled to me, and the three of us advanced to the mast and took the tarpaulin cover from the big pile of nets.

"Now to work, and God be with us!" cried Raphael, with the exaltation of spirit engendered by dedicated toil, and he began lowering the end of the net into the dark waters below us.

We worked in silence. It took a long time, lowering the nets from the deck into the low swell of the waves, plashing gently against the hull.

"You can tell now why he wanted us here!" Raphael chuckled, winking at the rest of us. Still, the manual lowering of the nets was the kind of work that not only warmed the body but cheered the mind as well.

"There's nothing like the sea to heal all ailments!" declared Avinoam, standing up from the now emptied net-space.

"It's like a drug!" cried Israel, his response to Avinoam's versicle. "The drug of joy and freedom!" he concluded, in a thick, vibrant voice.

The boat circled and began hauling in the nets, heavy with fish. All the horse-power of the motor was not enough to lift them onto the deck, and it stalled repeatedly, treating itself to a short breather before mustering its energy and resuming with added vigour, with a frantic surge of anger. At one moment, we were afraid the nets themselves might collapse under the weight and the four of us set to, exerting our muscle-power in support of the struggling motor. The crisis passed and the mechanism stabilised, throbbing equably as it hoisted the nets with their booty, metre by metre.

The nets were silver with fish of all species and sizes, but among them all one particular specimen stood out: a long-bodied fish, of superior weight, struggling doggedly in the meshes of the net.

"This is a new variety of bonito!" Raphael exclaimed, stooping over the net, drops of sweat still sparkling on the nape of his neck, testimony to his recent exertions. "This one comes from Turkey," he declared, adding: "The Turks have been enjoying these for long enough, so God has sent some of them along to us, the Jewish fishermen of tomorrow!" He chuckled pleasurably.

Within an hour the nets had been raised and the deck was swamped with fish, writhing and tossing, their bellies silver in the chilly moonlight.

"I've never seen such a thing in all my life!" Raphael said, and Avinoam added his own comment:

"Even in films you don't see a sight like this, not even in cartons!"

"Haven't we spent long enough standing around and philosophising?" Israel protested, his voice shaking with excitement and adrenalin. "Let's drop the nets again!" he cried.

"Don' be in such a hurry!" Raphael forestalled him with a blocking gesture of the hand and a frown. "Big eyes," he added in a more genial tone, "don't mean big happiness! Let's do some sorting out here first, see what we're dealing with – and then we'll drop the nets again. And if the yield is similar to this one, we'll call it a day! Give thanks and go back to the shore. And God will give us a decent return. No need for envy, or greed, or exploitation!" he warned in an authoritative voice, and with a raised finger he added:

"Because then all the pleasure disappears for good, and satisfaction turns to servitude... We have to retain our purity of mind." His tone was restrained, but emphatic.

"I don't see the point of all that," Israel objected, his strange ebullience waning and his face falling: "What I mean is, everyone has his own idea of what he needs, and nobody's going around snooping and checking up. So if fortune's been kind to us – why should we be scared of it, or turn our backs on it?"

"It's a question of moderation!" Raphael insisted, "And if you're not satisfied with what God puts in your hand – I'd rather waive my share than catch more fish than we need. Fish – they're living creatures too!" he pointed out, "So if you want to make a respectable living out of them, make sure you do it right. Don't be a glutton and a murderer!"

"Aren't you being a glutton and a murderer now?" Israel asked with a sneer, pointing to the fish writhing at his feet.

"No," Raphael declared – "it's our livelihood. Take what you need and any excess – put it back! That's the hallowed practice of the true fisherman."

"The true fisherman is a noble soul!" added Avinoam solemnly.

Israel conceded defeat. "We'll do as you say," he said with

resignation. "We'll sort these out – and then decide!"

We filled the lockers with superior fish.

"This is a special night!" Israel exclaimed, bemused. "When I went out with you," – glancing at Raphael and Avinoam – "even after three hauls we didn't get as much as a third of this lot!" He pointed to the packed lockers. "It's a special night, a night that's blessed from every angle."

On Raphael's advice and with Avinoam's consent, we lowered the nets one more time. The catch was such that the lockers overflowed; most of it was left unsorted on the deck.

"We should count our blessings and have done!" whispered Raphael, in a tone of deep agitation, matched by the anxious expression on his face.

"I'm as hungry as a gypsy at the fair!" Avinoam announced suddenly. "Let's go on a bit further, find a quiet spot to heave-to, and have a bite to eat!" he suggested.

"I've brought flasks of coffee and tea," Israel announced.

"And we've brought sandwiches!" Raphael contributed.

The motor was started up again on full power and the boat moved on, prow erect and a double trail of white foam marking its rapid progress.

After about an hour the vessel came to a halt. The coastal strip was plunged into darkness that was perforated by faint pin-pricks of distant lights. The stars above shone in all their splendour, so big they seemed to be drawing closer, while the moon receded further into the heights, as if disdaining the world beneath. Its light remained –silver and chilly.

We sat in the fore-section of the boat, just behind the prow, protected by the high bow-panels from the strong gusts of the off-shore winds. The tea was piping hot, the sandwiches tasty. We ate and drank calmly.

"I've heard," Raphael turned to me, "that you left your home, abandoned your wife and came here to live alone..."

"That's right," I replied.

"How do you manage?" he asked, making a vague gesture in the air.

"In what sense?"

"You know what sense!" he chuckled, almost choking on his sandwich, and added emphatically. "That is what I'm talking about!"

"Relationships... all that stuff..." Israel took it on himself to elucidate, earning a nod of assent from Raphael.

"And how do you manage?" Avinoam demanded to know, turning to Israel.

"There is someone... I have a steady relationship with..." he replied with some embarrassment. "It seems to be working out."

"And you, Adon?" Raphael persisted.

"It isn't an issue for me," I answered him, taking a deep swig of the tea, its invigorating heat a welcome and appropriate antidote to the chilly air of the night. The motor was silent, and the boat drifted on the gentle swell, the sea stretching away calmly with veiled face to the far horizon.

"It isn't a question of issues!" Raphael protested.

"What is it then?"

"Pleasure," he declared. "How is it possible to get by without that kind of pleasure! It's the greatest of all pleasures, isn't it? Living without it, what a terrifying thought that is! What taste or purpose is there?"

"It seems to me you're exaggerating a bit," Avinoam interjected in a hushed voice, as if talking to himself, staring intently at the sandwich in his hands. "But," he added in a louder voice, looking up, "in a general sense – there is some truth in what you say."

"An infantile truth!" I countered with a light laugh, and the three of them simultaneously raised startled eyes to stare at me – whether bemused by the unexpected remark, the choice of words or the tone of voice.

"What's that supposed to mean?" queried Raphael, taking his third sandwich and making serious inroads into it.

"Real pleasure is the kind that will never enslave you, that you're not dependent on in any sense at all," I replied, my words reverberating around the confined space of the fore-deck. After a short silence, Avinoam declared:

"What Adon's saying, that's true as well."

Again the deck was plunged into silence. It was broken by Raphael, turning to me with a quizzical look in his eyes:

"That's a different subject altogether!" he insisted, with a strange air of regret, "In fact," he added in a lower voice – "in the heart of every male, there's sometimes a yearning to be liberated from that thing, to be in control of it..." And, inconsequentially or so it seemed, he went on to say:

"Pain and suffering – they call them pleasure and happiness, because they're easily attainable; true happiness – that's called pain and suffering, because it's always out of our reach!"

"Is there really no way to get to it?" Avinoam asked, addressing his question to me.

"There certainly is," I replied.

"And is it tough and complicated, inaccessible to average guys like us?" he persisted.

"Not at all."

"Can you give us some idea of what it is?" – Avinoam was not yet satisfied.

"The way is simple," I replied. "From an objective point of view, nothing could be easier."

"And it is?" the young man pressed me.

"Giving. Always and forever, giving, without desire, without seeking reward. Filling the heart with the desire to give, that – and that alone!"

The three of them tensed, listening with rapt attention.

"Inside, in your hearts, be prepared to give, give and give only," I continued. "Anyone whose heart is filled with the true desire to give – fears nothing, longs for nothing, doesn't know disappointment or despair, doesn't burn with hate, isn't eaten up by jealousy. Desire doesn't dominate him, he's happy at all times, in any place, any situation, happiness that nothing can match – he's worthy of the great love of God, and is rewarded with it, immediately!"

My speech was done. The silence that followed it was imbued with a pleasurable sense of calm introspection, a pure serenity.

The first to stir himself was Raphael, speaking in an unexpectedly mournful voice, not typical of him at all:

"The truth is that everyone envies you and would like to follow your example – but it just isn't possible!"

He stood up from his place, shook a crumb from his sleeve, tightened the coarse leather belt over the thick sweater, and with erect pose, taut as a highly tuned string, walked back and forth on the deck, stirring gently under his feet.

For a long moment he stood facing me, silent, head bowed, hands clasped behind his back. Then he turned slowly, walked briskly towards the stern of the boat, careful not to tread on the slippery, shiny bodies of the fish, and having arrived there, shouted hoarsely, without turning in our direction:

"We're going home!"

With an energetic flourish he started the engine, stood up straight and shielding his mouth with his hand, shouted to us:

"Conversations like these just inflame the imagination. There's no point or profit in them! As soon as we land, I'm going straight home to my wife!" His voice was coarse, as if challenging itself, and it ripped apart the silence of the night that was spread all around like a veil.

The fish, as it turned out, fetched a reasonable price. Raphael, who handled the sale and held the cash, deducted from the overall sum the cost of fuel and general running costs, including depreciation and tax, and handed it over to Israel. The remainder he divided equally between the four of us. The reckoning up was done in the early hours of the afternoon, in Rahamim's café.

I received a quite respectable sum. Israel was content, but Raphael himself looked gloomy and depressed.

"What's your problem?" Avinoam asked him, without looking up.

"I went home and sorted out separate beds," Raphael replied in a dejected tone.

"What does your wife think about it?" Israel asked with interest.

"She's content," Raphael declared, "always content!" And he went on to explain with a hint of scorn and veiled reproof: "She says OK to separate beds. She says OK to separate rooms"

"A good wife!" Israel exclaimed, impressed.

"No reason why she shouldn't be," Raphael responded with a sour smile, adding: "She knows better than anyone that I won't stick to it... She'll wait, patiently. She knows when she's well off!" He sighed, and concluded: "My wife has nothing at all to do with this whole business... I'm the one who's to blame!"

"There's no point blaming anyone," I turned to him. "There's a time for everything. Your time hasn't come yet, and you've nothing to reproach yourself for. When it comes – things will sort themselves out!"

"You mean," – Avinoam turned to me – "without yearning for the great love of God?"

"By means of yearning for the great love of God!" I replied.

We went our separate ways.

A SHARED PARTY WALL

Friday afternoon, Rahamim's café was closed. I left work early and went down there to give the place a thorough cleaning. I cleaned the fridge, the gas stove and the ancient baking oven which had rusted over years of disuse. I rinsed pans and kettles, and scrubbed the floor, the walls, the tables and benches. All this took some time, but in the end the whole café gleamed, including the thick walls and ancient floor-tiles. Even the air seemed more limpid, lashed as it was with myriad flashes of dancing light, like the sparkling air of a dewy meadow on a fine spring morning.

It took considerable effort to close and lock the glass-panelled door of the café, using the long key – which looked like something you might use to secure the gates of a medieval fortress. I turned to my left and walked slowly along the beach, feet barely touching the sand, eyes looking out to sea while seeing nothing, and my body moving on, yet ceasing to exist, leaving only my real self – the enlightening, infinite happiness from which the world emanates, in which it moves and into which it will melt and be gathered in – when it deigns to awaken from the futile dream of its illusory existence.

A surprise awaited me at home. My neighbour sat in the outer room, a sour expression on his face. He rose to meet me, held out a moist hand to shake mine, warily, and tried to smile ceremoniously; it was a positive and well-meaning effort, but clearly there was something in him at odds with the smile, as if he considered it out of place.

"Would you like tea?" I offered.

"No!" he said morosely, and then hurriedly softened his refusal: "I had some not long ago. I've eaten too... we are neighbours after all!" Again he smiled that twisted smile tinged with embarrassment. He seemed unable to control the twitching of his legs.

I crossed to the inner room, turned to the kitchenette, brewed enough for just one cup of tea, poured it out and returned to the front room where my neighbour was sitting on the sofa and waiting for me with commendable patience.

I prayed and drank.

My guest cleared his throat as a signal that he was about to speak, and he began:

"It's a strange life you lead... the way you pray, it's not like Christians, or Jews, or Muslims even! What I mean is – the Jew never prays without a cap on his head, and your head's bare! The Christian never finishes a prayer without crossing himself – and you don't cross yourself! The Muslim washes before praying and bows low to the floor – and you don't do that either... It's a strange kind of praying.

"All the same, you should be careful!" he warned me in a conspiratorial tone. "Speaking as man to man, as neighbour to neighbour..." – he continued in a nasal whine which also, strangely, managed to convey an immature, chirruping sound, simultaneously repellent and pitiable – "you're mixing with some dangerous types! I've seen them all, exchanged words with them all. Sometimes – just a word or two, sometimes – a proper conversation...

"Like that weird guy who was looking for you some time ago... not so long ago, in fact. I saw him, watched him and sized him up, spoke to him too... Dressed all in black, with this tiny moustache – quite comical really! Dried blood on his lips, and on his face... a real mess! You'd think he'd just been thrown out of some bar. But he wasn't drunk!" he asserted with irrefutable confidence, thought for a moment, and decided his story needed a more thorough grounding:

"It was early in the morning, and you weren't at home. You'd gone to work," he explained, and resumed his account. "He didn't smell of anything, no whiff of alcohol I mean... blood, yes, there was a smell of that... and his eyes were popping out of their sockets, sort of miserable, as if he'd been crying. He was here, in front of the house, walking to and fro and looking really agitated, nervous, or maybe he wanted to go in but didn't have the nerve.

"When I went out and asked what he was doing, he trembled all over, and answered in a cracked, grating sort of voice, like someone with a really dry throat. He was asking about you..." – the raconteur's turbid glance hovered over my face, dissatisfied with my reaction, or lack of it: "I disappointed him, disappointed him badly. You could tell that from his face, when I told him you'd gone about your business. I took pity on him, suggested he should try calling at your office. I explained to him how to get there... but he just stood where he was, as if he'd taken root, about a quarter of an hour, looking absolutely stunned, pole-axed... in the end – he went."

My neighbour lapsed into silence, staring at the floor, in tense anticipation of a reply. When this was slow in coming, he looked up with a kind of self-conscious gravity and asked:

"You know him?" – the look in his ugly little eyes was positively indignant.

"No," I answered him, having summoned to the surface of my memory and paraded before my mind's eyes all those acquaintances of mine who bore the slightest of resemblances to the figure described.

"At the end of the day," I added with a smile, "he'll find me!"

"It was quite a long time ago," my neighbour reminded me, trying to fix a date on it. "A month...maybe more..." Again, he studied my features intently.

"It seems he doesn't need me any more, in that case," I replied, and stopped concerning myself with this individual, whoever he might be.

My neighbour weighed my words, examined them analytically, digested them and no doubt arrived at some creative conclusions which satisfied him, for the time being at least. After a long silence he spoke again, this time with emphatic composure:

"I sit at home, by the window, facing the alley – I've nothing else to do. Sometimes – I read books. Social Aid contributes something. I am slightly disabled, as you know," he explained without looking at me – "in the upper storey." He grinned to himself, raised a long finger and tapped his temple. "I pretend to be worse than I am, so they'll pay up! Why waste public funds on roads and buildings and street-cleaning and libraries... it should go to some living person who can enjoy it!" His pale face lit up with what was supposed to be a leer of diabolical cunning.

"I lead a quiet sort of life," he continued, regaining his composure. "Sitting at the window and looking out at the alley, the neighbouring houses and their residents, some normal, some eccentric... coming and going, angry or happy... seeing all, knowing all – and keeping it all inside!" – he exclaimed with an aggressive kind of relish, alarming himself into an abrupt change of tack:

"Up to a certain point... I have a wife and children," he informed me, as if this were adequate justification of his caution and reserve. "Boys who are still young, and girls who haven't reached puberty yet," he revealed in a sombre and reflective tone. "I have to keep an eye on them, so they don't go astray... I really wish we could leave this ghastly, godforsaken town altogether – this freak-show of criminals and whores and drug-dealers. But that would cost money, and Social Aid isn't that generous..." He sighed, staring around at the walls of the room, wondering whether to carry on and reveal more of his secrets, things liable to harm him if falling into the wrong hands – or to keep mum.

"I go out to work too... sometimes," he resumed, in a hushed voice. "Delivering papers and sometimes – fizzy drinks... I see you down there, in that café, old Rahamim's place, the guy who has no children. I know that too! I keep my eyes open!" he boasted. "An open eye – is the elixir of life!" he declared, coining an epigram of startling originality and creative genius. And with a strange intensity, its motivation unclear, he went on:

"And what I wanted to say – with all due respect for your intellect and your principles – is that you should show some consideration for your neighbours! I show consideration for you, and you ought to do the same!

"The landlord's related to my wife and, if I can put it this way, I'm not just one of his lodgers, I keep an eye on his property too, make sure the fabric's in a decent state and the tenants are the right kind of people! Not that he pays me anything. He did try once, but I turned it down, got quite shirty with him. He apologised... and he's been apologising ever since! I ended up feeling sorry for him.

"I did get paid once... for work that I did, of course. That was when people used to pay for work, even within families!" he stressed, hesitating, and lowering his eyes. After a long moment he raised them, still avoiding mine, and went on to say:

"I'm very fond of my wife. I could almost say I love her, but it's a word that so over-used, especially in films, in a cheap and titillating sort of way. The point is, I can't imagine life without her, I just can't!" His voice was rising, inflected again by that grating and repellent chirruping sound.

"And what strikes me as strange is your behaviour!" The note of reproof was heavy and unmistakable, but he made no effort to look me in the eye. "Leaving a wife, at your age, with children and grandchildren!" Pausing only for a deep breath, he continued:

"On the other hand, there's no doubting that what you did took some courage…no doubting at all! It's like cutting off a living limb with your own hands… I don't know what you're proving with this or what you intend to prove, but the act itself is exceptional in its own right – the kind of courage that not everyone's capable of! And even if the limb is rotten," he reverted to his former image, "cutting it off with your own hands?" His amazement sounded sincere: "It's virtually impossible. There are quite a few people who would like to follow in your footsteps, because relationships with women can go either way… As a matter of interest, how did you do it?" – he turned to me and asked bluntly.

I didn't answer. He shifted awkwardly in his seat, and after a brief moment of silence he added: "I came here to raise a different issue altogether, something entirely practical!"

"And that is?" I prompted gently, sipping from the tea that had cooled.

"The business of the open door!" he cried in an angry outburst that he made an effort to restrain. "I've nothing against it in principle, nothing graven in stone… I wish we could all leave our doors open, without fear. But it just isn't an option!" he exclaimed, with that strange chirrup, testimony perhaps to intense emotion, and concluded vehemently: "So long as there are children in the world!" He fixed me with a stern look, demanding my exclusive attention.

"What do children have to do with this?" I asked him.

"They're nosy and inquisitive, and they love mischief and playing games!" he replied patiently. "In my own home I can supervise them, but your house, with its permanently open door, is another matter!

"Just imagine it," he cried. "They get in here, the little varmints, and meaning no harm, just as part of their game," – he changed the tone of his voice and put on a look of childish innocence, to underline the point – "they turn on the gas… and afterwards, forget to turn it off. Someone comes in, an adult or another child, strikes a match… what is the result of that going to be, eh?" he berated me with fatherly indulgence.

"You're absolutely right," I replied, "if you're talking about wayward children who have no supervision on the part of their parents." And at once I added: "But dangers lie in wait for children everywhere, in the street and in their own homes. That's not a reason to abandon your beliefs and flout your principles."

"Belief in the open door?" my guest queried.

"It represents a great hope," I explained.

"And if I try every possible form of persuasion, if I plead with you, go down on my knees, confess that I'm far from being an ideal parent... my disability holds me back... I can't run after my children, can't bring them up the way other parents do..." He studied the expression on my face tensely.

"Please!" he cried suddenly, with unexpected heat and fervent sincerity: "Put a lock on your door! Do me a favour, in the spirit of that great hope that you mentioned!"

He lapsed into silence, focusing on me a look that was dull but at the same time steady, and surprisingly resolute.

"I'll get it done today!" I assured him.

His look softened, and something like a faint smile twisted his thin, colourless lips. "What about your beliefs and principles?" he asked with a hint of derision creeping into his voice.

"This way I'll remain true to them," I replied.

"What a way with words!" he chuckled suddenly, the tense lines of his face easing, sparkling with bright and tender light. "I knew you were an educated guy," he added, "This business of writing books – that means something! Although I admit – I haven't read your books! I've seen them, flicked through them, and it doesn't seem they're written for people like me. In fact, I read a lot. Papers too. Not all the way through though, as little as possible. You have to be careful, 'cos the papers are full of filth! Gossip and cruelty, smutty scandal and titillation, lies and exaggeration and plain arrogance. That's just reality! – you might say, to which I would reply: It's newspaper reality!" he declared triumphantly, before restraining his exuberance and adding with total gravity:

"My children – they've been in here any number of times. I didn't come here to apologise for that. To a child – an open door is an open invitation," he drew out another original epigram from his sleeve – "You the one who's to blame! I came here to talk things through with you," he added, "and if you were obstructive and rejected my appeal, I meant to go to the landlord who, as I told you, is a relative on my wife's side, which confers on me the obligation to keep and eye on his property..." and here he hesitated suddenly and mumbled something unintelligible. And after a long pause he went on to say:

"But I got things in the wrong order, and instead of starting with you and going on to him, I started with him. I didn't tell him I was going to talk to you… I hadn't made up my own mind at that stage… But tonight, Friday evening, the eve of Sabbath according to the Jewish religion, it's boring at home – wife doing housework, the streets empty, nothing to look at, nothing to think about. I couldn't even find a book worth reading in the library. So I said to myself: How about a conversation with an educated guy!

"And so what if you are educated?" he added, with a provocative, defiant air. "You weren't born an intellectual, but you worked, invested effort…" and he added, with confidence: "If I invested the same effort, I could get somewhere! I'd be an intellectual like you, I might even overtake you! Only God," – he spoke with sudden reverence, his voice lowered, "can do things without effort. And that changes everything! Seeing as it follows from this that the aspiration to imitate God has to be fulfilled without effort, and taking it a step further, it follows that no intellectual can get close to God, ever!" And he added with warmth, and more than a hint of complacency: "This is a subject I prefer not to dwell on!

"And as for the business itself," he resumed in a candid and fluent tone of voice – "because of your open door, weird people are coming and going. I don't know if you even know them, all of them…anyway, today, there were children paying a visit. And immediately after that visit – to my utter and unpleasant surprise – I saw them carrying packets of chewing-gum, a packet in each hand… Work it out," he suggested amicably, "four children times two – eight packets. I looked into it straightaway, and what emerged? It was here, in your house, that the rot started! They found money here – ten tenners!" He drew nine crumpled notes, of ten shekels apiece, from the pocket of his baggy trousers, and from another pocket produced a fiver and five one-shekel coins."

"This doesn't belong to me!" I declared.

"The money you mean?" He treated me to a cunning glance and added at once: "I know – you're going to tell me you're not in the habit of leaving sums like this lying around… you'll probably claim that you're broke! I know how the money got here, and I'll prove to you it's yours. I'll bet it's a debt that's been repaid. Take it!" He proffered the notes and the coins.

"The first rule of wisdom – is to check!" I commented.

"If this isn't your money," he retorted, "give it back to me. Go on, take it! Don't you trust me?" He scanned me with an indignant look, ready to flare up at any moment. "Haven't you caused me enough grief with those kids?"

"I'm sorry about that!" I said, meaning it. "But I really don't mind the chewing-gum being charged to me," – and while saying this, I put the little bundle aside having taken two coins from it and put them down in front of him. "That's one shekel for the chewing-gum," I explained, "and another one for the next time!"

"Are you trying to humiliate me?" he snorted, "Make me a laughing-stock?"

"Not at all," I declared in a thoroughly friendly tone. "I don't want to see the children punished... I'd much rather they were happy, and that would make me happy too! I say this in all seriousness, it's my earnest request!"

For a long moment he thought this over, his head slumped on his chest. Eventually he looked up at me, his face brightening again, and he spoke in a tone of endearing, childish happiness:

"I can see that you're sincere. And I've been boring you with all my chatter... but it was a burden I had to unload! And you, you're the understanding kind! There's no one here to talk to... and this disability of mine, it's a real one... and it isn't just upstairs, it's in the legs as well... and the wife – not the most stimulating of company, does her duty and that's it! The kind of person you can be fond of, as indeed I am... but a conversation with her – that will just make both of us angry! And I... I don't get out of the house much. It's a mundane existence. Looking, yes, taking an interest, watching different people and trying to figure out what makes them tick, speculating, reading books... but that isn't enough! A conversation with an intellectual, a writer of books – that's something else entirely... it brings relief. Can't you tell how relieved I am? It's more than that – I'm refreshed." And scanning me with a strange look of relish in his dull eyes, he reverted to the former topic:

"This habit of the open door – is a habit of arrogance... testimony to arrogance. Laziness too!" he declared in a manner brooking no contradiction. "Listen to me!" He leaned towards me again, a soft radiance lighting his face: "I've weighed this up thoroughly, from every angle and perspective – renounce arrogance, and you'll be a free and upright man! On the other hand," – he was suddenly pensive, his heavy brow wrinkled – "it's good that things have worked out as they have... I wonder what I'd have done if it hadn't been for the open door business!" He glanced around the room and focused again on the surface of the table.

"You know," – he spoke as if starting a new story, or an interesting chapter in a story already begun: "I used to come in here too... just, out of curiosity...and to keep an eye on the children... make sure they didn't turn on the gas or fall on some nail or a forgotten knife – so they'd come to no harm and do no harm. The house, my house I mean, is only next door. We share a party-wall! So the effort was worthwhile, from my point of view as well." He chuckled, studied my face carefully and added:

"I know exactly who brought that money and stuffed it under your pillow... where the kids found it. You're not going to tell me you're in the habit of leaving money lying around... anyway, not in an obvious place like – under the pillow!" he exclaimed with a complacent sneer, looking into my face again before proceeding to reveal his secret knowledge:

"The money was brought here by that skinny girl, the one who tries to act tough... whenever I see her, my heart goes out to her!"

"Why is that?" I asked with interest.

"How can anyone mistreat a child like that?" he retorted with feeling, and added: "Because she is a child, believe me, a child. In spite of everything she knows and everything she does or has done, everything she's been through! But you know all this better than I do... One look's enough for you!" he concluded with an unexpected flash of envy.

"One look is enough for you, too, isn't it?"

"No!" he protested with an emphatic gesture, "I need to investigate. I don't rely on faces. And I know a lot about her. I've heard what she's told you, here. The walls are thick, but that doesn't matter if the voices are loud enough – and I've worked out the best place to position my ear for the optimum effect." He spoke with dignity, as if this were a standard procedure requiring no further explanation, modestly recounted by an admirably conscientious master-technician.

"You've been eavesdropping!" I snapped at him.

"Yes," he assented, standing up from his seat and adjusting his belt to prevent his baggy trousers drooping any further, and in what was supposed to be an authoritative voice, with recurring traces of that repellent and pitiful chirruping sound, he said:

"As for you – you get that lock repaired and be quick about it! We haven't yet reached the Golden Age of mankind, the so-called era of 'ease and security'. Then they won't even build houses, and it'll be 'every man sitting under his own vine and fig-tree' as the Good Book puts it. As long as they're building houses and fitting locks on doors – we have a duty to lock them!"

He extended a damp hand in a clumsy gesture of friendship and went prattling on:

"And don't forget to visit the landlord! I've managed to work him up into a foul temper. It's true, time soothes and helps us forget, but sometimes: he who waits – weeps!" Having produced another of his original epigrams, he continued smugly:

"I'll hand over that shekel to the children. They'll be very happy. And I'll tell them you're a good man – as indeed you are!" He nodded, acknowledging the sagacity of this remark, and went on to elucidate, with his peculiar brand of doleful enthusiasm: "You've listened to every word I've said, listened with true dignity, showing not a hint of weariness or impatience! By my life, you're a good guy – the best of men! Or the maddest of them all!" He left the house.

Before evening came, I mended the defective lock. The next morning, I rose early, and after the customary exercises and tea with honey, made my way towards the south-eastern sector of the city, where I knew I would find Lili. The money she had left under my pillow was in my pocket. This was a free day and I had time on my hands.

HOUSE AND COURTYARD

In all cities of the world there exist quarters whose inhabitants know one another very well and yet pretend otherwise, neither greeting one another nor returning greetings. An outsider straying into these parts is immediately conspicuous and is dogged by hungry and inquisitive looks, studying and assessing the details of his features, his gait and his clothing, while avoiding eye-contact with him. Sometimes these looks are angry, protesting indignantly at what is seen as a violation of boundaries, sometimes they are softer, as if apologising for something obscure that requires apology, and sometimes they are haughty. But all of them, the sharp and the indignant, the apologetic and the haughty – follow the outsider intently, the deeper he penetrates into the interior of the quarter. And if the outsider makes it to the very heart of the quarter, it is inevitable that someone will approach him – usually an older woman, whose curiosity has got the better of her and who has time on her hands and the very best of intentions. The woman stops him with an imperious gesture or a simple exclamation and puts a question such as:

"What are you looking for?" or "Can I help you?"

In my case it was a girl of ten or twelve years old, with two companions of the same age, following me at a respectful distance. Finally, unable to restrain her curiosity, she quickened her pace, hopping and skipping on an invisible rope, caught up with me and stopped chewing her nails for long enough to ask me, with bright eyes – a little bashful, yet inquisitive:

"Who are you looking for?"

For my purposes, the little girl's intervention was timely, and her practical question entirely appropriate.

"Shuki," I replied with a smile.

"Shuki?" The girl seemed to flinch and her face clouded over, as if she regretted not having resisted her impulsive curiosity.

"You don't know him?" I asked in a deliberately casual tone, offering her a way out of her awkward predicament.

"There's no one doesn't know Shuki!" she replied at once, assertively, as if her pride had been hurt, and in a changed tone, her voice lowered, she added: "But I don't know if there's any point you going there... He's not at home. His mother – she's paralysed!" she explained.

"I'd be very grateful if you'd show me where his mother lives!"

My request surprised the girl, but she seemed to take it as a compliment. She gave me a bright look of childish innocence, tried in vain to adopt an air of grown-up cunning, and without a word, turned abruptly and gestured to me to follow, gladly accepting the role of my guide on the journey to the house where Shuki's mother lived.

The outer gate was substantial, its lintel shaped like a flat and broad arrowhead. After repeated knocking, which wasn't answered, the gate swung open before me with surprising ease. Beyond it, stretched a narrow yard. A couple of chickens were rooting about among the gravel-stones strewn on the parched and yellowing ground, seeking tasty morsels invisible to the human eye. A startled cat fled to a corner, climbed nimbly up the exposed pipe of a jutting tap, and somehow reached the top shelf of an ancient, disembowelled wardrobe, where he crouched and surveyed his surroundings keenly.

At the rear of the courtyard stood a long building with a domed roof. Thick walls testified to its age, and it was obvious that little had been done in the way of maintenance, apart from an occasional, and incompetent, replastering job. The door of the house was open wide, revealing a dark and dingy interior.

I closed the gate behind me carefully, and for some reason the cat found this reassuring. He abandoned his attitude of surveillance, relaxed, stretched his limbs, settled down and began to doze.

I approached the building until I stood in the entrance. A long, cavernous, domed hall was revealed to me. At the far end were four or five beds of assorted types – iron, wood, formica-covered – with neat but unmatching quilts and coverlets. Four dark, low-lintelled passageways, without doors, opened on the hall on both sides, while the fifth, evidently leading to the bathroom, had been fitted with a door. Near the entrance, where I stood, were some sunken sofas which had lost most of their stuffing, a jumble of armchairs and two or three narrow tables.

To the right of the beds, in a big, padded armchair, sat an old lady, with dense curls of grey hair descending on her shoulders, resembling a clown's hat – a spectacle both grotesque and pathetic.

One of the old lady's eyes was closed; the other, smaller than its sister, had a frozen and glassy look but seemed capable of seeing. Her tight mouth was tilted to one side – a typical residue of a stroke. She was dressed in a shabby gown, her arms lying limply on the sides of the armchair. One leg was stuck out in front of her, bare and puffy, mottled with prominent, dark blue blotches, and the other folded beneath her, covered in some flowery fabric, pyjamas apparently.

I nodded to her, although I had the clear impression she wouldn't be capable of responding, not even with a reciprocal nod. However, I knew she could see me and my movements and I reckoned my greeting was likely to dissolve any superfluous tension, actual or potential.

At the old lady's feet, a young woman was cleaning the scarred, concrete floor, crouched with her back turned to me, using a mop and a precarious-looking bucket.

"Lili?" I called to her softly.

She sprang to her feet with a start, as if she'd trodden on a sharp needle, turned and let out a cry:

"Adon!" – it was an exclamation of total surprise, bemusement, fervent, wild protest and happiness that was wilder still. "What the Hell are you doing here?" she snapped, attempting a display of anger and resentment. "And I'm – dressed like this!" She ran frantically to one of the hall's doorless exits.

I approached the old lady and from close quarters repeated my nod to her. It seemed something faint and distant stirred at the base of her frozen eye, in response – or with the will to respond. Without saying a word I bent down and continued the job of cleaning the floor. The water was cold, the mop defective. I wrapped the squeezed-out rag around it and began drying what was already wet, then carried on with an orderly routine of dipping, squeezing and mopping. Half of the hall had been cleaned when Lili reappeared in her traditional garb – jeans and a dark masculine shirt.

"Adon!" she cried in genuine alarm. "You're insulting me, offending me… us!" she corrected herself hastily and glanced desperately towards the old lady, pleading for support. But the other seemed to be ignoring her completely and made no response at all.

"No need to take offence!" I replied. "When a job needs doing – does it matter who does it?"

Lili swooped on me and insisted on taking the mop from me. I picked up the bucket and went to the tap outside, to replace the dirty water with clean.

Before long the floor was cleaned, its moisture glistening, fresh and benevolent.

The old lady stirred in her armchair, and when Lili hurried to stand before her, she uttered vague fragments of words in a shrill voice, and in her one open eye a searing flame was ignited, which at first sight could have been interpreted as a violent surge of anger.

"She wants to thank you," Lili translated.

"I'm grateful too!" I replied, approaching the old lady and repeating the words in a louder voice. Lili, so it seemed, was used to her and her speech, and could decipher these abrupt, raucous screeches clearly and accurately. And the crone yelled another series of strange staccato sounds into Lili's ear, she translated:

"You're a wise man! But your wisdom is nothing compared with purity – purity of heart!"

"Every creature has a pure heart," I retorted and added, "even if he ignores it. The truth that is in every creature," I continued, "is God, and from this it follows – the heart is pure!"

"Does that include Shuki?" – Lili translated a series of agitated squawks.

"Him too," I declared.

"And Shuki's father and his brother too?"

"Them too."

"But you don't know them!" – the screeches grew louder, with a perceptible note of bemusement.

"I don't need to!" I insisted. "All are equal – you and Lili and Shuki and his brother and his father, and me. God is in all of us!"

"Strange words!" – the clamour subsided.

"True words!" I declared with pleasurable certainty, and to this there was no response.

Lili had got over her initial surprise at my visit and was all radiant with the soft lustre of a strange and steadfast willingness – to be other than herself. To be whatever might be demanded of her, but not herself. And this seemed to relax her, infusing her with delight from the sole of the foot to the crown of the head.

"Would you like some tea, Adon?" she offered in a vibrant voice, her eyes as bright as a spring morning.

"I would indeed!"

The tea was served on one of the low, uncoordinated tables. But before fetching the tray, Lili was called back by the old lady, who intoned in her ear a long series of disjointed sounds, rising and falling, sometimes angry, sometimes gentle and conciliatory.

I took deep, steady draughts of the warm liquid. Lili sat beside me, on the broad, sagging sofa, and didn't touch her cup, instead thirstily imbibing something hidden that floated and shone in the clear void of the vaulted hall.

Her brow reflected back a distant ray of light that crept in from somewhere and left its mark on its pure, childish dome. Her eyes seemed filled with reverent joy, the joy of finding what the fleshly eye yearns for in vain, to expose and explore it to the ultimate.

"You know," she began hesitantly, the note of radiant gladness in her voice gradually subsiding, "the old dear was talking about you... she had a lot to say... you must have noticed, before I came in with the tray. She told me I wasn't to leave you, I should bind myself to you always, in thought and in feeling, and so on..." She picked up her cup and without drinking from it, went on to say:

"She told me that you're my last hope, and for her part she's prepared to do without my services and go to her end, which she knows can't be far away... She says she'd rest easy if she knew I was by your side, or rather, you were by mine.."

"I've brought you the money," I said in an abrupt change of subject. "And I'm asking you not to do things like that" – my voice was gentle but firm. "It's not as if I needed it!"

"You did need it!" she cried defiantly.

"No! That was all sorted out!"

"After the cash-card business?" she asked incredulously.

"After the cash-card business."

She sighed a bitter sigh of disappointment:

"You might as well know – that money is kosher! That is," she hastened to add, "Shuki knows about it. In fact, it was his idea! Well, not directly... but you see, I knew something like this was going to happen and so I asked him, what would he think if I lent you a hundred. He smiled and nodded his head!" Amazed at her own disclosure, she added:

"It's a rare thing for him – smiling, I mean. That kind of a smile – without malice, or scorn, or ulterior motive..." She looked up at me, her big eyes reflecting unexpected gravity and resolve, and cried:

"You'll offend him, offend him badly!" – and in a softer, more conciliatory tone, with a sidelong glance she added: "If you don't take the money..." – before concluding with a sudden surge of her former vehemence, her eyes flashing: "There's no way I'm taking it back!"

"Shuki won't be offended, not in the least!" I assured her. "If you don't want the money, I'll give it to charity!" I spoke clearly and calmly, and she knew I meant every word.

"You're so stubborn!" she protested, knotting her brow and suggesting in a completely different tone, an air of helplessness and resignation: "If you like... we'll go out to the market round the corner... The house is empty!" she added, putting her cup down without drinking from it – "no groceries here at all, hardly anything to eat! It's hunger that's killing the old lady, not paralysis... It's true, she never cries, never utters a word of complaint, but all day yesterday she didn't eat at all! Let's go out and buy her something, but not right now, not straightaway. I want to make sure she's okay, and Shuki isn't coming round. He winds her up, you see, gives her all kinds of grief...

"She used to have a wheelchair," she went on to relate – "and he just couldn't wait to get her out of it – and sell it! And then they brought her a replacement, an old one, donated by some bunch of do-gooders. But she refused to sit in it, pleaded with them to take it back... they paid no attention, didn't believe what she was saying – saying through me, that is. They thought I was exploiting her; either that or I didn't really understand what she was getting at. So they left the chair. Shuki arrived, and an hour later – no chair..."

"When he has money," I asked her, "or rather, when he had it, did he treat her differently?"

"No!" she replied vehemently. "Exactly the same. He winds her up, curses and abuses her and she gives as good as she gets... but I don't pass on her answers. Sometimes I tone them down, because when it comes down to it, she's upset about him, really upset. He's her son after all, the only one who isn't doing time! Deep down she loves him and feels guilty for ever bringing him into the world. And he knows it too, and he yells in her ear: 'I'm only here 'cos somebody raped you, so who was it, eh? Who? Who?'

"He's a menace when he lashes out," she continued. "He terrifies her" – she pointed to the armchair – "for myself, I'm not afraid. I know how to handle him. And he wasn't always like this...

"The old girl's afraid of his enemies, and says the only safe place for him is behind bars, and the sooner they lock him up, the happier she'll be. And she believes it's only a matter of time, and she's getting impatient..."

"You said he wasn't always like this," I reminded her.

"When I met him," she replied, "he was different. Maybe not that different," she added hastily, "but then, what kind of a guy he really is, deep down, no one knows for sure, not even he himself...

"When we got together," she resumed, "he spent a lot of money on me. Took me to shows, parties, trendy night-clubs, introduced me to his mates, underworld bosses like Joe and Benny and Gabriel. He introduced their girls too. He bought me expensive clothes and showered me with jewellery... and three days later he came back in a rage, took it all away and sold it... I can't say I was that disappointed.

"One of those bosses, wall-eyed Gabriel, he murdered. Not personally. He sent a hitman. But before that, he'd killed his girl, Rita – a skinny, cheeky little tart she was, pinching clients and ignoring all the warnings. So he murdered her. Slit her throat. That's his favourite method. It was then that his mother had her stroke."

"Who told her?" I asked.

"Nobody told her. Nobody would have dared."

"So how did she get to know?" I persisted.

"She didn't!" she retorted, with a kind of dull obstinacy.

"You said that following the murder, she had the stroke," I reminded her.

"He murdered her here!" She pointed to the scarred floor of the room, its moisture infusing a little freshness into the fetid, enclosed air - "Before her very eyes!"

"Maybe," I spoke hesitantly, "he didn't mean..."

"He meant it!" she insisted. "He could have killed her anywhere, but he dragged her here. His father was here too, and his brother. And another of his lackeys. They didn't bat an eyelid, they even helped him dispose of the body..." Lili fell silent for a long moment and then spoke again:

"He ordered her to wipe up the blood on the floor. She was going to do it... and then she just collapsed, and that was the stroke and all the rest of it."

"And you – where were you?" I asked.

"At the other end of the room," – she pointed – "curled up on one of the beds. Hearing it all and not seeing anything. Head under the blankets, and eyes closed. But there was no need to see..."

"Full of surprises, isn't he," I said.

"Shuki?"

I nodded.

"Yes," she agreed with a kind of irresistible melancholy that wiped away any last traces of her former animation, and added in a low voice:

"He cried once... the one and only time I ever saw him cry. He came to me. I was in a hotel. He waited till the client left, and came in. It was a grey, heavy, depressing sort of morning, the way mornings usually are in cheap hotels and derelict buildings. He came in looking pale, without a word – and burst into tears. He was wailing and whimpering, his face twisted and his shoulders heaving. I didn't ask what was up, 'cos he wouldn't have told me. Anyway, it was obvious he hadn't come here to unburden himself. He just wanted to weep in some corner where no one would disturb him. He went down on his knees, laid his head on the soiled bed-sheets, and went on howling. When he finally managed to get a grip on himself, he told me..."

"Told you what?" I asked.

"The whole story. Unbelievable. I wouldn't have believed it myself, if I hadn't heard it with my own ears, and seen some evidence on the ground. He told me – about a cat!" Her lips twisted in an awkward smile:

"It happened when he was on his way home. He wasn't stoned, and anyway this was before he turned into an addict. He was wrapped up in his overcoat, as it was winter, with rain pouring down and a strong wind off the sea... and he heard the wailing of a cat – a kitten, really...

"He turned around in the dark, hunted for the kitten and found it. For a long time he was wondering what to do with it, and then that kitten – a ginger, he said – came towards him, nervous and shaking all over, and rubbed against his legs.

"That really shook him, though he wouldn't admit it. He said that's when he knew the kitten had been abandoned, and was suffering and was bound to die unless someone took care of it right now... He decide to be that someone...

"He took the kitten under his coat, enjoying – so he said – the warmth of the body and the regular purring, expressing contentment and gratitude to the one who had taken pity on him and was caring for him.

"But that's only the beginning of the story. He brought the kitten home, laid it on the table, ran out and roused some of his neighbours, got milk, warmed it, cooled it, and fed the kitten. And then the kitten started throwing up...

"Shuki didn't know what to do. He warmed more milk, and tried again. Same result. The kitten was writhing around in agony, puking over and over again...

"According to the way Shuki tells it, he felt he'd been entrusted with some kind of mission centred around this kitten, but it seemed to me," – she offered her own opinion – "he was fond of the creature, too fond perhaps, and didn't want to admit it, as that would be an admission of weakness.

"So Shuki took the kitten, and ran to the vet's house in the next quarter. All this at three in the morning. He hammered on the windows and the doors... he knows how these things are done. The cops use the same technique when they're raiding us..." she commented sadly and continued:

"He threatened, cursed, pleaded, made a scene... till the vet opened up to him. A balding, fat sort of guy, couldn't care less, doesn't know what feelings are, more like an executioner than someone who's supposed to be looking after animals. But in this case, he showed himself in a different light!

"He started off arguing with Shuki, not impressed by his threats and trading curses with him... but when he saw the kitten he went all soft, forgot Shuki, forgot himself, took the kitten in and treated it. Cleaned up the muck and the puke, and shoved some pills in his mouth, and after a while he sighed and said: 'He doesn't stand a chance. Well, maybe there's some hope for him, but he's so small!' He advised Shuki to keep the animal warm with his own body heat.

"Shuki took the kitten and ran home like a maniac, went straight to his room and got into bed, cuddling the kitten, and peering at him anxiously from time to time, checking he was still alive.

"It seems this kitten," she took a deep breath, as if tiring of the lengthy anecdote – "had those big, innocent, pure sort of eyes… and as time passed they showed nothing but dumb pain and an appeal for help. Shuki was going crazy, he didn't know what to do. He was holding the kitten close, stroking him gently – and praying!" For a moment Lili peered into my eyes, smiled to herself contentedly and went on:

"He was letting out heart-rending cries of agony, with solemn promises and pleas, vows and threats too – as you'd expect of him. Just before dawn he fell asleep, and when he woke up, he found himself cradling not a sick kitten, but a corpse. It shook him to the roots of his soul; he refused to believe the animal was dead and tried everything he could think of in the attempt to revive it. And when nothing helped, he lapsed into despair.

"He realised – so he told me – that God had abandoned him completely. There was no helping him now. He, Shuki, was the worst of sinners and God would never answer his prayers and forgive him. His only intention was to punish him, as he deserved. But he, Shuki, would never understand, he refused to understand – why this God chose to punish him through the suffering and death of that poor and pitiable kitten.

"I didn't know what to say to him. I'd had a pretty rough night myself…but seeing how much he needed a boost, I said:

'God didn't want this kitten to die. There's no death in God, He's beyond it. And I'm sure the soul of that miserable kitten is resting now in God's warm embrace…'

"And you know," – she turned to me, her face alight with wonderment – "he looked at me, and there was a sort of faraway look in his eyes and a new kind of peace – he believed it!" she exclaimed, with an exaltation that faded rapidly, continuing:

"He was soon back to his normal self. Told me to get dressed, took me to the corner of a garden near the sea – a bit more neglected then than it is now – and showed me the place where he buried the kitten, a little, flat patch of ground… and he knelt down there, bowed his head…

"And when he stood up, all the tears, and the remorse, and the grief, had disappeared, leaving no traces behind. In his eyes, I saw the diabolical leer again, the leer that had abandoned its post for one night, the night I saw Shuki cry for the first time in his life and probably – the last!"

The tea was going cold, but I drank it anyway. Lili made an effort too, taking a few long, slow gulps. She put the empty cup down on the table and continued solemnly:

"And now, everyone's abandoned Shuki... except me. And despite everything that the old lady said, and maybe in spite of some deep-seated desires of my own – I've no intention of leaving him. At the end of the day," she added, head lowered and eyes staring at the floor, "he's just a kid, that's all! A bad, naughty kid, but still a kid... His luck's turned sour... the world's full of guys like him!" She sighed, lifting her head and turning to me with deep sadness in her eyes, a voice full of pain:

"He's sick, Adon! Shuki is sick. He doesn't know it yet, or he's pretending he doesn't know. Either way, he's going to find out soon enough. He's got a fever. He's burning up... all the time, day and night. And all kinds of ugly growths springing up all over his body, and showing no sign of subsiding, but expanding, spreading. I'm afraid. I'm almost convinced this is something really serious, a critical condition! He doesn't want to admit it – but most of the time he's tired, so very tired! It's true, he's cursing and abusing and sometimes lashing out, like before, but even his violence...is lacking something these days...." – she paused briefly, speculating – "the devilish malice, perhaps, the sadistic lusts... something is melting in him and I don't know what it is! I have to stand by him!" she exclaimed, an exclamation clearly addressed to herself, a rigorous attempt at self-conviction – nothing more or less. Suddenly she looked at me again with eyes full of gloom, and in a hushed tone, but deep and slightly hoarse, she added:

"What I really want is to be with you, beside you, at your side..."

"You are with me," I assured her, "so long as you are capable of dispelling sorrow and gloom from your heart! Because my essence is delight, true delight without beginning and without end, pure, everlasting love, illuminating the world! And whoever is a part of this – is forever in me and I in him."

We went down to the local market and bought provisions – vegetables, fruit, fish and meat. We returned to the old lady's house and deposited the supplies in the larder – one of those dark and dank passage-ways, ending in a blank wall, with a few crude, unplaned planks nailed to it. On returning to the main hall, I paid my respects to the old lady and wished her well, and she answered me with a series of emotional shrieks. I turned to Lili, but she refused to translate the contents for me.

We left the narrow courtyard, and stood in the gateway. The chickens were still clucking as they rooted about in the gravel, and the cat sidled between us, rubbing our legs. Then his attention was drawn to some enticing, shiny object, and leaving us behind, he proceeded to subject it to a keen and cautious inspection, wary of arousing its wrath or, worse, causing it to disappear.

The day was turning to evening.

I held out a hand to Lili, for a farewell handshake, and sensed a strange awkwardness suddenly arising in her, unease and tension setting all her sinews on edge. She lowered her head defiantly, and it was clear beyond any doubt that she had seen something behind my back – something or someone deeply disconcerting to her,

I turned. Just a dozen or paces from us, stood an elderly monk, of the Orthodox Church, surveying us with clear, calm, feline eyes, and waiting.

"Is that him?" I asked her.

"It's him!" Lili replied without looking up. "He's been hanging around here for days like a tomcat on heat. As for me – I've had enough of all that stuff. I don't want to see anyone! Not even him! I don't feel comfortable with him around... something burning in me, hatred perhaps... and so much grief... As for you," – she lifted her eyes and fixed them at the level of my chin – "take no notice of me! Be on your way, and let this randy old goat grapple with his filthy lusts... I know how to deal with types like him, put them in their place!"

She looked up suddenly and shot a chilly and proud look at the old man, then shook my hand warmly and disappeared into the house.

A CYLINDRICAL HAT

I turned to go my way, and at once heard the patter of light feline footsteps behind me; it was that old man, in the dark cassock and the high cylindrical hat, the well-known symbol of the Greek Orthodox Church.

I didn't alter the rhythm of my walking, and he had no option but to quicken his own pace. He finally succeeded in catching up with me in the first of the southern alleyways, veering off in the direction of the coastal strip.

"Excuse me, Sir! Be so good as to excuse me, Sir!" His Hebrew was fluent, but tinged with a foreign accent.

I stopped and turned to face him.

He stood there as if rooted, his face, flushed from the effort of pursuit, smiling at me – a smile that was broad and ingratiating and at the same time natural, absolutely natural, a smile seeking to awaken attention and respect, and if at all possible – a little affection too.

"How can I be of assistance to you, Sir?" I replied in the same formal style.

"Aha..." He seemed a little confused and awkward, going on to say, inconsequentially, and abandoning formality, apparently without being aware of it: "I don't mean to be a nuisance. Your time may be precious... in fact I'm sure it is! Whose time isn't precious? As it says in the Scriptures: 'You shall account for every second of your life in the flesh!' In our Scriptures, that is!" he thought it necessary to clarify, the smile still fixed on his face, and at the same time he took a step forward, apparently inviting me to follow suit; what he had to say could be revealed while we were in motion, thus minimising the waste of my precious time.

I complied anyway and walked calmly beside him along the winding alleyway, descending gradually towards the sea. A breeze rising from the west blew softly in our faces.

"What do you want?" I repeated my question, likewise reverting to a more familiar style. His smile became broader still, as he shrugged the shoulders behind the shabby black cassock, fingered his cylindrical hat and, still pattering along beside me, said in reply:

"It's nothing special... something quite trivial perhaps. I'm still wondering if it's even worth mentioning..." He looked away quickly, but not quickly enough to hide a hint of decidedly sinister intent, somehow focused between his thick, grey-streaked beard and his undulating moustache.

"He who keeps his mouth and his tongue, keeps his soul from trouble!" I quoted playfully.

"Ah, King Solomon!" he noted complacently. "Proverbs of... Yes, yes, the wisest of all men... and yet, perhaps not the wisest after all... I mean, keeping a harem of a thousand wives and still not being satisfied, protesting bitterly at your lot... nothing very wise about that, oh no!" Without any connection with the foregoing, he turned to me suddenly and said:

"Don't believe everything she tells you about me – that little whore, I mean. Women like that have vivid imaginations and they like to boast about all kinds of affairs – when in fact it's all hot air!" His feline eyes tensed, and their penetrating glance studied me closely, to gauge the impression that his words were making on me.

"Judge not that you be not judged – that's something else you'll find in your Scriptures, and it's a rule you're already breaking! How dare you apply such derogatory terms to anyone? Are you better than she? Who are you, anyway?" And in a gentler tone I added: "If I don't believe her, why should I believe you?"

"Ah..." He skipped over a little stone, tugging at the fringes of his cassock, an impulsive gesture expressive of nervous tension. A look of alarm flashed across his broad, round-cornered face, which had meanwhile regained the rosy-cheeked blush that seemed to be its natural hue.

"You sages! Like Solomon himself..." he muttered as if talking to himself. "There's no standing up to you... and what you say is germane indeed – why should you not believe her, but believe me?" He repeated my question, misquoting it slightly, and went on to ask, in a clear and almost childish tone: "And why should you believe her – and not me?" And he proceeded to supply the answer:

"I'll tell you why..." Again he turned to me abruptly as we walked on, and his face, which had moved closer and for a moment was very near to mine, was revealed in precise detail: soft and puffy, laced with blue veins and prominent red capillaries, testifying to his weakness for intoxicating liquor; his purple nose, heavy and fleshy, told the same story.

"The reason is – this will lead you into a dilemma, or dilemmas…that you'll be incapable of resolving… and the question I wanted to ask… in fact I've already asked it, but you didn't take it that way… the question is – has she said anything about me?" He fixed me with a keen, sidelong stare.

"She hinted at something I already knew about," I said.

"Ah," – his face fell and suddenly he began to quicken his pace, as if scared of something or pursued by someone.

"Goodbye!" I said, with every intention of parting company and going on my way, but he hastened to forestall me:

"No, no," he urged. "I ask you most earnestly, my plea is laid before your feet!" He managed to give his speech a poetic inflection without it sounding artificial. "The church, where I officiate, is just here, not far away I mean. Would you care to come inside, Sir? We can drink something, tea or coffee, or liquor if you prefer. Oblige me, Sir, please! It won't take up much of your precious time, and I would be offended, truly offended, if you were to refuse." He spoke with an air of mounting confusion, lurching from the formal to the familiar and back again, but there was no doubting the sincerity of his impassioned pleas.

"Were you to refuse, I would think to myself that you have gained an erroneous impression of me, Sir!" – he declared with a vigorous wave of the hand – "Without giving me the opportunity to present evidence, advance certain arguments, try to justify myself… if indeed it is within the capacity of flesh and blood to be justified. I am after all only flesh and blood, all of me… as you are, so am I!"

"Not only flesh and blood," I commented.

"What is there besides flesh and blood?" he asked, turning sharply into a side alley.

At that moment we stood before the high gates of the church, vaulted steel gates, resplendent in their fresh black paint, with four little crosses, two to each panel, picked out in silver against the dark background.

The monk tried to open the gates and realising they were locked, impatiently pressed a hidden bell.

"What is there besides flesh and blood?" he repeated his question mechanically, in an attempt to keep the conversation going, while he waited tensely for a response to his ringing.

"The truth that is in man," I replied.

"What truth is that?" he persisted, shifting his weight from foot to foot, as if a chill had suddenly descended on the earth and was threatening to freeze his limbs.

"His divine nature," I declared.

A little hatch opened in the gate. Someone peered through it for a long moment, and then the hatch closed and immediately one of the panels of the gate swung open silently and we stepped inside, into an expansive courtyard, as broad as it was long and padded with grass. A mighty cedar, ancient and grand, stood proudly at its western end. Behind the regal cedar, a church was visible, its high walls gleaming white, and beneath the canopy of the tree was a long table made of simple wood and arranged around it – about a dozen garden-chairs of modernistic style.

"Dimitri!" the monk turned to the gate-opener, a hunched little man in a shabby jacket, his red and swollen nose showing that he too was not averse to the fermented fruit of the vine. "A bottle of arak for me please, and whatever this gentleman prefers."

"Tea," I replied.

"Tea!" he passed the message on to his minion.

Dimitri shuffled away across the lawn and disappeared behind the broad trunk of the tree. We sat down at the long table and a few minutes later, the bottle of arak was set before the monk, with a glass and a dish of sliced pickled cucumber, and before me – a cup of tea, the rich colour of ripe dates. Along with the cup was a jug of hot water, for refills if required.

The beadle performed his duties with measured movements, and without a sound; he seemed to be gliding around rather than walking on two feet, and when his work was done, he slipped away out of sight.

The day was turning towards evening; shadow covered the great courtyard and only the broad canopy of the tall cedar was still absorbing the last rays of the sun, glowing like a crown of pure gold.

The monk, or priest, poured out some of the clear arak, filling his glass, then picked it up with his left hand and poured it down his throat with an emphatic toss of the head. He clicked his tongue, passed a puffy hand over his moustache and the portion of his beard that was already wet or was liable to be so, took a slice of the pickled cucumber, crumbled it and chewed it with his few teeth, clicked his tongue again with an air of restrained pleasure, and finally broke the silence:

"I feel very sorry for her," he announced, as his opening gambit. "She's a slut of course, but she has a good heart... a sensitive heart. At first, I wanted to help her somehow... I was willing to pay if only she wouldn't go astray... if she'd stop going with others, I mean. Ah, what a fool I was, an incorrigible, gullible fool! I almost went as far as to steal the collection money! My first idea was to allocate a reasonable sum of money to this young lady... and maybe more. To open some business in her name. The Church, thank God, has ample resources that aren't put to any use. It doesn't take that much ingenuity to divert some of it, when it's for a good and charitable cause!" He grinned to himself and studied my face with eyes that were beginning to show the dull flash characteristic of alcoholics.

"I made it conditional on her changing her religion. When I saw that wasn't going to happen, I was prepared to go ahead anyway, without any conditions. I was going to lay a stack of money at her feet... and she raised no objection... and the moment came when the money was ready. And then I realised that he, that vile whoremonger, had his beady eyes open and meant to line his own deep pockets and not leave her a cent. So I saved the money, dedicated public money that should never be spent for secular purposes, carnal desires and the like..." He took a deep breath, poured another glass and emptied it, gobbled another slice of cucumber, clicked his tongue, wiped his moustache and went on in a cracked voice, a tone of bitter passion:

"Everything she told you about me – is the absolute truth!" And he added sadly:

"She's not a liar, she doesn't know how to lie... A wanton to the marrow of her bones – with a heart untouched by evil. Absolutely! Innocent and pure...

"In fact," he changed the tone of his voice and infused it with something sounding like enforced awakening – "all creatures are like her! Innocent and pure. Except for those who devote themselves to sin and wickedness, because in sin and wickedness they find their pleasure and their human dignity...

"You look at me now – and what do you see?" He smiled to himself, that broad, tender, unique smile of his, which was not lacking in goodwill and lustrous light. "Do you see an old sinner? Flesh and blood riddled with licentiousness? A fallen monk, who took vows and failed to keep them? If that's the way you see me, it's only because you want to see me that way. It's your pleasure, your personal, repressed pleasure! And if you see me otherwise, that's your choice and your pleasure too... How do you see me?" He suddenly lifted his oval, rosy-cheeked face, topped by the cylindrical hat, and fixed me with his glassy feline stare, demanding an answer.

"I don't see," I replied.

"Are you blind?" he expostulated.

"Far from it."

He wrinkled his brows for a brief moment, scanned me with a watery look and turned away, entwining the little fingers that poked from the sleeves of his cassock, giving him the ludicrous appearance of a clumsy doll dressed in a black kimono.

"You're going too far!" he protested, head lowered and eyes staring fixedly at the well-kept lawn, turning grey in the twilight. It seemed he had misinterpreted my implications, but I made no attempt to put him right; his time had not yet come.

"And maybe," he added pensively – "you're right, and maybe not! Anyway, I see myself as what you might call... an average sort of person. Not a saint, but not the worst of sinners either!

"In fact," he raised his hoarse and crackling voice, an admonitory finger jabbing the clear, evening air as he shifted to another tack: "Monasticism is just a challenge to God! Impertinence of the most reprehensible kind!"

"So why did you choose it?" I interjected with some vehemence, taking a deep draught of the tea in my cup while it was still hot. It had retained its fragrance and the taste was exquisite; clearly the work of a virtuoso in the art of brewing tea.

"I went with the flow," he admitted sombrely. For the first time since I had met him, his face looked utterly dejected.

"You have to understand... or know, I should say..." he continued, holding his oval head erect, trying to dispel from his face some of the gloom that was vibrating in his voice: "Once, a long time ago, I was married. Married to a healthy, affectionate woman, full of warmth and vitality, and not averse to sensual pleasures... suddenly – she fell ill and never recovered...

"I was shocked, furious at the world and everything in it, blazing with destructive rage… Someone had given me a precious gift that I loved and cherished. I guarded it like the apple of my eye and knew happiness such as I had never known before, and suddenly, this someone came back and stole her from me, tearing her from my embrace, grinding her down before my eyes and turning her to dust!

"It was a cruel thing!" he declared, reverting to a more fluent and coherent tone: "Unbearably cruel! But it was more than that, it was weird! I was consumed by curiosity,

painful, irresistible curiosity! Desperate pursuit of knowledge, I suppose you could call it. With all my heart and soul I wanted to understand the motives of this 'someone' who when he chooses – gives marvellous gifts, and when he chooses – takes them away. Steals them, in fact! Without any warning or a word of explanation, grinding them down before your eyes and consigning them to oblivion…"

Even as he spoke his temperature was rising, his eyes flashing angry sparks all around, but he controlled himself with an effort, shook his head with its drooping beard and went on to explain:

"So I became a monk. I wanted to get close to Him, as close as I could, make His acquaintance, get to know Him really well, ask questions, demand answers. I wanted to fathom out what's in His mind and to understand!" he exclaimed, staring at the empty glass gripped between the fingers of his little hand, and continuing:

"At first it all went smoothly. I couldn't bear to look into a woman's face, and that made things easier. The very idea was loathsome! You see," he put his glass down and gazed at me intently: "All women, the whole race of them, were as nothing compared to her! In facial terms alone – the face of an angel couldn't radiate such love and warmth. So, I couldn't look into a woman's face… to me they were like the vile sewage that thirst forces you to drink when the pure spring has dried up…

"And then I became aware that there was more to women than just faces – it was the rest of them that I couldn't resist! I realised at once I was incapable of resisting it, and there was no point trying to be subtle about it – going to confession and mortifying the flesh, and trying for absolute detachment from the tangible world – because I knew the tangible world inside me would never give me any peace, ever. Thoughts of sin are worse than the sin itself, your sages say – and they're right!

"So I needed the modest services of those brazen hussies... Wherever I go I seek out girls of that kind for their services. In exchange for money, of course, a reasonable fee. I believe 'harlot's pay' is the technical term. That way, we both profit: she has her money and I gain some peace of mind – my deceitful, lost and unruly mind, that is so often disturbed! And when peace of mind is disturbed, the service of God is impaired too!" And he saw fit to elucidate further:

"Instead of being focused on that undeniable, higher truth, that nourishes the world and gives taste to our existence here, that is the sole purpose of life on the earth, that is all joy and blessing – my mind is distracted, and vile images float before my eyes..."

"There is one thing I want you to understand," he added earnestly: "Nobody is more utterly convinced then I am – of His existence! This isn't some faith that needs to be propped up on tottering pillars every now and then. The convictions that I have are unshakable! There is nothing higher.

"A worldly sinner – that's what I am and it's all I have to offer Him, but a worldly sinner who loves Him in spite of everything, and will never stop loving Him, in spite of everything... and even if He doesn't want me, I won't stop... I can't, I'm just not capable! Because there in nothing in me other than my love for Him – as it has always been and always will be!" He had begun whimpering softly, and his clumsy body was shaking beneath the broad, shabby cassock. A sprinkling of tears moistened the surface of the varnished table.

At this point Dimitri returned. He approached us as silently as ever, gathered up the utensils with leisurely movements, and before disappearing, announced:

"The reverend gentleman is due to conduct the evening service. Soon the congregation will be sending a deputation, to fetch him!"

"Wretched sinner that I am!" the monk hissed, wiping his eyes with the sleeve of his cassock.

"God loves sinners!" Dimitri retorted, gently but firmly.

"You're a sinner of one kind," cried the monk, treating his acolyte to a meaningful look, "and I'm of another kind entirely! You may yet be absolved, whereas I..." He waved his hand dismissively, turned to me and added in a tone of bitter resignation: "I'm one of those sinners who believe in Him absolutely and love Him to the end..." He rose from his seat to escort me out.

When we reached the high gate, he addressed me again:

"Please tell her, Sir, that girl, not to leave me like this, not abandon me! And if she's found some other course to follow, she should send me one of her friends. It doesn't matter who... I'm not choosy. She'll be performing a sacred duty; without that release I'll be incapable of serving God as I should – with undistracted mind, broken heart and true humility! I'm not asking you to respect me, Sir," he added. "I'm not a man but a coarse, rutting beast! At the best, a miserable, pitiable beast and at the worst – a vile insect not even worth the effort of stamping on... Salvation – is way beyond my reach!"

"I don't think that way," I told him earnestly. "Love is the only way to salvation. Love is all-conquering!"

He studied my face with an air of utter incredulity. Then suddenly, a faint light, a distant glow of wonderment blended with reverence, was ignited in his eyes.

"You are right, Sir," he declared, "Love is indeed all-conquering... but what of the vow that was broken?" he asked in a tremulous voice, with trepidation that still preserved within itself a tiny space for hope.

"This was a vow too stringent for you," I replied. "Keeping to it was beyond your capabilities. A man has to know what he's capable of, and what he's not capable of. That way he won't be lying to himself, which does the most serious damage to his divine nature... It's never too late!"

"Never too late for what?"

"Leaving the monastic life and taking His love with you into the secular community. The way of monasticism is not his way!" – I declared with finality, shaking his childish hand warmly, and walking out through the imposing gate of the church.

MOSHE LEON

At an early hour of the afternoon, on leaving my workplace and before making my way to the café, I went down the broad main avenue with its white-washed buildings, its vibrant traffic and its pungent miasma of exhaust-fumes, turned into a short and narrow alleyway and paid a call on Moshe Leon.

His office was of impressive proportions, located above the expansive premises of a jam factory, one of Moshe Leon's many business interests. He himself sat behind a desk resembling a banqueting table, capable of accommodating a couple of dozen guests with ease.

Moshe Leon was rocking in a leisurely fashion in a massive, high-backed armchair. He smiled at me and extended a giant hand – heavy and gnarled, the hand of a former locksmith. I shook it and sensed surprising tenderness in his grip; it was almost limp, sickly – a symptom of premature old age perhaps.

"Glad to see you!" he intoned in a thick voice, as if talking through a loudspeaker, but sounding sincere: "Please, take a seat!" He pointed to a smaller armchair on the other side of his desk. He pressed a button and spoke into a meshed grille on the desk-top.

"Coffee?" – he turned his grey eyes to me, eyes that seemed small in proportion to the head and the dimensions of the body, reminiscent of the eyes of a whale.

"Tea," I replied.

"Tea," he repeated into the grille, "and white jam!" He turned to me again, with the broad, habitual smile on his square, heavy-jawed face and asked: "How does that sound to you?"

"Sounds fine," I replied.

"Excellent!" he cried, and did a mime with his hands of rolling up his sleeves – a legacy, no doubt, of his locksmithing days – and said:

"I hear it's not all going smoothly with you – relations with your neighbours, I mean."

"I wouldn't put it like that," I replied. "I admit, your relative had something to say about my unlocked door..."

"My relative?" he grinned, and added: "Well, why not? All human beings in all corners of the world are one big family, and that's especially so of the Jews – 'always standing by one another' as our revered sages put it! As for the unlocked door – not a good idea!" he declared with some vehemence, his smile deepening as he continued:

"I know this is a kind of hallowed principle, a part of the great dream of mankind for a bright future, something about universal tolerance. Humans wouldn't be humans if they didn't have such a dream..." He clicked his tongue, and a shadow of bitter disdain passed over his face. "Unfortunately, there's a flaw in it. You know what they say: 'The hole attracts the mouse, and the open door – the thief'... But that's your business! What concerns me is the damage to property, unnecessary damage to rented property. One way or another, there's always damage and destruction. This is something that affects rented property most of all – the tenant feels he has no responsibility for it. He's here today and tomorrow – somewhere else!" he concluded with a kind of good-natured shrewdness.

I listened in silence. The lack of response on my part seemed to make him uneasy, and he hastened to clarify things:

"Adon, may I call you Adon? You of course may call me Moshe... I don't often get the opportunity to meet an understanding sort of person, grab some real conversation with him... I mean, someone whose ears are open to things, who takes things in the right spirit and isn't offended by some straight talking – which in this instance I reckon was necessary, and has served its purpose, and will go on serving it!" He smiled his broad smile at me again, then suddenly cocked his head as if remembering something of vital importance, although for the moment its connection with the foregoing was unclear:

"You sent Nessim to me, the one who wears a skull-cap. Funny guy!" he said, with lingering emphasis on each of the syllables of 'funny' – as if to express the full depth of his bemusement: "He seems weird to me, but maybe I'm wrong and there's lots of others like him. He could be like me, like all of us... maybe we're all 'Nessims' at heart..."

"What about him?" I asked.

"He's looking for an apartment," Moshe Leon replied willingly, and added: "with energy, determination, faith... and desperately hoping he won't find it! Every apartment I've offered him, he's found something wrong with it. It's as if he wants a spacious apartment at a nominal rent, and that's what he's after, in all seriousness!" He paused for a moment as if weighing something up, as if he needed to filter and sieve what he was about to say to make it more palatable. He resumed in an even tone:

"He interests me, and he makes me curious too. To satisfy my curiosity I offered him a place, just like that – a spacious pad at a knock-down rent," – he smiled a thin, surprisingly innocent smile and explained: "To try him, of course! And then – the thing I least expected to happen – he agreed! Naturally, I had to call the deal off. He immediately offered more, and went on increasing it until it came close to a reasonable price. I felt sorry for him, or maybe I was a bit ashamed of myself, for the way I'd been messing him about, and I accepted the offer.

"We drew up a memorandum, I took a deposit from him, and we went to a lawyer... at least, I did. He didn't turn up!" he exclaimed, as if still bemused by the turn of events. "And to this day I've been waiting for him, to come and take his deposit back. I don't need it!" He shifted on his padded seat of supple leather, was silent for a long moment as if putting his thoughts in order, then turned to me and said in a persuasive tone:

"Next time you meet him – send him along to me. Or he could see my secretary, if he's too shy to face me. I just want the whole business finished!"

At that moment there was a knock on the thickly padded office door, and after a loud cry of "Enter!", the door opened and a thin man, with a moustache and thick side-curls, the sleeves of his check shirt rolled up, came in carrying a tray with everything that Moshe Leon had asked for – tea, coffee and jam.

With care appropriate to the ritual, the man laid the tray on the desk, bowed in an ingratiating manner, straightened up and stood there tense as a bowstring.

Moshe Leon inspected the tray, nodded his satisfaction and the minion proceeded to complete his task He stooped again and set out the broad coffee-cup and the standard tea-cup, little bowls of jam and an array of gleaming teaspoons.

"Thankyou!" Moshe Leon dismissed him and he took the tray, retreated to the door, walking backwards, and disappeared.

The host leaned forward and handed me the tea-cup, then nestled back in the embrace of his armchair, pulling the coffee-cup towards him. To my surprise, even this minuscule effort was apparently enough to inject a hint of pallor into his square face.

He took the coffee-cup in his right hand, holding the decorative saucer in his left, and took a deep and satisfying gulp, clearly intent on extracting the maximum possible enjoyment from the experience.

I followed his example, and having sipped the tea and replaced the cup in the saucer, I said:

"The business with the door has been settled. Since yesterday evening – the door has been locked."

"In other words," he retorted, somewhat taken aback, "it isn't an issue of principle after all! And I was thinking in my innocence," he continued with head bowed, as if talking to himself, "we'd be having a proper debate here, putting forward arguments and counter-arguments, introducing conclusive evidence, exchanging barbed speeches, turning up the temperature – it was going to be interesting! I'm not sure you understand what I'm getting at!" He shot me a scornful-inquisitive look from under his brows.

"I think I do," I replied, tasting some of the jam that had crystallised on the spoon, an indication of its superior quality. "I reckon you're feeling sorry for yourself."

He followed my example, licked some of the jam and asked, putting the spoon down:

"Sorry for myself? What's that supposed to mean?"

"You're disappointed. No grand tirades today!"

"Aha," he scanned me with a long look, "you picked that up... Anyway", he continued in a lighter tone, intended to mask any residual resentment, "you're right!" He picked up the spoon again, rolled it around in his mouth like a child licking a sweet on a stick, put it down on the edge of the dish and said:

"I... have a favour to ask of you... some unfinished business with a certain government office located in Jerusalem. There's been no movement on it in half a year. It's probably been entrusted to some petty bureaucrat, who even as we speak is sleeping peacefully at his desk...

"To get to the point," he knitted his brows as if gathering together his disjointed thoughts, "I'd like you to undertake a particular mission for me. Not complicated, not at all! I want you to go to that office, present the documents in person, get them signed on the spot

– and be done with it, once and for all and in the best possible way! Of course," he hastened to add: "This will be in exchange for a reasonable fee! Anyway," he continued, I've done my calculations and I know that even for a little job like this, a lawyer, any lawyer, however junior he might be – would take me to the cleaners. You, on the other hand," he continued, laying his huge hands flat on the polished desk-top: "will get two months exemption from room-rent. How does that sound to you?" His tiny eyes studied the lines of my face – with a combination of curiosity and amusement.

"Is this why the man who calls himself your 'relative' told me I should come to see you?"

"That's a part of it," he replied, and added with emphatic dignity: "Of course, there was the business of the unlocked door..."

"And that was your excuse?" I suggested.

"Not exactly," he retorted, and after a moment's thought added: "You could say I saw a bandwagon coming and hitched a ride on it!"

The black telephone beside him emitted a few tuneful notes. He picked up the receiver, and in a well-practised tone, not lacking a degree of asperity, pointed out: "I told you not to put any calls through!" and carefully replaced the receiver.

"This business trip to Jerusalem," I reminded him. "Could you be more specific about it?"

"By all means!" he replied, producing three closely typed sheets of paper from a drawer outside my field of vision, plus a couple of memoranda, and proceeding to acquaint me with the contents...

The issue was so trivial it could easily have been ignored, or forgotten altogether.

"For something like this you're prepared to pay money?" I pressed him.

"Adon!" he leaned towards me, with an air of friendliness and complicity. "It's a matter of principle! I'm a man of principle!" he exclaimed, "and I shall spend my money as I see fit. It is my money after all!" He grinned and leaned back in his black leather padded armchair, which exuded a heavy and sombre feeling of solemnity.

"There's no arguing with that," I concurred.

"You'll do it then?" he asked with interest.

"Willingly," I replied, thinking of the overdraft.

"I knew you'd agree!" he declared complacently. "In fact," he added, "I know all kinds of things about you... Without any effort on my part, without having to investigate you," he saw fit to emphasise – "information just flows in, by itself, like water running down a hillside... I daresay you know things about me too?" It was part question, part statement.

"No," I replied.

"For example," he studied my face keenly, with more than a hint of apprehension – "anything to do with, let's say, my state of health?"

"Nothing at all," I said, and his relief was almost palpable. He sighed deeply, made an abrupt sideways turn in his swivelling chair, and without looking at my face, showing me only his cetacean silhouette, he commented:

"I know for example about the cash-card – and the big overdraft."

"And because of that cash-card, you invented this assignment?" I shot at him, smiling brightly.

"You see," he laid his linked hands on the table and turned his grey eyes towards me, "I didn't want to offer you a way out of debt, just like that. That kind of gift would be like giving charity to a beggar. I wouldn't feel comfortable, and somewhere along the line, I'd have felt cheated. Giving money away and getting nothing in return – I'd be a fool in my own eyes. It would sour my life for years – however long I have left..." His mood turned ugly for a moment, but he quickly took up the reins again and continued in a steady voice:

"I invent what I choose to invent... in this case – there was no invention. The business in Jerusalem is real and genuine, as you saw with your own eyes when you read those papers. But it's not particularly urgent. So here I have the opportunity to invest in a profitable deal, and also give it a veneer of respectability, offering you a decent recompense for your pains. I've no doubt at all that decency is something you're thoroughly committed to... Am I right?

"Absolutely!" I declared, amused.

"So that," – he held up both thumbs – "is why I acted as I did." He pondered for a while, raising his left hand and supporting his temple on the splayed fingers. "I suppose this could all be bluff! Self-deception!

"Probe anything too deeply," he continued in a tone that he had some difficulty keeping steady, "and ugliness is revealed. Under everything. You mentioned self-pity. For my part, I'd add arrogance and hypocrisy... Am I right?" – he fixed me with a penetrating glance.

"No," I replied. "The truly arrogant, hypocritical and self-pitying will never admit this to themselves. Those who are honest with themselves and admit, with deep sorrow and remorse, to being arrogant, hypocritical, self-pitying – there's a lot of hope for them!"

He scanned me with a prolonged, grey and heavy look, then, clearly intent on diverting his thoughts from the previous topic, addressed me rather brusquely:

"So, do you accept the assignment?"

"With pleasure," I repeated my assent. "But I can't do it immediately. It won't be for another two weeks at least. Two weeks or a month.

"Two weeks, or a month, or two months – makes no difference either way!" he declared. He picked up his cup, sipped slowly and fell silent for a while, staring straight ahead of him.

"You know," he continued, sounding thoughtful but in a louder voice than was characteristic of him, "I exploit people... a lot of people. I exploit you too," he added brightly, "though you don't seem to notice it. In fact – even if you did notice it, it wouldn't do you any good! Where are you going to go? Which way can you turn?" he asked himself and replied at once:

"For the kind of rent you're paying, you wouldn't find a run-down hovel! But I'm still making a profit out of you, a reasonable profit I might say, and at some point or another, in the heart I mean – I'm laughing at you. Not in a derisive, or arrogant, or hurtful way, but laughing, just laughing. A good-natured laugh maybe, or a foolish one, but that's all. You're not offended?"

"No," I replied, smiling.

"And that's the whole point..." – he knitted his brows which, strangely, seemed to be exuding tiny droplets of sweat. "You're not offended, so why bother laughing at you? It all comes down to pleasure, you see, and pleasure without inflicting harm is no pleasure at all... In the final analysis, I'm not laughing at you – you're the one who's laughing at me, am I right?" His eyes bored into mine with a look of feverish inquiry, a sickly lustre.

"I'm not in the habit of laughing at anyone, or deriding anyone," I responded in a clear voice, without a trace of pomposity or pretence.

"That's impossible!" he protested.

"Nobody," I continued emphatically, "is capable of laughing at anyone other than himself. Anyone who claims otherwise, is simply deceiving himself!"

There was a long pause while he considered this, his heavy chin resting on his open palm. Then, lowering his hand and replacing it on the polished desk-top, he sighed for some reason and said:

"How little we know about ourselves!" He hurried to amend this: "The fact is, we're really deceiving ourselves with evasive statements like: 'how little we know about ourselves'! We know ourselves inside and out!" he declared, and after a moment's silence, added:

"I was really looking forward to this conversation between us, the opportunity to share my thoughts with an understanding sort of guy, exchange some sophisticated ideas... In fact," he went on to say, his face seeming to lighten – "all I really wanted to do was humiliate you! That was my intention.

"And as it's turned out," he cried in a tone of genuine bemusement, "I can tell that my objective hasn't been realised. And I have the uncomfortable feeling that the humiliated one is me. And this prompts me to ask myself another question, utterly different from any question that's been posed up to now, and from a totally different angle! The question is: wasn't this in fact my explicit intention – to be humiliated and not to humiliate, to be humiliated by you?" He gave me a chilly, distant look, resentful but well controlled, and concluded: "And I know the answer, and I don't care to reveal it!"

"In principle," I retorted, unimpressed by the heavy expression on his face and the aggressive look in his eye, which had subsided in the meantime – "the answers to all questions are known to each and every man..."

Here he hastened to interrupt me with acute, uncharacteristic alertness:

"All the answers, to all the questions?"

"All the answers, to all the questions," I echoed him, and added: "so long as the senses don't come in and cloud them."

"In other words," – for some reason he sighed with relief and his face began to emerge from its mask of gloom – "man is always prevented from knowing any answer to a question, because he's always held back by his capricious senses!"

"Which he is capable of overcoming," I rejoined, "if he really wants to."

He looked up with an abrupt movement, almost with an air of pride, his heavy face lighting up suddenly:

"It's better to leave things as they are, let lively sensuality stay in the driving-seat. That's what man really wants!"

"It depends on the man," I replied firmly.

He picked up the spoon, licked off the remainder of the jam, put it back in the empty dish, then swallowed what was left of the cooling liquid in his cup as if it was strong liquor, and put the empty cup beside his saucer.

"I really wanted this conversation!" he announced solemnly. "The things I heard about you gave me the strong impression that with your help I could find the answer to all kinds of vexatious questions... you have to realise," he added – "I'm surrounded by a herd of fools..."

"That depends on who's looking at them," I commented.

"And I'm the biggest fool of them all!" he declared, disregarding my interjection, and added at once with uncharacteristic fluency:

"They're all fools – at home and at work, in the factories I run, and in all my other concerns. And the bureaucrats I have to deal with are the same, to say nothing of some of my tenants...

"You have to understand. I've had to use all kinds of tricks and strategies to get hold of these apartments and at the same time avoid tax liability, getting round prohibitions and bending the rules, wriggling between the laws like a snake! And I've succeeded: a real triumph!" His eyes shone with a grey, distant, autumnal light.

"All methods seemed legitimate to me: favours of all kinds, bribery – crude and open or subtle and disguised – intimidation and threats where necessary, or wheedling and pleading, and as a last resort – legal claims, lengthy proceedings...

"And it all went smoothly and I always came out on top, whatever the circumstances. And a constant stream of cash flowing into my coffers... on behalf of fictitious clients and sub-contractors that I invented. And everyone knew and no one said a word; only too happy to enjoy the honey that came their way...

"Like this jam factory that I set up. I used to turn a blind eye to the rubbish that the workers were sticking in the jars. Then, I dismissed them all, had to go to industrial tribunals, all the way up to the High Court.

"So we had a clean product. And production didn't go up or down, and demand was static too. The idiots went on buying the stuff the way they always had, as if they couldn't tell the difference between the clean version and the old version, the one the workers used to dilute…"

"With urine, you mean?"

"With urine," he confirmed. "When workers reckon they're hard done by, they find original ways of registering their protest."

"You knew about this – and you didn't stop it?" I asked.

"I knew," – he hesitated – "too late… I sacked them. And the new ones I took on – behaved just like their predecessors. And the ones I replaced them with too! Until I changed the system, without anyone noticing! Piss or no piss, the dopes went on buying and I was the biggest dope of the lot, 'cos I didn't get anything out of it at all. I made no profit from the clean or the dirty version. I tried exploiting the workers, tried being nice and conciliatory towards them and that did me no good – nor did sacking them.

"You might as well know," he raised his hand as if warning me not to interrupt – "there was a time when it occurred to me to make them shareholders in the factory, shareholders with full rights and obligations, without demanding any investment on their part. And then I realised this would be the height of folly; they wouldn't appreciate it and I'd only end up worse off…

"The question, why do I do this? – arises from time to time, and the answer isn't: don't do it! The answer, as you said, is well-known to me. And I'm afraid of it, afraid to take the mask off. Show myself naked and exposed – to myself. You," he looked up at me heavily – "can you guess?"

"You want me to guess?" I asked.

"Try!" He slapped his hand on the table, as if proposing an ambitious and dangerous wager. There was a hunted look in his eyes, as if he was flinching from something unseen, heavy, menacing. I answered him calmly:

"You're running away. Escaping. All the time – you're on the run."

He froze, his little, cetaceous eyes scanning the lines of my face, and scanning them again. After a tension-laden silence, an extended silence, he muttered in a cracked, barely audible voice:

"From what?"

"From yourself," I answered him without any change in the tone of my voice.

He struck the wooden desk with unexpected force, and let out a grating cry:

"What madness!"

"It's the only kind of sanity that the senses are capable of offering," I replied genially.

"You're suggesting," he said in a faltering voice – "we should get away from the senses?"

"Control them," I answered him.

"And then?" – the grating cry again.

"Outside and inside – will look different."

"So what's going to happen, outside and inside?" he demanded with asperity, in mounting agitation, breathing heavily.

"The outside and the inside will stop dictating your behaviour." I met his gaze steadily.

He snorted and fell silent, and having succeeded in getting a grip on himself, gave me a softer look, which was almost a smile, and asked:

"Don't you belong to some mystical sect?"

"No," I replied.

"Don't get me wrong," he felt the need to explain – "I've got nothing against mystical sects. I don't care if one of my tenants belongs to a mystical sect or a religious denomination or just the Greens... so long as he doesn't fall behind with the rent!" He chuckled amiably and added: "I trust I've made myself clear..."

"Admirably!" I echoed his chuckle.

"As for myself," he began hesitantly and then continued, aware that he wasn't risking anything – "I tried transcendental meditation... for a while. And I stopped. I got the feeling the people running it were just out to make a fast buck. Absolutely nothing to do with mystical enlightenment. Pity!"

"There are other movements," I pointed out.

"One disappointment's enough for me! They were talking about things they didn't even begin to understand!" He shot me an inquisitive glance.

"If the senses are getting in the way," I responded – "they won't have the faintest shadow of an idea."

"Honestly and truly," he said after another pause – "I've nothing against sects, even clandestine sects... not that there's many of those around these days. But there's no doubt you'd be paying me a compliment if you let me in on your little secret! I admire people who put their trust in me!" His look was alert and intent.

"You're making a big mistake!" I declared, my voice strong and vibrant. "I don't belong to any sect whatsoever. If I belonged to a sect, I wouldn't have hesitated to tell you even before I rented your apartment."

"How disappointing!" he exclaimed, and suddenly burst into rolling, resonant laughter:

"That 'Jewish Purity League' – they're going to be really disappointed! What a show that's going to be! I can already see the offended look on their bearded faces. They don't trust anyone, not even themselves, not even their God, in spite of their hare-brained notion that they're under His tutelage and doing His work.

"I believe you!" he continued, sounding thoroughly amused. "But they won't believe me! And there's a funny side to that too... they're world-class experts in threats and extortion! We'll watch the show and I hope we'll enjoy it and not be disappointed. Anyway, you take care! They've latched on to you – they've even got a record of your pulse-rate. They won't hesitate to strike at a moment of distraction or weakness... and they always hit below the belt!" His face shone with fresh, unexpected vitality.

"The whole of this meeting," he added in a light and amicable tone, "this whole conversation, was arranged for this purpose! I exploited your neighbour's gossip about the unlocked door – as an excuse. Knowing about your cash-card helped as well...

"Don't get me wrong," he went on, glancing at me obliquely – "I admit that everything I've said, including my offer, has just been a spring-board to get to the main issue – the revelation of the truth that I so much wanted to have revealed – not for the sake of that narrow-minded clique, but for myself, first and foremost for myself – but the offer is still valid.

"As for the conversation that we've had, I've enjoyed it and I've learned something from it too. And going back to the subject of mysticism, it was members of that association who pressed me to meet and talk to you. Speaking for myself – I despise them.

"And they know it too. Grit their teeth and say nothing. The tales they could tell about me are nothing compared to the tales I could tell about them. Anyway, if you had belonged to some sect, I'd have told them. I always play a fair game! That's my way of shafting my enemies, and there's no shortage of them. Strange as it may sound, that's the way I like it! It makes me feel younger, ready for a good scrap... the idea of ever being left without enemies – what a ghastly thought!" For a moment I had the impression that he was talking to himself, veering between pleasure and sorrow and utterly oblivious to his surroundings.

"I have friends too. Not many, I have to admit. I mean, friends that I consider friends. Not that they see themselves as my friends. No, there aren't any like that. Not even in the family. People who can be trusted, I'm talking about."

He raised his little eyes and looked at me steadily:

"You're one of my friends. Whether you like it or not – that's how I've got you pigeon-holed!"

"If I had been a member of some sect," I pointed out lightly, "that pigeon-holing wouldn't have helped me!"

"The two things are quite unconnected!" he declared solemnly, and it was clear he meant it.

"Anything can happen to a friend of mine, his fault or otherwise, but that doesn't

stop him being my friend, because the pigeon-holing is one-sided, imposing no obligation whatsoever on the 'pigeon'... But," he hastened to add, as if the previous sentence needed toning down, "I'm glad you don't belong to a sect. And it's not for your sake that I'm glad – it's them that I'm thinking of. This will take the wind out of their sails. And all the surveillance, and the detective work and the eavesdropping and all the money spent – wasted! They're very sensitive about money, they bow down to it, like in the days of the Golden Calf!" He chuckled dryly, stared at a point behind my shoulder, and commented:

"I'm already enjoying the look on their faces... looking forward to the shock, the devastating impact... the wet frog they'll be forced to swallow! And now it's time for us to part company, my dear friend Adon! What an extraordinary name you have!" He seemed suddenly exhausted, utterly drained, his wrinkled face grey and beaded with tiny drops of sweat. His pale eyes tried, in vain, to retain some vigour and humour. His shaking hand probed and found a little button on the desk, and he pressed it.

In the frame of a side-door, blending neatly into the padded surface of the high wall, a middle-aged woman appeared, her face pale and dignified.

"Ask the gentleman to sign the memorandum of agreement that's been prepared," he said, indicating with a movement of his big, close-cropped head that I should follow in the lady's footsteps.

"What agreement is that?" I asked.

"A two months rent moratorium in exchange for your trip to Jerusalem. I trust you'll have an enjoyable journey," he said and saw fit to add: "I'm not in the habit of leaving loose ends!"

"I might not have agreed!" I pointed out, with a smile.

"Then we'd have chucked the memo in the bin, wouldn't we!" was his hearty response.

We parted with a firm handshake.

The memorandum seemed reasonable enough. He had already signed it. I added my signature, took one of the copies and went out into the alley.

WEDNESDAY AFTERNOON

On the Wednesday, during the second week following Rahamim's departure for his vacation, at a late hour of the afternoon, as I was setting out the rinsed cups and glasses, an intense feeling of foreboding rose up in me, and rapidly grew heavier. Air seemed to refuse to penetrate the compressed lungs, the beating of the heart slowed, the limpid light in the empty void of the café seemed to thicken, and my eyes dimmed.

The hand that held a cup, about to put it down on the shiny enamel tray, remained suspended in the air.

I calculated swiftly. Three possibilities were open before me: to leave the café at once, to lock the door and shut myself inside, to ignore it, paying no attention to the whole business – and whatever was likely to happen here in the next few minutes – and carry on as usual. Time was pressing, and demanded rational consideration and a firm decision.

I smiled a tender and hearty smile into the illuminated void of the café, glanced at the heavy glass door which unlike its predecessor – secured by means of a whole series of heavy iron bolts and bars – was dependent on a single keyhole. The long key was lodged in the hole, on the inside. To run and retrieve it or leave it where it was? – the thought that flashed through my mind was bizarre and without logical foundation.

I placed the cup upside down on the clean enamel tray. The decision had been taken and the foreboding retreated, dissolved and disappeared as if it had never been. Lungs breathed easily, the heart beat with the rhythm of radiant delight, the true and immortal delight.

As I turned to look at the half-open door, Shuki appeared on the threshold.

For a long moment he stood there as if rooted. He seemed to be weighing something up, thinking it through, silently, like someone whose decision isn't yet ripe, and who still has time to change and reconsider. And this in the light of significant changes in the terrain, which simply haven't been foreseen from the start, nor taken into account. With the light of the lamp and the darkness outside, he seemed to be standing on the borderline between them, a black, thick shadow.

When he finally stepped forward into the café, still without saying a word, his face was exposed to the light – tormented and contorted, unshaven. A number of tiny, reddish-pink swellings sprouted around his lower lip. His flat forehead was beaded with drops of sweat and his eyes blazed as if gripped by a fever, darting around in their sockets endlessly, aimlessly, like little animals caught in a trap. His hands and arms were trembling – held stiffly against his body in a tense and unnatural pose, as if seeking support for themselves or perhaps, some evidence that they were still there and in working order. Shuki himself seemed to be walking as if in a dream, unconscious and relieved of any responsibility, especially towards himself. His shabby shirt was torn, and there was a fresh cut in his trousers near the right knee.

"Adon", he began in a heavy whisper, "I didn't come here to get rid of you! Not tonight, anyway… Forget what I said before! That was just empty pride talking… although," – he chose to point out stubbornly – "I'm a man of my word and one day… I shall definitely carry it out! But, not now…" he added, "no, not now…" – his voice crackled, hoarsely.

"I came to ask for help! After all, Adon is always ready to offer help – without checking the small print, without arguments and excuses and demanding evidence… Adon isn't out to make an impression. Impressions aren't what he's about!" – he chuckled a brief, venomous chuckle

"I need money!" he declared, his voice seeming to clear. "A considerable sum," he added – "and you're going to give it to me, 'cos you have no choice! Neither have I. And time is short. Time is running, running out… And there's a few things I have to tell you, so you'll understand what's going on here and just how urgent it is!" He was making an effort, an effort he was trying to conceal, to add vigour to his voice while retaining its relative clarity:

"I tried to steal some money. I broke into a clothes store. In the centre. A big boutique. With cash registers. Usually, they're crammed full of notes. Today the banks are closed, and the money stays in the registers. I had it all worked out! Like a Swiss watch… I'm an expert in these things!" – he declared with desperate bravado, like a cockerel, plucked of his last feather, naked and forlorn, perching on a branch and stretching out his neck, attempting to crow as before.

"I stole a car... it's outside! It's going to be evidence against me... I didn't have any choice, you see, and time is pressing!" He was panting now, uttering staccato, guttural sounds like someone liable at any moment to lapse into unconsciousness. Despite this he managed to maintain a reasonable clarity of voice:

"I broke through the lot!" he cried. "Shop, doors, cash registers... and on the way out I smashed a display window – just to set the alarms off! But those storekeepers are mean bastards!" he yelled, incandescent with bitter rage, taking a deep breath and explaining:

"They only left coins in there. A few paltry cents... I picked them all up, I was that desperate... Look!" He drew a handful of coins of various sizes from his deep pocket and flung them at me.

The coins scattered on the ancient floor of the café, tinkling metallically, and rather melodiously as they rolled, turning on their faces, spinning on their axes, and finally coming to rest in whichever corner they had reached.

"And then I decided you were my last hope!" – he tried to wink at me sardonically – "My only hope! For a long time now I've been stalking you. I know every move of yours, everything you do for work or for relaxation – when, where, how... I know your route from your workplace to the café and from the café to your home – I know it to the last stone, the last crushed blade of grass!

"It wasn't to ask for help that I've been doing all this thorough surveillance," he declared with an air of superiority – "and without you having the faintest idea what I was up to!" He repeated his venomous chuckle and reckoned he was obliged to clarify: "There are some people who haven't betrayed me. At least – in theory. And they do me favours. Still. I'm not going to demean myself, crawling after you like that seedy detective in the movies... What I'm doing now is degrading enough. But I can face it.

"I know everything about you!" he cried with turbid enthusiasm. "At every moment of the day – I'm with you!" he added solemnly – "Living, breathing, thinking... trying to think, I should say... And all this, so I can keep my promise to you!" The sickly flash of his eyes swept over my face, his expression bearing the clear, intense imprint of sheer malice. "Remember?" – and without waiting for a response he continued, his voice a little hushed:

"I promised you I was going to murder you!" – and in a different tone, tense and alert, he added: "When the times comes, in a place of my choosing and a situation of my choosing... and I'll leave you no chances! You'll have nowhere to run! No 'line-up' in the world is going to save you this time, or any other power come to that..." He was wheezing like a cracked pair of bellows, exhausted by the effort of speaking. He wiped sweat from his brow, before resuming, foam glistening at the corners of his blue lips, and fringing the necklace of livid growths on the lower lip:

"You can't keep dodging me! I need a fix! I'm going mad. I'm already mad!" he yelled in real pain. "Any moment now, I'll be going berserk! I'll smash everything in sight, rip it to shreds, commit arson, violent assault and murder without a twinge of conscience. What do you think of that, eh?" – he repeated his piercing shriek.

"Adon," he looked up at me with tormented eyes, flashing maniacally: "You must help me! And quickly. They're already on my trail... I left traces... a lot of traces! The security alarm and the stolen car and the witnesses, plenty of witnesses! And I have to have that fix. I need the money!" he cried, suddenly dropping to the floor and shuffling towards me on his knees, sweaty hands raised in supplication, whimpering in a voice that was barely holding back the tears:

"Help me, Adon! I promise I'll change my ways! It's a promise. My solemn vow! I won't steal, I won't murder. Your life is given back to you, so make the most of it! I won't hurt you. As long as I live. Despite my former promise, from this moment on – it's cancelled absolutely. Help me! I won't hurt anyone else either. I'll set Lili free. Once and for all. She'll be yours, yours exclusively. Which is what she wants, deep down, despite anything she says or does... I know, I know that wonderful heart of hers! She'll be yours forever. I won't do her any harm, on the contrary, I'll protect her forever, if I have to die in the attempt. I'll protect you too... all the vulnerable people. Shuki will be a changed man! As he always wanted to be and as he really is! Try me, Adon! Try me! Give me money!"

I approached him, gripped him under the arms and pulled him to his feet. As he leaned on me trembling and feverish, it seemed for a moment he was about to burst into tears. I slapped his shoulder encouragingly. He recoiled from me, scanned me with a manic look and cried:

"Will you give me?"

"I've no money of my own, except a few coins that won't be much use to you – and other people's money – I'm not going to touch," I explained.

His face crumbled:

"What can I do?" he asked like a scared, helpless child.

"In my humble opinion, you should go to the police station and turn yourself in. They'll look after you. They'll take account of your special circumstances."

Shuki glowered, bowed his head and withdrew further from me.

"What about the cash-card?" he asked in a cracked voice.

"Cancelled!" I replied.

"You're not touching the money in the cash register?"

"No," I answered him softly but firmly.

"If that's the way it is," he looked up, and on his face, the colour of earth, there was a twisted, venomous smile: "I'll take it myself! That way your hands will be clean!" he added, with emphatic scorn.

"The money was entrusted to me," I smiled back at him – "and I shall look after it!"

"You mean that seriously?" He looked me up and down, appraisingly, and suddenly his expression stabilised; the fever seemed to flee from his face and it was as if all the limbs of his body were charged with an unseen force of brute energy, strong as steel, reflected in the cold, menacing flash of his eyes, staring at me with assured contempt.

"I'm being completely serious," I answered him without altering the tone of my voice, gentle and firm as ever, and leaving no room for any doubt.

"In that case," Shuki began solemnly, with emphatic slowness, drawing out every word – "things are looking different, entirely different..." He smiled his confident smile again, all malice and the hedonistic love of evil – and yet at the same time, incredibly, there was a distant flicker of something hesitant, and purely human.

With a sharp and vigorous turn and measured tread, neither deviating nor hesitating, he approached the heavy glass door, closed it with a slam, locked it with the key inside, extracted the key and stuffed it in his trouser pocket. And when he turned to face me again, his arms were stretched out sideways, like the winds of a big bird of prey swooping on its victim, and in his right hand – the flashing blade of a razor.

His face had changed beyond recognition: where before there had been contortion and torment, suffused with despair and acute awareness of failure – all was now animated, keen and alert, suffused with evil assurance, smiling a smile of provocative malice.

"Adon!" he cried in a clear, level voice, almost jauntily – "Your life in the flesh is coming to an end!" – and he took a few short steps towards me, without lowering his arms. His gait was agile, tense, like a choreographed dance – or perhaps the way that a tiger stalks an antelope, before pouncing.

"I think," he added without shifting his gaze from me – "you're really helping me! Fulfilling all my expectations... delivering me from depression! And this will be to your credit, your very great credit, when in just a few moments from now you'll be knocking on the gates of your Garden of Eden... if you really believe in it, that is!" He grinned.

I didn't respond.

Some distance from me, propped against the counter, were the broom and the floor-mop, with its solid aluminium shaft. Without attracting his attention, I shifted to within half a pace of these implements. Both were now within reach.

"As for me," Shuki continued as if talking to himself – "Hell will be fine by me! What I should say is I'm used to it, here, in this world!" He took another step forward, his eyes scornful, predatory. "In the next world," – he kept the train of thought going – "there'll be no surprises for me! I hate novelties!" He chuckled his venomous chuckle, this time suffused with a sure sense of supremacy and victory.

"I could take the money without touching you!" he announced suddenly, advancing on the cash register with two brisk hops, making no sound at all.

I exploited the moment and without hesitation, grabbed hold of the floor-mop and with just one quick sideways step, blocked his path to the register, with my back to it, and facing him.

"Aha!" cried Shuki. "You really think that if I wanted to take the money without touching you – I'd have told you?" Again he laughed that cold, contemptuous laugh of his, emerging from immeasurable depths..

"You don't know Shuki!" he hissed – "And you're going to leave this world without ever getting to know him!" A trace of disappointment crept into his voice, which might have been sincere, or adopted to give stronger emphasis to his crude mockery and confidence. "I'm not really interested in the money any more... not that much!" he corrected himself in time, with a thin smile. "Now I'm finding something else... surprising... no, not surprising..." he amended, taking another step towards me – "I'd call it sensational! Positively sensational. The pleasure I get from shooting up," he explained to himself, "isn't the most potent pleasure in the world! I thought, till this very moment, I was addicted to drugs, dependent on them, an eternal slave... without atonement, without a saviour... And now, you see," he gestured with his eyes, pointing to himself with the flashing razor – "I'm having fun! I'm different. I feel the thrill flowing in my blood-stream and inflaming all my hormones, the greatest of all thrills! The hardest of all hard drugs couldn't even compete! No more drugs! Look – I'm weaned of drugs!" He poured out the words in a low voice, in a kind of heavy, lascivious whisper, crude and menacing, inspired by loathing of the world and indefinable evil.

"I shall slit your throat," he informed me calmly, in a level tone, as if revealing an intimate secret to a dear friend – "the way only I know how! A clean job!" he boasted, brandishing the razor a little closer to me – "I shall put this blade to your throat, and it will be easy and smooth and as fast as lightning! And your blood will flow!" he declared with obvious elation – "On this floor, and on the counter, and on the clean cups you've arranged so nicely, and it's going to splash all over the cash box – which I shall empty to the very last cent" – his eyes burned with a venomous flame – "I'm going to spend it all too – this very night! And this I shall do with the utmost pleasure, knowing that you went to your end in a state of misery, depression and despair, having failed to conserve your friend's money. This money that was entrusted to you out of stupidity and incomparably flippant irresponsibility!" He chuckled, made a threatening gesture with the hand holding the razor, and advanced another step or two, circling me.

"God, what a pleasure this is!" he uttered a cry of vibrant ecstasy, high-pitched and piercing the void of the café like the screech of a night-bird swooping on its prey – and retracted it immediately:

"Why should I call on 'God'? He abandoned me years ago... It's Satan I should be invoking!" He circled around me, forcing me to move with him.

"But," he went on, "I don't believe in him either... is there a devil greater than Shuki?" – he fired the question into the empty, silent void of the café and without waiting for a reply he continued: "And if I'm the devil, why should I call on him. And I... I tell you this," he addressed me with a surprisingly earnest expression, a childish appeal for trust – "I'm not Satan... and God really did abandon me, deserted me... But the pleasures that He's endowed me with!" – he had some difficulty curbing his enthusiasm – "Perverted, yes, and flawed, but pleasures all the same. He has a special way of doing this... I don't mean your God!" he berated me and added at once with a change of tone and expression: "He's not mine either. I have neither God nor Devil, I don't even have myself... Just these pleasures, that I'm addicted to, enslaved to them to the marrow of my bones! And they're burning me alive on their satanic pyre and I... I love it! Always finding new kinds of experience to enjoy! Don't you agree that in this very thing, the endless quest for new forms of pleasure – there's something of the truly divine?"

He gave me a quizzical, steady look, grinned – and lunged.

I took a firm grip on the aluminium tube and fended him off with a vigorous and decisive movement. He reeled backwards, slipped on the tiles which were still wet and fell, almost losing his hold on the razor.

Somehow he got back to his feet and confronted me again, shaking, arms and legs splayed, still gripping the open-bladed razor, eyes dancing in their sockets, full of despair and gloom. I advanced on him, the shaft of the mop still in my hands, held horizontally. He retreated a pace or two, with a light and calculated movement, retaining something of his predatory agility.

At that moment the silent void of the café was ripped apart by a series of thunderous blows landing on the outside door. The knocking didn't let up for a moment but grew ever louder and heavier, discharging deafening fusillades.

I was following Shuki's movements and paying no attention to the commotion outside. The same couldn't be said of him. With a quick, sidelong look he immediately understood the significance of the blows that were shaking the door of the café.

"The cops!" he exclaimed. "Like I said, time's running out, and it's all over... No!" he yelled as if rebuking himself – "It's now or never!" and with this battle-cry he went for me again, the razor poised in his hand. I had no difficulty fending him off with the mop. He lost his balance and fell, rolling over on the floor until his body collided with the locked door.

I approached him; his contorted body was flailing about in his desperate attempts to stand and resume the attack. Through the glass door I saw policemen – some in uniform and some in the unmistakable attire of the "plain clothes" branch. One of the latter drew a revolver and seemed intent on shooting the lock.

"Wait a moment!" I shouted, waving my arms. He saw me in time, and changed his mind momentarily, although it was clear that the idea of shooting out the lock still appealed to him.

I bent over Shuki. He was fully conscious, acutely so. His expression seemed to have cleared completely. With surprising awkwardness, with a kind of apologetic smile, he inserted a shaking hand into the pocket of his trousers, drew out the long key, with an effort, and handed it to me:

"Go on," he said in a cracked, abrupt voice – "open up..."

I took the key and helped him to his feet. He put the razor in his pocket and walked with me to the glass door.

The whole pack of policemen, uniformed and in mufti alike, swarmed in at once, pushing me aside and pouncing on Shuki; within moments his hands were encased in gleaming handcuffs.

The detective who had intended to shoot the lock, the revolver still in his hand, was having difficulty controlling his nerves; with the heavy butt of his magnum he began pistol-whipping Shuki about the head. Shuki fell down but managed to get up again, a thin trickle of fresh blood streaming down his cheek and dripping to the floor. Without saying a word, Shuki turned to the detective who had assaulted him, and spat in his face. The other wiped the spittle from his cheek and tried to attack him again but his colleagues restrained him, pinioning his arms and separating him forcibly from their prisoner.

Taking advantage of the confusion, Shuki turned back to me with a strange smile, a blend of arrogance and goodwill, and declared in a hushed but clearly audible voice:

"We shall meet again, Adon, and then – it will be the end!" He didn't know how right he was.

Initially, Shuki was charged with breaking into the boutique, stealing a car and resisting arrest. But about a week later, a far more serious indictment was lodged against him – the double murder, dating back three years, of the notorious pimp Gabriel and his girl Rita. As I subsequently discovered, one of the new gangster bosses, having decided to be rid of Shuki once and for all, exploited the opportunity and pressurised one of his former "boys", who had been a witness to the murder, to testify against him. Rather than charging him as an accessory, which could have led to imprisonment and possible reprisals at Shuki's hands, the authorities granted him immunity as a State's witness.

RAHAMIM'S RETURN

I went down early to Rahamim's café, as this was the day he was due to return from his extended vacation. I was determined that the café would be set up in good order to welcome its proprietor back. But there wasn't a lot that needed doing; already the rinsed mugs and tea-cups glistened on the trays and the rest was likewise clean and neatly arranged – kettles, jugs, cutlery, plates, stove, brass cylinders containing tea, coffee, sugar, juices and condiments.

I shifted a few tables and benches into their regular positions, tipped bucketfuls of water over the ancient, cracked tiles, and they smiled back at me with a cheerful air of contentment. Two gentle rays of light filtered through the pair of skylights, placed high up at the apex of the arched ceiling, laying broad bands of brown and blue on the tiles, the colours of the thick stained glass. Through the broad, wide-open door the sea was visible; bright surf riding on the backs of the rising waves, breaking on the beach and rushing on, whooping like a mischievous child pursued in a game by his doting parents. The salty sea air, fresh and free, redolent with the delights of unexplored distances, wafted into the café and filled all the empty spaces.

Rahamim arrived at a late hour of the afternoon. He was affable and relaxed, and even the colour of his face had changed – turning pink and shiny, reflecting a sunny mood. His broad smile exposed the flash of a gold crown as he shook my hand, warmly and energetically:

"Thank you!" he cried. "I thank you with all my heart! It's been wonderful. To get away from it all, if only for a short space of time... and more important – to miss it all!" He surveyed the concrete walls of the café with a glance of deep affection, and tears sparkled in his mottled eyes.

"I'm so glad to be back!" he declared in a vibrant voice – "and once again, thanks!" He moved on to inspect his counter.

"And how is your wife?" I asked.

"She enjoyed it too!" he replied. "Admittedly, she never stopped talking... you see, it's not often we're together like that... twenty-four hours a day, for a whole month! At first I listened, then – I pretended to listen... in the end – I stopped even doing that. But she didn't seem to mind, and she just carried on. I get out to meet people, you see, in the café I mean, while she's stuck within those four walls, year after year. Mind you, recently she's had guests to look after – Nessim and his family. But that's only a recent development."

"How is Nessim?" I asked.

"He's fine..."A slight frown wrinkled his brow and quickly disappeared.

"Still staying with you?"

"That's right," he confirmed, adding hastily – "but it seems he's planning to move."

"Has he found an apartment?"

"No," Rahamim replied, while checking out the stove, igniting a flame, adjusting it and finally extinguishing it.

"Where's he moving to, then?" I persisted.

"He's going back," he declared, bending down and inspecting the contents of the little fridge at the corner of the counter.

"Back where?"

"To his old apartment," was the reply. "It seems," Rahamim added – "that something's changed around there. But he'll still be coming here. In fact, he should be turning up some time in the next hour, maybe less, and he can tell you himself. Not one of the world's most reticent men!" Rahamim smiled. He inspected the floor, and was impressed:

"That's been thoroughly cleaned!" He flashed me a look of gratitude, adding: "In fact, the whole place is spotless! You've been working hard..."

"That was the deal," I replied.

"You deserve a bonus!" he commented.

"We had a deal!" I responded. "We should stick to it – both of us!" I added, smiling.

"If you say so!" he exclaimed, as if accepting the verdict, and immediately went on to say in a clear, almost aggressive tone: "I want to tell you something in all seriousness." He looked up at me with eyes that seemed to have sunk deeper into their sockets, but were as wise, sincere and understanding as ever – "Whenever you feel like it, you're welcome to help out here!"

"It will be my pleasure!"

"On one clear condition..." He scanned me with that radiant and steady look, guarding against any attempt to cavil at his words, or to take them in the wrong spirit, and disappoint him.

"Which is?" I inquired.

"You accept payment!" he insisted, trying to keep on holding my eye.

"That's a different matter!" I commented, and in a tone that was vibrant and forceful in equal measure, I suggested: "Let's agree that when I'm short of money, I'll work here for pay, and when I don't need it, I'll come along and help you out – a favour between friends!"

He scrutinised the lines of my face with a quizzical, somewhat stern look, then bowed his head and declared:

"Your offer – does you credit! I accept."

We shook hands again to seal this new accord.

About an hour later, Nessim appeared. He too was in a perky mood, and even his thin lips were tensed from time to time into a rather bashful smile.

"I've been to see Moshe Leon," I told him, having responded to his polite greeting.

He was sitting close to me, by the thick glass of the wide-open door, with its vista of the sea kissing its horizons, all energy and glorious freedom.

"Yes," Nessim confirmed that he had heard this and added: "He took a deposit off me!"

"He wants to give it back."

Nessim stared at me, utterly bemused:

"How many times have I asked him to give it back! And he's been giving me the runaround... in fact, he claimed that until he managed to let the apartment that the deposit had been paid on – there was no point going to him and asking for it!"

"Maybe the apartment has been let," I commented, a hint of puzzlement creeping into my own voice.

"He's converting it into a warehouse," Nessim retorted. "He's a cunning guy all right, a schemer. All he likes to do – is play with people, put them in awkward situations, see how they react... and sometimes – throw an unexpected punch. I danced to his tune until that meeting we were supposed to be having with his lawyer. I shafted him!" – Nessim chuckled, a hoarse, colourless laugh – "I took great pleasure in shafting him – so he'd know even little people like me deserve respect!" And in a changed voice, he explained:

"As for the deposit – it's a paltry sum! I don't need it. I hope it gives him heartburn! He'll pay it back eventually... when he catches up with me. In the meantime, he can chase me. It won't do him any harm! He needs the exercise! I used to run after him, and he'd avoid me or simply refuse to see me. In a word – he chucked me. Now it's his turn. When I see him, I always suggest he leases the apartment again... not that I mean it..." he thought it necessary to stress – "but it's an excuse, or more like – a way of bugging him! 'Cos I owe him that, and how! The laughs he used to have at my expense! But that's when I was interested. I swallowed it all. Said nothing. Pretended. Inside I was telling myself: I'll be getting even with you, dear boss, I'll be getting even!

"When I suggested he let the apartment again, like I said, without any serious intention on my part – he used to shake that heavy, square head of his to show his categorical refusal and he used to say with all the authority and gravitas of a boss and a dictator, someone whose word everyone obeys: The best I can offer you is a stable! – implying I'm some kind of animal that doesn't deserve inclusion among the sophisticated elite of society, and should be content with a shed!"

"And though he fancies himself as a gentleman and an aristocrat," Nessim continued in a tone of bitter derision – "to this very day he's refrained from paying the debt that he owes me. He could send it by messenger, or through you, even! It's another of his arsenal of tricks – to get me back into his office, face to face, and preferably – on my knees...

"So I'm exploiting this to my own advantage," Nessim's face suddenly lit up with a kind of distant, but tangible satisfaction. "It wouldn't ever occur to him to suspect anything," he chuckled. "What really matters is, he's not going to forget me! He's going to remember me in vivid detail, and I don't care if it's for good or bad. So he'll recognise me straightaway, and if my name is so much as mentioned in his presence – he'll know who's being talked about. 'Cos he's a man of wealth and influence... and there's no knowing when a solid citizen like you or I will need someone like that, a Moshe Leon, with his wealth and his influence... As our sages said: The wise man is he who sees what is hatching!"

"I hear you're intending to move back to your former apartment," I commented, deciding it was time for a change of subject.

"In the very near future!" he replied and added: "Conditions have changed, the circumstances and everything..." He glanced at me briefly, quizzically, and went on to say: "A new boss has turned up. He knows his business, knows how the job's done, all the stuff he has to take on board, shows some consideration... And my former role and status, obviously, mean that I'm in demand! I'm talking about my presence, my advice, my contribution..." he explained.

"People in the neighbourhood told him about me, and he was impressed. And he came to see me, turned up in person at Uncle Rahamim's house and brought presents – for me, the wife, my daughters and son. He didn't forget anyone. Expensive presents too. He must have spent five hundred on us, maybe more!

"You can tell he's a guy with class! Solid foundations, I mean. The kind you can rely one. He even said he was sorry I'd had to leave in such a hurry. Things like that won't be going on any more! he told me. He was laughing when he said it, but you could tell from his dignified manner that he meant it, the word of a man of honour. Things like that won't be going on any more! – meaning there'll be no more ructions of the Shuki variety. He himself, the new boss, is healthy and normal and like I said, he knows his job. And he's not on drugs either – not an addict, not even a user. Sure – he makes a handsome profit out of human weakness, but he doesn't touch the stuff himself. He's immune!"

"I've heard about him," I commented quietly, adding: "He's the one who put pressure on one of Shuki's former 'boys' to act as State's witness in the double murder charge that he's facing."

Nessim turned to me and scanned my face with wide-open eyes. This information came as a total surprise to him. But finally he regained some composure, adopted a secretive look, lowered his eyes and responded with clear reluctance:

"That was him?" and at once he saw fit to add: "In fact, there was no need for that."

"Why?" I asked.

"Haven't you heard?" – he looked up and studied my face again, this time with thin scorn and a clear expression of superiority.

"I've heard nothing," I said, providing justification for his repressed satisfaction.

"Shuki," he began, the tone of his voice solemn and emphatic, as he keenly checked the impression his words were making on me – "Shuki is in hospital!"

"Has he been assaulted?" I asked.

"Not by any human agency," he went on to say with the same childish solemnity, without relaxing his scrutiny of my face, milking to the very limit that strange, teasing pleasure that any imagined superiority is liable to confer upon the one who feels it.

"By whom then?" I went on to ask, unimpressed.

The answer came promptly:

"By the One who sits on High!"

"He's had an accident?"

"Some accident!" he chuckled again, but as I asked no more questions, a lukewarm, colourless silence fell between us. For me the conversation was over, but not for him.

"Shuki has fallen victim to that disease – that terrible new disease, the one that gays go down with..." he muttered, as if he couldn't remember what it was called.

"Aids." I finished the sentence for him.

"Haids," he echoed, inaccurately, and as if offended by his failure to remember the name of the disease, fell silent for a moment before continuing:

"Not that Shuki was gay... perish the thought! But he sometimes messed around with men who were! He tried out all the bodily pleasures – without recognising any limit. He was addicted to them, and in the end they destroyed him. The wonder is that he lasted as long as he did. Stupid sod!" He tried, again without success, to adopt a tone of resigned tolerance.

"Not long ago," I reminded him – "you wouldn't have dared call him that, even in your own head!"

For a moment he was taken aback, evidently confused, and he looked down as if working something out in his mind, before finally lifting his tiny eyes again, putting the artificial smile on his face and asserting with all the confidence he could muster:

"That time is long gone! We, we're living in the present. And the future is before us. And the fear of this man, that he used to impose over the whole neighbourhood and outside it too – has faded. It's been wiped away as if it never was. Mention of his name these days arouses only tolerant smiles… and relief. In the not so distant past – as you say – his name alone was enough to transfix people with dread. Times change!" he concluded with a sigh of relief – "and so they should!

"Incidentally," he turned to me again abruptly, with a keen look, masking a hint of menace: "Not long ago he sent one of his hitmen to the neighbourhood… and he searched and searched, but couldn't find the one he was supposed to be sorting out. At first we thought he was after the new boss, or the boy who grassed on him, who's under the full protection of the new boss. And the boss took all the necessary measures, quietly, under the surface, in the cleverest of ways – admirable really!" Nessim was unstinting in his fulsome praise of the new boss.

"Until they all realised it wasn't the boss he was out to get, or the boy who grassed. So they let him go on looking. And he went on looking, turning this way and that, inquiring, demanding, subtly and openly, using all the clever professional tricks these guys keep up their sleeves – and still couldn't find him!" Nessim grinned again and added smugly:

"Shuki," it seems, "had gone off the rails completely! He gave him a duff description, or the wrong name, or both. Maybe he couldn't remember the name of the man he so wanted to waste!" He fell silent a moment.

Rahamim, who had approached in the meantime and taken a seat beside his nephew, caught part of what he had said and interjected:

"And how did the episode end?"

Nessim smiled what could almost have been described as a cunning smile, and replied:

"The one who was looking, the hitman I mean, finally began asking questions openly, without any caution, asking everyone who was prepared to answer him – about a thin man, short of build, nasty and argumentative, who calls himself 'King' and goes around pretending to be some kind of holy man, living somewhere round there… When the word got out, everyone laughed…"

The day was turning to evening. A pale star, close by, began spreading its silvery gleam on the infinite blue of the sky, which had deepened and without any perceptible transition, turned from royal blue to solemn purple.

One after another, singly or in small groups, café customers started arriving and entering the hall, shaking Rahamim's hand and giving him the traditional welcome, asking after his health and his wife's, the faces of all radiant with the pleasure of seeing him again.

The café filled up, and when a round moon climbed at the fringes of the sky, solemn and stately, the place was already packed.

The fishermen were all here, as were some neighbours and acquaintances of Rahamim's whom I'd never met before. And they were all served tea or coffee, according to their preference and custom, on the house, and they drank pleasurably, with eyes half-closed. They exchanged a quiet word or two, plying Rahamim with questions about the Dead Sea, its landscape, sky and shores, and the therapeutic qualities for which it was renowned worldwide, and asking whether his wife had been cured and how this famous sea, situated at the bottom of the world, had affected him, personally. And in fact, this last question was superfluous, since the colour of his face confirmed more eloquently than any words the truth of everything said in praise of that strange sea, where no one sinks and no fish swim. And they also asked Rahamim if he had missed his café, all assuring him they had missed him sorely. Not that the drinks served in his absence had tasted inferior, far from it – the speakers shot me sidelong glances of friendship and appreciation, adding that he, Rahamim, was a fixture among them; they were used to him just as he was used to them – habits, smiles, speech, styles of drinking and smoking – as if the café, Rahamim and they, were one single entity.

And Rahamim, for his part, admitted he had missed the café and its customers, although he had enjoyed it there, and the issue of his wife's health had been paramount. Still, he was overjoyed to be back among them, sitting with them between the benign, familiar, concrete walls of the café, and serving them their favourite drinks, according to their taste, and drinking with them as in former days. Since at the end of the day, they and he and the café were one – and the absence of any component impaired the whole. And he invited them all to another round of drinks, announcing that this festive evening, everything was on the house.

The atmosphere in the café was warm, suffused with pleasure and sated with vibrant brotherhood and friendship, such as few of them had known before or even imagined possible. They realised just how dear Rahamim was to them, as dear as the good, solid and ever-welcoming walls of his café.

And Raphael said:

"Sometimes, something needs to be slightly impaired, so you'll be all the happier when it's made whole again!"

And Avinoam answered him:

"Alas for the happiness that depends on the impairment of something!" and he turned to me with a significant look, inviting a response.

"Happiness that depends on something or is given by someone – isn't happiness at all!" I declared.

"What is it then?" asked Israel from his shady corner.

"Pain," I replied.

"Why is it pain?" Raphael asked with interest, and Avinoam too was tense and alert to hear the answer.

"Because of the dependence on 'something' or 'someone'…"

"What of it?" – rose the anonymous voice of someone who had squeezed into the shadowy, southern corner of the café, his features obscured by the gloom.

"Because when the 'something' or the 'someone' lets you down – your happiness is lost!" Avinoam hastened to reply on my behalf.

"Well, memory remains," the occupant of the dark corner persisted.

"Which is the perpetual pain of the loss of the happiness, that was irrevocably dependent on 'something' or 'someone'," I replied.

"And another kind of happiness exists?" Rahamim joined in the conversation. I turned to face him.

"The other happiness is the only one," I answered.

"Few experience it, if any do at all!" Raphael commented obstinately.

"And the one who hasn't experienced it," I turned to face him full on – hasn't the faintest idea what happiness is!

"And what can be comprehended except by means of the senses?" – the voice of Gabriel was heard from a corner, and Nono, sitting beside him, supported him in his exclamation with vigorous shaking of the head and waving of the hand.

"The truth!" I declared.

Silence descended in the café.

Suddenly, Avinoam tore apart the silence with a high and

impassioned cry:

"Adon! Take pity and be kind and show me the way. Where is it?"

"In your heart!" I declared.

"And what must I do to live beyond the reach of the senses?" he implored me.

"You must love!" – was the answer.

THE MOTHER

I returned home late, went to bed and for a long time was unable to sleep. From time to time, Lili's name would rise to the surface of my consciousness, appearing in elongated, print-style letters, and vanish, leaving behind it a trail of agitation and anxiety.

In the morning, after the routine exercises and breakfast tea, I left the house, went to the nearest public call-box and, having informed the secretary that I'd be absent from work today, set off towards Shuki's neighbourhood.

This time I wasn't shadowed by little boys or girls; there were no old men asking questions, or old ladies staring curiously. Occasionally I encountered the puzzled, slightly indignant look of someone wracking his brains in the effort to remember where and when he had previously come across a face resembling mine.

Without any difficulty I made my way to the house where Shuki's revered mother lived. The gate was half open, hanging slightly askew; one of the hinges had broken or rusted away. I pushed it carefully and entered the yard, which at this hour of the morning seemed to be striving to retain the last moisture of the grey mist that the sea, close at hand, had obligingly bestowed upon it. The chickens scrabbled in corners on both sides of the house, and the cat dozed in an open drawer of the broken wardrobe.

Directly in front of me, deep inside the house, through the wide-open door, I could make out the frozen form of the mother, sitting motionless in her heavy armchair, her one open eye studying my face, with painful intensity. And then I sensed that beyond the fearful paralysis – there was entreaty in her unwavering gaze, and a silent scream. And as I approached her, the flood-gates of that eye were opened, and it filled with tears, streaming down her wizened, earth-coloured cheeks in the tracks of their arid wrinkles and dripping from her pointed chin to her flowery gown.

Hanging round the crone's neck was a clean cloth, like a baby's bib. With great care, with a light and gentle movement, I wiped the tears from her cheeks. There was a flash of intense astonishment in the depths of her open eye, immediately followed by a stubborn effort at self-control. It was an effort that proved successful, and the flow of tears stopped.

Again the old lady scrutinised me with her frozen, still moist eye, and suddenly she let out a screech that could be interpreted as "Thank you".

"Don't mention it!" I replied. "It was nothing."

"Nothing?" – I could just about deduce from her next screech.

"How is Lili?" I asked, with careful enunciation.

No answer came. Instead, tears again filled her eye, and this time she was incapable of stemming them, in spite of her desperate efforts. Again, I wiped her face gently.

That single eye, frozen as it was by paralysis, reflected a sudden surge of mounting tension, which suddenly exploded in a howl – not so much a howl as a fearful scream:

" 'Opital!" the cry echoed in the empty hall.

"Hospital?" I asked, checking my translation.

A short, impatient yelp confirmed this:

" 'Es!"

I gave her a moment to relax before asking, focusing intently on her open eye:

"Which hospital?"

The air of dull tension and mounting stress returned, culminating in a couple of abrupt shrieks which this time were more easily understood – the name of a well-known hospital.

I thanked her profusely.

And after a relatively short pause for recuperation, the old lady quavered something which I interpreted as: "Go to her, hurry!"

"I'm going!" I announced, adding in a tone meant to inspire confidence: "Don't you worry!"

Before going, I thought I should check the state of the house, where she was now left all alone. I went to the larder, finding a reasonable stock of food. The house itself had been cleaned quite recently. The old lady's cry caught up with me:

" 'Bours 'elping!" – and the more impassioned repetition:

" 'Bours 'elping. Go 'er, 'urry!"

I must have grown accustomed to her idiomatic screeches; I had no difficulty translating this as: The neighbours are helping. Go to her, and hurry!

I bent down silently by her paralysed legs, and kissed the hand that lay dead and blue-veined on her faded floral gown.

"I'll take care of Lili! God be with you!" I said, as I rose, turned and left the house – never to return and never to see her again.

Later that morning, after a long crawl by urban bus, and another, inter-city service which seemed equally reluctant to complete its journey and be parted from its passengers, I was walking the long corridors of that central hospital.

The young lady at the information desk answered my question in the affirmative, while giving me a long and meaningful look. She left her cubicle, clearly willing to help, and explained in detail, and with broad hand-gestures, how to find that distant corner where the patient was quartered.

On the upper storey, at the end of a broad and dingy corridor lined by the cold doors of tool cupboards and bed-linen closets, segregated from the public wards, I found the little room and in it a single bed.

From the broad and raised pillow of the bed, a pair of wide-open eyes peered out, the expression of quiet despair and resignation in them receding and diffusing in a beam of light, and something resembling hope, buried at their depths, coming back to life in a vivid surge of delight.

"Adon!" Lili cried, making an effort to sit up in her sick-bed. And all those silly and artificial rigid veils were mercilessly shattered and shed one after the other, in the bright light of sincerity. And their place was taken, for perhaps the first time in this life of hers, by something of her real radiant essence, so pure, so vulnerable and so submissive.

I approached her and held out my hand. She pulled hers away in alarm, as if recoiling from fire, and cried in a vigorous tone of desperation and fear:

"No!" – her voice was cracked and hoarse – "The disease is contagious! That's what they say. In fact, they don't know how it's transmitted," – she softened a little – "but it is contagious. There's no doubt of that! Champion sinners and total reprobates – they're the ones who go down with it..." She grimaced with quiet bitterness, but managed to overcome it, and it was replaced by a young and thin stream of pleasure.

"It isn't transmitted by shaking hands!" I assured her, adding by way of evidence:

"If it was, the doctors and nurses would catch it too!"

"They wear gloves when they treat me," – she smiled – "double layers of gloves!"

She laughed heartily and added: "You're probably right about hand-contact... but I wouldn't want to risk it. Still, if you insist..." Her eyes glowed with a distant lustre.

"I insist!" I replied, smiling.

Without shifting her gaze from my eyes, awkwardly, bashful as a little schoolgirl offering the teacher a flower she has picked for her, for her especially – she held out her hand to me.

I clasped it warmly, a purifying touch.

Once more assailed by that dumb fear she hastily withdrew her hand from mine, and put it well out of harm's way, under the nape of her neck.

I studied her. Her face had changed beyond recognition, having turned very gaunt, suddenly and in a strange and frightening way. Her domed, pure and juvenile forehead was more prominent than ever – like the brow of a skull above empty eye-sockets. Her eyes, big and shining, had sunk very deep.

"I'm not a pretty sight!" she commented with a faint air of bitterness that she hastily erased. "But this is me..." she declared with an apologetic smile and added: "Now, you understand. And as far as I know, my condition's just going to get worse and worse. Tumours will be the next phase... I hope you're not around to see that!" she said earnestly. "When I see you, I'm filled with happiness, a pure sort of happiness that's all light, all song...

"You see," she went on, "when I see you, and especially, seeing you now – I have the feeling that I'm part of a song... I'm inside a song... one of the lines... the last line maybe, but it's like all the others and when it's combined with them – it can never be erased. And this line of mine, you see, together with all the others, has something important to say to this suffering world, something to inspire it with hope, tidings of salvation...

"This salvation and the triumphant tune of this song," – she looked up at me with her horribly sunken eyes, studying me intently – "they are you..." Her cheeks burned, high, aristocratic cheeks, with only skin to cover their delicate bones.

She scanned the lines of my face meticulously, repeated the process, and apparently what she saw gave her profound satisfaction. In her big eyes the pleasure intensified, cramming them until a veil of moisture covered them. She turned her head on the pillow and chuckled – a limpid and joyous chuckle of a special kind, like the laughter of someone who has longed for the sea year after year, and all of a sudden – the sea opens out before him in all its glorious expanse and caresses with its generous breezes, redolent of poetry and of freedom, the face of its beloved.

"Why don't you sit down?" – she pointed to a rickety chair.

I did as she suggested, moving the chair closer to the bed and sitting beside her.

"My heart," she began, "will soon burst – from happiness! And you know the reason for this happiness?" she asked, all radiant.

"Not yet," I replied with a smile. "But I'm prepared to hazard a guess. If that's what you want, of course!"

"Yes, yes, I'd like that! Try!" she cried mischievously, with thin and clear note to her voice, like the rustling of the wind among flowers in the spring, light radiances descending at evening on the waters of a calm and deep lake. The voice that used to be her voice, repressed over the course of the years, silenced as if it had never been, subdued and trampled underfoot as a symbol of weakness and lack of faith in her surroundings... and here, towards the end of her short life, it was showing itself again, pure, clear and overwhelming in its sincerity. "Try!" – she repeated the challenge, with teasing, playground emphasis. "You'll be stumped!"

"Well," I retorted, "I don't think I'm going to be stumped, but let's have a go anyway... The reason for your happiness," I continued with affected solemnity, studying her face which was turned to me in tense attentiveness – "is you!"

" It's me? What's that supposed to mean?" she asked in genuine bemusement.

"You – are happiness!" I declared confidently.

"That isn't what I meant!" she objected. "But..." – she smiled – "you don't like being wrong, do you! So let's say you got a little bit of it right! But the real reason, and it may be mundane, belonging to this world but still – the most important reason, is something else!" She peered at me, and the delight returned to her eyes, radiant as the silvery shimmering of the stars on a moonlight summer's night. There was a plea there as well, wanting me to play the game and ask her the "reason" – so that due solemnity would not be offended, and I could be kept in suspense.

"What is the reason then?" I inquired obediently.

Lili shifted her hand, clutching the back of her neck, which was horribly lean and scrawny, its skin transparent.

"The real reason I'm so happy," – she suddenly turned serious, her eyes lowered and looking away from me – "is that I never slept with you! You know," she added hastily, glancing at me anxiously, "I wanted to! It was the strongest impulse I ever felt. I've never, never known anything like it. I wanted to give myself to you, like they say in books. Willingly, happily, maybe even..." – she pondered for a moment, the look in her eyes entirely sincere – "out of love. I wanted to sacrifice something to you. And I had nothing to give you – other than this body that I despise so much, that I find so hateful and repellent...

"I wanted so much to sacrifice something to you," she repeated, looking away again, "and I didn't know what. There was nothing worth sacrificing... the body, and you didn't want that, neither did I, maybe..." She turned to me with sudden animation, but also with the wondrous equanimity that derives from pure sincerity:

"Can the spirit be sacrificed?"

"No," I answered her.

"Why not," she persisted.

"The spirit, or the soul – is a part of the divine, for ever."

She thought this over, weighing up my words with care, before saying:

"In the Mission, they taught us about the great and terrible Day of Judgment, when the Messiah will come and separate the souls of the righteous from the souls of sinners... those rewarded with everlasting life, and those doomed to eternal damnation..."

"What they omitted to teach you there," I commented, "is how to tell the difference. I mean, who are the sinful souls and who – are the pure..."

"That's quite simple," she replied calmly. "The sinful souls are those who have given way to their impulses, and the pure – are those that haven't!"

"Those are the unhappy souls," I rejoined, smiling

"Which ones?" she asked tensely.

"The ones who haven't contended with their impulses."

"You mean – the ones who haven't given way!" she retorted, as if setting the record straight.

"The one who has contended with his impulses," I answered her gently – "has given way to them. The one who hasn't contended with his impulses, hasn't given way. It's reasonable to suppose," I continued, "that souls which haven't contended with their impulses, will be declared sinful souls and will go down into the outer darkness, whereas all the others will be gathered into God's embrace, having known the bitterness of life and failed to cope with it, because this is beyond the capability of flesh and blood. It's only by the grace of God that impulse can be overcome. Flesh and blood alone," I concluded with emphasis, "can never get the better of impulse."

Lili was listening open-mouthed, impressed as a little girl hearing a fairy-story.

"Have you earned this grace?" she asked finally.

"If I am master of my impulses," I replied, "it means that I have earned it."

"There aren't many who earn it!" she sighed wistfully.

"Everyone who truly longs for it," I stressed, "will earn it!"

"It seems I haven't longed for it," – she declared with a faint air of bitterness – "or I haven't longed for it enough…"

I decided to conclude my remarks on a somewhat solemn note:

"For those obsessed with notions of Heaven and Hell, the Day of Judgment will be a truly marvellous day! A day of surprises, and enlightenment, and revelations of divine grace and divine love. Sinners will be comforted," I explained, "and granted full absolution. Those who have never sinned at all – or like to think of themselves that way – will be put back into the melting-pot of flesh and blood – because they haven't yet experienced it as they should and have failed to learn its lesson, the most important lesson of all."

She gazed into my eyes, delving as deep as she possibly could, holding on and not letting go, intent on staying there forever. Her look was all innocence and purity, and readiness for sacrifice of a kind unknown to me, and love beyond measure. We were silent for a while, as the entire space of the narrow room was radiant with clear and limpid light, such as the eyes of the flesh can never witness.

I scanned her face: the face of a skull with yellowing skin, transparent as parchment, stretched over bones in a desperate attempt to disguise their fragility and protect them. A few thin blue blood-vessels, for some reason refusing to submit, were visible beneath this slender skin, which within a short space of time would be providing a meagre repast for hungry earth-worms.

Lili turned her eyes away, sighed a strange sigh of relief and asked if I had visited Shuki's mother.

I told her. I mentioned the mother's insistence that I go to the hospital at once, and the assurance she had given me that the neighbours were looking after her.

"I very much hope that is so!" said Lili, the anxiety showing in her face. "It all depends on the new boss," she added. "If he prevents her getting help... she'll die in that armchair like a cat nailed to a fence!"

"He has no reason to be unkind to her," I opined, "now that Shuki has been neutralised." I immediately regretted having mentioned Shuki, as I didn't want to burden her with the issue of his illness. But my caution was unnecessary; she knew.

"Poor Shuki!" she exclaimed, and after a long moment of silence went on to say: "He infected me... on purpose, I think. He knew about the disease, and he knew that he had it. And he said nothing. Maybe – not even to himself. And being the kind of guy he is, he went ahead and infected me! At any rate, he made every effort to infect me – and it looks like he succeeded...

"Shuki is such a coward!" – she smiled suddenly, and her yellow face shone again with the faint gleam of distant conciliation, and hidden pleasure – "He's afraid of going to Hell by himself. Even there he wants me standing beside him, to protect him from the tormenting devils!" She grinned, was silent for a moment, then looked up at me with deep-probing eyes and asked:

"Will he too be saved on the Day of Judgment?" – she sounded doubtful.

"If he longs for salvation," I replied, "even if he keeps it a secret, in his heart!"

"There's no one who doesn't long for salvation, deep down in his heart!" she declared solemnly and added: "Even the Devil, I think, secretly longs to be saved!"

"All those who truly yearn for salvation," – I stressed the word truly – "will be saved!" I smiled at her.

"I'm so happy!" she cried, returning my smile, and she added in that surprising buoyancy of spirit: "And what they taught us in the Mission, that God is love – is the truth. Because only love could take pity on worldly sinners such as me, and with boundless grace, send someone like you to meet me in the filthy path that I've been following!

"As for Shuki," she continued with a change of tone – "he's not to be blamed for infecting me! I'm sorry for the nonsense I've been talking! Besides, in the way of life that we lived, Shuki and I, and in my vile profession – how can anyone be sure who did the infecting? It's possible, you see, even a reasonable assumption," – she seemed to be casting about for a fixed point to lean on – "that I infected him and not the other way round... unintentionally, of course.

"But, as soon as the situation became clear to me, I stopped, gave it up altogether, you see – I left the profession, for good! I felt so happy!

"You see," – she made an effort to sit up in her bed and spoke with animation, in that special variety of exaltation of spirit, infused with confidence, which calls to mind new and redeeming faith, until now repressed and subdued and not to be revealed – "even in this disease you can recognise the great and true love of God. It has opened my eyes to the light, and the doors of my heart – to the truth!

"If it hadn't been for the disease – I couldn't have imagined it possible to stop, ever to be free of that devil's dance! And now, the moment has come and He Himself, who in the Mission they taught is love – is showing you, out of love and tenderness, like a compassionate father – that it's not only possible to stop, but it's your duty to stop, right now, so He can shine in your heart... And as for me, that was the only way I knew, and I'm coming out of it, and there are no words to express my joy!

"I have to admit," she added in a changed, more stable tone of voice, "these pains and torments – they're not a simple thing... and they belong to this world, which is the real Hell, the one and only, the melting-pot of flesh and blood..."

She looked up at me again, her eyes blazing, but in their lustre there was more than the flame of debilitating heat – her eyes reflected a strange uplifting of spirit, the exaltation of one who has, in truth and innocence, denied himself for the sake of something immeasurably sublime.

In the narrow room, with its white sheets – starched and cold hospital sheets, silence reigned.

It was Lili who broke it, saying suddenly, her voice remarkably even: "I'm very glad you came – but you must go now!"

"Visiting time isn't over yet," I pointed out.

She smiled mischievously:

"I don't have visiting hours!" she explained. "Even the nurses steer clear of me, the doctors too. I suppose they have a point. This disease is such a terrible plague, fearful pain – followed by certain death! You just can't imagine anyone being crazy enough to accept this with love... and all I can do is try... Now I'm begging you, pleading with you, kneeling at your feet – I'm asking you to go! There's an attack coming on, I can feel it!" she cried out in despair, and found the strength to explain: "The pains, you see! I don't want you here... don't want that!" she declared with such asperity as she was still capable of, but seeing the expression on my face, she relented:

"All right! If you insist on helping, call the nurse, get her to inject me with whatever it is she injects... call the nurse, hurry!" Her face contorted, and her frail, skeletal body writhed under the thick blanket. Her forehead was awash with sweat. "Such terrible pain!" she cried, in a ravaged voice, unlike her own, in a desperate attempt to overcome something vile, intimidating, the fearful herald of Hell.

Spasms racked her, bloodless lips quivered, and eyes opened wide in terror, showing something resembling resignation, and with it the readiness to submit to any condition however dreadful, and the heavy shadow of cold despair.

"Call the nurse!" It was a faint cry, like the wail of a kitten under the wheel of a speeding car.

I went out into the dark corridor, calling out in a voice that echoed like thunder around the cold marble hospital walls: "Nurse! Nurse!"

Eventually I was answered.

After the injection, Lili sank into a spasmodic, fitful kind of slumber, tossing in her bed, occasionally opening her big, scared, glassy eyes to stare into the void.

A LAST ATTEMPT

Tuesday, towards evening, my neighbour knocked on the door and without waiting for any response, pushed it open and hobbled inside.

I left the cup of tea that I had just poured to steam on the low table in the outer room. To my look of emphatic surprise, the uninvited guest replied with an awkward smile and an apologetic shrug of the shoulders.

"I knew you were at home," he announced – "so I didn't wait for an answer! Some kid's been looking for you. Here he is!"

This was a boy of about fifteen years old in cheap jeans, a faded and shabby shirt which had once been garish, and flip-flop sandals that didn't suit his big feet.

"Mister Adon?" he asked, in a solemn and respectful tone that probably wasn't his natural style.

"Yes."

"He sent me…" he hesitated and glanced at the neighbour, whose head was tilted towards him in hungry curiosity.

"Well?" I said, encouraging the boy with a genial tone and a bright smile.

"Shuki's relations, his neighbours I mean," he corrected himself – "one of the bosses…" – again he shot a sidelong glance, charged with deep suspicion, at the neighbour who was drinking in every word that he said.

"Go on," I urged him, implying that the man standing there, roasting himself on the coals of his curiosity, posed no threat or danger.

"Shuki is in hospital," the boy informed me. "He wants to see you. As soon as possible. That's what they told me to say – as soon as possible! So that's what I'm telling you!" he concluded, as if this was a point worth stressing.

"Tell the people who sent you that I'll be with Shuki in about an hour," I replied – "and thank you, thank you very much!"

The boy left and the neighbour, still standing there, found a point of absorbing interest on the floor. Finally, rebuffed by my silence, he turned and hobbled to the door. On reaching the threshold, he looked back at me and exclaimed:

"Don't forget to lock up!"

Shuki had been allocated to a special ward – for terminal cases. The policeman, who was supposed to be guarding him, sat some distance away from him, at the end of the corridor, not even bothering to keep within eye-contact. This in itself gave some impression of the hopelessness of the prisoner's condition.

Shuki was barely recognisable: his face was hideously bloated, resembling not so much a human face as a horror-mask or the painted features of a carnival puppet. Instead of lips, the face was split by two long rows of repulsive growths. Swellings covered the eyes, reducing them to narrow, sardonic slits. The distended nose was a dull violet colour.

"Adon!" he cried, recognising me – his voice crackling and sibilant, like the hissing of a snake. I was clear he had no control over it.

"Adon!" he repeated his cry, with perceptible effort. "I had the right to call on someone. Before... before... you know what I mean!" He raised his arm in a gesture of aristocratic resignation. Even his hand had lost its normal shape.

"Not nice to look at, am I?" – he grinned sourly, reading the expression on my face. Behind the narrow slits the pupils of his eyes were in constant motion. "They tell me that on top of everything else, besides the basic disease, I've got a dose of gangrene... a kind of complication of the disease... as if it wasn't complicated enough already..."

I could sense that, behind the hideous mask forced on him by the disease, Shuki was still smiling his scornful and arrogant smile, with an undertone of restrained bitterness.

"I asked them to call you," he resumed, mustering all his reserves of energy, sounding more tense than ever – "so listen, Adon! I have something to tell you, something important..." The pupils of his eyes focused on me through the narrow slits, and despite his desperate condition, or perhaps because of it, they reflected all the changes of mood and temperament affecting his mind. Anyway, it was impossible to be unaware of the wild and fiery look suddenly ignited there.

In mounting agitation he whispered:

"I planned to murder you... it was the most important thing in my life! Not only since I've got to know you. It's obsessed me for as long as I can remember! Take my word for it!" He paused, while his breathing returned to a more stable rhythm, and added:

"It was like being possessed by a dybbuk! And I put up no resistance... Not that I didn't dare!" he stressed – "I didn't resist 'cos that's that the kind of person I am. I don't go in for resisting Shuki... you see what I mean... I'd much rather go along with him, all the way! Wherever he goes. It's my joy and my pleasure!" He paused for a moment, summoning strength, and continued:

"This vision that I've been cherishing all this time – the joy of removing you from the world – doesn't seem very practical just at the moment..." He swallowed spittle, in an effort to moisten his parched throat, and his croaking voice, anxious to carry on and not lose his train of thought:

"I have to talk quickly," he added urgently. "There's some liquid medication they're trying out... on me that is. And a few other poor sods... two I think... or maybe three..." – he was trying to be precise. "Anyway, it's a whole litre of the stuff – injected straight into the vein. They don't give us kid-glove treatment here. One way or another – it's all hopeless... so there's nothing to lose, no compassion to be wasted – unless, I suppose, it's out of compassion that they're shooting that liquid into us. They say it relieves pain...and so it does – for an hour or two, and that's it. It's like – how can I put it? – going to Hell and back.

"When the pain kicks in – you forget everything...schemes, dreams, the lot... it's what they call dancing to the Devil's tune! And he's an expert in the art of torturing the soul and inflicting pain on the body. I and the other miserable wretches, we've given him a refuge, a place to shelter..." He took a hoarse gulp of air, sounding strangely like a cracked pair of bellows.

"In a little while... No, not so little..." he murmured, before drifting off in another direction: "I wanted them to inject me the moment you arrived. You see, according to my experience, we have an hour at least. I'll do the talking... and if need be, I'll listen too. But I don't think there'll be any need... I've never listened to you in the past so there's not much point starting listening now... when there are just a few hours left..."

It was clear that he had something important to tell me, but whatever it was, he seemed in no hurry to reveal it, or perhaps he was being inexplicably cautious. For the moment, he poured out his bitterness on the things that oppressed him directly – the disease, the discomfort, the treatment.

He tried to take a deep breath of air, but somehow this failed to work. A faint wheezing sound indicated he was incapable of supplying his lungs with the volume of air required, and he abandoned the attempt, continuing in his quavering voice:

"I'll never understand how you could do that, in the café I mean – coming to me and picking me up – helping me onto my feet I should say. At that moment – you ruined everything! If you remember – that was the moment I handed you the key... of my own free will and with my own hands... A moment I won't forget, even if I wanted to! Maybe, there was light in it. But this light was too intense, dazzling, painful! That light dealt me an unforgivable blow!" He was almost shouting now, trying to sit up in his bed, in the grip of a fever that set his whole body shaking.

"And this multiplied my hatred of you, sevenfold, or maybe that should be seventy-seven... Not straightaway, but afterwards. After I was arrested, and that dumb detective was getting his jollies clobbering me round the head with his pistol-butt..." – his voice had turned to a snorting, hissing wheeze, a danger-signal perhaps, and he took another break, finally continuing:

"You know, I didn't feel the blows. All, all of me, to the last fibre of my body – was anger, frantic anger, and nothing else! That's why I got up so quick. I was burning with murderous, overwhelming anger! Not against that dope but – against you!" He licked what had once been his lips and ploughed feverishly on:

"When I spat in his face, and I did a good job of it too, well aimed and with just the right degree of force – I meant it for you! And I was really disappointed that you were out of my range... and to this day I'm angry with you, to this very moment... and it seems I'm going to carry on, I'll be furious and wrathful to the last moment and beyond it... What do you reckon to that?" he hissed.

"My opinion is the same as yours," I answered him calmly.

"What's that supposed to mean?" – he snorted, demanding clarification.

"You're going to leave this world in a state of fury and wrath."

"And that's bad?"

"It's very bad," I retorted – "but there's nothing I can do to change it."

"Nothing I can do either," he muttered, adding hastily: "Even if it was up to me, I'd refuse." Big red bubbles of thick saliva, mixed with blood, appeared among the tumours on his face.

"Why don't you do something like," – he said carefully, articulating every word distinctly – "spit at me...in my face. That way, at least, I'd have a reason to be angry, a motive for my rage! I'd feel somehow vindicated, over my hatred for you, and that wretched aspiration, that still burns in my bones and gives me no respite, to murder you... remove you from this world... So do me one more favour, on top of all the favours you've done me up to now!" His voice was entirely serious, and I had no doubt he meant every word he was saying. There was a long moment of silence.

"Spit at me!" he hissed suddenly, commanding or pleading, or both, in a sharp, venomous king of whisper.

"I won't do that," I declared calmly.

"You want me to be tormented – doubly, fourfold? Have you no compassion for me?" – he fumed – "Those hallowed principles of yours!" He tried once again to take a deep breath, before repeating his demand:

"Spit at me!" – the whisper became menacing, like the hiss of a cobra poised to strike, and through the narrow slits the pupils gleamed in a yellowish, toxic, fire of evil. The moment passed, and it all subsided. He seemed to be reconsidering.

"No, no! 'Cos then I'd roasted by the flames of Hell, burned alive by hatred, hopeless!" And after a long pause, and some laboured, regular breathing, tuned to the murderous rhythm of a rapid pulse, he snorted again:

"You know, even in the café, when you defended yourself with that funny mop, that aluminium rod, when you pushed me away..." the growths on his lips puckered, in the effort to form a grin, or perhaps a smile:

"Even then I was sick... to tell the truth – I was seeing you double! What an unmitigated nightmare this disease is!" – he growled, irrelevantly, continuing: "But I saw, that you are flesh and blood... and I was glad. 'Cos at long last I knew for certain, with absolute confidence," – he invested considerable effort in emphasising this –

"that no supernatural power is going to protect you…. and I knew too, deep down in my heart, that one day you're getting your throat cut… not by me," he admitted gloomily, "but by someone acting on my behalf… my envoy!" He drew strength from his hidden resources and concluded: "I'll get there – somehow…"

He sighed a rusty sigh, tried to move a limb but abandoned the attempt, evidently defeated by the pain, and raced on as if in the grip of a dybbuk, as if roasting on a spit, as if afraid something would stop him in his tracks before he arrived at the point:

"Well, I can see that I was wrong – seriously mistaken! Something supernatural does stand between you and the world, something stronger than armour-plating or a castle wall, something that concentrated, vitriolic hatred is powerless against, impotent…" The rows of tumours quivered, and red foam licked them again. He went on to say:

"Yes, I see it clearly! And the truth is – I still don't believe in it, I refuse to believe in it. 'Cos I don't know what this thing is, what it's called, what it even could be called…" – the growling grew louder – "Do you have a word, or a sentence, that could define this thing, whatever it is?" His lungs wheezed, and his pupils focused on me with tense expectation.

"Love," I said.

"Oh, that again!" – he sounded defiant, as if trying to shake something off or repel it – "I'm already sorry I wasted my only privilege on you… the privilege of one single visitor before the end… and maybe," – he added suddenly – "that's exactly what I had in mind…" His head slumped sideways, and he tried, with a clumsy, uncoordinated movement, to reach out with his deformed hand for a glass of water perched on the bedside cabinet.

I took the glass and held it to his mouth.

As he drank, intense pain was evident in the contortions of his body under the thick blanket. With an expression of alarm, etched deep in the pupils behind the narrow slits, a kind of frantic desire for escape was blended, a mute appeal for help. His ample forehead was beaded with big drops of sweat. When he had finished, I wiped away the remnants of the liquid from the necklace of growths, using a towel hanging at the bed-head. The tumours themselves were soft, like the young flesh of a baby.

"That wasn't a smart thing to do!" he said, agitated for some obscure reason. "Sometimes, it seems to be you're stupid, stupid! A total idiot! King of the idiots!"

"That may well be so," I replied, and in the same relaxed tone I asked: "Why wasn't that a smart thing to do?"

"You could have been infected! Actually – I rather wish you had been! But I know you're not going to get infected, you're not the type... Anyway, that isn't what I had in mind. Listen carefully!" – he commanded with vehemence, in an authoritative tone, despite his whispering, diminishing voice, and the unflagging effort that he had to invest in making it heard:

"The idea of murdering you has never left me for a moment, to this very moment..." he chose to stress. "Conspiring against you kept me awake and alert, even in the bloody prison! It was all very simple – someone was going to slit your throat. He agreed – and then did a bunk. That's when I began to get superstitious... something I'd never bothered with before, but it seemed the fates were against me. And I never stopped scheming... and the truth is, up to this very moment... and even when I decided to waste on you this last privilege, a visitor and a comforter... I've been hatching plots, you see..." – he made a futile attempt to stabilise his voice, and even pump up the volume, before reverting to his faltering whisper:

"I knew you were going to hand me the cup... and that's why I asked the nurse to leave it there, where you'd see it. You'd reckon I was thirsty and, without being asked, you'd hand it over.

"Well, you see," he continued in a reasonably modulated tone, though his breathing was laboured and superficial – "in one hand, I'm holding electrical wires with the ends exposed, keeping them apart. With the other hand – I was going to touch your hand, giving me the cup, and at the same time join the wires together. And what happened?" he hissed as if reproaching himself – "I got confused! Instead of joining the wires – I pulled them and they came out of the socket. You see – wires hanging in the air, no use at all..."

I glanced at the socket on the other side of the bed; the rigid plastic cover was detached, with loose wires hanging, stretching to the bed and disappearing under the blankets.

"Maybe now," he croaked horribly, as if his lungs had turned into heavy blocks of gravel, air whistling through their tiny perforations – "you'll change your mind about me – and spit in my face!"

I tugged cautiously at the wires, which glided slowly from under the blanket, and I saw that the ends were indeed exposed, capable of electrocuting anyone intent on electrocution. Shuki's hand followed them with a slow, dreamy motion, and remained suspended outside the bed, powerless. I took it and put it gently back into its place.

"Thank you," he said feebly and added: "I reckoned that with a bit of luck we'd be going together, you and I... you to Heaven, and I to Hell... and maybe you'd manage to grab hold of me and take me with you... ha, ha, ha!" He experimented with a laugh, but the sounds he produced were more reminiscent of the rustle of industrial sand poured into tin containers.

"Or maybe it would have been the other way round – I'd be taking you to Hell with me!" He snorted pleasurably. "That would have eased my suffering no end! What a shame it didn't work!"

"It wasn't a scheme that was ever likely to work," I pointed out.

"Just my bad luck! But don't you forget," he added, "you ruined my life! You took her from me. Stole from me the only soul that was loyal to me! Loyal to me," – his croaking was sounding plaintive now – "despite all the harm and the heartache I inflicted on her... and you robbed me! Took from me the only one who ever stood by me!"

"She's ill," I reminded him in a thoroughly neutral tone.

"Critically?" he asked with interest.

"Critically."

"The same disease?"

"The same disease."

"I infected her!" – a vivid spark of relief and profound satisfaction flashed in the depths of his pupils, trapped in their narrow slits – "For once, fortune has favoured me!" he declared with a triumphant snort, exuberance tinged with some strange and unexpected air of tenderness.

"She won't be either yours or mine!" he added complacently, his breathing seeming to ease and stabilise.

"If you see her," he continued, "tell her I haven't forgiven... No!" He hesitated, considered, and retracted this: "Don't tell her anything. Don't mention me... it's over!" He gargled horribly, fear flooding his pupils, which seemed to be trying frantically to escape.

"And now," he wheezed – "go! Sod off! I can't understand why I'm acting this way with you! I could have murdered you a thousand times. My dearest wish was – to murder you! I've behaved like an idiot... you won't understand this...or maybe you will. But I'll never understand it myself. There's something diabolical here, or it could be the opposite – not diabolical but divine. The hand of God is in this... and before you go, if you really are a man, come here and shake my hand!"

I approached him, gently took his arm, so thin it was barely recognisable as an arm, and as black as pitch, and delicately I shook the shrivelled, shapeless thing that had once been a hand.

Shuki closed his eyes. A distant emotion drifted across the swollen mask of his face, like a defiant ripple on the surface of a treacherous swamp.

"Love..." he muttered dreamily, – "that guy, the one I sent to sort you out, who took himself off – I gave him information about you that didn't fit. He really didn't know who you were... I confused him. Deliberately. I suppose he gave up and vamoosed. Funny, don't you think?"

"Instead of my name – you gave him the name 'King'" I pointed out.

"So I did!" He grinned with pleasure that he made no attempt to conceal. "Well, 'King' isn't that far from 'Adon', is it? I set him a riddle, but he just wasn't smart enough to crack it! Still, he had a clue to work from, a subtle one, right?"

I squeezed the lump of flesh I was holding in token of assent and agreement, leaned down and kissed his domed forehead, glistening under its patina of cold sweat, and left the ward.

Next day I heard the news: that evening, about two hours after my parting from him, Shuki had breathed his last.

JERUSALEM

One fresh morning early in the spring I travelled by bus to Jerusalem, to sort out the paperwork entrusted to me some time before by Moshe Leon, my landlord, in exchange for a two month remission of the rent on my apartment.

On both sides of the road pine-trees, swaying gently like dreamers, bestowed their sharp and delicate fragrance to the void, gilded in its transparency, and to the travellers speeding by them. Young trees, awakening to the great hope that bridges the chasm between deep blue skies up above, and the rigid, silent earth below.

I arrived at the appointed hour, waited in a relatively short queue, exchanged documents, signed receipts, exchanged hearty smiles with the old men and old women sitting behind rickety formica tables, and left the anonymous building. A bright sun shone above me, a breeze rustled, and open spaces kissed broad horizons.

I returned to the bus-station and before buying a ticket, went into the cafeteria. While making my way to one of the tables with my "self-service" cup of tea, I sensed someone staring at me, relentlessly.

This was a stocky, broad-shouldered individual, of elderly appearance, in tattered clothing, with a rounded moustache and a thick, unruly beard which was mostly grey, as was his hair which had not been trimmed for some time – and he was fixing his eyes on me – his bright, glassy, feline, smiling eyes.

As I stared back at him, bemused and trying to remember where we had met before, he approached me with confident gait and held out to me a tiny, soft hand, like the hand of an infant, appealing for charity. I drew a small purse from my trouser pocket, opened it and dropped a few coins into the outstretched hand, still unable to remember where and when I had met him. I was about abandon the effort – after all, the man was undoubtedly a beggar, whose sole purpose was to obtain money, and since this had been given to him, there was no further business to be done between us; the episode was closed.

And then I heard him address me, in a low but thoroughly familiar voice:

"Are you in good health, Sir? Do you not recognise me? It's a shame that I, at my age, recognise you," – the man pressed on, veering from the formal to the familiar and back again – "you are younger than me, aha! Although not by a wide margin... ten years perhaps... no more! And you still have no idea..."

"The monk from Jaffa!" I exclaimed in a ringing tone, looking up at him and scrutinising him closely, meticulously – a heartening sight indeed.

"He and no other!" he declared with a variety of stolid pride, or perhaps, a hint of the light of the freedom that he had acquired from somewhere or other. Serenity of a kind suffused his face, and yet this face was vibrant with life and with a perceptible, faint sense of contentment – not complacent but cautious, as if probing in the darkness, with a rigorous still to be faced.

He held out his hand again, horizontally this time, not in alms-gathering mode, and shook mine firmly.

"Will you drink tea or coffee with me?" I suggested.

"Not here!" he replied with the bright, inoffensive decisiveness that he had acquired for himself by virtue of his new profession.

"If it be your pleasure, Sir," he continued, with his typical switching between formality and informality, and vice versa – "if you'd like to come to my house, a modest abode to be sure, one rented room, but what used to be called, a warm and hospitable home... It would be my delight, my utmost delight," – his eyes pleaded – "to entertain you!"

I had time to spare and I went with him.

The room was spacious and dimly lit, with meagre furniture. At one end – a kitchen and a lavatory. As we entered, we heard a dull racket from the kitchen, the clatter of crockery on a marble slab.

The door separating the kitchen from the extended room opened and a middle-aged woman stood in it, smiling brightly and wiping fleshy hands on a bright, clean apron. She removed the apron, hung it behind the door, came to meet us and greeted me:

"You are most welcome!" she declared with deliberate emphasis on each word, and shook my hand warmly.

"It's the man from Jaffa," – my host hurriedly introduced me –

"the one I told you about. I had a conversation with him some time ago… an important and fateful conversation. I'm sure," he continued, "there isn't the slightest doubt in my mind, that then he was performing a divine mission!" – he pointed with his childish finger at the high ceiling – "In fact, there is no one who isn't an emissary of the superior powers… and we must be ever alert and attentive, to hear the word of God that such people speak, to think it through properly and fulfil it with love… and then we shall be rewarded, so that our existence in this world has not been in vain!" He spoke in haste, almost with impatience, and at the same time he took care that every word he spoke be clearly heard, resounding in the hearts of his audience, and stamping on them the impression he intended. His expertise in preaching was clearly a legacy of his days in the ministry of the Church, when he used to deliver his homilies from a gilded pulpit.

We took our seats at a long table, covered by a clean, blue nylon cloth. A cool Jerusalem breeze blew softly from the window, which opened on a tiny garden with a bed of violets and young rose bushes.

After a short, polite silence I asked:

"And how is your Orthodox Church reacting?"

"It isn't!" he answered me succinctly, before adding: "Because there's nothing to react to!"

I could see that he was waiting tensely for me to ask more questions, in my eagerness to have the situation clarified in its entirety. He clearly found the business somewhat entertaining, as well as a source of personal satisfaction.

So I complied with his wish, with the comment:

"I don't understand!"

"Aha!" – he smiled serenely, rubbing his childish hands together pleasurably: "The monk from Jaffa doesn't exist!" he exclaimed loftily, with an expansive gesture intended to denote total and utter finality. "Instead of that," he went on – "what you see before you is a loyal and devout Israeli citizen, of Greek origin… I'm a citizen!" he repeated his enthusiastic pronouncement – "New in every respect! New on the outside and on the inside!" he declared emphatically and added in a more balanced tone: "According to the documents…"

"What documents?" I queried.

"Forgeries!" he replied triumphantly, and went racing on: "You remember the beadle at the church, that Dimitri, the smoothie – he's an expert in the business... he has contacts too... extensive contacts!

"In fact," – he reverted to a more level tone – "it was his idea, his ingenious suggestion!" His round face lit up and he glanced at the woman, who sat there all the while, listening alertly and companionably, identifying with every smallest movement in the muscles of his face.

"As for me, I had a different idea, an inferior one – to disappear! Just disappear! Take off the cassock – and disappear... and then Dimitri came along and fixed everything for me – from aleph to taf, as you would say, or from alpha to omega, in our version – and it has to be said, and it's greatly to his credit – without taking a cent from me! He even contributed something himself... and through his contacts I found this room, and this wife. He arranged the marriage too – what a man, what versatility!" he asserted with an apologetic smile and went on at once: "He has to be the envoy of the Almighty! He's a shining revelation, of the highest order, a revelation of the true love, love of Almighty God!" His eyes shone with a kind of awe and reverence, his voice rang out, melodious and earnest.

"What about the clergy?" I asked, – "All those who knew you – after all, in your outward appearance you haven't changed much!"

"I haven't changed at all!" he declared and added: "They all know! I even participate in Sunday services, here, in Jerusalem, the Holy City... They all know," he insisted, – "from the humblest of novices to the Patriarch himself – and they say nothing!" he concluded, the shadow of a cloud passing over his balding, wrinkled forehead.

The woman stood up from her seat and went to the kitchen, stayed there a while and returned carrying a flowery tray of lacquered tin, and on it, steaming cups of tea and a fat-bellied kettle.

"You've waved goodbye to arak as well?" I asked.

"To arak as well!" he asserted, "And to everything else that I'm finally having to see in the true light..."

He hesitated at this point, and I prompted him:

"Which light is that?"

"The light of His love, the Almighty that is!" he answered me in a low voice, with a hint of the joyful reverence that is stored away in the depths of the heart.

He crossed himself, his face turned to the eastern wall of the house. It was only then that I noticed the perpetual lamp burning beneath the icon placed there.

"Take note and observe," he began with uncharacteristic equanimity: "I've changed direction, stopped acting a lie to myself... as you were kind enough to point out back then – it's something I'm just not equipped for!" he concluded with a heart-felt cry.

"What aren't you equipped for?" the woman asked, her voice as soft and melodious as his.

"Monasticism!" he replied, and without looking at her he added:

"I married a wife... and that's a test, a severe test. Admittedly," he went on in a changed voice, with a trace of regret, "I left it a bit late and I don't suppose I shall ever have children – but life has changed and is utterly different!" And with a stiff smile, he proceeded to specify: "There's an accumulation of uncharted troubles, disappointments, and black depression. And that's what I need!"

"Why is that?" I asked with frank astonishment.

"Because, finally, I am aware of His guiding hand, I hear His answers to my pleas, know His wondrous love, given in response to my plaintive, discredited love... and He relates to me, sets me tests and trials, the most severe that there are!

"I'm sure you're familiar with this," – he turned to me abruptly – "the sense of emptiness, of choking, of a dark, heavy grey cloud which has no name, in which there isn't the smallest chink of hope, which sucks all your vitality and poses before you that penetrating, endlessly repeated question: What's it for? What's the purpose behind all this? Meaning – life in the flesh, in this world... and this happens especially to the married man, to one who has taken a wife and is sharing his whole life with her... he, and he especially, is prone to face that moment of standing before a dark and yawning chasm..." He peered into my face for a moment and added in a rush:

"Because here is the ultimate disappointment. What seemed to you destined to soothe your pain, to provide a full answer, medication for all your ills, turns out to be incapable of soothing its own pain, healing its own ills, which exceed even yours...

"What seemed to you to be a support, needs supporting itself, day by day, hour by hour, moment by moment. And all the support that you offer, is not enough – it can never suffice because it is rooted in flesh and blood... and as we know – such support is nothing but an illusion which doesn't exist at all, never has and never will!" he declared, lifting his tea-cup with a flourish as if it was a glass of arak that he intended to empty with one swig. And sure enough, he took a deep gulp before continuing:

"And then you get to Him... there, when you stand on the edge of the abyss, gaping before your stumbling feet, the void of your black emptiness and your cold despair, which more than anything else is capable of killing what is called the 'will to know God' and corrupting it horribly... and with it your longings for Him and your love of Him.

"There," he went on to say, "on the edge of cold despair, in the empty void, in which there's no air to breathe, nor any desire to breathe, when your whole being is turning into a single and overwhelming desire, 'to end it all!' – He comes and with one fatherly caress, which is all yours, delighting in His love of you, his faithless son, slanderous worm, unworthiest of all men – brings you back to the battlefield, life in partnership, with a wife!"

"And yet in spite of all this," I interjected, as if summing-up – "you've stayed married and you don't regret it.

"And I shall stay so to the end of my days!" he retorted decisively, returning to his tea-cup with a repeat of that inappropriate, boozer's flourish.

"I'm faithful to my wife and devoted to her and thereby – I'm serving Him! My mind is at ease and my baser instincts are in retreat... and I'm seeing straight in front of me.."

He took another sip of his tea and concluded:

"I live off charity – the charity of people... and love... His love, the Almighty, His boundless love!"

"We are commanded never to lose hope!" I commented, in a vigorous tone.

"I'm not losing it!" – his face was regaining the vitality that had surprised me in the bus station cafeteria, where we met by chance, or perhaps – not by chance at all.

"We both have one great hope!" the woman interposed in her soft and melodious voice, her warm eyes sparkling in the dim void of the room. "We," she added, "are united in our belief in Him," – she pointed to the icon on the eastern wall of the room, – "and that is enough and more for this life, this human life in the flesh!"

The rest of the tea we drank in silence.

When I stood up to leave, the former monk accompanied me to the door.

"To be – is enough!" – he looked into my face with a sad, remote smile. "I'm learning to be content with little," he added, – "and this profession of mine, most ancient of all professions, is both the true balm for heartbreak, and also the way by which He will descend and come to you... and whereby you raise your eyes to Him, eyes yearning for Him in perpetual hope... and whereby, when the day comes – you will ascend to Him."

"Peace be with you!" I said, waved to the woman who was peering over his shoulder, and went out into the street.

I hadn't gone far when he suddenly detached himself from the threshold where he had been standing watching me, ran after me, clutched my sleeve, looked earnestly into my eyes and said:

"I used to bless people... will you bless me now?" – and saying this, he knelt at my feet.

I laid my hand on his shock of greying hair and in a clear voice intoned:

"Live for ever in His love!"

He stayed on his knees for some time, oblivious to the curiosity of the few passers-by using the narrow street at that hour of the day, while the woman stood in the doorway of the house, looking on impassively.

AMELIA

Amelia resigned from her post in the least likely of all possible ways – by means of a letter to management, a copy of which I received. She gave no reasons for her resignation, made no effort to invent excuses. She sent a two-line announcement, on scented writing-paper, that with effect from such-and-such a date, she would no longer be an employee of the institute. There were no expressions of regret, or of gratitude.

There was consternation in the institute over "this terrible waste" as it was described by its official representatives, over the "total lack of consideration and logic" and over a "hasty" and "impulsive" action on the part of the "afore-mentioned employee". Admittedly, in statements such as these, heard repeatedly in the offices and corridors of management, there was an element of stark institutional truth: Amelia had progressed to a position of considerable seniority, and by resigning in this way she was waiving, knowingly and willingly, all her rights, including redundancy compensation. Only those workers who had shared an office with her, and been in close contact with her, were not overly impressed by the "hasty" and "impulsive" elements in her conduct. They smiled at me genially and tolerantly, and one of them, one of the veterans, took it on herself to put me in the picture:

"The manager gave her a hard time," she began.

"The manager's on leave," I retorted, – "has been for three months!"

"You think that's a coincidence?" – she looked at me in gentle amusement, as if speaking to an overgrown child, lovable no doubt, but still naïve and needing things spelt out. She was kind enough to explain:

"The manager's due back in work in a few days from now. And then Amelia will be dependent on him. She's decided to get her move in first."

"And how is the manager?" I asked.

"He's sinking further and further into depression, and drinking too much. He asked for and got a divorce from his wife, and he's rented a small apartment. It's in an exclusive square, but he never goes out of his front door. Why don't you visit him?" she added suddenly. It seemed a practical suggestion.

I visited him.

As I was on my way to his apartment, I tried to refresh my memory of the events that had transpired since I was told that he was going on extended leave – three months that were scheduled to expire, it seemed, within the next few days. His deputy, an energetic but taciturn individual, had done his best to maintain the status quo in the institute, both in terms of stability of manpower and working practices.

At the time, I hadn't taken much interest in the manager's reasons for suddenly deciding to take a holiday, which from a point of timing at least, was unusual. I remembered there had been whispers on the subject at the time, but I made a point of ignoring them, and rejecting unequivocally any attempt to involve me in the gossip. And now, Amelia too was leaving in an unconventional manner...

These days, I hardly saw her at all. The few times we happened to meet in a professional context, I was struck by the deepening pallor of her face and her troubled, rather mournful look, invariably averted. Following her promotion, she worked in an office far removed from mine. There were no complaints about her work, or her competence, or her conduct. For this reason, perhaps, we seldom met, except for chance encounters in the corridor at the end of the day, when we would exchange conventional farewells.

The door of the manager's apartment was half-open. I knocked and hearing no response, I pushed it lightly and went inside.

Directly facing me, on a padded stool, the manager sat by a low, oval table, gazing fondly at an opened, half-empty bottle of whisky.

The hand which at that moment held a full glass, sparkling with a pure lustre, a crystal glass apparently, rose steadily towards his lips. He gave me a look that was blank, almost apathetic.

"Oh, it's you, Adon!" – he exclaimed in a weary voice, lightly tinged with scorn, then wiped his thick moustache on the back of his hand, set the empty glass on the oval table, and with a listless flap of the hand, signalled to me to sit opposite him.

I pulled up a chair from the corner of the room, and sat down in silence.

"I'm impressed!" he drawled impassively, without looking at me. "Impressed!" he repeated in the same tone. "I might have known you'd be around. You're always there when disaster strikes – right in the thick of it! Ha! Ha! Ha!" – he uttered a colourless laugh, stood up from his seat, took a faltering step, disappeared for a moment behind the internal door, evidently leading to the kitchen, and returned with another glass, similar to his.

"Oh," he said, remembering. "I was forgetting what a puritan you are... Smart guy! A man of principles... In the circumstances I can't offer you anything but cold water... I have nothing else!" And he returned the way he had come, exchanged the empty crystal glass for a cup of cold water, set it down in front of me and returned to his padded stool.

I took of the sip of the water, which had a slightly sour, stagnant taste to it, as if it had been left too long in the fridge, for days, perhaps weeks.

"Are you up to date with what's been going on?" he asked without looking at me, pouring more whisky into his glass; it overflowed, splashing the check table-cloth.

"No," I replied.

"I thought as much!" He smiled a flaccid, foolish smile. His unshaven face looked swollen, his eyes, evidently inflamed by some infection, had reddened from the inside, and from the outside seemed to have sunk into their sockets. He wasn't wearing his spectacles: perhaps he'd swapped them for contact-lenses, or perhaps he didn't need them for purposes of intoxication. He stared blankly. His hands shook.

"That bitch Amelia!" he began, interrupting himself after every word, enunciating with deliberate gravity. Suddenly he looked up, scanned me with a quick look and declared:

"Don't you dare call her a bitch! See, you've been warned! Only I'm allowed that! Not that she is a bitch, but I'm so desperate...I don't know what else to hang on to..." His face crumpled and he seemed to lose the thread of his thoughts, but managed to recover himself.

"There's no doubt, I'm a swine!" he exclaimed with a grimace. "I don't know myself any more..." He smiled a mournful sort of smile, covering something deeper, something disguised, nagging.

"She, you see..." – he gripped the edge of the table, as if making an effort to resist the glass and the liquid in it – "immediately after her husband was sentenced... even though I'd dropped my charges against him..." he hesitated – "Did you know he'd been sentenced?"

I nodded. I knew that Valery had been jailed for two years, plus two years suspended.

"She didn't want to accept me!" he cried as if refusing to believe it. "Imagine it!" he added: "I go to her laden with sweets and cakes and exotic fruits, and the tokay wine that she likes and my favourite whisky, and a massive bunch of flowers!" – his voice rose momentarily into a wail, but he stabilised it again: "You see, we always dreamed that once he was inside... we'd be free to live as we please. You get it?" His voice seemed to quaver and lose some of its vigour, and he continued with a sigh:

"She, she rejected me! Despite all the presents and the flowers... and no explanations... it was a pretty crude rebuff, you know..." He was silent a long moment, his hands to his temples, eyes staring at the floor.

"I wasn't expecting that!" he admitted with dignity, and in a quite even tone of voice. He lowered his hands and rested them on his knees, lifted his head and looked at me steadily:

"I couldn't even get inside – she slammed the door in my face and locked it from the inside. All my urging and my impassioned pleas, appeals for forgiveness and compassion, and the threats and the promises – couldn't we just talk, a short, civilised conversation to clear the air, that was all I wanted – none of it was any use... She just didn't want to know..." He lowered his eyes, measuring the level of the liquid in the bottle in front of him. His back was stooped and he looked much older than he really was – ageing, broken and shabby.

"It was like that, you see, all so sudden – no explanations, no warning, nothing! I was stunned. No, not stunned," – he corrected himself. "I was thunder-struck. In the end I went wild and started kicking the door... nearly knocked it off its hinges. I really bombarded it. Then I chucked all the packages, and the flowers, at the closed door... like a kid..." He checked the impression his words were making on me, and lowered his eyes again. "There were cream-cakes, chocolate, fruit, all mashed up together – it was like modern art! A broken bottle, wine all over the place... what a vile mess!" he declared with a kind of irate sorrow, and at once, with no perceptible transition, he smiled and even tried to laugh – "Ha, ha, ha, ha!" – that colourless laugh of his, heavy and frayed at the edges. Having suppressed it, he added earnestly:

"I returned the same way I came, empty-handed. I looked for a reason. I thought to myself – this is the shock of her husband's conviction – it will pass! Time heals everything! I brought it on myself – no tact, no patience, going after her like an animal on heat… what a swine! Instead of giving her a break… even a short one. Time to digest the facts, assess the situation, let her weigh things up, come to me of her own accord, at a time of her choosing! A born swine!" – he tried to convince himself, seeking my assent, and when this didn't come, he declared:

"I swear to you, in good faith!" – he adopted a style utterly foreign to him – "My only reason for going there was to comfort her! And I can't be accused of tactlessness, not really! If she'd accepted me, taken me in, I'd have been prepared to stay out – out of her bed, I mean. I wouldn't even have touched her, not touched her at all…" He shifted on his stool with a degree of discomfort.

"That's the way I see it today, that's what I believe today," – he lowered his eyes, sighed, picked up his glass, took a sip from it and put it back in its place. He was clearly intent on maintaining some lucidity.

"Then," – he looked up and stared at me, a faint glimmer in his eyes – "I'm not sure I'd have been capable of being that considerate. If she'd accepted me, taken me in… I wouldn't have left just like that…" – he averted his gaze – "without some debauchery of one kind or another. And she knew that," he added, almost in a whisper, looking at me directly again. "She knew it, from experience. She knew – and hence the firm rebuff…

"And by the time I got home – I was feeling almost encouraged by the way things had gone! I told myself that this kind of thing would only sharpen the anticipation, make for a more intense, and satisfying experience…

"And then came the second encounter. A real encounter this time – face to face. I turned up empty-handed, with a gloomy look on my face, as if I'd come to offer condolences… She opened the door to me, and I got a cold, formal sort of reception. The expression on her face was about the same as mine – maybe a bit more sincere.

"We have to put an end to all of this! she tells me straight off.

"All of what? I ask her, keeping that silly, sympathetic expression pasted on my face.

"Contacts, meetings, conversations! – she says coldly. I reckon it's a kind of coldness that comes to her naturally.

"And why's that, if I may ask? I ask.

"I've realised – she tells me, like a romantic heroine from some cheap novel – that the only soul I really love – is my husband. I'm ashamed of what I've done to him, and I don't know if he'll take me back. He's already suggested we should separate. And if he insists – then we'll separate. But I'm not going to betray him any more – she tells me, in a cold and unequivocal sort of voice. And just to make sure that I've got the message, she adds – whether he's by my side or not!

"Listen, I told her, all these words, these high-flown words of yours, they mean nothing, you know, they have no grip on reality… you have a body and it demands its due! You can't stand by all the solemn vows you've made and it's better to get down before it's too late from the high tree that you've climbed, and stop trotting out a lot of romantic clichés that belong to the last century… you should be looking ahead, with maturity! I've always loved you…" – he paused for a moment – "and at that she looked up and shot me a frigid, murderous stare and came out with:

"You never loved me! You came here just to take, to satisfy the animal in you, and that's it. You don't know what love is! – she threw that in my face and then, in a lower voice, as if coping with a heavy load of doubt, as if peeping into the recesses of her soul, she declared – And it seems I don't, either…

"At least I'm going to try… – she went on to say. I want to love! And this desire in itself gives me some peace of mind. A radiant sort of peace, like nothing I've ever known before. I'll do anything for Valery! – she announced – and you'll just have to try to understand me… – she was talking in a special, persuasive tone of voice, not the soft kind that can be taken one way or the other, but firm, 'steely' I'd call it – And the most important thing of all, you try to love! Your wife and your children, I'm talking about. But leave me alone!

"Imagine it, she's standing there, solid as a cold, marble statue, indifferent, ruthless and all her body-language telling me, none too subtly, that I should get up and get out of her sight!" – the manager cried, as if unable to believe it even now – "Rejecting me, you see, something I never imagined in my worst dreams! And I suppose that's why I felt so hurt... worse than hurt, humiliated! The truth is – I reckoned I was lost! Losing something I'd never be able to reclaim, something beautiful, precious, important, special... something, it seems, that till now I hadn't appreciated, hadn't given it its true worth... something that would leave me alone in the empty void, naked and helpless in a hostile world, something that would send me plunging into the depths, sinking in utter despair, from which there's no outlet..." His voice grew fainter and for a long moment he was silent, as if considering something inwardly, vacillating between options.

"You wouldn't believe it," he went on grimly – "I pleaded with her... like a child, like a baby. I nearly fell down and knelt at her feet..." He described a broad gesture with his undamaged hand – a motion which could have been interpreted as an expression of resignation, of rising above the level of the trivial – or of the bitterness of despair.

"How do you know – I turn to her and I'm yelling now – that I don't love you?

"Everything you do tells me that! – she declares in a practical sort of voice, with some appropriate gestures thrown in. Your behaviour – is the very opposite of love! And then she seems to be offering me a lifeline: If you learn to turn your behaviour round, I mean, do the exact opposite of everything you've done up to now, then I'll believe that, just maybe, I've misjudged you a bit! But it's a project that's doomed from the start... you're incapable of loving! You're no better than an animal on heat, with behaviour dictated by the basest instincts!

"You see," the manager continued, speaking now with a kind of icy restraint, attempting to bury beneath it a storm of emotions – "she's standing there like a princes, and I'm seething with desire for her, burning up... so much desire I'm scared by it myself and maybe... admiration too, and something like affection, love even – and all this because she's turning me away... like a lovesick adolescent." He sighed, and shook his head this way and that, as if trying to dislodge something troublesome from his face.

"And if in spite of all this, I can prove to you that I love you? – I shot at her with a hollow-sounding voice, like a drowning man clutching at straws, looking at her the way a spurned dog looks at his master, petulant and aggrieved.

"She was gracious enough to meet my gaze head on. She glanced at me, studied me with a look! You hear that? She gave me a look – a look of pity! If something like that had happened to me before, with another woman, I'd have been hurt to the depths of my soul, incurably offended... I'd have run away – and stayed away!

"Are you following all this?" – peering at me from under a wrinkled forehead and contorted eyebrows – "It's possible you have no experience of women – but I've had plenty, a rich variety! And I tell you, a look like that is worse than overt scorn, a look like that is eloquent and unequivocal testimony that you're worth nothing more in her eyes than a rotten tree-stump... even less than that. In her eyes, you're not even worth spitting at! You don't rate at all. It's not only hurtful and humiliating, it crushes you!" he asserted in a tone of despair and resignation.

"All the same," – he let out a deep sigh, like a terminally ill patient – "under those circumstances, I was grateful even for that kind of a look, you see, a look that's worse than overt scorn, worse than a spit in the face... that's how far I'd sunk!" He fell silent for a moment, fidgeting with his glass. Then he raised it slowly to his trembling lips, took a moderate sip, just the one, wiped his moustache and hastily returned the glass to its place.

"Don't try! – that's what she told me, but her voice wasn't cold and pragmatic any more – but compassionate, like her eyes. And this was the genuine article, the kind of compassion you might feel for a maggot after you've stamped on it. It disgusts you, but there's some regret there as well...

"And in the state I was in then, after all the wheedling and the spitting in the face – I clutched at the straw that was offered to me, at that compassion rooted in disgust, and I made a solemn declaration:

"I'll not only try, I'll do it – I'll prove to you, not just in theory but in practice too, that I love you, and it doesn't matter how you choose to take it! It makes no difference, it isn't important!

"And then – incredible as it sounds – I stood up, and without turning back, as if pursued by a thousand devils – I fled for my life while I still could. You see," – he raised his red, inflamed eyes to me, eyes reflecting a load of ineffable dejection – "a certain idea came to mind, a brainwave, perhaps... at the very moment I was declaring I'd prove my love to her – the idea arose. Till that moment I'd just been babbling a lot of senseless words, not meaning anything, my only motivation being – to carry on being by her side, to guarantee my place close by her, my physical place I mean, so I wouldn't be forced to leave, forced to get up and go, expelled, shame-faced, into the unspeakable depression that awaited me, I knew, in the world outside, without her...

"And that idea flashed up, sparking in the deep recesses of my impure soul... I remembered that during one of our previous encounters, she'd gone through the same routine – claiming that I didn't love her, didn't know what love is... but you see, this was when we were in flagrante, bodies entwined, with all the intoxicating delight that entails... and at a time like that, words are meaningless. You just say them, and no one takes them seriously. But I remembered that on this occasion, she made the usual accusations and then added a very specific rider: if I wanted to prove that I loved her there was only one way – to separate from my wife and marry her... and she, for her part, needless to say, would set about divorcing her husband...

"At the time," – the manager continued his vivid account – "the idea seemed crazy, out of touch with reality. I paid no attention to it, and I was sure she wasn't putting it forward as a viable course of action. It was just the kind that's said in those circumstances, nothing more than that.

"So, going back to the situation I was in then, like a beaten dog – when all that I wanted was just to hold on to her, to keep on seeing her – while the knowledge that she was slipping away between my fingers, now of all times, when the way was absolutely clear, with that brute of a husband of hers behind bars and neutralised – was driving me out of my mind! It was driving me out of my mind!" – he saw the need to repeat with particular emphasis, as if it meant so much to him, and the trauma had been so decisive, that he couldn't resist deviating from the point at issue. And deviating still further, he added, reverting to his familiar strident chirrup:

"I've been in a manic state ever since! To this very day..." – his voice beginning to veer out of his control – "everything I do or don't do – is an act of mania, a manic act!" Suddenly he scrutinised me with a surprisingly stable look, and asked: "Do you agree with me?"

"No," I answered him, smiling.

"Would you mind elucidating?"

"That can't be the end of your story; there must be more!"

Pensively, he clutched his glass again, as if it served him as an anchor in the stormy sea of his emotions, and said, as if talking to himself:

"There is more... the moment I got home to my wife and children, I starting trashing the place. I threw things at the walls, smashed plates on the floor, threatened my wife, kicked my kids out... I was in a real manic state! Oh yes, and then I asked for a divorce..."

He took care not to meet my eyes, a caution that was quite superfluous: my eyes were focused far beyond him, beyond the walls of his apartment, beyond all walls and apartments, and anyone looking into them at that moment would see nothing but the bright reflection of something reminiscent of the vault of the sky on a clear spring morning.

"And what could my wife do?" – he spread his fingers in a gesture of helplessness – "I sent a lawyer to her, a slippery type who was well up in the whole business, and he got me a divorce within a remarkably short space of time. About fifty days after that last meeting – I was free as bird, officially; 'Domestic Circumstances – Divorced' it says on my I.D. card, not 'Married' any more." He rummaged in the back pocket of his trousers, to provide documentary evidence of this statement – evidence which hadn't been asked for and which had no bearing on the current issue.

"For fifty days I didn't go near her, didn't speak to her, for better or for worse... I was just sending her flowers, every week. And because they weren't returned, I began to feel hopeful, a little more confident... Not only that, I was aware of a kind of happiness taking me over, as if the world around me was a brighter place, and I could respond to it in the same way... it seemed to me that at last I was experiencing something real, that I was breaking through the constricting bonds of banality, dispelling notions that hitherto had aroused in me a blend of reverence and disdain, extricating myself from a repellent morass of futility, a futile life... I was finally beginning to know myself...

"And so, after a gap of fifty days, I showed up again at her apartment – the divorce document in my pocket, a big bunch of flowers in my hand, and a silly, dreamy smile on my face... and I got the same reception as before, the same long, quizzical look – so much more murderous than scorn, overt or hidden,   infinitely more venomous: a look of cold compassion, that gives nothing away, involuntary compassion, the most demeaning kind that there is...

"My bouquet was grudgingly received. I found out later that the flowers I'd been sending every week had been dumped on one of the neighbours... but let's keep things in order! She didn't even glance at the document...I read it out to her, in a quaking voice. I doubt she took any notice, or heard a single word. Standing there like before, a marble statue – cold and angry and indifferent, and worst of all – distant, distant, out of reach! For ever and ever, for all eternity...

"I nearly lost my senses, nearly fainted... yes, I nearly fainted, like a hysterical female... anyway, I must have blacked out for a moment, and everything was spinning around me... I had to grab the table for support and she didn't react at all. She said just two words: Too late!

"I tried to ask questions, to understand something of what was going on, to draw some conclusions, invent excuses for myself, even pointless excuses! I tried to seize on some signal, encouraging or discouraging – a sign of recognition, at least – and get to the bottom of the business that had become so complicated, decipher some of the complexities of her mind, probe as deeply as I could... I piled up words, mountains upon mountains of words, words with no meaning to them, hollow words, words of despair – despair that there was no point in disguising any more – like the adolescent spurned by the idol of his sad imagining...

"Tears welled up in my eyes... yes, in these eyes of mine that never knew anything other than the tears of tasteless laughter, angry laughter and schadenfreude, bestial satisfaction... and then, then came a turnaround. She condescended to grant me another sentence, something that had been said and chewed over often enough in the past, but she insisted on reviving – after she'd been kind enough to wipe from her face the look of involuntary compassion and repressed revulsion. She must have decide that the surest way to be rid of me, was the way of honesty, the direct, unmediated truth, unequalled in its brutality:

"You don't know what love is! – she declared, while walking to the door, opening it wide, taking up her position beside it and waiting. And I knew she wasn't going to leave until I left her apartment... that small apartment, devoid of furniture, devoid of a husband, devoid of a dream!"

He stretched out his hand again, picked up the glass with a resolute movement, poured the fiery contents into his mouth, and slammed it down on the table,

"You don't know what love is!" – he quoted angrily, in a hollow voice, turned to me abruptly and asked:

"What's your opinion?"

I took the cup of water, drank my fill, put it down half-empty on the low table and replied:

"She was telling the truth!" – the tone of my voice was affable, but firm.

"Why do you say that?" – he uttered a strange, indignant and pitiable screech, like the cry of a mouse hit on the head with a heavy implement. Hurt, resentful, he demanded to hear some conclusive answers.

"The man who knows what love is," I began calmly – "is always happy!" – and without waiting for an answer I added: "When you meet a sad individual, addicted to drugs or drink, you can be absolutely sure, without a shadow of a doubt – that person doesn't know how to love, and doesn't know what love is!"

"It isn't that he doesn't know how to love," – he interrupted me with a raucous cry ,– "the point is that he isn't loved!"

"Only the one who knows how to love – is loved! Because he doesn't ask to be loved. The genuine lover doesn't seek the love of others, and that's why he's loved. The sole desire of the true lover is that the object of his love will be happy. It doesn't matter to him where this object sits, or with whom. Does the other know of his love, or not; will the other befriend him, treat him with interest or indifference, despise or appreciate him? And if for the sake of the happiness of this loved one – he has to go far away – he will do this with joy, although he knows he will never again see his loved one, or hear his loved one's voice – until the end of all generations!

"The true lover is always and forever happy, and a world in which such a true lover is to be found – is a fortunate place!" I concluded, emphatically.

"How does he do this?" the manager asked with a kind of bemusement, devoid of vitality and yet, with a tense wakefulness, a readiness to engage in rational thought.

"The true lover," I answered him, – "gives! Always and everywhere, in all circumstances.

"What do you mean by 'gives'?" – he persisted.

"Everything that he does, he does without asking for reward!" I replied.

"That's going to bankrupt him pretty damn quick!" – the manager declared, as if this was an incontrovertible argument.

"Nothing could be further from the truth," I retorted. "There's no wealth to compare with his! And the reason why? – He is unsullied by expectation!"

"Another sermon!" – the manager's heavy head suddenly sank, and his voice was tinged with veiled bitterness – "No one could match up to standards like those!"

"That's why the human race appears the way it does – consumed by fear and inner despair, wallowing in dejection, not knowing what love is, not knowing how to give!"

Silence fell in the room.

The manager sat on his padded stool, his head between his hands, his breathing heavy and laboured, rasping with intense emotion.

"So according to your logic," – he said after a long pause, his voice cracked and quavering: "I'm supposed to be glad that Amelia's left me!"

"Yes, if you really love her!"

"And why do you say that?" he persisted.

"Because it's her explicit wish, and her happiness depends on it," I replied.

"And if she's wrong, and she doesn't know where her true happiness lies?"

"Let her work that out for herself" – was the answer.

"The way you're showing me is kind of..." – he strove to find the appropriate word, finally compromising with – "exceptional!"

"You've tried the non-exceptional – and where has that got you?"

He rubbed his face with his hands, reluctant, for some reason, to reveal it. After a long pause, he commented wearily, morosely: "I do want to give!"

"All you want to do is take!" – I corrected him, and added: "When you give, you'll know the joy of giving, which doesn't depend on anything."

"What do you have to do, if you're going to give?" He looked up suddenly, turning his inflamed eyes to me.

"Eradicate self-pity, once and for all!" I replied.

"And in practical terms?" he demanded to know, with a sudden surge of alacrity.

"Ask Amelia's forgiveness and then stay out of her way – don't even send her flowers! If she asks anything of you, do it joyfully and don't expect anything in return. Go down on your knees before your wife and children, and admit to being the lowest wretch on the face of the earth. If there's anything left that you can salvage by going back to them – go back and salvage it! Don't delay! See yourself as you really are – an arrogant, hypocritical scoundrel, wallowing in self-pity, an incorrigible egotist who wants only to take, grab and plunder, to enjoy the pleasure of the moment and in fact – to enslave yourself to that illusory pleasure and sink into the clinging mire of depression and inescapable despair!"

I glanced at his face: it was taut, tormented, sober.

"Sadness and gloom," I added – "are symptoms of self-pity. Pure joy – is the expression of a love that isn't dependent on anything."

"And love that is dependent on something?" he was curious to know.

"There's no such thing," I declared.

"You mean it doesn't exist?"

"I mean it's the opposite of love."

We were silent again.

He stared at the wall of his little room, tastefully furnished, admittedly, and decorated with a degree of artistic flair.

"I'm glad you came!" – he spoke again – "What you said... there's something in it... worth hearing and bearing in mind... putting it into practice, that's something else entirely!" – he grinned – "I'll give it a try..." His grin became a broad smile, a cunning smile, with a hint of a sneer around the edges. "Not that I don't believe it," he added hastily, as if to counter the unfavourable impression – "I believe. But," he added, trying to convince himself – "I'm not sure how to put this... it would be a pity to give up on sorrow and grief, and self-pity!" His voice sounded lucid, and his broad smile was candid and sincere.

"Without them," he continued, "how would we know what love is – I mean the love that isn't dependent on anything, of course! Besides – a world without sorrow and grief and self-pity would be a boring place, not what we're used to at all!" He checked the expression on my face with a quick glance and went on:

"Well, I like the world the way it is now, and it would be a shame to lose it!" He looked at me keenly, awaiting my response.

"Everyone's wishes deserve respect!" I retorted, smiling: "If sorrow and grief and self-pity are important to you – stick to them and rejoice in them, just don't pretend to be miserable!"

"But that's what makes those things worthwhile!" he cried, with sudden vehemence: "If I don't pretend to be miserable – what's the point of sorrow and grief and self-pity?"

"You must do whatever you see fit!" I shrugged, drank the rest of the water in the cup, and stood up from my seat.

He followed suit, swaying unsteadily, and held out a quivering hand to me. His face was grim:

"Be so good as to tell them there.... at work, I mean... I'll be back in a few days. How is Amelia, by the way?" he couldn't resist asking.

"As far as I know, she's well," I replied, adding: "She's left the institute."

"What?" – he stiffened as if bitten by a scorpion, clutching his head between both hands, shocked and devastated.

"She resigned," I explained.

"That's terrible!" he cried: "My last hope – gone!" He lowered his voice, hands still clutching his head. "You shouldn't have told me, not like this – out of the blue!" He lowered both hands gradually and stood hunched in the middle of the elegant room, eyes staring at the floor.

"No point in going back to work now!" he muttered, addressing his words to the thick carpet and his shuffling bedroom slippers. "If she's resigned – I'm resigning too!" he added impulsively, looking up and staring into the middle distance, without seeing me.

True to his word, he resigned and emigrated to the U.S.A. where, rumour had it – he eked out a meagre living as an accounts clerk, employed by a distant relative and footwear manufacturer. He gave up drinking altogether. His family was left in penury, but his wife refused point-blank even to discuss alimony orders or the like. Instead she looked for work and found it in the same institute that had employed her husband, as a book-keeper of the humblest rank. Our paths didn't cross. It was said of her that she never stopped smiling, and her smile was innocent and sincere.

In the end, Amelia withdrew her resignation, asked to have her job back and was reinstated. She visited Valery in prison regularly, and he too was allowed out occasionally for home visits. Later, Amelia struck up a friendship with the new manager and was often seen in his company. She explained, to anyone who wanted to know, that she wasn't the type who could cope with lonely nights or a silent house. She was promoted, given a section of her own to run and severed her ties with former workmates and with my department. After that, I heard no more of her.

MARY

At one of the most pleasant hours of a modest afternoon, shading into twilight, I was strolling calmly in the street that skirts the market, my face towards the sea, and I had almost reached the traffic-lights, when someone behind me called my name:

"Adon! Adon!" – his voice was urgent and unfamiliar; it seemed he had been running in a desperate attempt to catch up with me. When I turned round I saw a man in middle age, strangely attired: a dress-shirt – thin blue stripes on a white background – a bow-tie constricting a stiff neck with a prominent Adam's apple; his shabby jacket, somewhat resembling an old-style tuxedo, was unfastened, and tight, dark-striped trousers impeded his running. A thin moustache adorned his upper lip.

At first sight, the man made a bizarre impression, out of tune with his surroundings and a stranger to his time – a sort of antique reproduction brought to life. As he came closer, a distant figure began to take shape in my consciousness, a familiar figure, lacking the moustache and wearing an overall patched with dark oil-stains...

"Gaby?" It was part question, part statement. I smiled at him.

"In person!" he cried triumphantly. "He and no other!" And while still panting heavily, and his face flushed following the unwonted exercise, he added: "I'd be very grateful, I implore you most earnestly – could you come with me, Sir, and spare me a few minutes of your time – just a few minutes!" His plea was impassioned, and in his dark, puffy eyes there was a look of wounded entreaty, and suspicion lest he had unwittingly offended my dignity.

"I have a story to tell you, Sir... a story that obsesses me. You, Sir, I am sure, will prove understanding!" – he repeated his appeal.

"I'll come, on one explicit condition," I replied.

"And that is?" – Gaby tensed, apprehension still showing in his eyes.

"You stop addressing me in such a formal style!"

"Consider it done!" – the suspicion fled from his face and he glowed like a high school pupil who has passed an exam – "just so long as you agree to come with me!"

We went into the familiar shop, the shop that was formerly Israel's. No radical changes were perceptible. In fact – it had hardly changed at all. But the atmosphere was different: lighter and more congenial, an air of unlimited willingness to adapt and an openness to change. Perhaps this was accentuated by the recently painted walls – a light beige, almost pink, with gold horizontal stripes.

"I heard you acquired the shop at a reasonable price," I began.

"The price wasn't exorbitant," he concurred, calling to his assistant:

"Shimon!"

From deep inside the shop, from behind the thick, heavy curtain which was still as I remembered it – a youth appeared, wearing an oily overall and with a convict-style cap on his head. His face was round and chubby, featuring small, dark eyes and a silly smile.

"Bring tea for Adon, coffee for me – and don't forget the lokum!"

At a light run, surprising in view of his rotund frame, he left the shop and disappeared for a while. By the time he returned with the tea, the coffee and the lokum, we had almost completed the polite dialogue that was to be the preamble to Gaby's "story".

Anyway, we sipped the warm liquid and tasted the lokum in companionable silence, although there was still a faint sense of unease between us.

"The price was by no means exorbitant," – Gaby repeated his earlier remark, with emphasis, "but Israel was in the grip of a strange kind of mood, it was like a mania to get rid of the shop – as if it had turned into a millstone round his neck... and he offered to sell it to me on condition I could raise the money – which I did, borrowing from all kinds of people, relatives especially – and give it to him cash in hand. And he had to grit his teeth, 'cos he didn't like the idea of his assistant, his lowly protégé, taking over the place. He was the one who studied at the technical college after all, whereas I got no further than high school, and I taught myself electronics. All the same, I was better at the business than he was – and he knew it...

"Don't get me wrong!" Gaby continued with some vehemence, his still-smiling face turning a shade darker: "As long I can remember, I've dreamed of acquiring this shop, but in different circumstances, a different atmosphere... without Israel going off to be a fisherman, and his sisters going abroad to marry suitors they didn't know, had never seen, chosen for their religious pedigree..." He drew in his saliva, and swallowed it with an emphatic gargling movement, larynx bobbing up and down.

"I was very fond," – he stammered, lowering his dark eyes – "of Mary, the eldest. She was a woman of character! In fact," he added, – "it was more than just affection! A number of times I got to have conversations with her. Of course, that was without Israel knowing, or her late-lamented father...

"She'd listen to what I had to say, chuckle a pure, musical sort of chuckle, shoot a hot, deep look at me, a look full of emotion... not exactly emotion," he mused, hands flailing helplessly as he searched for the right word and failed to find it – "Not emotion exactly, something stronger and more expressive than that..." Suddenly his eyes lit up, his quest crowned with success:

"Melancholy!" he cried triumphantly. "A look all suffused with melancholy! A searing kind of melancholy, that's both desperate resignation to a certain situation, and also a cry from a wounded, bleeding heart, a cry for help!" He fingered his clean, resplendent bow-tie with a nervous, awkward gesture.

"Then she'd go home – having heard what she heard, and chuckled her chuckle, without saying a word, turning away and leaving... so it was really just a monologue, although from another point of view I think it may have amounted to more than that. I didn't know it then, and I don't suppose I ever will!" he continued, still weighing his words carefully, but after these meetings – and there were more than just a few of them – I was always left hurt and depressed, day and night... until the next meeting, a month later... or sometimes more. I couldn't sleep, couldn't eat...couldn't even breathe, without remembering her, thinking of her, dreaming...

"And so, in my wildest, boldest dreams, I used to see myself as proprietor of this shop, dressed like a toff..." – he fingered the frayed cuffs of his elderly tuxedo, which gave him the reasonably authentic appearance of a handyman in a cheap hotel – "making an impression on her and at the end of the day – asking for her hand... But all of this was just a juvenile, pointless dream, one that would never come true..."

"Why didn't you talk to Israel about this?" I interrupted him.

"I was afraid," he admitted: "He was jealous for his sisters, as his late father was too. Only the mother was prepared to compromise on the issue of husbands for her daughters – after that crisis, I mean, when both of them married whoever it was they married and were divorced… She, the mother I mean, was prepared to consider even a suitor like me…"

"How did you know the mother was prepared to compromise?" I asked.

"I took the opportunity to drop her a few hints… back then," he explained. "And do you think nothing came of it?" he asked, without looking up at me, and promptly answered his own question: "Something came of it! Mary began visiting the shop more often, turning up unexpectedly when she knew Israel wasn't there. And then we talked. We talked, as they say, in depth, in breadth, and at length, if you follow me…"

"No," I retorted, "I don't follow you."

"We spoke in depth, that is, with wisdom and logic – the years pass by and a woman is destined to be a wife and a mother, especially – a mother! And at a certain age, the opportunity is lost… We spoke in broad terms, about the kind of affection that goes way beyond affection, and I implied that in my specific case it went way, way beyond! And we spoke about the long-term perspective, and the attractions of living as a couple, in mutual understanding and partnership…" He forced a smile and continued:

"If you follow me, the word 'love' doesn't come easily to my lips… I'm sort of bashful about using the word, incurably bashful. I preferred to call it 'affection that goes beyond affection'. However, I'm absolutely sure she knew what I was on about, had me figured out… and anyway, she was a pretty perceptive sort, with finely tuned intuition…"

"And all this, without Israel's knowledge?" I asked again.

"It was kept a secret from Israel," he answered me in a confident tone: "He never suspected anything." He stared for a long moment at the ceiling of his shop, his hands groping for the pockets in his narrow trousers and trying to find a refuge there – failing and hanging limply at his sides.

"If you follow me," he went on to say, "she somehow grasped what I was talking about, and used to listen earnestly. And finally, one day, she gave me an answer, saying that, seeing it from a logical perspective, she was prepared to have another try at marriage – not necessarily referring to me, personally – she made that clear – but as a point of principle. On the other hand, this 'affection' that I was talking about – this 'affection going beyond affection' – was a strange concept to her, as she had never experienced anything like it, although she'd been married and divorced... and if I agreed to this, to take her as she was, not fully understanding the affection that I was constantly mentioning, and despite her bitter experience of marriage – she was prepared to give the whole thing careful consideration, weigh it up seriously... What do you think my answer was?" – he suddenly turned his dark and puffy eyes on me.

"I assume you said you were ready and willing," I replied, accepting the invitation to guess.

"Much more than that!" he declared, his face, for some reason, taking on a grim expression: "I embarked on a detailed assessment of the future, sketched the whole picture for her, poured out all my feelings, assured her she'd never regret her decision, if she really had taken the decision I was referring to, and we'd raise a family, and so on, and so on..." His body stiffened, as if trying out a more upright and rigid posture.

"Yes, I spoke with enthusiasm," he asserted with a faint trace of bitterness, swallowing a sigh, before resuming: "Pure enthusiasm, I should say. And this seemed to impress her, or at any rate... it set her thoughts moving in a certain direction. She promised to think it over seriously. And then she stopped coming to the shop.

"So, time was passing. And I don't think I was being hasty or impatient, but the uncertainty was weighing me down. With the help of mutual acquaintances I made contact with the mother, and her reply was – I should be patient." He drew a delicate handkerchief from an inner pocket of his tuxedo, wiped the foam from his lips and continued:

"Meanwhile – everything was going wrong for Israel. He didn't like his profession, just saw it as a soul-destroying source of income. As for the shop – it wasn't that he wanted a quick sale before he had time for second thoughts, which is his version of events, the fact is – he was sick of the place! Or maybe he saw it as a one-off opportunity... to squeeze some money out of me...

"And then I began to grasp that my juvenile dream was coming to fruition, taking shape – it would soon be realised! And I started making my preparations, talking to banks and relatives and checking the ground with all of them, jotting down all the figures – I was poised to pounce!

"What can I tell you?" – Gaby sighed, creasing his narrow forehead. "I could see the whole business working out, everything coming together, and I was so happy, exhilarated – inside and out – rubbing my hands with satisfaction...

"And then, just at that very time, would you believe – along came the matchmaker, with offers for the delectable Farhi sisters... and here the story gets complicated." He was clearly embarrassed, making another attempt to stick his hands into his narrow pockets, failing again and planting them on his knees instead.

"That night, after the matchmaker called and reeled off his persuasive spiel, and the girls listened and were persuaded – Mary came to me..." The steady flow of his words was interrupted. He tried to lick off the remains of the lokum that had stuck to the toothpick, broke it between his teeth, put the fragments back in the dish, and continued:

"I live in a small apartment, just a room and a half, in the northern part of the town. That night, at around midnight, or a little before, someone knocked on the door... a delicate knock... I have a bell, but I disconnected it because children used to mess about with it, waking me up from the midday nap that I was accustomed to... children, if you see what I mean, always enjoy embarrassing and ludicrous situations, and that's why they get up to all kinds of mischief... And what could be more embarrassing and ludicrous than a middle-aged man, living alone, dashing to the door when the bell rings, half-asleep – pyjamas flapping, the wrong slipper on one foot and just a sock on the other... anyway, in my part of town – this is reckoned the ultimate in comedy...

"The bell was disconnected," – Gaby reverted to his primary theme, having exhausted the topic of children and their mischief – "so anyone who calls round has to knock on the door... and she – knocked!" he cried with a strange, triumphant kind of exuberance, which did nothing to stem the under-current of bitterness and grief accompanying the whole of his narrative. "She knocked delicately at first but then, when there was no response... I wasn't sure whether to go to the door, or ignore the nuisance, let it go away by itself. It wasn't usual for kids to bother me at this time. And when I didn't open the door, the knocking got louder, it was a real fusillade...

"This made me all the more nervous, and I didn't dare open up, even though I was awake and unusually for me at this time, hadn't gone to bed yet... I had a strange sense of foreboding. She went on trying, and I couldn't ignore it any longer... and besides, I was starting to get curious. So I peeped through the spy-hole... and when I saw her!" – this with a cry of alarm, as if he was reliving the moment – "I hurriedly put on something more decent, a clean dressing-gown, nearly new... I've got quite a collection of them..." he seemed to think it worth pointing out. He swallowed saliva and continued:

"I opened up and she came storming in, into the half-room that serves me as a bedroom, and sat down on the end of the untidy bed. Maybe she didn't notice the mess, or maybe she did, but anyway she gave me that look of hers and in a clear and resolute voice, a voice I barely recognised, she asked:

"Do you remember our last conversation?"

"I remember it well, I replied immediately, unable to hide the tremor in my voice.

"My answer – she declared – is yes!

"For the second time that night, she focused her eyes on me, but this time it was completely different... in this look there was something bold and radiant, something frank and decisive... This was, at the very least, the look of a queen!" He stared again at the ceiling, rubbing his hands on his knees, with an air of deepening gloom.

"I stammered something," he muttered eventually. "I don't remember what..." After a long and pregnant pause he went on to say:

"For my part, I started weighing up this sudden, strange turn of events. With lightning speed I was measuring up one against the other in my mind – Mary, as opposed to the shop... which in a just a few days from now was going to fall into my hands like the proverbial ripe fruit..."

"Why one against the other, why not one and the other, Mary and the shop?" I queried.

"That's how it began," he continued, evading a direct answer to my question, his voice sounding flat and emptied of vitality. "A strange beginning," he admitted – "and the end was stranger still. Beyond anything that could be imagined.

"At that moment, for some reason, I began looking at Mary in a completely different light. The majesty and the dignity that she used to radiate, that used to intimidate me – seemed to have faded away.

Either that, or I was doing my best to ignore them... and succeeding. There was something dismal in her demeanour, or perhaps I should say I found something dismal there, utterly dismal... I began shying away from her and shaking off the feelings that I had for her. In short – I began to be ashamed of that 'affection beyond affection' which I felt for her and which in my naivety I had found in her too, and ashamed of my blind willingness to marry her, without her finding in herself something resembling sincere feelings for me. With the brazen manner of this nocturnal visit, an act of degradation and servility, it seemed to me – she had destroyed the legend I created of the invincible, unattainable woman – and of this fortress only a pitiful ruin remained. Suddenly I felt like an over-tolerant master wronged by a serving-wench... and yet in spite of this, something impelled me to put her to the test:

"Do you still have nothing in your heart resembling sincere feeling for me? I asked in a friendly voice, that was meant to disguise the chilly sobriety that had taken me over, and that I was ashamed of – thinking I knew in advance what her answer would be. I did know her well," he assured me – "a woman of principles who would never demean herself by saying anything other than the truth! And her reply, when it came, astounded me:

"I have sincere and true feelings for you, genuine and powerful feelings, straight from the heart. I'll be a good and devoted wife to you, and I'm prepared to prove it to you here and now.

"And what do you think, Adon, what do you suppose in your wildest imaginings, that she did?" – he asked in a dull, choking voice.

He took my lack of reaction as meaning that I understood him, and could indeed imagine Mary's desperate ploy.

"And then," he cried – "it finally became clear to me that I didn't want her, didn't want her at all! The only thing I wanted was the shop, my exclusive property, without any partners... least of all a shrewd and capable partner like Madame Mary!"

"And because I respect myself, if you understand me, Adon – I asked her to stop demeaning herself. If you understand me, Adon," he repeated mechanically, "what flashed into my mind then, and even now I still believe it absolutely – was the thought that she was entirely intent on demeaning herself – sinking to the lowest level of degradation, and if possible, further still."

His voice wavering, he continued:

"I don't know if you're following all this, Adon, but what she did – or rather, what she tried to do – was a particular kind of suicide. Not simple suicide but something worse – spiritual suicide. A kind of self-abasement that there's no escape from, no turning back."

He glanced gloomily into my face, wiped his lips with a clean handkerchief and added:

"I told her to get dressed, and wait for my answer some other time.

"What other time? – she asked, with hope still in her voice, a childish hope... I'm supposed to be going abroad, and time is pressing! – she added softly.

"I can't put a date on it, not at this moment, I said, feeling myself blushing for shame, but continuing with pomposity that surprised even me: When I feel the time is right, I'll let you know!

"And then she finished dressing, put on a coat, and something round her neck... a hat as well – and went away in a hurry, leaving the door wide open, and disappeared from sight, never to return...

"So now you understand," – again he turned his baleful eyes to me – "what a swine I have been, what a stupid oaf! That dream, the dream that was coming true, putting on flesh and bone and sinew, the icon of womanhood that I admired and adored and felt so much more than affection for – evaporating into nothing. No! Worse! Destroyed, wrecked to the foundations – by me. With my own hands I ruined and destroyed... trampled it all down with clumsy feet, stupidly, irreparably...!

His body shook. He made an effort to regain control of himself and was silent a long while. As was I.

He resumed his narrative, once again staring at the ceiling and the beige-pink walls with the horizontal stripes:

"About an hour later, at two in the morning, I ran to their house... I didn't run, not exactly... what I mean is, I called a taxi, and all the way I was urging the driver to put his foot down, and we were careering along the narrow alleyways, like a chase scene out of the movies. The late hour was a help to us," he explained – "no other traffic, no people, no animals... It took us just a few minutes to get to that narrow passage, and from there I continued on foot.

"The main gate was open, the inner door, the entry to the house, was locked... I knocked on it like a maniac... It was Sylvie, Mary's younger sister, who opened up to me. I went inside, no, I didn't just go inside, I burst in... like a wild beast. Blundered straight into her room..." He glanced at me for a moment, scanning my expression.

"I knew which room was hers – I'd dreamt about it often enough!" he commented dryly. "I asked her forgiveness, went down on my knees, kissed the floor that her feet walked on..." He turned to look at the display window, through which people appeared as walking shadows. The light of day had faded, and a soft dimness was spreading through the interior of the shop.

"She didn't respond – not with a word or a gesture, not a smile or a sneer. She sat there on her bed, frozen, in a thick, broad-sleeved gown.

"As for me, I decided I was staying put. It was the only way I could even try to repair the damage I'd done, though I knew it was utterly hopeless...

"And then Israel came in and tried to eject me. Not in a nice way either..." – he scanned my face again with that blank look.

"He hit me... punched me in the face and kicked me in the ribs, again and again. My mouth was bleeding, my nose... twice I went down. Twice I got up again into a kneeling position... and she still wasn't moving a muscle. And then the mother appeared... and she managed to get me out of there! That's one tough lady – in words I mean, not physical strength. Some of the curses she came out with made me blush! She's a witch, a genuine witch!" he declared, without any change in his voice or the expression on his face: "Intimidating, casting terror into every foolish heart... and that's what my heart was then. Maybe not only then... maybe it always was and always will be!" he added bitterly, and with more than a hint of touching innocence,

"And next day, if you get my drift," he continued – "Mary wasn't there any more, or her sisters... nothing to dream about. All that was left was the shop, with me in charge, dressed up like a tailor's dummy, just what I always wanted. Everything was falling into place... I even made my peace with Israel, although I didn't dare ask him about his sister. To be honest, the desire had gone too. And I was being offered various other brides – young, docile, submissive types – and I turned them all down. Not that I'm a prude! I get what I need once a week – at a price," he explained confidentially. "I'm afraid of marriage, and I don't know why..."

"Why have you told me all this?" I asked, getting up to leave.

"A good question!" he said, "And there is an answer to it! She mentioned you. At that moment when I was sprawling at her feet, after I'd passed out twice under Israel's onslaught... I heard her say Adon – softly but very clearly. It was like hearing her through a veil: Adon – she said – Ask Adon. If he says I have good cause to change my mind – I'll do as he says! Ask him. You haven't much time. About three hours from now I'm due to leave this house and this country.

"So, I ran to your house to consult you, as she recommended. I found the place all right," he said, sounding indignant – "but I didn't go inside, or even try to. The allotted time had run out and you – you'd gone to work. Or so your neighbour told me.

"That neighbour of yours, he's a funny guy," he commented, "gammy leg and all... It seems he'd been looking out of his window for ages before he spotted me. And then he wanted to know what I wanted and who'd sent me there, as if he was interrogating some criminal."

I remembered the neighbour's report of a "comical" man with a little moustache and blood on his face, looking for me one morning.

"A funny guy!" – he smiled an awkward and apologetic smile – "He said all the weird people in the world come to you. It seems I'm one of them..."

I parted from him with a handshake. He didn't accompany me to the door of his shop. He stood by the broad table, in the gloom – tense and still, as if rooted to the spot. He was staring down at the floor, his hands dangling and his long face fading into shadow.

PURE AND RESOLUTE

Early in the spring, Lili's condition took a turn for the worse. I used to visit her every day after leaving work in the early afternoon and stay with her, depending on her condition – for an hour or two, and sometimes, late into the night.

She lay in the same little room, isolated from the other patients and medical staff. The treatment she received was diffident – characterised on the one hand by anxiety to relieve pain, and on the other by determination to give her as wide a berth as possible. The disease alarmed members of the medical profession, who hadn't yet figured out what it was and knew nothing of its causes or modes of transmission, other than the sexual. For purposes of visiting, the situation had its advantages. No one cared how much time I was spending with her, no one came to tell me that visiting hours were over and I must leave, as would be the case in other wards and departments of that hospital.

Sometimes we talked at length; sometimes we lapsed into prolonged, profound and blissful silence. Sometimes – a nurse had to be called.

Her body was fevered and shrivelled, and she had the physique of a ten year old girl, critically ill and racked with hunger. In a strange way, her voice kept its clarity, as did the look in her eyes, which never tired of checking the impression made on me by her outward appearance. This insistent scrutiny invariably satisfied her.

Soon after Passover, one day when there was still something of the radiant solemnity of spring in the air, I was walking down the bleak corridor as I did every day, when I was aware of a strange kind of sensation. A presentiment of separation, blended with exquisite sadness and at the same time – a thinly flowing stream of happiness, distant indeed but steady, glistening in my heart.

When I opened the door of the little room, crammed as it was with gleaming medical paraphernalia – heavy oxygen canisters, machines checking the performance of other machines, thin metal plates clamped to the chest, designed to sound a warning siren, should the need arise, in the distant observation centre, where nervous medical personnel were monitoring her condition – I felt an abrupt change had taken place, both in the atmosphere and in the condition of the patient on her sick-bed. Whatever had been here yesterday, or the day before, was no longer, and what had replaced it was entirely new, post-dated – clear, succinct and unavoidable. Things had been decided, and time had packed its bags and gone; its job done, it wasn't needed here any more.

Lili gave me a scared look from under the light, state-of-the-art oxygen mask, anxious, as usual, to check the impression made on me by the mask and the mass of tubes attached to it. She relaxed at once, and a faint spark of joy – distant, admittedly and strange, out of kilter with the place and its atmosphere, took up residence in the depths of her eyes and showed no intention of budging from there.

Gently I took her fevered hand, the transparent skin barely covering her brittle bones, the bones of a child, and held on to it.

She smiled a smile of quiet contentment, which changed the expression of her face and erased the resemblance – which the eyes of the flesh were incapable of ignoring – to a hairless skull with deeply sunken cheeks, truncated nose and distended nostrils, turning black with encrusted blood – infusing it instead with freshness and astonishing serenity. With her free hand she removed the mask and inhaled the air in the room with pleasure. She put a silencing finger to her lips, to dissuade me from urging her to replace the mask, and said:

"I'm ashamed..."

"Of what?" I asked her gently, in a tone expressing nothing but light, the light of absolute truth, which is all love.

"Of being so happy!" – she smiled and went on to say, with as much clarity as her cracked voice allowed – "Happy to be seeing you... happy that you're holding my hand... or what's left of it! You should be so lucky!" She smiled at me rather bashfully, holding my gaze with a look of stubborn mischief.

"When I met you for the first time," she went on to say, her sunken eyes still fixed on mine – "you made me feel uneasy... very uneasy, I should say. You made me ashamed," she explained – "and I didn't know I was still capable of that. I was ashamed of the way I was… ashamed you were the way you were… ashamed of…of…" She stammered, her eyes boring into mine, and stumbled on: "You know, I always dreamed… about you. Between one filthy episode and the next…" She puckered the dry skin of her lips in sudden aversion, looking away, and then back again to my face:

"I dreamt simple things… that you were walking beside me, not knowing how much I longed to touch you. And it was such a delight to me, even when I was wrestling with the impulse to touch you, and you knowing nothing about it! And all this – in a dream…"

"You've told me about your dreams before!" I pointed out playfully.

"There have been plenty of them!" she agreed, adding: "I haven't told you all of them, not this one…"

I reckoned it was time to put the oxygen mask back on her face, and gestured accordingly. She took the hint and sighed, giving the matter some thought.

"There's no need!" – she smiled gently with the withered strips that were once her lips. "It's already been decided," she added, and saw no need to elucidate.

"And you may not believe it," she continued with an effort – "but that prohibition that I imposed on myself, not to touch you – opened up a way for me to touch something much deeper, much more true! You see," she explained – "ordinary contact has to stop at a certain point… and that is its saving grace! The other kind doesn't need to stop… it's something that's beyond time, that words like 'pleasure' or 'delight' or 'satisfaction' don't apply to… 'happiness' or 'grace' come closer…" She lapsed into silence and seemed to be listening to the frantic rhythm of her heart, pounding away in her emaciated, skeletal chest. After a long pause she continued:

"And if I look for something close, more fitting…" she hesitated and seemed to be veering from the subject: "Of all the English that I learnt at the Mission, there was one word that impressed me especially, and it's stuck in my memory. The English word blessing – do you know it?" Her voice faltered, and her eyes demanded a response.

"I know it," I assured her, with warmth and interest. I had almost forgotten that I was still holding her hand, and she surprised me by suddenly giving mine a squeeze.

"I'm entitled to do that!" she announced in a faint voice, but in a strangely cheerful tone: " 'Cos tomorrow I won't be here and I can't squeeze your hand even if I want to... Or perhaps – can I do it?" she asked me in all seriousness, waiting tensely for an answer.

"No," I replied. "After separation from the flesh – it isn't possible..."

"I'm not sure I agree!" she interrupted me with a note of gaiety: "You should know, in those dreams I wasn't content with just holding your hand... I wanted to kiss you too... that was the dream and I'm not ashamed of it. 'Cos it never happened and it's never going to. It's better that way... and holding hands – is enough for me. But if you ask me, it seems to me that after that – what did you call it?" she asked, a glint of frivolity reflected in the orbs of her big eyes.

"Separation from the flesh," I reminded her.

"Separation from the flesh," she repeated with relish and added: "That seems to be an apt expression... when that happens I think I will be able to kiss you after all... and there'll be nothing you can do about it, 'cos I'll be hovering in the air above your head..."

She studied the expression on my face, the response in my eyes, her manner suddenly earnest, and then looked away. The transparent eyelids, laced with little blue veins and bare of lashes, seemed incapable of covering her big pupils, apparently unaffected by the disease.

After a prolonged, serene silence, she linked her tiny hand, still holding mine, to her other hand and said:

"I do have one serious favour to ask..."

"Name it!" I replied readily.

"I want you to put flowers out for me..." she said with unexpected awkwardness, despite the tender gleam of purity reflected in her eyes. "From time to time," she added with more confidence, "a bunch of flowers... let's say – once a year! But if you forget, it's no big deal!"

"I won't forget!" I answered her, my voice steady and reassuring. "So long as this ludicrous flesh is walking on the suffering surface of this earth!" I saw fit to add.

What had once been lips stretched into a gentle and apologetic smile, against the frame of her delicate skull-bones.

"There I go, making demands on you again!" The disjointed sounds of a faint chuckle, a chuckle of pure pleasure, accompanied these words.

"Don't leave me now!" she said suddenly, with an involuntary spasm, as a veil of fear clouded her face. Her hands clutched my fingers tightly, like the talons of a dying bird. The spasm passed, and she regained composure enough to laugh softly:

"I knew you wouldn't leave me!" she said and released my hand.

After a moment's silence, she continued in that melodious tone of hers, soft and distant and yet with every word carefully enunciated and clearly audible:

"If I'd known, when I first became ill... but everything comes in its own time! It seems I can't be such a sinner after all, not as long as you're sitting beside me! I almost believe that... and I'm ashamed. I'm so ashamed!" she exclaimed in a choking voice. "I'm so happy... and I'm not worthy. That's the bitter truth – I'm not worthy! There's been some terrible mistake here!" she said suddenly, a heavy pall of gloom clouding her eyes.

"No mistake!" I declared with a confident smile.

Her withered hand, the hand of a woman a hundred years old, again sought for mine. When I held it out, she took it solemnly and pressed it lightly against what was left of her lips. When she released my hand, simultaneously withdrawing her own, pure moisture glistened in the orbs of her eyes, eyes radiant with the wonderment of joy unbounded.

"Call the nurse!" she quavered, looking around her for the oxygen mask. I put the mask on her face, and went running to find the nurse.

She came with obvious reluctance, without saying a word injected something into Lili's arm, on which there was virtually no flesh left, and went away immediately.

After a series of gasps and hollow, abrupt sighs, in which it was impossible to detect even the faintest spark of anything resembling hope, Lili relaxed fractionally. She was clearly making an effort to control her pain, growing ever more severe and acute despite whatever it was that had been shot into her arm.

I laid my hand on her domed, childish forehead, and this seemed to help a little,

She didn't speak. Silently she wrestled with herself while her staring eyes, agape in dumb terror, were fixed on the dazzling white ceiling. Her breathing was abrupt, her body writhing as the pain threatened to rip apart her lucidity too.

Shortly after midnight, there was a surprising change in her condition: the pace of her breathing slowed, the spasms stopped and the fear in her eyes gradually withdrew, giving way to a distant look of tranquillity, while a faint smile, tender and radiant at the same time, was etched on the dry and solid line of her mouth. She took the oxygen mask off her face.

There was a change in the atmosphere of the room. The sharp gleam of the metallic instruments seemed to soften. The alien chill of the cramped space faded and vanished. And a different light, a light pure and resolute, despite the calm infused in it and the delicacy of its lustre, spread through the room, lit it and swamped it utterly. It penetrated and suffused everything, shone in everything, was reflected by everything and at the same time – it dissolved everything: the walls were there no longer, nor the ceiling, nor the floor and the instruments, no bed, no little bedside cabinet, no neon bulbs, no high and unfeeling skylight.

Lili's head was visible somewhere, in a space that was infinite and yet – tangible and close; beyond reach and yet – solid and defined; filling everything and yet – outside everything; immeasurable and yet – real, radiant and revealed. The face was pure and bright, its smile – like a young sun, shining on a spring morning, a smile effulgent with wondrous joy, enchanted and delicate...

Voices rose, limpid, harmonious sounds, distant at first and drawing closer, clear and melodious and telling of joy, of unbounded rejoicing.

The face changed, its beauty the beauty of the sublime, the absolute and the ineffable, such that flesh and blood will never know, nor experience.

"How wonderful all this is!" she exclaimed, her voice blending evenly into the chorus all around. And there was nothing in her wonderment to suggest that she was surprised, on the contrary: she had earnestly hoped for this and yearned for it all her days, and this alone she had recognised long ago, and she was glad, for it was returning to her and she was returning to it, returning home. And this was unlike anything she could ever have imagined in her distant past, which had been utterly erased from her memory, as if it had never been.

"Still here?" She turned to me and her eyes, set in the gilded frame of her serene face, searched for my eyes and found them.

"The flesh stays behind," I answered her with a softness to match the strains of the melody swelling all around us.

"The spirit" – I added – "is always in Him."

Her life in the body was no more.

www.ingramcontent.com/pod-product-compliance
Lightning Source LLC
Chambersburg PA
CBHW072256020726
47501CB00002B/289